DEMON'S DAUGHTER

"You're bleeding," Dro said in a quiet voice across from me.

I looked at her, slowly sheathing my knife, trying to act like that simple movement wasn't pure agony to my shoulders.

"I'll be all right," I rasped out, my breathing still heavy from the fight.

She took a tentative step closer to me. "I'm sorry, Constance. I was trying to get there sooner, but–"

"You know the rules," I told her. "Leave the fighting to me."

Dro was tougher than she looked. She had to be, given the way we lived. But deep down she was just too gentle, never wanting to hurt anyone or anything. She wasn't comfortable with a weapon in her fist or blood on her hands.

Not like I was.

Dro frowned and looked at my injuries again, taking another step toward me. She didn't hesitate, reaching out and pulling away the collar of my shirt to see the wicked wounds on my skin. Her frown deepened and she gently touched the broken skin on my shoulder. Her hands began to glow a strange golden light, and she began to heal me.

There were many words a person could use to describe Dro. Special. Gifted. Strange. All of them were true, because she wasn't human. I wanted to pretend she was, but it was impossible to do when she healed my injuries with a single touch. Or when she told me she could read other people's thoughts if she concentrated enough. Or when she heard, smelled, or saw things way before I did. Or when she had the nightmares and burst into flame.

None of it changed my love for her, but it did scare me. More than I wanted to admit.

DEMON'S DAUGHTER

A CURSED NOVEL

AMY BRAUN

This is a work of fiction. All of the characters, organizations, and events portrayed in this novel are either products of the author's imagination or are used fictitiously.

DEMON'S DAUGHTER
A Cursed Novel

Cover Artwork: Derange Doctor Design

Paperback ISBN: 978-0993875823
ASIN: B0851QJ243

ALSO BY AMY BRAUN

Cursed Series

Demon's Daughter

Dark Divinity

Damnation's Door

Dark Sky Series

Amber Sky (prequel novella)

Smoke Sky (prequel novella)

Crimson Sky

Midnight Sky

Obsidian Sky

Areios Brother Series

Storm of the Gods

Hunt of the Gods

Fury of the Gods

Betrayal of the Gods (coming soon)

Standalones

Storm Born

Path of the Horseman

Needfire (novella)

For my friends and family.

The worst pain a man can suffer: to have insight into much and power over nothing.
  Herodotus

I believe I am in Hell, therefore I am.
  Arthur Rimbaud

PROLOGUE

If the monster was going to take my sister, it would have to kill me first.

I was covered in blood, not all of it my own. My ears rang with the sound of agonized screaming. I tasted copper from the blood in my mouth. I smelled death and smoke everywhere. All I saw was fire, and all I felt was fear.

But it was trying to take Dro. It was trying to take my little sister.

I shook as I stood, my body swimming with pain from being clawed and thrown around the camp. I looked around, trying to find Dro.

So many people were dying. Burned, ripped apart, shredded, eaten. There was so much blood...

I forced my legs to work, not looking at the torture, death, and fire in a place that had once been filled with laughter. Not wanting to see it, but knowing I would remember it forever.

Then I saw her. The only little girl with white hair in the camp. I ran faster, gripping my father's hatchet tightly. A red-skinned monster pulled her along. She cried and shrieked for me to save her.

And I would. I was her big sister. I kept her safe.

My heart thundered against my rib cage, pulsing with anger and fear. I had no clue what I was doing. I didn't know how to stop the monster. Only that I had to.

Dro's icy blue eyes found mine, wide with terror. "Connie!" she screamed.

The monster hit her across the face, sending her sprawling onto the grass. I ran faster.

It was turning when I slammed into it, sending us both onto the ground. I tried to hit it with the hatchet, but it was so much stronger than me. It punched me in the chest and knocked me onto my back. I rolled on the ground to avoid its claws. It snapped its sharp teeth and hissed at me. Somehow I found my footing and swung the hatchet again. This time I hit the monster in the arm with the weapon. Black blood gushed out of its wound.

The back of the monster's hand cracked against my face, sending me crashing onto the charred ground. I panicked, my breathing ragged. I'd lost the hatchet and was looking for something, anything, to fight back with–

The monster screamed.

I twisted on the ground, eyes widening. Flames engulfed it. Not a normal, red and orange fire, but a fierce, white-hot flame a hundred times hotter than any bonfire I'd ever been close to. The heat was sweltering, a thick, humid air that coated my throat and made it hard to breathe.

The white fire burned the demon, turning it into black ash.

The white fire came from my sister's hand. My sister, who'd also been wrapped in fire.

She looked at me, crying and consumed by flames. "Help me, Constance."

CHAPTER ONE

I have a nasty habit of constantly waking up with one hand under my pillow, grasping the hilt of my hatchet like the lifeline it is, coated in sweat and feeling as tense as a wire.

But that wasn't what woke me.

It was the smell of smoke from the burning bed next to me. The one my sister currently screamed in.

I shot out of the bed like a bullet from a gun, getting as far away from the white flames as I could. Despite the horrible screams she made, I knew Dro wasn't being hurt. Or so she always told me.

Our bags were by the motel door, ready as usual. I'd slept in my clothes, so I didn't have to dress. I grabbed my knives from the table, holstering them in the sheaths on either side of my ribs, and threw my black military jacket– my lucky jacket– over my shoulders. I hooked my hatchet to my belt, shoved on my boots, and glanced at the bed where Dro still screamed.

The fire had moved from the bed to the walls, to the curtains, and then to the ceiling. The cheap, peeling wallpaper blackened and rained down around her, like black snow in a whiteout.

Dro suddenly stopped screaming. The nightmare was over.

She realized what was happening around her, and that it was time to leave. I waited by the door, our bags in hand. She jumped off her burning bed, completely unharmed by the fire. It sloughed off her like a second skin.

It never got easier seeing her burning like that, but when you're about to be smothered in what literally feels like ten thousand degrees, there are only two things that should cross your mind: Get out, and get out now.

Dro threw on her jacket and boots while I yanked open the door and took off down the hall. She would be right behind me. She always was. She knew the drill.

The rest of the motel residents screamed and shouted for help as the fire moved from room to room. I swerved around them as much as I could, but some I had to shove out of the way. Not very nice of me, but they didn't know what caused the fire. I did. Getting caught wasn't an option.

At the bottom of the second story, I could see the motel owner. He roared in outrage and panic. He would probably going to blame us for what happened to his place once the hysteria was over, since we'd shown up covered in dirt and blood, demanding a room with no questions asked. Not that I was going to admit the fire had started in our room. We hadn't exactly planned it.

We raced across the street, the motel now engulfed with brightly burning red flames. Dro no longer burned, but the devastation remained. It only lasted as long as she stayed conscious and in control, which happened about five times out of ten. There was no safe way to predict when Dro would be in control, and when she would simply lose herself.

It would take firefighters hours to put out the blaze, and even longer to figure out the cause. Not that they'd come to the proper conclusion, because cases of teenage girls spontaneously combusting weren't normal.

But on the other hand, my sister had never been normal.

Even if they had a psychic on hand to see the truth and make them believe it, it wouldn't matter. We would be long gone by then.

I ducked into a narrow alley behind a cheap, "genuine" Southern-style diner. It smelled like grease and stale French fries, but it was better than smelling something burning. Or sulfur.

I pressed my back to the wall, steadying my racing heart. I looked up at my sister. Her breath came in shuddering gasps, her arms wrapped around her pale body.

A dull sadness pulled at my heartstrings. I hated seeing Dro this way. She blamed herself for what happened. A thing she hadn't been able to control, a curse she had been born with.

"Are you okay, Dro?" I said in a rush.

She looked down, gripping her elbows tightly and bent over like a hunchback instead of a sixteen year old girl.

As sisters went, Dro and I couldn't look less alike. She was still a growing young woman, becoming increasingly beautiful with each passing day. Only a few inches shorter than me with perfect skin, once chubby from childhood, now stretched over her bones. Her hair hung long in shining, white ripples down her back that never held any hair dye we tried to use to disguise her. Her lips were full and perfectly shaped, her cheekbones high and noble on her heart shaped face. Her eyes glowed an icy blue, piercing and striking against her snowy, angelic appearance.

My skin a brownish gold, and I was more of the athletic body type, my curves smaller and not worthy of a sculpture the way Dro's were. My black hair had been cut close to just under my chin because I hated when it got in my way during fights. My lips were thinner and my face longer. My eyes were the same deep brown our father's had been. What I lacked in beauty, I made up in strength. My muscles were refined and powerful, my stomach and legs taut.

Dro told me I was beautiful, but I knew she said it only

because she thought the best of me. Even when I became the darkest, most violent version of myself.

"It's my fault," she whispered, not meeting my eyes. "I burned it down. Someone's probably dead by now."

I moved from the wall and placed my hands on hers. "Look at me, little sister." She did, familiar tears streaking her face. "You didn't mean to do it."

She hadn't. Dro wouldn't hurt a fly, even if that fly was buzzing half an inch from her face and trying to get into her eye. Dro helped people. She cared about them. She never hurt them on purpose.

Not like I did.

I wish I knew what to tell her so she would believe me. I didn't want to think of myself as a bad sister. A bad person, yeah. I had made some nasty enemies over the last few years, and I'd never been able to see eye to eye with the law. But I put Dro before anything and anyone else. She was the only person who mattered to me, the only person I would do anything for. She was the one who kept my head on a swivel when I thought I would to lose it. And I was the reason she hadn't lost all hope and given in to whatever was chasing us.

We still didn't know what they were. Six years living under the radar, four of which were spent working for one of the most ruthless, vicious drug cartels of Mexico, hadn't exactly afforded me a lot of time to brush up on my monster knowledge.

Though it did teach me how to fight, how to avoid the cops, and how to inflict severe pain on my enemies. Whether they were human, or something else.

I glanced down the alley, making sure nothing was watching us, then glanced at my sister.

"What did you dream?" I asked.

She winced, but she wasn't crying anymore. "The usual. Monsters torturing me, burning everything I touch, ripping people apart with my bare hands."

Her voice started to shake again, edging toward another break down. While I would have let her cry it out anywhere else, this wasn't the place or the time.

"Come on," I soothed. "Let's get out of here."

I started turning out of the alley when the smell hit me. Rotten eggs. The scent of monsters.

CHAPTER TWO

The air ripped open like a wound, shuddering and pulling apart to reveal the red, flaming misery of another world. Fire licked at the air, peeling out of the cut. I couldn't tell for sure, but my guess was that I was looking into Hell.

Out of the tear came a skinny red monster. A Red, I called them. Six feet tall with a scrawny humanoid shape, blood red flesh and vicious black claws on its hands and feet. Its thin, oily hair hung around its head and in front of its ugly pointed ears. Its eyes were almond-shaped and pitch black, its lips peeled back in a savage snarl that revealed a row of serrated teeth. The moment I smelled me, it charged.

Reds were fast. Very fast. But so was I.

As soon as I saw the wound in the air open up, I threw off my backpack and started reached for one of the slim, throwing knives in my jacket. I'd killed these things before. I just had to be smart and quick.

I ducked down as it swiped its claws at me, stabbing my knife into its stomach. The monster growled with rage instead of pain. I stabbed it again and again as quickly as I could, hoping to damage it before it could get a shot in at me, or get to Dro.

From the corner of my eye, I watched its clawed hand swing toward me. I pulled back and twisted away, the claws skidding along the back of my jacket. I dropped to the ground and kicked its legs out, but the Red tucked and rolled instead of staying down.

I tried to scramble to my feet when it pounced on me.

My back slammed against the ground and my head cracked on the pavement. I winced and stabbed the monster in the ribs over and over. It snarled and buried its claws into my shoulders. I let out a cry of pain as the nasty talons hooked into my flesh. The Red used the claws to lift me up and slam my head onto the pavement. Then again. And again. And one more time just to make sure I would be bleeding.

The world spun around me, but I still tried to fight. The monster opened its jaws, rearing its head back to strike—

A sharp knife plunged into the back of its throat. Dro stood behind the Red, twisting the blade with a disgusted look on her face. Thick black blood rippled down its shoulders.

The Red got off of me and raced for her, but I shot to my feet. I nearly collapsed from the wave of vertigo, but I knew how to fight through pain. The monster had Dro pressed up against a wall with nowhere to run.

I rammed my knife into the Red's back, making it stiffen in pain. I kept stabbing as it whirled, throwing out its hand. I narrowly leaned away from the slap then drove forward again and shoved the blade into its heart. I stabbed as fast as I could, twisting the knife until it finally went down.

By the time I delivered the last stab, my arm was almost numb. It throbbed with pain and was soaked in hot, sticky blood. Monster blood burned, but I hardly felt its sting through my adrenaline.

The monster began to dissolve.

Its chest caved inward, as if crumpling under its own weight.

The skin turned black and crusty, turning to ash. Then it evaporated and blew away, like it had never existed at all.

Not for the first time, I wondered what the hell had just happened. I didn't know what these things were, never had time to learn. But then, I didn't care so much. If it threatened me or Drop, I killed it. I liked when things stayed as simple as that.

I stood up and straightened my back, beginning to feel the full extent of my injuries. My head was swimming, the hairs at the back of my neck felt sticky, every muscle ached, my shoulders were throbbing with pain from being clawed, and the demon blood burned on my arm.

Still, I'd had worse. Not that I counted this little encounter as a positive thing.

"You're bleeding," Dro said in a quiet voice across from me.

I looked at her, slowly sheathing my knife, trying to act like that simple movement wasn't pure agony to my shoulders.

"I'll be all right," I rasped out.

She took a tentative step closer to me. "I'm sorry, Constance. I tried to get there sooner, but–"

"You know the rules," I reminded her. "Leave the fighting to me."

Dro was tougher than she looked. She had to be, given the way we lived. But deep down she was just too gentle, never wanting to hurt anyone or anything. She wasn't comfortable with a weapon in her fist or blood on her hands.

Not like me.

Dro frowned and looked at my injuries again, taking another step toward me. She reached out and pulled away the collar of my shirt to see the wicked wounds on my skin. Her frown deepened and she gently touched the broken skin on my shoulder. Her hands began to glow a strange golden light, and I felt my skin tingle as she healed me.

There were many words a person could use to describe Dro. Special. Gifted. Strange. All of them true, because she wasn't human. I wanted to pretend she was, except normal people couldn't heal injuries with a single touch. Or read other people's thoughts if she concentrated enough. Or hear, smell, and see things way before I did. Or have nightmares that turned her into flame.

None of it changed my love for her, but it scared me. More than I wanted to admit.

I winced as her magic worked on my damaged flesh. It didn't exactly hurt, but it was uncomfortable. Like taking a dip in icy cold water and then immediately splashing into a hot bath. The pins and needles feeling sent a shock to my nerves and my brain saying something was wrong.

No shit, brain. Thanks for reminding me.

Being a bit uncomfortable was a small price to pay for what she was doing, and I knew it would make Dro feel better.

She moved onto the back of my head and I couldn't help but stiffen. It just felt so *wrong*.

"Sorry," she whispered.

"It's okay," I told her, forcing my shoulders to drop and relax, despite the prickling in my skull. "Don't think I'll ever get used to it, but I'm grateful."

Soon enough, Dro finished healing my wounds. Aside from the dirt and bloodstains on my clothes, I looked normal. Well, as normal as I could, considering how rough I was on clothes. That my jacket survived all it had seemed like a miracle to me.

Even though she only had a few minor scratches, I made her heal herself. I'd been overly protective even when we were kids, and it had only gotten worse as we got older and our lives spiraled out of control. There was nothing I wouldn't do for Dro. Nothing I wouldn't steal, no law I wouldn't break, no human or monster I wouldn't kill.

I would burn the world to a cinder to save Dro.

After she healed and I'd concealed as much of the blood as I could under my heavy jacket, I rearranged the bag on my back and walked out of the alley with my little sister behind me. The town was small and while the fire crews were on their way, it would take the sheriffs a few more minutes to get here.

More than enough time for me to steal a car and find somewhere else for us to run. When Dro had a nightmare, it meant monsters were close. I didn't want to get into another fight if I could avoid it, even if they weren't the things I feared the most.

Monsters scared me. Lawmen and faces from my past scared me.

But Dro scared me more.

CHAPTER THREE

We drove to Amarillo, which was only a fraction bigger than the last town we had been in. Amarillo was a sleepy place with some paranormal hunting groups, so Dro had suggested going there. I might have a blasé approach to our little monster problem and be more accepting of her abilities, but Dro desperately wanted to know what she was. Couldn't say I blamed her, but I knew better than most that knowing never changed the past.

Regret was no friend of mine.

We spent the first day in Amarillo doing research. Dro went to the library and checked out books while I waited in the car. I'd been ready to go in with her, but I was a wanted criminal. I couldn't exactly go into a public building and hope I wouldn't be recognized.

While I was waiting, I used the electronic tablet that had been in the car I'd stolen to read up on the Wanted lists on the U.S. Marshal website. A sketch of my angry face and a list of all my crimes were still posted there.

Aggravated assault. Drug trafficking. Breaking and entering. Assault with a deadly weapon. Aiding and abetting. Kidnapping.

Possession of firearms. Theft of varying degrees. Arson. Manslaughter. First and second degree murder. Underneath the ever growing list was a note for a hefty reward of twenty-five thousand dollars for my capture.

I checked news sites to see what my old bosses, the *Espanis de Sangre*– the Blood Thorns– were up to. A shoot out with honest cops that left four officers dead with their badges nailed into their hearts. A bus full of children who were kidnapped, the boys forced to shoot their teachers and join the Thorns while the girls kidnapped. The severed, veiled head of a rival gang leader's newly wedded daughter on a bed of roses on his front porch.

So they're having their typical Monday, I thought bitterly, my stomach churning.

Remembering the things I had done for them brought up bad, unwanted memories. I was no saint, but I'd never murdered a child or a bride. I'd done horrible things, and one day I would pay for that. I deserved to.

And I did it all for Dro. Because I was stupid. Desperate. So damn sure I could escape.

Self-loathing ate at me like acid. For a brief second, I imagined another life. One where Dro found a safe place to stay, her nightmares ended, her powers under control. I could leave her there, see that she stayed happy, and then turn myself in. Maybe I could reduce my sentence by telling the Marshals all I knew about the Thorns. And I knew *a lot*. Maybe not much about their current events, but enough to seriously damage their organization. Maybe it would be enough for me to see Dro from time to time.

Or maybe the Blood Thorns would find me first and take their revenge.

Dark thoughts would only sour my mood further, so I decided to be productive. Opening a new tab on the tablet's browser, I did a couple of image searches of the Red monster. All

I found were pictures of a stereotypical red, horned devil. Nothing specific enough.

After about half an hour, I gave up on the monster search and starting looking for a description of a creature with the same powers that Dro had. I came up with nothing. Whatever she was, she might be the only one of her kind.

I'd known she wasn't normal when I found her...

To celebrate my fourth birthday, my parents took me camping to a park just outside of Temple Texas. They were getting ready to cook dinner when I wandered from the campsite and heard a baby crying in the forest. I followed the noise, and found a pale baby lying in a patch of earth that smelled like rotten eggs.

I couldn't stand the loud, sad cries she made. Mom would know what to do. I wrapped her up in my coat and soothed her as best as I could, rocking her back and forth and even singing to her. Mom liked to sing to me when I got upset. She stopped crying, then opened up her big blue eyes and stared at me. Her pale, chubby hand reached up and batted against my chin.

A smile broke out onto my face.

I had always wanted a sister. I'd overheard my parents talk of wishing they could have another kid, but Mom couldn't get pregnant again for some reason. Feeling light-hearted and happy, I walked back to the camp. Mom had just stepped out of the trailer and was pulling on her jacket, while Dad stood waiting for her, his eyes wide with panic.

They watched me step out of the forest, holding a baby and smiling.

"Mom, Dad, look! You can have a baby now! I can have a sister!"

They scolded me for running away and taking a baby, but I

showed Dad exactly where I'd found her. I couldn't leave her. Someone needed to look after her. She was so small.

And loud.

My parents wanted to give her back to her family. We were poor. Really poor. The rusted, hundred dollar camper and a trip to the RV Park was the most Dad could afford for a vacation. He was a construction worker and Mom worked two jobs. They wanted to bring her to an orphanage, but Dad had a criminal record and now that he was trying to start over, the last thing he wanted was to do paperwork that would get him in trouble.

But I couldn't let her go. Someone had left her there to die, and I'd heard stories about what happened to kids who went into orphanages. Some were lucky. Most weren't.

We waited for someone to claim Dro. Dad even asked other campers if they'd heard someone missing a baby. When no one claimed her after three days, we adopted her. Mom and I doted on her, and Dad often fell asleep with her in his arms.

I suggested the name Andromeda because I saw it in a book about constellations, something my teacher taught us in the first grade, which my parents managed to slip me into a year early. Andromeda was a Greek Princess who had been chained to a rock for a sea monster to eat because her mother, Queen Cassiopeia, bragged about Andromeda being more beautiful Poseidon's water nymphs. The hero Perseus saved her, killed the sea monster, and together they lived happily ever after. I figured at least the first half of that story matched Dro's appearance in the woods, and my parents liked the name.

We knew she was different, but we never knew how much until the weird things started happening. Like her knowing things about the neighbors. Healing my cuts and bruises with a single touch. Sensing things way before I could.

The horrible nightmares, which only got worse as she got older...

A GENTLE RAP on the car window startled me and made me jump about a foot in the air. Dro stood outside of the car, an awkward grin on her face. She walked around the car and got into the passenger's seat next to me.

"You looked really intense just now," Dro said, closing the car door. "You okay?"

"Yeah," I replied. "You just scared the crap out of me."

She grinned. "I was trying to get your attention. Guess it worked." Her grin faded a little. "You look tired. Do you want to get something to eat?"

"Not sure that's a good idea, little sister. We're fugitives, remember? Fugitives always get found in diners."

"Come on, when was the last time we had a good breakfast?" She was smiling at me. "I know you want bacon."

My stomach rumbled at the thought of food. We ate whatever we could whenever we could, but Dro was right. It had been a very long time since we'd eaten outside of a motel room or a stolen car.

"Come on, Connie," Dro coaxed, sensing my hesitation. "One quick breakfast at a cheap, greasy diner. We can pretend to be normal for once."

Those were the magic words: *We can pretend to be normal for once.*

My stomach grumbled again. It had been almost a year since I'd filled it with bacon.

"All right. But we follow the rules."

Dro nodded, white hair bouncing against her shoulders. "Nothing over fifteen dollars and we make sure the restaurant is empty."

I nodded back at her, tossing the tablet into the back of the car. "Okay. Let's start pretending."

Dro had picked out a mom-and-pop diner as soon as she'd left the library. Confirming she'd planned this by exploiting my love of bacon.

I pulled the door open and walked ahead of her, bells tinkling over my head.

It was a kitschy diner with red and white tiles on the floor, faded red booths and chipped tables. Light shone through the wide, greasy paned windows, illuminating the poorly printed signs boasting the *"Best Breakfast in all of Texas!"* A cool grey counter top with plastic bar stools was set up across from the booths. Behind it was a silver walled kitchen I couldn't see into very well. There were two doors, the one we had walked into, and another at the other end of the diner.

I didn't like this place at all.

It looked harmless enough, but all I could only see two visible exits and too many windows. I couldn't see what the people in the kitchen were doing. They could call the cops or the Blood Thorns and I wouldn't have a clue.

"Con?" she asked from beside me.

I turned my head slightly so she would know I heard her. "Yeah?"

"Are you going to be okay?"

"Of course," I told her, shifting the bag on my back.

The kitchen door opened with a bang so loud I reached for the hatchet on my hip. I pressed myself closer to Dro, ready to throw her behind me.

Not that the woman who came out of the kitchen looked like a threat. She looked more like Dolly Parton, all curly blonde hair, big eyes, and peppy attitude.

"Mornin' ladies!" she said in a chirpy Texan drawl. She smiled so wide the cherry red lipstick she wore turned into two curved slashes on her face.

I didn't trust anyone that happy.

My sister moved in front of me this time. She was a lot better around people than I was.

"Good morning," Dro said politely. "We'd like to get some breakfast, please."

"Sure thing, sugar! Take seat anywhere you like." Dolly's eyes shifted over Dro's shoulder to me, some of her smile fading. "Your friend okay? She looks a little upset."

I crossed my arms and held back from laughing rudely. Dro smiled for me. "She's fine. She's just not a morning person."

This time I did laugh, shortly and icily. Dolly looked at me with hesitance, but Dro took over again.

"We'll take one of the booths."

"Sure thing, darlin'. Menus are on the tables. I'll get you back in a second."

Dolly turned on her heels and clacked her way back into the kitchen. I watched her, trying to see who else was beyond the swinging door. I wanted to know who Dolly was talking to and what she said about me. If there was someone back there I needed to be worried about. If–

Dro tugged at my elbow. "Con? Where do you want to sit?"

I looked around the diner again. There was no decent place. No corner I could sit in and watch all the exits. I looked at the booth on my left, the closest I was going to get to a corner.

"Here's good," I said, shrugging off my backpack and tossing it onto the seat. I sat down and moved into the corner by the window. Dro sat across from me and picked up a plastic menu. I glanced at my own, but barely registered what I read. I kept flicking my eyes up toward the kitchen whenever I saw a hint of movement. A barrel-chested man in a white apron came into view beyond the counter. His face looked a little chubby, but he was big. Ghosts of tattoos covered the part of his arms I could see. He might have been holding a knife. I couldn't tell for sure, since he didn't seem to be looking at me.

The kitchen door banged open again and Dolly returned with a pot of coffee. I stayed watched her from the corner of my eye. *Normal, normal, pretend to be normal...*

"This should perk you right up, darlin'," said Dolly as she poured some steaming black coffee into the mug near my wrist. I pulled my hand back and let her do it.

"Are you girls ready to order?" Dolly asked, purposefully looking at Dro and avoiding me.

"Yes, can I please get the chocolate chip pancakes and the mixed berry salad with a glass of orange juice?" Dro asked.

"Of course, sweetheart," Dolly replied, jotting it down on her notepad. She turned her big brown eyes on me. "And what can I get you?"

"Ham and cheese omelet with a side of bacon and potatoes," I said, tossing the menu down the table and taking the mug of coffee.I took a careful sip. It was scorching hot and a little bland, but I hadn't had coffee in a long, long time.

"That's a lot of food for one girl," Dolly said, trying to be nice to me again.

"I have a good metabolism."

I didn't add that I burned calories by fighting monsters and running for my life. Honestly, I would have been happy with just kickboxing and Muay Thai.

She looked at Dro again, clearly liking her more. Everybody did, and that was fine with me.

"I'll be right back with your order," Dolly said before scurrying off to the kitchen.

Dro looked across the table at me impatiently. "I thought we were trying to be normal," she chided.

"That is my normal," I countered, taking another sip of coffee.

"Normal people are a bit more polite."

I blinked. My sister sighed and shook her head. Dro loved

me and I loved her, but when it came to social skills, we were in a never-ending war.

"Did you find anything out?" she asked me after a moment.

"Nope," I said, thinking back on my research in the car. Focusing on the research, and not the memories and shame of my past. "Just a bunch of sites saying that the Reds are demons. You?"

Dro shook her head, leaning back in the seat. "Not really. Most of what I came across suggested demons, too." She looked at me. "Do you think that's what they are?"

I shrugged. "Wish I knew, Dro. I'm not sure there's anyone we could ask, either."

"There must be someone here. A demonologist or paranormal investigator we can ask. Amarillo is supposed to be a hotspot for that kind of thing."

"Assuming they know what the hell they were talking out. We can't waste time dealing with charlatans and hoping for the real deal."

Bells tinkled harmlessly behind me. I turned sharply in my seat. Two parents with a young boy and younger girl walked in. The kids were tired and restless and the parents were trying to contain them. Dolly came back out of the banging kitchen door to greet them. I was ready to rip the fucking thing off its hinges. Dolly led them past us to another booth. The little girl caught sight of Dro and stared with wonder. Dro smiled and waved at her. The girl giggled.

The kid reacted the way everyone reacted around Dro, but it was unwanted attention. Having a beautiful, pale sister with snow-white hair and ice blue eyes made it difficult to stay under the radar.

When the family was seated three booths down, Dro looked at me again. "What if we went to a priest? They'd know for sure if we were being chased by demons, and they would know how to prevent them from coming after us, or at least tell us what they could want."

"We prevent them by killing them, little sister.

And I'm not sure we'd like knowing what they want."

Dro narrowed her eyes. "It doesn't matter if we don't want to know. We have to find out. I'm not going to die not knowing what I am or why I'm being hunted."

I matched her sharp gaze, nerves forgotten. "Don't say stuff like that. You're not going to die. I'm going to keep you safe, just like I always have."

She sighed. "This is so much bigger than us, Con. I can feel it. I'm not asking you to believe everything you hear, but we aren't going to get anywhere if we skip obvious options."

The kitchen door banged open again, Dolly coming towards us with huge plates of food. Dro's eyes lit up, but I looked past them to the cook, the way he was chopping down with his knife. I'd seen similar motions when I was with the Blood Thorns. A blade slicing into flesh and removing it from the bone, blood gushing out like a fountain, a tortured man screaming for mercy–

I tensed again, nearly jumping when Dolly placed the plate of food in front of me. I glanced up at her, not hearing what she said because I was still shaking free of my memories. Dro said something nice to get her away from our table. A small smile played across my sister's lips as she looked at the mountain of chocolate chip pancakes and berries in front of her. She picked up her fork and knife, cutting into her food.

I looked down at mine. The omelet was cooked pretty well, brown singed egg folded over and over with greasy ham and cheese seeping out of it. The potatoes were crispy and dark. The bacon was perfectly cooked and smelled like heaven. Every bad thought I had about the diner began to evaporate. I grabbed my utensils and started eating.

Maybe it wasn't the best diner in Texas. I hadn't been to enough restaurants to compare. But to me, this was five star cuisine. It tasted homemade, reminding me of the Sunday breakfasts Mom used to make when she wasn't working. I looked up at my little sister. She was in bliss, the small smile that I loved on her face as she devoured chocolate chip pancakes.

For a minute, we had the normality Dro wanted. We didn't have to say anything. We could just sit there with each other and let everything else fade away.

But then the kids started arguing and I snapped out of my trance. I kept eating, but my eyes focused over Dro's head as the mother of the family said something to her kids with a sharp tongue. I couldn't hear what they were arguing about, but the little girl was trying to get out of the booth. What was she trying to run from? Was she just being stubborn, or was there something wrong that she saw and I missed?

My eyes ran over the diner again, my body stiffening and my pulse starting to quicken. I'd lost sight of the cook. Was he in the back of the kitchen? Had he looked at me and recognized me? Was he calling the cops? I'd made Dolly nervous. She must have said something to him by now.

I focused on my food, forcing it into my mouth and chewing more than tasting. The far door of the diner kept opening and closing, filling up with the morning seniors and hungry regulars. I kept my head down, but we were going to have to leave soon. Dro noticed this too, taking a break from her pancakes to eat some of the berry salad.

The doorbells tinkled behind me again. I twisted in my seat, hands loose and ready to go for a weapon. Two large men walked in. One wore a plaid shirt with rolled up sleeves and dirty denim jeans while the other one wore a black Creedence Clearwater Revival shirt and light blue jeans. I saw them both look at Dro, staring at her with wonder and amazement. Creedence whispered something I couldn't hear to Plaid, and I felt the tension build in my muscles yet again.

What were they saying? Did they think they could try

something? Would they listen if I told them to stop looking at Dro and fuck off? How fast would I have to move to stop them? Could I reach a knife in time if they left me no choice?

They took their eyes away from Dro and beamed when Dolly's chipper voice called them over. I watched them sit at the long booth across from us. Only Creedence looked back at Dro.

"Do you want to leave?"

I looked across the booth at my sister. She'd eaten about half her food, but stopped when she saw how uncomfortable I'd become. I looked down from her concerned blue eyes and poked some of the potatoes with my fork.

"No, it's okay," I said. "Just wish it were the two of us."

Dro looked at me with a frown on her face, but I pretended I was all right. That I didn't hate places where I couldn't see everything. That I didn't like the cook. That I didn't have a minor anxiety attack when the doors slammed open and someone I didn't know walked inside a place I was unfamiliar with.

Pretend you're normal, Constance. Give Dro her wish.

Maybe I could have kept faking for another five minutes, if Creedence and Plaid didn't have such loud voices and a habit for gossip.

"Did you hear about the bodies they found in El Paso? Can't imagine what kind of animal could tear up a body like that. Sammy said the body was shredded like red confetti."

Dolly laughed loudly with some of the seniors. The regulars were talking over them. The kids started screaming at each other. The parents raised their voices to calm down. The cook slammed things around in the kitchen.

"What about that execution a couple days ago? Guy had his intestines torn out and wrapped around a damn bouquet of red roses."

My heart started racing. The Blood Thorns were two days away from us. The monsters were even closer. They were on our trail. The monsters could sense Dro, and the Blood Thorns knew how to track me. We were going to be found unless I did something. Unless I moved us out of the town and headed somewhere safe.

But nowhere *was* safe. I might know how to run from the Blood Thorns, but the monsters? I didn't know what they were. I didn't know how to keep Dro safe from them. I didn't even know what she was and why they wanted her so badly.

Dro reached across the table and placed her hand on mine. I'd been shaking and hadn't even realized it. I looked up and inhaled, the havoc of the world starting to dissolve around me. Dro tried to smile, to hide the concern in her bright blue eyes. She squeezed my hand.

"I don't know about you, but I can't eat another bite. What do you say we get this all to go? I'm sure it'll last for a couple days, and I know how fanatical you are about leftovers."

I let out a laugh, though it sounded forced. Dro smiled, gave my hand one more squeeze, then signaled Dolly for the check and to-go boxes. I reached into my pocket and pulled some crumpled bills from our reserve cash. We wouldn't have much more after this. As I tossed the money on the table, I glanced at my sister and thought about what she'd said about trying to talk to a priest.

Deep down, she knew I would give in. Dro didn't ask for much, and whenever she did, it was for a good reason. I preferred to be blissfully ignorant. It was easier than knowing the truth. But now that the idea of demons seemed more real, I couldn't deny the curiosity building in the back of my mind.

Even though I knew that if we were dealing with demons, we were in way over our heads.

Dolly walked over, handing us the boxes. "Where's the nearest church?" I asked out of the blue.

The middle-aged blonde waitress looked at me like I was from the moon. "Church?"

"Yeah, the place you go to pray and stuff. Where is one?"

Dolly hesitated, then said, "You can go to Father Colin at the Church of the Redeemer, up the street and two blocks to the left. He should be there now."

I gave her a nod and started dumping the food into the Styrofoam cartons. I moved quickly while Dro charmed the waitress. I just wanted to get out of here before I had another minor panic attack. As soon as we slipped out of the booth, I headed for the door and stood next to it, glancing around the diner to see if anyone was going to try anything while our backs were turned.

Dolly was talking to the cook. Creedence and Plaid were gossiping, Creedence taking the occasional look to Dro. The seniors and regulars hadn't even noticed us. The family was calming their children down. The little girl turned in her seat and waved at Dro. My sister waved back, then left the diner. I followed behind her, catching up to her side.

"So Father Colin at the Church of the Redeemer, huh?" said Dro.

I shrugged. "Guess so."

A faint smile passed my sister's lips and she wrapped her arms around me in a quick hug. "Thanks, Connie."

I stifled a laugh. "Don't thank me yet. We haven't even met the *Padre* yet."

"I meant thanks for breakfast."

I glanced at her uncertainly. "The food was good, but it wasn't what I would call ideal. Or normal."

"Maybe, but for a moment it was." Her smile softened. "Besides, it seemed normal for us."

She was right. But I wasn't sure if that was a happy thought or a depressing one.

CHAPTER FOUR

I'm a skeptic. Given all the paranormal and outright insane things I had seen and endured, I shouldn't have been, but it was a habit I just couldn't break. I needed facts and proof. I couldn't just blindly accept something because it was dressed up with pretty words and magic.

So I don't like churches. I don't like religion. I don't believe in God. They were going to kick me out as soon as they got a look at my dirty jeans, roughed up military jacket, and unwashed hair. And that would be before they realized I was carrying four throwing knives in my jacket and a hatchet on my hip.

It was mid-morning by the time we made our way up the steps to the Church of the Redeemer. Dro stared up at the tall white steeple at its top while I thought about what I could do in Amarillo for money. Maybe we'd be able to get some quick work in and make a little more cash or get us another decent Southern meal. Maybe I could sneak onto a construction crew or something. I had no intention of going back to my criminal ways, not unless we *truly* got desperate, but I didn't want to carve my way through a bunch of red tape either. Paper trails were not my friend. We had eighty-five dollars left, and that wouldn't be enough to get us to... wherever the hell our final destination was.

Dro pushed open the doors to the church and walked inside with me right behind her. The church was what you might call 'modern gothic.' The nave was wide with dozens of long, well polished pews, the curving roof over my head seemed to actually stretch up to Heaven. Stained glass windows glistened with rainbows of light. At the end of the nave was the lectern, with a tall pulpit and a gleaming brass organ behind it. I guess it was a nice church, but I also thought it was a little pretentious.

Dro dipped her pale fingers into the bowl of holy water near the door and crossed herself, saying one Hail Mary. I considered the water, then decided against it. My fingers would never be clean, and I was already going to Hell. A dab of water wouldn't be enough to save my soul.

"Hello?" Dro called to the empty church, her elegant voice echoing against the walls. "Father Colin? Are you here?"

Out of one of the doors on the far right corner came a man in a black priest cassock. He was older, maybe his late fifties, his skin tanned from being in the sun on his off days. In addition to the crisp, white collar around his throat, he wore a long silver rosary that rested against his slightly chubby middle. He greeted us with a warm smile and kind blue eyes.

"Welcome, children," he drawled. "It's always good to see young folk coming to pray in the name of our Lord."

I almost laughed at him. He just sounded so damn corny. I coughed instead, Dro shooting me a look over her shoulder to keep me from saying anything rude for the moment. She turned back to the priest and smiled.

"We're looking for Father Colin. A waitress at the Blue Sky Diner said we could find him here."

He grinned. "You've found him."

She sighed. "That's great. We could use some help."

"Come for confession, child? I'm glad you wish to cleanse

yourself of any impure thoughts, to absolve yourself of any sins and redeem yourself in the eyes of the all gracious God."

I didn't like the way Father Colin looked at her, his eyes quickly running up and down her body. Maybe he needed to confess something to God.

Dro probably noticed his wandering eye, but she didn't say anything. "Not exactly, Father," she admitted. "We have some questions."

"Of course. Tell me what's on your mind."

Dro hesitated. "What can you tell us about... demons?"

His smiled vanished. "We don't speak of demons in the house of the Lord, child. Not unless we're speaking of cleansing them."

"I understand that but, I…"

Oh, no, Dro, don't…

But my sister trusted too deeply. She was too honest. She wanted help so badly.

"I can sense things about people. I have nightmares where I do terrible things." She hesitated again. "I'm wondering if I might be possessed."

I looked at the back of Dro's snow-white head. At least she hadn't said that she could supernaturally heal anyone's wounds and spontaneously combust into fire hot enough to melt metal in two minutes flat, but more subtlety would have been nice.

"Then we'd better test you and see," Father Colin said, blue eyes no longer friendly. "Follow me."

"Where are we going?" I asked.

The priest looked at me. "To the back of the church. I need some privacy."

"No," I said. "Whatever you have to do, you can do it out here, and in front of me."

"Con," Dro started.

I cut her off with a single look. "I'm not going anywhere. And you're not possessed."

"But–"

"No 'buts.' "

"The girl wants to be tested, then she has the right to be tested," said the priest.

I gave him a look so cold he flinched. He probably thought I was the monster. He wasn't totally wrong. Father Colin quickly looked at Dro again. She probably didn't look like anyone he'd ever seen before. There weren't many pale girls with snow-colored hair in Texas, and if there were, none of them looked quite like my little sister.

As soon as he realized I wasn't going to leave, he turned and walked to the stage beyond the pulpit. Dro and I sat on the bench in front of the organ as he took out a Bible, holy water, and Eucharist crackers. Dro sat nervously with her hands on her lap, while I leaned back against the organ and tucked my hands under my armpits, ready to go for a weapon if the priest did something unsanctified.

Threatening a man of God was low and I didn't want to do it, but Dro's safety came first.

Father Colin dripped some holy water onto the top of her head, then gave her a Eucharist to eat. When nothing happened, he showed her the cross on his rosary and spoke some lines from the Bible. Still nothing. He frowned, then closed the book, held it to his chest, and looked deep into her eyes.

"Do you speak with the Devil?" he asked. Dro shook her head.

"Do you go into obscene fits and rages?" She shook her head again.

"Do you speak unusual languages?" Another shake of her head.

"You claim to sense things about other people. What kind of things?"

She opened her mouth to speak, but stopped, looking at me. I shrugged. This had been her idea and I wouldn't talk her out of it, because I didn't have any better ideas myself. But I gave her a steady look that let her know I was here for her, and would keep her safe. Dro looked at Father Colin again.

Her eyes narrowed in concentration. The priest stared at her without emotion, ready to dismiss anything she said.

Then she spoke.

"I… I promise not to say anything outside of here," she started.

Father Colin frowned at her. "What do you mean?"

She looked at me again. I stood ready, and nodded. I knew how ruthless people could be. I could hardly judge him.

"You… You keep some of the money from the collection bowls for yourself. You're jealous that Mr. Harrison has a BMW. You lust after Jebediah's youngest daughter," she said quietly, as if these were her sins to confess and not his. "You asked her to come to the church to see you alone, and when she didn't feel the same way you did, you got angry and–"

I'd been watching the priest's face the whole time Dro had been pulling out his dirty laundry. He went through a whirlwind of emotions. First, there was shock. Then horror. Then anger. And finally, fear.

"How do you know this?" he interrupted in a panicky breath.

"I don't know how it works," Dro said desperately. "Please, I'm trying to find out, I–"

"Only a spy or worshipper of the Devil would create such lies!"

Father Colin's shout bounced off the walls of the church, making it sound even louder. Dro jumped and I straightened, getting in front of him and reaching for the hatchet at my hip.

"That's a pretty harsh assumption, *Padre*," I said, warning in my voice.

He looked at me, but pointed at Dro. "Only demons can read minds and speak false truths!"

I gave him a blistering look. "My sister doesn't lie."

He grimaced. "Then you consort with the devil's ilk," he snarled.

"Stop jumping to conclusions," I snapped. "She's in a church. You used the holy water. She ate the Eucharist. You asked her if she was possessed. She told you she was different. So answer her question."

"I did," Father Colin spat, glaring at her again. "She is the spawn of the devil."

"What if she were a prophet?" I asked. "Did you ever consider that possibility?"

He looked at me like I'd slapped him. If he kept his attitude up, I just might.

"A prophet of the Lord would not resort to vile, wretched lies to prove they were in God's service," he said as if everyone knew that. Maybe he was right, but Dro had tried to get him to listen to her. Revealing his secrets was the best way she could do that.

"I'm sorry. I just want to know what I am," she whispered from behind me.

She sounded so small that I actually turned to look at her. Dro's blue eyes stared down at nothing, worry and nerves creasing her forehead and making her seem older. My heart ached to see her so scared. I was about to go over and comfort her, but the priest opened his mouth again.

"I do not suffer demons in my church," Father Colin growled. "If she were possessed, I could help her. But she shows none of the typical symptoms. Whatever she is, it is unnatural, and she does not belong in a house of God."

I tightened my hands into fists. "Fine by me," I muttered. "Come on, Dro. Let's get out of here."

I waited until she walked past me before following her. The priest turned in front of me, giving me a sharp look.

"If either of you breathe a word of what she said–"

I put my hands on my hips and let his eyes drift down so he could see the knives and hatchet I carried.

"You'll what?" I challenged.

Father Colin backed off. Our stay in Amarillo would be shorter than I thought. I shouldered past the priest, who moved back farther than necessary. He was an asshole, but I wouldn't hurt him. I didn't need to. Let him stand behind his pulpit and jump at shadows. I didn't care.

Dro was waiting for me on the steps outside of the church. She sighed and wrapped her arms around herself. Any happiness and peace she might have felt at breakfast was gone. I debated going back in the church and smacking Father Colin, but instead I stood next to my sister and tilted my head to look at her.

"You okay, Dro?"

She nodded, clearly lying to me. "I just thought he'd want to help us."

"Maybe he wanted you out of there so he could work on an alibi in case you go to the cops," I said.

"I still plan on doing that anonymously," she said. "He shouldn't have gotten away with some of the things he's done. Elizabeth was so scared, she probably never told anyone what he did to her."

Elizabeth, the name of the daughter the priest had traumatized. We had never met her, probably would never meet her, but I couldn't help but think about the last Elizabeth Dro and I had known when we were kids...

If Dro was too shy for her own good, Elizabeth was too chatty for her own good.

Mom had just left for work and Dad was on his way home, but for about an hour it would be just Dro and me. She was five and I was nine, and we decided to play outside for a little bit. We weren't supposed to because we didn't live in a nice neighborhood, but the sun was shining and we didn't have school that day. I was playing with an old soccer ball while Dro played with some dolls Mom had given her from the Salvation Army.

Then, Elizabeth showed up.

There wasn't anything wrong with her, except that she was super annoying. She was my age, and she never stopped talking. Some days I wanted to scream at her to shut up. Other days I wanted to stick my fingers in my ears and say, "I'm not listening, I'm not listening!"

I refused to turn into Elizabeth's life-size Barbie doll, never wanting to wear dresses or do weird things with my hair, so Elizabeth went after Dro.

"Hi Constance!" Elizabeth said, her voice irritatingly chipper. "Why are you playing with that boring ball? Is this your sister? Are you Andromeda? Why do they call you Andromeda?"

I groaned. Hurricane Elizabeth had touched down. Dro gripped her doll tightly and looked at me nervously. She was shy around new people and watched how I talked to them. If I was nice to them, she knew they were okay to talk to. If I was mean to them, she knew to stay away. Elizabeth was like an alien to her. She wasn't bad, just loud.

"Hi, Elizabeth," I said in a tired voice, kicking the soccer ball on my way over to where Dro sat on the grass. Elizabeth wouldn't hurt my sister, but Dro would relax the closer I was to her.

"Does she talk? You can talk, right?"

I sat on the grass next to my little sister. "Yeah, she does. You're asking too many questions, Elizabeth. Calm down."

"But she looks so weird," Elizabeth said, plopping down on the grass in front of Dro and placing her elbows on her knees so her hands could hold her chin up. Dro stared at Elizabeth curiously, but the big eyed- ditz wasn't done asking her million questions yet.

"Why is your hair white? Are you an albino or something? Shouldn't you have red eyes? Do you get sunburned really badly?"

Elizabeth just went on and on and on. I wondered when she would run out of breath.

"Can I ask you a question?" Dro said suddenly.

Elizabeth finally stopped talking. She gaped like a fish, then smiled so hard I thought her face might crack in half.

"You do talk!" Elizabeth started off again. "Ask me, ask me, ask me!"

Dro looked at me like she wanted my permission. I shrugged. I didn't know where she was going with this, and I wasn't the boss of her. Dro shifted nervously, then looked at Elizabeth.

"How come you stole Jenny's doll when you broke yours?"

Elizabeth paled and started gaping again. I stared at my little sister.

"How— Who told you about that?!" Elizabeth shrieked.

Who indeed, seeing as Jenny lived two blocks away and had never met Dro.

"Nobody," Dro confessed. "I just know it."

Elizabeth shot to her feet, pointing an accusing finger at my little sister. "You're a liar! A rotten little liar! You'll be in big trouble if you tell anybody!"

I pushed to my feet and quickly stood in front of Dro. My fists were balled at my sides. Elizabeth stopped shouting. I was known around the block for being a tough kid. Boys bigger than me had tried to bully me, and I had sent them home in tears.

"Go home, Elizabeth," I said coldly. "Leave us alone."

She hesitated, wanting to argue and get her way. I wouldn't budge. Elizabeth pouted, then spun on her heel and stomped off. As soon as she passed a couple houses, I turned and sat on the lawn across from Dro. My little sister plucked the dress of her doll, trying to focus on something other than Elizabeth's words.

Dro had always been a little weird. But I'd never expected this.

"You okay, Dro?" I asked.

She nodded, but didn't look at me and said nothing.

"How did you know about the stolen doll?" I asked after a moment.

"I don't know. I saw that Elizabeth had a bad secret, and then I knew what it was." Dro looked at me, big blue eyes filled with sadness. "You don't believe me, do you?"

I hesitated. Dro was my sister. She knew that I loved her and would do anything for her. But she'd known something nobody but Elizabeth could have known, and it made me nervous.

It also made me wonder more about where Dro had really come from...

"I JUST WANTED A LITTLE HELP," Dro sighed. "I didn't think he would be so..."

"Awful?"

"Yeah."

I wrapped my arm around Dro's shoulder and tugged her to my side. She nestled against me, grateful for the comfort. We stayed that way for a moment before she glanced up.

"Storm's coming," she remarked.

I looked at the sky. Dark clouds were building quickly. I frowned. The monsters could only come out in darkness and while they hated the sunlight, I couldn't take the chance that they would hunt us in a storm. I wasn't thrilled about saying in Amarillo, but now we didn't have a choice. We were low on supplies, needed food, and I had to find a new car. Or at least new license plates.

"Come on," I said. "Let's get back to the car. We'll try somewhere else. Maybe we can find a demonologist."

Dro pulled back to meet my eyes, hopeful and confused. "Really?"

"Yeah. Like you said, the people here love that kind of stuff."

Dro smiled thinly at me. I smiled back at her, wishing I had more assurances than doubts.

CHAPTER FIVE

F inding a demonologist wasn't the challenge. The challenge was finding one whose shop didn't look like a cross between an apothecary and a circus tent.

Signs boasting "real" fortunetellers and "Spirit- Searching- Saturdays" were posted on rundown shops on streets hidden away from public view. Dro spoke with some shop owners to find the addresses for all the demonologists in Amarillo. We stopped in every single shop, and I walked out less impressed every single time.

Granted, I didn't know much about them either. But I did know that when someone avoids answering questions and tries to sell a five hundred dollar demon hunting kit complete with anti- demonic possession pills, the nicest thing to do is walk out of their shop and never come back. Dro forced me to be polite, but with each offer and attempted up-sell, all my faked politeness deteriorated.

By the sixth shop, I was out of patience. I was about ready to tell the owner that I had been fighting monsters since I was fourteen years old, carried a small arsenal with me, and had seen and killed things that would make him piss his pants.

Dro could sense the hostility pulsing off me as I debated slapping the anti-possession pills out of the shopkeeper's hand. She touched my arm and smiled at the shopkeeper. His eyes sparkled with wonder.

"Thank you for your time, but I don't think this is what we need."

She smiled at him again then pulled me toward the exit. I glanced over my shoulder at the shopkeeper to make sure he wasn't doing anything suspicious, then walked with my sister down the street. I reached under my jacket and pulled up the hood of my sweater. The quick moving storm clouds had darkened the street, people rushing along to get inside from the lightly drizzling rain, but I used the hood to keep my face hidden. There was no way to hide Dro. Amarillo didn't have any stores that sold wigs, and we had a bad habit of losing them when we ran for our lives.

Dro sensed people staring at her through the shops or car windows. Even the people jogging past with papers or umbrellas over their heads gave her a second look. I glared at as many of them as I could see. Dro hated it when people stared at her.

I walked close to her, blocking her from as many eyes as possible and distracted Dro by asking how many were on the list. She picked the crumpled piece of paper out of her coat pocket and looked at it.

"Just one. It should be up here."

I took the piece of paper from her and read it. *Garcia Preternatural Associates.* A father and son who promised extensive knowledge and incredible results. Which I would believe when I saw. She shoved the paper back in her pocket while lifted my head when the rain started falling harder.

"Okay, they're our last stop. I'm not liking the weather."

Dro grinned and nudged my side. "Usually you're jumping for the chance to shower."

I rolled my eyes. "Usually I'm not freezing. Come on. If we move fast enough, we might be able to make it out of the storm."

We didn't make it out of the storm. It became a full on downpour by the time we reached the two-story bungalow with white siding and a wooden porch. A plastic sign that read *Garcia Preternatural Associates: Family Owned and Operated since 1997* was staked into the front lawn. The windows were curtained, golden light glowing from behind them and letting us know that someone was home.

The sight of it reminded me of the house Dro and I lived in as children. It had been so long that I'd nearly forgotten what comfort looked like.

Memories threatened to push into my head, but I stopped them before the sadness crept in.

We stomped up the porch, soaked to the bone. Dro clutched her drenched jacket around her body, shaking with cold. The joints in my hand were stiff and filled with an icy burn. I yanked open the screen door then gripped the doorknob. I twisted it to find it was unlocked, so I pushed it open.

"Constance!" My sister protested, but I was already in the house.

Everything smelled like sage. The walls were painted an off-white color, making the hall seem wider than it was. A couple tables with tissue boxes and decorative vases were on my right under a large silver cross on the wall. At the farthest end of the hall was a closed door. The staircase was on my right and a living room on the left. I started to walk toward it when someone entered the hallway and nearly ran into me.

He stopped while I stepped back, my arm wrapping around Dro and pushing her behind me. This new person looked about as harmful as a marshmallow, but pretty faces lied just as easily as ugly ones.

This kid was definitely pretty. A little thin maybe, but his gold skinned face was smooth and unmarked. If it weren't for the dark stubble on his face, he would have looked like a very tall ten year old boy. He had a mop of curly black hair and gentle brown eyes. He smiled, friendly and nice, if weirded out by our entrance.

I didn't trust him.

"Uh, you ladies look a little lost," he said. "And like you need some towels."

"I'm so sorry," Dro quickly said, glaring at me. "I thought she would knock."

"The door was open and the sign was outside, so I figured they were open."

When my defensive expression didn't change, he looked over my shoulder at Dro. His eyes widened, and I could practically see his heart skipping a beat.

Human beings are naturally attracted to beauty, but things got messy when men lusted too heavily after her, or women tried to beat her on sight out of jealousy. That was when I got involved, and they paid a serious price.

But I didn't get that sense from this kid. At least not yet. I could feel Dro moving behind me, her nerves raw and evident.

"We truly did mean to come here, and we were told you took walk-ins, but we should have called ahead. We just couldn't find a phone. But if you want us to simply clean up the floor and go..."

He kept staring at her. I wondered if he recognized her from the Wanted lists, where she was listed as my accomplice, but doubted it. If he had, then he would have had to recognize me. Instead, he didn't even notice that I was the wall between him and Dro. He was too amazed by her.

"No worries," he smirked. "I'll get you some towels. I might be able to find some spare clothes for you to borrow so the ones you're wearing can dry out."

Dro smiled. "That would be great, thank you."

"Not a problem. I'll be right back."

"Wait a second," I said, before he could take off. "We're coming with you."

He frowned. "Look, I get that you might be clients, but you did just walk into our house." He sighed. "Lucky for you one of the shops you visited gave us a heads up you'd be coming. We're all pretty tight knit in that community. So yeah, we'll listen, but my dad made me clean the whole house yesterday. I'd really don't want to do it again."

My heart skipped at the idea of the other paranormal shops calling each other and letting this kid know we were coming.

Would they have warmed him that we were wanted criminals?

"She has serious trust issues," Dro explained. "But I promise we won't make any trouble. If you want us to wait here, we will."

He glanced at me with uncertainty, but agreed. "It's okay. Just take your shoes off, please."

Dro did so dutifully, and I reluctantly toed off my boots. The kid walked us toward the end of the hall. Every other door I could see had been closed and locked. Smart. They took walk-ins, but walk-ins weren't given free reign. He stopped at the far door and unlocked it. My hand slipped to my hatchet, my body tensing.

The kid flicked on the lights to a bathroom and rummaged around the linen cabinet for a pair of towels. He turned and handed them to me. I pulled them from his hands a little too aggressively, handing one to Dro before wiping down my face with the other. I shook out my hair, but kept my jacket on. There was no need to show the kid how many weapons I carried. I would have to empty my backpack at some point and make sure my supplies dried out. It sucked that we were going to have to throw out the leftovers from this morning.

"Do you guys want something hot to drink?" the kid asked.

We looked up at him. "Would it be too much to ask?" Dro asked hesitantly. "We've already been such a bother..."

He waved his hand. "Nah, not at all." He squinted at Dro, then pointed his finger at her. "Let me guess. Hot chocolate with marshmallows and cinnamon."

She blinked, grinning. "Good guess, especially the cinnamon part."

I looked at the kid suspiciously. Dro loved hot chocolate and marshmallows. But the cinnamon... How could he know that?

He turned his dark eyes to me. "And you probably want black coffee, maybe with some kind of alcohol in it." He held out his hands innocently. "Which I'm fresh out of, unfortunately. Dad and I aren't heavy drinkers."

He grinned his goofy grin again, but I was becoming more apprehensive about him. He must have noticed, because he cleared his throat and edged his way past me toward wherever the kitchen was before I could stop him. I watched his back for a moment before following him.

"Anything I should know about him?" I muttered to my sister for supernatural insight.

She shook her head, following the kid down the hall. "He seems okay, but there's something different about him."

"Different how?"

"I can't explain it, but he has something extra in his mind. But I can't read anything on him to believe that he'll hurt us. He's a good guy."

That remained to be seen, but I trusted Dro's instincts enough to give his kid a chance. Having her explain it to anyone, even me, had never really gone well...

ELIZABETH'S PARENTS called our Dad about five minutes after he got home. They said Elizabeth was crying and hysterical about what happened with Dro's knowledge about the doll and my mean attitude. After calming them down and hanging up the phone, he walked into the living room where we sat on the couch, waiting to get scolded. Dro hunched in on herself with her tiny pale hands in her lap, looking down guiltily. I sat next to her with my arms crossed over my chest, frustrated and bored.

Dad put his hands on his hips. He looked exhausted, his overalls and golden skin still dirty from working at the construction site. He hadn't even had time to sit down and eat dinner before problems started with his kids.

"Okay," he sighed. "Who wants to explain what happened?" He looked at me like I was the one to blame.

Usually I was, but not this time.

"Elizabeth is just being a big baby," I complained. "We didn't do anything."

"You said she stole something," Dad pointed out. "That isn't a small thing to accuse someone of."

I rolled my eyes.

"Don't roll your eyes at me, Constance. Tell the truth."

I pouted. I wasn't going to take the fall for this.

"It's my fault," Dro said quietly from beside me. "I shouldn't have said anything. I didn't mean to look, but..." Dro shifted back onto the couch and pulled her knees up to her chest, wrapping her arms around them and looking smaller than even a five year old should. "It was an accident," she whispered.

Dad looked at her strangely, glancing at me for answers. I said nothing. I might have seen what happened, but that didn't mean I understood it. I still didn't know if I should believe Dro or not.

"What was an accident? Elizabeth's mother told me you said Elizabeth stole a doll from that girl Jenny, but how do you know it belonged to Jenny?"

Dro hugged her knees tighter to her chest, biting her lip and holding back tears. Dad walked over to the couch and sat down beside his adopted daughter. He put his arm over her tiny shoulders.

"I'm not mad at you, Andromeda. I know Elizabeth is... a bit much, and I know that neither of you took that doll. But I don't know how you knew about it in the first place. I can't fix this unless you tell me the truth."

Dro shivered and Dad hugged her closely. "It's okay, sweetheart. I'll believe whatever you tell me."

My sister looked at him, blinking her icy blue eyes. "I saw it."

"You saw Elizabeth take the doll from Jenny?"

She shook her head. "Not in person. I saw it in my head."

Dad went still. "What do you mean?"

She shivered again, like she was about to cry. Dad kept his arm around her, but his dark brown eyes were uncertain. Usually I was the one he had to be wary of. Dro was a saint.

"It was like a dream. I looked at Elizabeth and I saw these pictures in my head. I saw her taking the doll from Jenny's house last week and putting it in her backpack when she wasn't looking. I just looked at her and knew."

Dad stayed motionless, his hand starting to leave Dro's shoulder. When it moved too far, Dro broke down and started to cry. I put my arm over her back and hugged her to me.

"I'm a freak," she cried into my shirt.

"No you're not," I told her.

"Then something's wrong with me," she sobbed. "Something's bad in me."

I pulled away from Dro to look into her eyes. Tears streaked her pale cheeks.

"Nothing's wrong with you, little sister. And you're definitely not bad."

Dro looked at me, desperate for an explanation. But I didn't have one, and I wouldn't lie to her. Dro started crying again. Dad's face crumpled, and he took her from my arms to hold her in his lap. She twisted and wrapped her arms around his neck, clinging tightly. He patted the snow-white hair on her back.

"It's okay, Andromeda," he soothed. "You must have heard a rumor or had a dream or something. Your sister is right. Nothing's wrong with you."

But as Dad looked at me, I could see the hesitation in his dark eyes, mirrors of my own. He didn't believe what he'd said anymore than I did...

"Con?"

I snapped out of the memory, having forgotten that I was standing in the doorway of a stranger's kitchen, staring into space. My sister looked at me warily.

"Are you coming?" she asked. "Yeah. Sorry. Got lost in thought."

Dro understood when I didn't elaborate. I didn't have warm or cuddly thoughts, and this would hardly be the time for nostalgia.

CHAPTER SIX

The kid led us to the kitchen, which looked small but cozy. He gestured for us to sit at the narrow island so while he worked on our drinks. I glanced at the dark stove, the stainless steel fridge covered in notes and reminders, the trinkets and the spice rack on the counter next to the microwave. The kitchen smelled like cinnamon, further reminding me of the home I used to know.

I fought against memories when he turned and placed our drinks in front of us. I glanced in the mug, breathing in the steam and smell of coffee. The coffee was rich, black, and deliciously warm. So damn good I nearly moaned. I could feel the caffeine waking me up at almost the same second it hit my tongue. Dro's hot chocolate smelled creamy and sweet, and was overloaded with marshmallows peppered with cinnamon, just the way she liked it. She took the mug in her hands to warm them up, looking at her smiling admirer.

"Thank you, Mister..." her voice trailed off, waiting for him to give his name.

"Whoa, don't call me Mister. That makes me feel like I need business cards." He grinned. "My name's Max."

She smiled. "Thank you, Max."

Dro reached out and touched his hand, squeezing it gently.

Max looked at her hand and suddenly pulled back. My hand went to my hip. Dro looked confused. Max looked at his hand and then at Dro, like he didn't know what he was seeing.

"What are you?" he asked her.

"I... I don't understand," she said quietly.

"You aren't human," Max said, speaking the dreaded words.

Dro looked at me. I had set my coffee mug down and got ready to move.

"That's a strange thing to say," I warned.

"Not if you have psychic talents," he told me matter-of-factly.

I huffed. "Right."

"Believe it, Constance."

I cut the sarcasm. He had my full attention, but his focus was entirely on Dro.

"I got a sense of why you were coming before you got here, and when you touched me, I saw a flicker of what you've been through," he explained. "You have demons after you. You have for years. That's why you really came here. To find answers."

"Demons?" Dro could barely hide the shake in her voice. "Are you sure?"

"My powers are the reason Dad and I started this business. He wanted to understand me, and the rest just kind of fell into place." His eyes widened and he started rifling through the pockets of his jeans. "I've got to call him."

"I don't think so," I warned. "You still have some explaining to do."

Max glared up at me. "What do you want me to say? I told you the truth, and you can't say you don't believe me. It'd make you a hypocrite, given what Andromeda can do."

God, how much had that single touch of my sister's hand shown him?

"Max, please," Dro appealed. "If you know something about me, about these demons, you have to tell us. They've been after me since I was a child. I have a right to know why."

This was the reason Dro negotiated with regular (well, mostly regular) people. She knew how to ask for what she wanted without pulling out a knife and threatening to cut off a body part. I tended to skip pretense and get down to business.

Max hesitated, then dropped his phone on the counter, wrapping his fingers around it.

"Okay, listen. I get senses about people and things without touching them. That's how I guessed about the cinnamon and alcohol and how I know your names. That knowing feeling is literally my sixth sense. But when I touch someone, I can get a flash of who they are. Sometimes if I concentrate enough while touch something, I can even see a little bit of the future. Mostly quick images and feelings, but with you it was more powerful than anything I'd ever felt. Not just the fear you've been feeling, but you have more raw power in you than... Than *anything*. More power than any human could possibly have."

"What does that mean?" I tried. "Do you know what she is?"

Max shook his head at me. "No." He hesitated, then added, "My Dad has taken me to some exorcisms, so I know how to sense demons. But you don't feel quite like that, Dro. You feel like something else."

Dro hung her head, running her hands through her snow-white hair. Hearing she was being chased by demons was one thing. Hearing that she wasn't human and something even a psychic had never encountered, was almost too much.

"Does your father know how to kill demons? Actually kill them?" I asked Max, needing answers while she processed his words.

Max started to shake his head, then stopped. "No. Yes. Kind of. If you want them expelled, he's your guy, but one-on-one combat?" He shook his head for real this time. "My dad knows the theories, but not how to practice them."

"Then you should call him. Tell him he can have a student."

Max blinked. "You want to learn demonology?"

Dro looked up at me. "Con, no, it's too dangerous."

I held her eyes. "Demons, Dro. Fiends of Hell. It's the best explanation I've heard so far. Granted, Max and his father will give us more evidence when they have it–"

"We will?" Max asked.

"–but if that's what we're dealing with, then I want to know more about them. I need to know how to keep you safe."

"You're making a lot of assumptions, Constance," he reminded.

"I am. But I'm also willing to teach him, and you, how to defend yourself against them if you ever come face to face with a real demon." I met his eyes seriously. "And trust me, you're going to be glad for the tips."

I didn't add that anything they had on demons might lead us to finding out exactly what my little sister was. That it was just as important as understanding the creatures on our tail. Maybe even more so.

Max hesitated again, probably regretting he ever sensed us coming. Couldn't say I blamed him. But I saw the worry in his eyes. He loved his father, and wanted to protect him as much as he could.

Chuckling, he picked up his phone again. "This will be an interesting conversation."

———

MAX DESCRIBED HIS FATHER, Manny, as a tough, smart man. I suppose he had to be, given that he was a professional demonologist and exorcist that expelled actual, real demons.

Despite Max's praise, I wasn't expecting the man who walked into the kitchen.

He was probably younger than I guessed, but I couldn't tell from the dark shadows under his eyes or the tired slump of his weathered face. His hair was gunmetal grey with bits of white around his temples. I could see the resemblance between Max and Manny in the shape of their eyes, lips and nose. Manny was a big guy, and only some of the bulk around his middle was fat. He looked like a man who'd endured a hard life, carried the scars of it, but came out as a survivor. I hoped I would be as lucky if I ever reached his age, but with the enemies I had and the reckless choices I made, I doubted it.

He glanced at us in the kitchen, his eyes lingering on his son that promised there would be a conversation about his choice later. Then he looked at Dro.

He stood stock still, assessing her as if he could tell by one look that she weren't human.

"She's okay, Dad," Max soothed. "I told you, she won't hurt us."

I sat behind the island next to Dro, watching Manny very carefully. He gave me a quick look, but his uncertain eyes kept moving back to my sister.

"Ladies, this is my father, Manny Garcia. Dad, that's Constance," he pointed to me, then moving his finger to Dro, "and her adopted sister Andromeda."

Manny raised his eyebrow. "Adopted? From where?"

"It's a long story," I told him.

"Dro's asked for us to help find out what she is," Max went on, "and Constance wants to become a better demon slayer."

"So you mentioned," drawled Manny, his accent rolling and familiar to one my father used to have. "Plenty of easy promises were made without me," he sighed, still considering me. "I'm assuming you've seen demons before?"

I nodded once.

"And you want to keep facing them? Keep killing them?"

I kept all emotion off my face. I didn't let him see the deep, dangerous anger that built up when I thought about the monsters and the way they had destroyed everything we'd ever known. How they'd broken down all the walls of safety we'd built with our parents. How they'd forced me to do things I would never forgive myself for.

I didn't let him see that I was tired of being afraid of the monsters, the Blood Thorns, life on the run. Of what Dro could do.

"I have my reasons," I said flatly. "And they aren't your business."

Max shrank back a little, and Manny regarded me coldly, probably getting ready to kick me out of his house, but Dro came to the rescue.

"What my sister means to say is that these demons, have been hunting us for years." Her ice blue eyes were haunted. "There have been times where they've almost killed us. She needs to learn how to fight them as best as she can, and I need to understand what I am and why they're after me."

Dro looked at Manny. "I don't know what we can offer you. Con's promised to help you learn how to protect yourself, and I'm trying to think of anything else. We don't have much, but we need any help you can give. We can't do this alone. Please."

I hated hearing Dro beg. It pulled at my heart and made me feel like less of the protective, providing sister I was supposed to be. I couldn't help but look back at everything that had happened to us, and wonder if I should have done something differently. If I could have kept us both from starving and begging and fighting a little while longer.

There was a long silence after Dro's request. I didn't like it. It gave them too much time to think rationally and throw us out. I resigned myself to it. I should have known better than to barge in here making demands. Hell, in their position, *I* would throw myself out.

"Dad, they came here because no one else would help them," Max explained. He looked at Dro and me. "Right? No one else believed you or took you seriously."

I did nothing, but Dro nodded. Max looked at his father again.

"Besides, Dro can help with your research. She's something the world hasn't seen before. She can–"

"Whoa, hold on a second," I spoke over him. "My sister is not going to be a guinea pig."

Max narrowed his eyes at me. "That isn't what I was trying to suggest–"

"Then you shouldn't have said it."

Tension built in the room. Manny moved closer to his son, ready to defend him if I decided to get meaner.

"Stop it, Con. I'll answer any questions you have, Manny," said Dro.

I looked at her. "Dro..."

"They aren't going to hurt us, Constance. I can feel it."

Meaning she'd used her powers to take a peek into their minds. But she'd only see what they were thinking now, at this single moment. When she wasn't looking, anything could change. Smart people knew how to hide their true intentions, saving them for when they would do the most damage. I'd experienced it a thousand times over back in my days as a Thorn. Everyone looked out for themselves first. The rest of us were left to choke on the dust they kicked in our faces.

I must have been scowling fiercely, because Manny's shoulders tensed when he looked at me. Dro turned her sweetest smile on him.

"I'm sorry about my sister," she soothed. "She's very defensive. But I'll be more than happy to work with you. It's the least we can do."

Manny regarded her with interest, becoming more and more intrigued by her. I watched him carefully, waiting for that sinister gleam to come into his eyes, or the hint of fear that suggested he would call the cops. Nothing on his face changed. This must have been sincerity, something I wasn't very familiar with. It made my fingers twitch, itching for the hilt of my hatchet to remind me that I could take control of the situation if I felt I needed to. Trusting others had never ended well for me.

"All right. I'll answer whatever questions you have. Tomorrow."

Dro bit her lip. Max cleared his throat. "They don't have a place to stay, Dad," he coaxed. "If they spend the night here, it'll be easier for everybody. They can sleep in the basement. They won't cause any trouble." Max hesitated when he looked at me. "Well, Dro won't. Constance... I'm not so sure."

I grinned.

"She won't do anything," assured Dro, fixing me with a glare. "You have my word."

My smile dropped. I didn't like when Dro made promises for me. It meant that I had to keep them.

"All right," Manny sighed, clearly as tired of this as we were. "You can stay one night so we can get some answers for each other." His eyes found mine. "I will tell you everything I know about hunting demons, if that's what you still want."

I crossed my arms. "It is, as long as you keep your end of the bargain."

Dro sighed heavily beside me and put her face in her hands.

Manny narrowed his eyes at me. "You don't put a lot of stock into the human race, do you Constance?"

"I haven't had the best experiences with them. Kind of hard to do when almost every single one has died or stabbed me in the back."

Another silence followed as I fell into a dark place. I tried to picture the faces of the people who betrayed me in the past, but there were more than I could remember.

And I was no better than any one of them.

"We won't betray you," Max sounded so honest.

He really did seem like a good kid, and I wanted to believe him. From the endearing look in Dro's eyes, she wanted to believe him, too. But if I had a dollar for every time someone said that to me, Dro and I wouldn't be homeless.

"Both of you should get some sleep," said Manny, the weariness still heavy in his eyes. "We'll start again first thing in the morning."

He made it sound less than promising, but at least I could tell myself we were making progress. Hopefully.

CHAPTER SEVEN

I woke up early on purpose. I didn't sleep much, having trained my body to wake at the slightest sound. I took the risk of having Dro sleep on the mattress next to me, like we had when we were kids. I slept near the edge of the mattress, my hatchet under the pillow and a knife on a box near my head.

After about four hours of sleep, I woke up and looked over at my sister to make sure she wasn't having a nightmare. She seemed all right, breathing evenly and calmly. But her nightmares were unpredictable. I could only pray she wouldn't burn down the house of the only people who had offered to help us.

And you should be more grateful.

I slipped out of the bed and grabbed my weapons, hooking the hatchet through one of the loops on the waistband of my jeans, sliding the knife into another. My oversized shirt concealed the blades.

I padded toward the stairs, glancing at Dro one more time to make sure her sleeping hadn't changed. She still looked fine, so I walked up to the basement door, pulled it open and left the room. I ran a hand through my hair to shake it out, stopping by the digital thermostat on the wall to check the time.

5:00 AM. *Ugh.*

I regretted not taking the time to check the rest of the house before we'd gone to bed. Still, now was just as good a time as any. I cringed at the idea of scoping a house again, but I wanted to know where the exits were. I wanted escape routes and a better understanding of where I was if something went wrong.

I made my footsteps as light as possible as I walked into the living room and let my eyes take it in.

Across from me by the window was a small white table with matching plastic chairs. In the middle of the room was a dark brown sofa and a matching love seat, a fake oak coffee table littered with magazines, coasters, and remotes for the TV across the wall. On the left of the TV stood a huge bookshelf with hundreds of books. To my right was a wide desk with a two leather chairs, one front of it and one behind. On the wall beyond the desk were framed certificates in psychology, theology and of course, demonology. The desk was covered with a computer, stacks of paper, a stationary set, and framed photos. I walked over to the desk and grabbed one of the photos.

In the photo, Manny had his arm over Max's shoulder. Max looked about ten years old, a huge smile on his face. I glanced at another framed photo that was the portrait of a lovely woman with deep eyes and a kind smile. Max's mother, I assumed. I wondered where she was. I hadn't seen if Manny had a wedding ring.

I put the framed photo back onto the desk and walked over to the books. There were a couple fiction works, but most of them were texts on demons. I read the titles on the spines, but they didn't mean anything to me. I was a fighter, not a scholar. All I wanted to know is how many stabs it needed before I killed it. Or where it should be stabbed. When it came to research, I didn't even know where to start.

"I didn't think you were a morning person," a voice said from behind me.

Half way through his sentence, I had whirled, my hands going to my hips. My shoulders tensed, as did the lazy smile on Manny's face when he saw the dangerous look in my eyes.

"Sorry," he said. "I didn't mean to startle you."

"Then don't sneak up on me," I said.

Manny frowned, his eyes darkening with disappointment. Normally I would have kept staring him down, but I remembered that I needed his help. Dro was always saying we had to be nice to people who were trying to help us, and right now I wasn't giving Manny any reason to. I relaxed, but kept my hands loose at my sides.

"Sorry," I said, adding genuine guilt to my tone. "I didn't hear you come in."

He took a careful step into his office toward his desk. "You should go back to bed. You look tired."

I stifled a laugh, glancing at the books. "My sister tells me that all the time."

"With good reason, I'm sure." Manny regarded me carefully. "You're safe here, Constance. No one is going to hurt you."

I crossed my arms and leaned against the bookcase. "Forgive me if I don't believe that."

Manny sighed. "You don't like to make things easy, do you?"

That got a sarcastic smile out of me. "Wouldn't have lived this long if I did."

"So you really have fought demons before," he stated.

I nodded, but didn't elaborate. I doubted even a demonologist would want to hear my horror stories.

"Usually I can perform an exorcism and expel a minor demon, but fighting a physical one..." He shook his head. "I can't imagine how hard that must be."

I pulled my arms tighter around my chest. "Trust me. You

don't want to. Even whatever tricks I show you might not be enough. They've barely enough enough for me."

Manny caught on that I didn't want to keep talking about it, and changed the subject. "I take it you're an armed woman." I held his eyes and nodded. "What do you use?"

I hesitated answering him. Manny and Max didn't seem to know I was a fugitive who used to belong to one of the most dangerous gangs south of the border, and I wasn't rushing to tell them.

Then he said, "I have a double-barrel shotgun under my desk filled with blessed rock salt and sage. Unless you're carrying a bazooka with you somewhere, there's nothing you can say that will frighten me."

I chuckled a little. I appreciated his honesty. Not only had he told me that he was armed and where to find his weapon, he said it as though he didn't care that I would be armed to the teeth.

He was earning my respect, if not my trust. "I have a hatchet and four throwing knives."

"A hatchet?" Manny said curiously. "Not the sort of weapon I would have expected a future demon slayer to have."

The humor left my eyes. "It was my father's."

Manny nodded, as though he understood. "I'm guessing that none of those weapons are silver or blessed."

"Honestly, Manny, what my weapon is made out of is the last thing on my mind when I'm fighting demons or whatever the hell they are. I'll use a fucking garbage bag if it means I can kill them."

"Hm. Well, faith and silver are your strongest weapons. Pure silver will injure any demon severely, but faith will repel them and keep them away from you."

"Right. I think I'll stick with the silver."

He tilted his head at me. "You want to fight demons but you don't want to have faith?"

"I'm a cynic. I don't have any reason to believe in a higher power."

He frowned. "Then you're only being difficult."

My face was stony, but inside my respect for him grew even more. I didn't mind being called difficult, since Manny had the guts to say it to my face. He was the type of person I could trust. I just wished my brain would let me.

Maybe I could try that nice thing Dro always went on about.

I grinned wickedly. "Oh, this isn't me being difficult. This is me being practical." He gave me a dry look, but I ignored it. "So. Rock salt and sage kill demons?"

Manny steadily moved back on topic. "Yes. It's even more powerful if it's blessed."

"Huh. Well, I guess since you're a demon guru, you would know if it would work. Rock salt is pretty easy to come by and make shells for, but what's so special about sage?"

"Demons are repelled by the smell. When it's burned it can cleanse and purify a house of evil spirits, but mixing it with salt and using it in a gun can make the shot extra powerful."

Which is why his whole house smelled like it. I glanced at the desk, then back at him. "Why not silver bullets? Or holy water or something? Wouldn't those work?"

Manny hesitated. "They do, but they are hard to come by, and very few people use them."

I stifled a laugh. "Not a lot of werewolf-hunters out there?"

"No. Not enough demon slayers."

I blinked at him. "Wait, there really are demon slayers out there? Actual, legitimate demon slayers?"

Manny took a deep breath, turning back around to walk over to his desk. He sat down in his chair, the framed photos facing him. I took one of the chairs across from him.

"I've only ever met one of them. It's not a profession with a long life expectancy."

"How do I get in touch with them?"

"You don't. His number is only dialed for emergencies. It's like 9-1-1, a number you pray you never have to use."

I narrowed my eyes. "I'd say that my sister and I being hunted by demons qualifies as an emergency."

"Please, Constance, if I thought he could help you, I would give you his number. But unless the situation is absolutely critical, I don't contact this man. He has other, serious problems to deal with. He doesn't have time for an apprentice."

Part of me wanted to keep pressing. Manny couldn't train me physically, couldn't give me the weapons I needed to fight demons, but a demon slayer could. The other part of me knew I wouldn't get anywhere, because there was nothing more Manny would tell me.

I leaned back against the chair, letting out a frustrated sigh. "Well, if I can't get help from a demon slayer, what help can I get from you?"

I asked it as politely as I could. Manny's eyes twinkled. I think he was starting to get used to me.

"Have you ever heard the saying that the pen is mightier than the sword?" he asked with a sly smile.

"Yeah,. But I prefer the sword. It's more efficient."

Manny didn't give me the hard, cold look I had expected. Instead, his eyes smiled.

"All demons have different powers. I can teach you how to exploit them. I'm not a demon slayer, but I have learned how to protect my family. Those are the kinds of lessons I will continue to learn."

We sat in a quiet understanding for a minute or two. Manny wasn't that different from me, after all. When it came down to it, he would do anything to keep his son alive. The shotgun under his desk was proof enough of that. My thoughts strayed to Dro.

"What about my sister?" I asked quietly.

Hesitance built in his eyes. Then he laced his hands together and looked at me over the desk. If it hadn't been for the softness and wisdom in his dark brown eyes, he would have looked like a teacher ready to scold a bad student.

"Tell me about her powers."

Christ, where am I supposed to begin? I thought.

Dro had powers as incredible as they were impossible. I didn't know if there was a way I could ease Manny into knowing about them. If he would even believe me when I told the truth. I took a deep breath. Manny was a demonologist who knew a demon slayer. He stayed patient with me and offered to help my sister. He would have been in his rights to kick us out of his house or call the cops. Hell, if he did that, he'd actually get paid for it.

Instead, he sat behind his desk, and waited.

So I picked out a memory, and told him...

ELIZABETH'S BROTHER, Miles, was like me when it came to his younger sibling. He protected her no matter what. When someone insulted or disrespected her, he got revenge.

I'd seen him stomping over to our house, fourteen years old, all temper and greasy skin. The local bully, he might have loved his sister, but he wasn't afraid to pick on girls or kids younger than him. We'd stayed away from each other, until Elizabeth tattled on Dro.

He'd come to our house looking for her, and found me instead.

"Your sister's a liar!" he shouted. "Make her apologize!"

"No," I shot back. "Dro didn't do anything. Your sister did. Get lost, Miles."

"Your sister's just a freak!"

"Don't call her that," I growled, clenching my fists.

"Bring her out here and make her apologize to Liz." He was

older than me. Bigger and stronger. He would hurt me, and then he would hurt Dro. I stood my ground.

"No."

I wasn't ready for Miles' fist when it hit my face. I dropped onto the ground, feeling bruised and dizzy. Miles grabbed my hair and pulled it, trying to drag me along the pavement. I found my footing and kicked back, my foot driving right between his legs.

He let me go and cupped himself, howling in pain. I tried to kick him again, but he tackled me and pushed me onto the ground. He weighed at least fifty pounds more than I did, crushing my chest under his knees. I couldn't move my arms, so I couldn't stop him when he started hitting me again. My head cracked harshly against the sidewalk. Blood coated my lips.

"Hey!" someone shouted furiously.

Miles was suddenly yanked off me and thrown back onto the sidewalk. He scrambled and tried to get up to fight again.

He stopped when he saw how angry my father was. "You like beating up on girls? What the hell is wrong with you?"

Miles had half a brain after all. He backed away from Dad. I pushed myself up into a sitting position, my hands still resting on the sidewalk. My head pounded, and I had to spit blood out of my mouth.

"Get away from my daughter. If I see you anywhere near my house or my family again, I'll show you what a real beating feels like."

Dad didn't talk about his past when I asked, trying to figure out why we left Mexico. Mom had only ever said that we were better off here, and that Dad had done everything he could to make a new life for us. She said never to ask him about it, and to be grateful for what he'd done. I was, but sometimes I wondered. But I'd heard him talk to Mom late at night, and knew Dad had done bad things before.

Miles scrambled to get away from my father. We were

probably going to get a complaint or another angry call from parents, but Dad would deal with it. He always did.

He watched Miles run home awkwardly, then rushed over to me, taking me by my shoulders. Any rage that might have been in his eyes before was replaced with concern.

"Are you all right, Constance?" he asked.

I nodded, stopping when it became too painful. I held back tears from the throbbing pain in my skull. Dad twisted so he could see the back of my head. I felt him gently peeling strands of my hair away. He cursed under his breath.

"Daddy?" a soft voice called from the house. "What's wrong with Connie?"

Dad kept his hand on my shoulder, starting to push himself up. "She got hurt. Stay with her. I'm going inside to get a first aid kit and call Mommy."

Dro was at my side before he'd even finished giving his instructions. She gasped when she saw the blood in my hair and on my face. Her eyes glistened with tears, her lower lip starting to tremble.

Dad put his hand on her back. "Constance will be okay, honey. Just stay with her and keep her awake until I come back."

She nodded, putting her arms around my chest. Dad got up and ran for the house. Dro tucked her head into the crook of my shoulder, starting to sob. I clutched her hands.

"I'm okay, Dro. It's just a headache." A very, very painful headache.

"You're bleeding," she whimpered.

"Yeah," I said. A grin twisted my lips. "But you should've seen what I did to Miles."

I tried to make Dro laugh, but she just cried more. She pulled away from me suddenly, staring at me with tears streaking down her face.

"I want to fix it," she stated. "It's my fault."

"No it's not. Miles was just being mean. It had nothing to do with you."

"He came here because of me, didn't he?"

I said nothing. Dro would know if I lied.

She sobbed again, then pressed one of her little hands on the back of my head while the other covered my mouth. A weird pins and needles feeling that buzzed along my wounds. I jumped back, away from Dro.

My little sister stared at me with wide eyes. I was about to ask her what had happened, but then I noticed the pain in my head was gone. I wiped my lip with my fingers. They came away bloody, but the cut was gone. I pressed a hand to the back of my head. My hair was still matted with blood, but I couldn't feel a gaping wound anywhere.

"I wanted to fix you," Dro whispered across from me.

I looked up at my sister, whose touch had healed me.

It didn't make sense. People didn't just randomly touch others and heal their injuries. That only happened in movies.

But Dro had done it for me.

I sat there and stared at her, not knowing what to think. She was on the verge of tears again.

"Are you scared of me, Connie?" she asked, voice barely above a whisper.

I shook my healed head slowly. "No," I said, hoping I sounded convincing.

When Dro started crying again, I knew I hadn't done a good job. I crawled across the pavement to sit next to her and hugged her tightly to my chest.

"I'm not scared of you, Dro. I promise."

She clutched my shirt in her tiny fist and sobbed. I kept holding her, but my mind raced. Dro knew about Elizabeth's stolen doll. She healed my cuts with single touches. How had she done it? Why had she been able to? What else could she do? Mom and Dad and I knew that Dro was special, that she was different. But this was something else. Something I hadn't expected, and couldn't understand.

She was still my sister though. I loved her and would stick by her side. Dro had been abandoned before, left alone in the forest to die as a baby. I would never do that to her.

I turned my head, resting my cheek on the top of her hair. I lifted my eyes and sighed, stopping when I saw that only one of the neighbors, the lady across the street, had stayed outside.

She was tall, thin, and beautiful. She was relatively new to the block, having moved across the street a couple years ago when the last residents suddenly decided to go on a really long vacation. The woman had golden skin like mine, her hair long and silky down her back. She wore a black suit with a pencil skirt and spiked heels. Long gloves were on her hands, reaching up to the elbow. She looked like a harsh, serious businesswoman. Or a funeral director. I think Mom said her name was Isabel.

And right now, she was stared at us. Or more accurately, at my little sister.

I'd caught her watching Dro a couple times before when we were playing outside. I hadn't thought anything of it, because everybody looked at Dro. But this wasn't one of the normal, curious or amazed stares. This was the look of a lion watching a gazelle from the long grass. Predatory and dangerous.

I held Dro tighter to me and glared at her.

Isabel glanced at Dro, then winked at me. She turned and walked back into her house, leaving me with a crying sister and a bad feeling in my stomach...

BY THE TIME I finished telling Manny every power Dro had, it was almost seven in the morning. He hadn't said anything the entire time I spoke, listening with rapt attention instead. I stared at Manny's desk, not seeing anything. Even though I had told

Manny the truth, the weight on my shoulders didn't feel any lighter.

Finally, I looked up at him. "Do you have any idea what she is, or what she might be?" I sounded small, almost childish. I hated myself for it.

Manny held my eyes. I couldn't tell if he was thinking or frozen with terror. Then he blinked slowly and sighed, his dark eyes turning sorrowful.

"No, Constance. I have no idea."

CHAPTER EIGHT

As a professional demonologist in Texas, Manny and Max had a lot of interesting clients. Dro and Max woke up a few hours after I had. Dro offered to make breakfast for all of us, whipping up some French toast so delicious Max nearly grovelled at her feet.

An hour later, their first client showed up. An elderly woman with kind eyes behind round glasses, dentures for teeth, and fire engine red lipstick.

She came for a palm reading from Max, apparently one of the few people who knew about his gift. Max was more than happy to do the reading in the living room. I watched with my hands on my hips. I'd known some tough old folks in my life. When it comes to holding a gun, age doesn't matter. A seven year old can hold a gun just as well as a seventy year old.

But Dro had assured me that she was okay. Some dark spots on her mind, but mostly from memories she wanted to forget. The woman focused on Max, chatting him and Manny up as Max read her palm. When she asked who Dro and I were, Manny had simply said we were interns. It was a lie as close to the truth as he could make it.

Max told the old woman what she wanted to know– which Bingo numbers she should pick and when her grandchildren would surprise her for a visit– and then left. At the door, she gave Max a peck on the cheek, leaving a huge red lipstick stain on his face. Dro giggled from behind me. The woman patted Max on the back and looked at us.

"You girls look after little Maxie, now. He's a good boy."

Max turned as red as the lipstick on his face. Even I managed a grin.

"Thank you, Mrs. Dawson. I'll see you next week."

"Not if your numbers are right, Maxie!" She said merrily before walking down the porch steps.

Max glanced at us when she was out of earshot. "She used to babysit me," he mumbled, rubbing at the lipstick on his cheek. "I almost got cavities from all the sugar she gave me."

Dro laughed again, taking a tissue from the box at the table behind us. She dabbed it in the water of the plant vase next to the tissue box and walked up to Max.

"Here," she offered, "I can actually see what I'm doing."

He grinned as she wiped the lipstick away. "I wasn't doing a good job?"

"You were kinda smearing it all over your face."

Max laughed, unable to take his eyes off my sister. She blushed and looked down. It only made him smile more.

I glanced over their shoulders, seeing a car pull up to the sidewalk in front of the house. I drew myself up tall, my hand resting on my hatchet.

As a man and a woman got out of the car, I walked past Dro and Max, putting myself in front of them. The couple glanced at a piece of paper in their hand, the sign on the lawn, then back to the house. They kept their eyes on the house as they walked toward it. They were a few feet away from the porch when they noticed me. The cold look in my eyes made them stop.

"We're looking for Manny Garcia," the man said.

"Why?" I asked.

The man almost flinched. "We called him a few days ago for an appointment, but something's come up. We need him now."

Max jumped up beside me. He held out his hand and shook both of theirs. "Mr. and Mrs. Kenway, good to meet you." I couldn't tell if he was seeing anything with his gift, because his face was expressionless. "You guys can come in. Don't mind her. She's a grumpy intern."

I gave Max a look so black that the smile dropped off his face.

"Let them pass, Con," Dro whispered from behind me. Her voice was serious, and I looked over my shoulder at her. "They're out of their minds with worry."

I trusted my sister, but made no effort to soften my expression. I pulled back into the house, hearing Max apologize and make excuses for my behavior. The couple walked inside, Mr. Kenway glancing at me with suspicion as they walked down the hall. His wife still hadn't noticed me. She looked exhausted, her eyes puffy and ringed red, like she hadn't been able to sleep after days of crying. Max led them into the living room, where I could hear Manny greeting them and offering what sounded like a condolence.

"They have a demon in their house," Dro whispered.

I faced her. "How do you know?"

"I sensed it from Mrs. Kenway." Dro looked at me with sad blue eyes. "It's attacking their daughter. They don't think she's going to live."

My hostility toward them lessened, if only a little. I took a couple steps toward the doorway, leaning in so I could hear what was happening.

The couple was sitting with their backs to me, facing Manny across from his desk. Max stood at his father's side, looking uncomfortable.

"We can't keep waiting, Mr. Garcia," said Mr. Kenway, his voice filled with desperation. "We need an exorcism today."

"That's a very tall order," replied Manny. "It takes time to prepare for an exorcism. To know exactly what is possessing your daughter and how powerful it is–"

Mrs. Kenway burst into tears. Her husband put his arm around her back and tried to calm her down, but it wasn't working. Exhaustion had finally broken her.

"Please," she sobbed. "Please, we can't keep watching her suffer like this. We'll do anything, pay anything, just please help her. Save her."

Manny said nothing, watching the woman cry. He looked away, his eyes finding his son. I remembered what Manny had told me earlier, how he would protect his family at any cost. Even from where I stood, I saw the flicker of pain in Manny's eyes. The look of a man who had lost someone he loved in a horrible way.

I started to understand why Manny's wife wasn't in the house anymore.

Manny inhaled slowly. "All right. I'll perform one tonight." He looked at them. "But I can make no promises. Even if I can get the demon out of your daughter, there's a chance it will come back. If someone has been possessed once time, it becomes easier for a new demon to find their body and take it over again."

The woman kept crying. "She can't keep living like this. She's our baby girl."

"I know," Manny said softly. "But I want you to know the risks. She won't be the same after this."

Mr. Kenway breathed heavily. "We'll deal with it. Just help her."

Manny nodded slowly. "Leave your address with me. I'll be there at five o'clock tonight."

Mr. Kenway reached forward and shook Manny's hand. "Thank you, Mr. Garcia. Thank you."

Manny smiled tightly. Max's smile was a bit more appealing as he led them out of the living room toward the door. Dro and I moved out of their way. Dro kept her eyes averted. She didn't like whatever her powers were making her see. Once they were out of the room, I walked to Manny.

"I'm coming with you tonight," I stated.

I could hear Dro's rushed steps behind me. Manny sighed and leaned back in his chair, rubbing his forehead. "Constance, I don't even know if it's an actual possession or if their child is just mentally ill. Those two things often get confused with one another."

"It's a real demon. Dro's seen it."

Manny looked at me, then at my sister. He knew about her powers now, and he was right in assuming that my sister didn't lie.

"I don't think it's a good idea," Manny argued. "Exorcisms are rituals that need powerful faith. You've made it clear that you have none. If anything, you could hinder the ritual."

"Or I could save your life," I countered. "You said yourself that you don't know what sort of demon it is. Are you taking that shotgun with you in case things literally go to Hell?"

Manny frowned, answering my question. I took another step forward. "I might not be a believer and I might not know a lot about demons, but I know how to kill them. I can stop them from hurting anyone else."

"This girl is possessed, Constance. Her body is being used as a vessel. The only way you can kill the demon is by killing the girl, and I will not allow you to do that."

He had me there. Almost.

"Fine. But you still need protection if this demon's as bad as they're making it out to be. If the girl loses it, no one else will have it in them to fight her off or keep her from killing you all. But I do, and I can."

Honestly, I didn't really care about the possessed girl. I'd never met her, didn't have a reason to be attached. It was the demon I wanted to talk to. I wanted it to answer my questions. To tell me what my sister was, or if it at least knew why they were chasing her.

"Dad," Max said quietly, now back in the room beside Dro. "Take Constance with you. This exorcism isn't going to go well."

Manny looked over my shoulder at his son. "You've seen the girl?"

"Yeah, from when I shook the father's hand." He winced a little. "It's not pretty. People are gonna get hurt. Constance can keep you safe."

Manny's dark, wise eyes found mine again. "If I agree to this, you follow my rules. You don't do anything without my say so."

I gave him a wicked grin. "I've never been good at following the rules, Manny."

He wasn't entertained. "Constance—"

"Fine, I'll be good. I'll even leave my weapons here."

I lied. I would leave *most* of my weapons here. My hatchet would come with me.

"I want to come too," Dro said.

I turned to face her. I never went anywhere without Dro, but... "Are you sure you want to do that?"

She hesitated, but nodded. "Maybe if I'm there, we can get some answers from the demon. It might react if it sees me."

"It might react badly," Max pointed out.

He wasn't wrong. The risk of Dro being seen and recognized by a demon wasn't one we shouldn't be taking, but we couldn't skip on a chance if one came up. If this demon could take over a human being, it might know something. I looked at Manny. It was ultimately his show, even if I wasn't going to quite follow his rules.

"Andromeda, think this through," Manny tried patiently. "I

73

understand you are impatient. But you might not like what the demon says to you, if it says anything at all. Are you prepared for that?"

A flicker of fear went through Dro's eyes, but she pushed it away and nodded carefully. Manny didn't push her, and even Max didn't try to talk her out of it.

"Okay. Five o'clock it is." He pressed his palms onto the top of the desk, then pushed himself up. "In the meantime, there's something else we can try."

DRO WAS UPSET that I told Manny about her powers instead of her giving her own descriptions, but Manny was more than happy to have her repeat them in more detail. My sister described how she sensed emotions, had a little bit of precognition, could heal physical wounds, and had horrifically detailed nightmares that ended with her bursting into flames, destroying everything around her.

Manny sat across from Dro as she sat on the couch, pale hands clasped in her lap. I sat by her side, Max on the other corner of the couch.

"And most of these gifts, they started before you first encountered the demons?" Manny asked. "When you were feeling scared or angry for yourself or for Constance?"

She nodded. "I learned how to heal and read people when I was nervous, but I can't control the fire or the nightmares." She took a deep breath. "Whenever I have one of them, it feels like someone is reaching inside my brain, ripping it apart to let something else in. I try to fight it, but I'm not strong enough."

My blood turned cold. She'd never told me that. It kind of upset me, but what would I have been able to do? I couldn't protect my sister from her mind. If there had been a way for me to get inside her head and fight whatever caused her pain, I would have done it without hesitation.

But I couldn't do that. I was human. The only special things about me were my quick reflexes and refusal to back down from anyone.

Dro glanced at me as if she'd read my mind. She took my hand in hers. "I didn't want to tell you, Connie," she said quietly. "I knew how it would make you feel."

I looked at our hands. Her pale skin against my gold tone. I smiled thinly at her. "It's okay, little sister."

It wasn't, but Dro and I knew that. We just didn't want to hear it.

"How would you feel about hypnotism, Andromeda?" Manny asked.

We both looked over at him.

"What good do you think that would do?" she asked curiously.

"It might allow us to see if a demon is taking control of your subconscious mind and force it to react while you are asleep. After your fires, a demon attack usually follows, correct?"

My heart beat a little bit faster. "You think they might be a signal to other demons? Letting them know where we are?"

"It's possible you're a victim of distant-possession. That's what Higher demons use to control their underlings," Manny answered.

"Does that mean that I'm a demon?" Dro asked in a fast breath.

Manny hesitated, but Max answered.

"No, there's no way," the young man said. "I would have felt it on you. Plus, you didn't react when you went to the church, sage doesn't repel you, and all the religious stuff doesn't work on you. If you were a demon, you would hate all of that."

She looked at them with uncertainty. "I'm not sure it's a good idea," she said quietly.

"I've done it with some of my clients before, Andromeda. Nothing has ever gone wrong."

"But I'm not like them," she pointed out. "What if I hurt you guys?"

Manny paused, but he controlled any nervousness. "Your sister will be right beside you. If Max sees danger, he'll tell me and I'll wake you up. I won't push further than you can go, Andromeda. You'll be safe."

Dro bit her lower lip, looking at me for guidance. Manny's idea interested me, and he was right about us watching over her, but I couldn't have a say here.

"It's your call, little sister," I said.

Dro took a deep breath and looked at Manny.

"Okay, I'll do it. But if I do anything crazy, anything at all, promise you'll stop me. Don't let me hurt anyone."

"We won't," Manny promised. "Now, lie down on the couch as comfortably as you can. Then we will begin."

CHAPTER NINE

Dro leaned back against the couch while Max and I shifted around her. I sat down with my knees close to her head. Max came off his side of the couch, knelt by Dro's head, and fluffed the pillows for her head to rest on. Dro smiled at him.

"Thanks, Max," she murmured.

He bowed low. "A beautiful princess should be comfortable when she sleeps."

Dro blushed. I choked back a groan. "Settle down, children," I chided. "We're trying to do hypnosis, here."

"Thank you, Constance," Manny agreed. He moved his chair closer to the couch. "All right, Andromeda. Whenever you're ready, I want you to take a deep breath and close your eyes."

She nodded, inhaling deeply and closing her eyes. "Now sigh it out."

Dro's chest began to lower as she exhaled.

"Relax yourself. Imagine a warm light starting at the top of your head. Feel it move down your body. Feel how warm and safe you are. Take another deep breath, then let it out."

Manny's voice was so reassuring and calm even I started

relaxing. Dro inhaled and exhaled again, falling into the rhythm of sleep.

"That warm light is filling your chest, moving down your arms and legs to your fingers and your toes. You are safe in your light. You have no cares or worries here. You are safe, and you can sleep in peace. Take another deep breath, and slowly release it. When I clap my hands, you will wake up. Do you understand, Andromeda?"

"Yes," she replied in a sleepy voice.

"Good. Take another deep breath, and sigh it out." She did as he told her. "Now Andromeda, do you know where you are?"

"Manny Garcia's house," she slurred.

"Do you know who is with you?"

"Constance, Max, and Manny."

"Do you know what you are?"

"A monster."

Manny glanced at me. I said nothing, but frustration built in my chest. I hated when Dro thought of herself as something she wasn't.

"Why do you say that?"

"I've killed people. Lots of people. Burned them to ash. Erased them from the earth."

Manny paused. "Why did you kill them?"

"He told me to."

My heart skipped a beat. I forced myself not to move.

"Who told you, Andromeda?"

"Don't know his name. He's a shadow in my mind. He wants me to kill them all. First he hurts me, then he shows me what to do."

Didn't matter that she didn't know his name. I would find this man. I would kill him.

"Who?" She didn't answer Manny. "Andromeda, who does he want you to kill?"

"I don't like it at first," she mumbled. "It's wrong. They

don't deserve it. Then it feels good. Having blood on my hands. Smelling fear. Tasting skin in my teeth."

Max let in a shocked breath across from me. Manny looked too nervous to continue. My heart beat frantically in my chest. Were these the thoughts the man was putting in Dro's head? I couldn't imagine these were hers. My sister was better than that. So much better.

But you don't know what she is. Deep down, she might be a demon.

I told that stupid part of my head to shut up, focusing on Manny's questions. Hopefully he could wrap this up fast.

"Andromeda, who does he want you to kill?" Manny tried.

The smell of burning fabric hit my nose. My eyes flicked down. Tiny white flames were starting to curl around Dro's fingertips.

"Dad," Max exclaimed, getting his father's attention.

"They're all going to burn," Dro said. Her voice was still sleepy, but there was a dark, terrifying edge to it. "They'll scream for mercy while the flames dance around them. Those who resist will be brought to their knees. It will be his. It was always going to be his–"

Manny clapped his hands loudly. Dro didn't wake up. The fire started growing in her hands, snaring around her wrists. Max shot to his feet and backed up. Manny stood up from his chair, swearing in Spanish. Dro was going to explode. We would never get away in time.

I had one option. One choice that might break her trance.

So I pulled the trigger on a bad memory.

I grabbed Dro's shoulders, digging my nails in hard enough to leave marks under her shirt.

"Remember Owl Creek, Andromeda," I shouted.

Her body shook and her eyes snapped open. No matter how distant she had been, the memory of Owl Creek would yank her back into focus. Thankfully, it worked here, too.

The fire in her hands vanished as her ice blue eyes met my dark brown ones. I relaxed my grip on her and sat back. She saw Max and Manny standing across the room, looking scared. Dro noticed the burn marks on the couch. Her eyes found mine again, widening in terror.

"Did I hurt anyone, Connie? Who did I hurt?"

I knelt next to her, putting my hand on the back of her head. "You didn't hurt anyone, little sister. You just burned the couch. We're okay."

"What happened? What did I say?"

I took my hand back. "You don't remember?"

She shook her head. "It's all black. I just remember falling asleep and waking up. What did I say?"

I turned to face Manny. His stunned expression would tell Dro something was wrong if we didn't give her an answer.

But I couldn't tell her the truth. It would break her heart, and fuel her belief that she was a freak. A monster. Everything that she wasn't, despite what her subconscious said. Dro had never intentionally hurt anyone. She never would. I had to keep her believing that.

But I couldn't lie to her, either. Manny had to do it for me. I held his gaze and for once, pulled down my emotional walls. I let him see how desperate, uncertain, and terrified I was. I let him see how deeply I loved my sister and how I needed help to save her.

"Nothing, my dear," Manny replied smoothly. "You said nothing we could use."

She frowned. "I didn't? Then why did I burn the couch?"

I turned to face her again. "You were starting to have a nightmare. Manny couldn't wake you up. So I did. I'm sorry about that, by the way."

Dro's eyes flashed with hurt, the same way mine probably did when I thought about that night six years ago.

Dro took a deep breath. "I'm glad you did it, Con. Thank

you." She looked at Manny again. "I'll fix the couch somehow. I promise."

"It's all right, Andromeda. We can just cover it with a blanket. Max, why don't you help her find one?"

To his credit, Max didn't hesitate. He looked at my sister with more caution, but he didn't seem to be afraid of her. At least not that I could tell. As Max passed me, he gave me a quick look that told me he wouldn't tell Dro the truth. I gave him a small nod in return.

Once they were out of the room, I walked over to Manny. "Tell me you got some kind of clue from that," I said.

"I'm sorry, Constance. But I didn't. She could be distantly possessed by a Higher demon, she could have nightmares influencing her subconscious," he paused, "she could very well be some type of a demon."

I stared daggers. "She is not a demon."

"Constance—"

"She is not a demon."

I remained grateful to him, but my tone made it clear that I would not repeat myself again.

"I'm trying to reason it all out for you, Constance." His voice sharpened. "Don't turn your temper on me."

Suddenly, I felt guilty. I liked Manny. He was tough, smart, trying to help Dro, and wasn't afraid of me. I'd invaded his life and he hadn't turned me out, when he'd had every right. He deserved better from me.

"Sorry," I said, admonished. "This situation's kinda stressing me out."

He still frowned, but the sparkle was back in his eyes. "Understandable."

I relaxed, even smiled a little. There weren't many people who could put up with my attitude for so long, but I was glad that Manny was one of them.

"So," I breathed. "What's the next step?"

81

AMY BRAUN

"Honestly, I don't know. I'm not even sure I can help her."

"Don't tell me you're quitting on your research now," I said, trying to be playful.

Manny's eyes were anything but. "Let me rephrase. I'm not sure that I *should* help her. You heard what she said. She's obviously being influenced by something we can't understand, and won't understand until we learn what's hunting you both."

"But you're not going to look into what she is," I said, just barely controlling my disappointment.

"No," Manny replied with a shake of his head. "I'm sorry, but I won't risk it to my son."

That was what it all came back to. Defending the ones we loved. Manny wouldn't take any risks for Max any sooner than I would take them for Dro. I understood. If I were in his shoes, I would have said the same thing.

"Then we had better start looking for demons," I said. "Starting with the one the Kenway's have."

CHAPTER TEN

I had seen horrible things in my life. Every torture, manipulation, and atrocity imaginable a human could inflict on another human. I'd been part of those atrocities, and would never forgive myself or sleep a full night ever again.

And I had seen more.

Demons sinking their teeth and claws into the flesh of people I knew, tearing them limb from limb, blood dripping from their teeth as black eyes glistened with murderous glee. Teeth and claws that would sink into me years later, leaving me scarred outside and in.

A screaming, burning sister who cried when she thought I wasn't looking.

Seeing a nineteen year old girl possessed by a demonic spirit definitely ranked among those horrible things.

The Kenways hadn't asked very much when Dro and I showed up with Manny and Max. My sister said nothing. She could feel the evil here. I tried to send her out, saying it wasn't too late for her to change her mind. No one would think less of her. But Dro refused. She wanted to help.

The parents had led us up to the second story of their house. As soon as we hit the top floor, we started hearing the shouting. Mrs. Kenway choked back tears while her husband opened the door.

It was worse than I imagined.

The room itself looked like a normal nineteen year old girl's room. White painted walls, a desk covered in papers and pens, a vanity table teeming with make-up and beauty tips from fashion magazines. Movie posters and school awards were framed on the wall. A white dresser covered with trinkets, memos from boys and best friends sat next to a mirror closet.

None of which matched the bed or the girl strapped to it in the center of the room.

The once white sheets were shredded and stained with blood, piss, and shit. The girl on top of the bed was covered in the stains, probably from having rolled around in them. Her pink T-shirt was torn at the collar and hanging off her shoulder, grey sweatpants sliding off her hips as she tried to pull herself free from the binds. Braided ropes were tied around her wrists and ankles, securing her tightly to the bed. The ropes had chaffed the girl's skin, covering her hands and feet with blood.

Just when I thought she couldn't look worse, she stopped thrashing her head from side to side and looked in our direction. If I didn't know better, I would swear I was looking at an animal rather than a human being.

Her straw-blonde hair was greasy and wild, her skin damp and death-pale. Her face was plastered with mucous from her eyes and nose. Vomit smeared the lower half of her face, mixing with the blood from her chewed, bleeding lips.

But her eyes were the worst. They weren't blue, brown, green, or a mix of colors. They were black from lid to lid. Just like a Red's.

The girl's parents moved into the room as their daughter continued to thrash and scream. Manny strode past me, and from the glimpse I caught on his face, he had seen this kind of thing before. It didn't seem to have gotten easier for him. Max and Dro were behind me, nervous about coming in. I can't say I blamed them.

I took a step deeper into the room.

The girl started howling in a language I'd never heard before. One that didn't sound human, and probably wasn't. Manny ignored it, getting set up for the exorcism. He looked at the parents.

"No matter what happens, you must not interrupt me," he told them. "One interruption could break any progress we make. Do you understand?"

Mr. Kenway sat by his daughter's bed with his wife. He nodded, holding back tears. "I understand."

Manny looked at me. His warning had been meant for me as well. I nodded stiffly. Manny looked at the girl. "Max, can you come help me, please?"

Max brushed past me. Manny looked at him. "Can you tell what it is?"

Max looked at the girl and focused. It was too dangerous for him to touch her. After about a minute, he looked at his father. "Some kind of Possessor, I think. But it's way stronger."

He said it grimly, as though he didn't think the girl would survive.

"What's her name?" Manny asked, pulling out a vial of holy water.

"Olivia," the father said.

"Olivia, if you can hear me, this will not hurt you." Manny threw the holy water on the girl's face.

Smoke rose up from where it landed and Olivia shrieked. I cringed a little, trying to think of something other than the girl.

So. I guess holy water really does work for something.

Max started reading from a Bible he'd pulled from his father's bag. His eyes flicked from the book to the girl thrashing on the bed. Her screams only became louder when Manny pulled a silver rosary out from his shirt, poured holy water onto it, and pressed it against Olivia's head. My heart pounded harder and harder against my ribcage every time she screamed. I focused on what Manny was doing, seeing what techniques I could use.

Silver. Check.

Dro shuddered behind me. I turned to look at her. "Are you okay, Dro?"

She wasn't looking at me, but she obviously heard me because she started shaking her head.

"I can see it," she whispered. "I can see the demon holding her."

I faced my sister. "What do you mean? See it how?"

Dro paused, trying to find the words to describe it all to me. "There's this black shadow around her, like a cocoon. It has to be the dem–"

"You!"

I snapped my head over to the possessed girl, hand reaching for my hatchet. Olivia sat straight up, pulling tightly against the bonds as she leaned forward. Her eyes weren't focused on me, though.

She looked at my sister.

"Where have you been? We've been looking for you everywhere, little girl!"

Olivia had two voices. One was a light, teenage girl voice. The other was a deep, raspy growl. The sound of it had my pulse racing. I tasted coppery fear on my tongue. Dro shrank back behind me as I moved in front of her. Manny hadn't stopped chanting, but Max was faltering, glancing at Dro.

"Why are you hiding? Come out here!"

"Get out of the girl," I told the demon, hoping to draw its attention from Dro.

The possessed girl snarled, turning her crazed face to mine. "I wasn't talking to you, *human*."

"Get out of the girl," I repeated. I had no clue how to carry out an exorcism, but I was talking to the demon. If nothing else, maybe I could distract it so Manny and Max could work on saving the girl.

Olivia pulled tighter on the bonds. Manny chanted louder and doused her with more holy water. She screamed again, her agonized shout turning into a rabid growl. Manny almost faltered, looking at me with wide eyes. He nodded, signaling me to keep it talking while he chanted. I pressed Dro into the hall and took a slow step forward.

"What do you want with her?" I asked.

The demon inside Olivia chuckled, sending a chill down my spine.

"It wouldn't be fun if I told you, human. But you'll find out soon enough."

I put my hands on my hips so no one would see my hands shaking. Brushing my thumb along the hilt of my hatchet calmed me down, if only by a fraction.

"Save me time. Tell me now."

Olivia smiled. An awful smile showing bloodstained teeth around a crusted mouth.

"No," it said. "I think I'll show you."

Olivia suddenly arched her back, bending so far backward I thought her spine would snap in half. I moved into a crouch, getting ready to spring. She opened her mouth and inhaled. Right when Manny slapped the rosary's cross to her forehead and poured holy water down her throat.

Olivia screamed, a deep, throaty roar that rattled the walls. Smoke seeped out of her throat like a dark fog. A black, smoky shape spiraled out of the girl's mouth like a tornado. The smell of wood smoke and sulfur hit me. I gave up on subtlety, whipping my hatchet out and holding it against my thigh, ready to swing it up at a second's notice.

But the smoke thing– the demon– didn't come after me. It

contorted until it formed a foggy head, a misty face, then lips that smiled cruelly. Manny and Max were yelling words from the Bible and hurling holy water like it was going out of style. The demon must have been vulnerable outside of a human body, because it yowled and twisted, slithering through the window behind the bed.

Aside from heavy breathing and crying parents, the room fell silent. I refused to let go of my hatchet. My nails dug into the wooden hilt. The girl wasn't moving. Her chest had stilled, her skin taking on a shade I knew all too well. The Kenways threw themselves over their daughter, crying and shaking her shoulders.

"Olivia!" they cried, trying to wake her up.

Dread filled my stomach when I looked at Max and Manny. They knew the girl was likely dead.

Someone gently touched my arm. I nearly jumped out of my skin. Dro lightly pushed me aside, slowly entering the room. Max and Manny stepped back so Dro could kneel beside the girl. She took the girl's pale hand in both of hers, lowering her head as if in a silent prayer.

But I could see the faint glow in her hands.

A minute passed before Dro looked up and backed away. One second later, Olivia gasped sharply and opened her eyes. Buckets of tears poured down her face. She cried as heavily as her parents did. The three of them wrapped their arms around one another, sobbing with relief. They didn't ask questions, didn't have the breath to thank Dro for what she'd done. They had their little girl back.

Dro walked back over to me and lowered her voice. "I had to do something."

I smiled. "I know, little sister. And you did great."

She gave me a sheepish look, then walked into the hallway to wait. Dro never sought charity for her actions. Knowing she had done something helpful was more than enough for her.

I I glanced at Manny and Max.

They looked at me with uncertainty, but I could see the pride in Manny's eyes. The glittering softness in Max's.

At that moment, I knew they weren't going to quit on us. And I couldn't have asked for more.

CHAPTER ELEVEN

Manny struck a new deal with me after Olivia's exorcism. We would stay in the basement for a few days while he went through every book he owned and called every contact he had to find clues about what my sister was. In return, I would go with Manny to exorcisms to kill any demon that might try and attack him or the person they were possessing. I could teach them a couple tricks to protect themselves, like I originally promised, but they also—correctly—believed I would be a terrible teacher.

It also helped that after the Kenways, Manny's curiosity about Dro amplified. He wanted to know what Dro was and why she was so hotly desired by demons almost as bad as we did.

Manny still wouldn't put me in touch with the demon slayer, but for the first time in years, we lived in an actual home. Dro had chosen to cook and clean the house. She liked doing because it made her feel normal, and she'd always been a hell of a cook. It almost made me feel guilty that I hadn't done anything but study and train since the Kenway exorcism. No one called Manny or came in for serious consultations. The only person who came in was Mrs. Dawson for her bi-weekly palm reading and doting on Max.

Not that I was about to complain. A day without demons was a day without demons.

Days turned into weeks as we learned everything about demons, memorizing every book on Manny's shelf. He didn't seem to be tiring of us. He was determined to figure out what my sister was, professional curiosity getting the better of him. He asked Dro questions and had her test minor powers, though they never tried hypnotism again. Once was enough, and we had no desire to press our luck.

Manny could tell me how to properly kill demons but he couldn't train me in combat. He let me set up a small gym in his basement where I trained with my knives and hatchet using dartboards and two-by-fours. I taught Max some self-defense moves while Dro got the more advanced training. She always beat Max when they sparred. But I don't think he minded very much, since sparring with Dro gave him an excuse to be close to her.

From dusk until dawn, everything was demon- related. I got bored, so used to running and fighting every second of the last few years, but I knew better than to take this peace for granted. Besides, I was learning. Every religion had their own kinds of demons, and Manny had information on all of them.

Possessors were what Manny dealt with on a regular basis. They were the demonic spirits that searched for a human body they desired, then latched onto its soul and took complete control of the victim. Even though they couldn't take a corporeal form and were weak outside of a human vessel, they were volatile and dangerous. It was tricky to stop them unless you damaged the person they were inside, which was almost never an option.

The red monsters Dro and I described were a crossbreed variation of Japanese *oni* and Greek *eurynomos*, but we stuck with simply calling them Reds. They were beings brought out directly from Hell by a summoning. While they could be controlled, they were savage and could easily turn their summoner into a snack. They didn't have any powers and were among the lowest demons in Hell, but they were not to be brushed off as an idle threat.

Demons came in a wide assortment of murderous varieties. Vampiric *lamias*. Malaysian *hantus*. Enormous Leviathans. Savage hellhounds. Too many to list, and way too many to kill on my own.

Faith was the strongest weapon apparently, a very powerful tool in exorcisms, but it wasn't something I could rely on. Mostly because I didn't have any.

Luckily, there were a variety of methods for killing demons. Holy water, blessed silver, salt, sage. Holy water was the only thing we had in abundance, but I was determined to get silver weapons somehow. Trapping a demon was possible, but you had to hope the demon wasn't too powerful to escape, and that it was going to speak English. Most demons only spoke demon-tongue.

Hell also had a ranking system. It started with lowly peons and imps, moving up to Knights, Presidents, Dukes, and Princes of Hell, and of course, the King himself.

Satan. The Morningstar. Lucifer. The one that nobody, human or demon, ever wanted to cross.

While we found out information on demons, we learned of the existence of cambion, the offspring of a demon, usually an incubus, and a human woman. Cambion could inherit certain demonic powers from their fathers, like super senses and strength. They could see other demons and if they became powerful enough, they could manipulate dreams and create hellfire, the blazing white flames that Dro burst into.

We were ready to call it then and there, until Max said one day, "Dro can't be a cambion. I would have sensed the evil in her. Besides, she seems to have divine powers, and cambion don't have those."

So it was back to the drawing board, where we stumbled upon the Nephilim, the children of angels and humans.

They were more rare than cambion (it was no secret that demons liked to fuck more), but perhaps more powerful. Nephilim could read minds, heal injuries, and create bursts of nearly blinding light. That sounded a bit more like my sister.

It always seemed to me that Dro was more angel than demon, and it made sense that demons would be out to kill her. Demons and angels didn't exactly make best friends. Still, I couldn't shake the feeling that we were missing something. Some of her powers still edged to the demonic side, especially the fire. I kept going back to what she had said under her hypnotism. Angels didn't usually talk about murder and carnage with glee. At least I hoped they didn't.

I doubted we'd tell Dro what she'd said during the hypnosis. She seemed content believing that she was half- angel instead of half-demon, so until we found out more, we left it at that.

After our brains were filled with demonology- induced headaches, I usually trained alone. Manny even bought me a punching bag and training swords. I was surprised, and told him he hadn't needed to do that. He just smiled and said I was getting too tough for dartboards and two- by-fours.

He wasn't wrong. As weeks became months, I got stronger, faster, more efficient in my strikes. There was no such thing as too much training. When came time to killing demons, I wasn't going to get a second chance. They weren't exactly charitable.

My sister, thankfully, didn't have any episodes. She drew closer to Max, something that made me wary and a little depressed. There was no way we could keep staying here. We were gambling Manny and Max's lives with the demons chasing us. The longer we stayed, the more we would care, and the harder it would be to leave.

But she was still a teenage girl with a crush on a cute boy, and Max wasn't the type to betray her virtue. Probably because he knew I would kill him if he did.

While they got closer to one another, I spent more time with Manny. He wasn't a replacement for my father, but he still treated me like a daughter. He was more like me than I originally thought. He didn't delve too deeply into the past, and he never held many assumptions over my head. He also refused to quit on me, no matter how dismissive and stubborn I became. Even when we argued, he made me break my own rules, and become more attached.

I liked being around them. I liked waking up in the same place every morning. I liked Max's witty attitude and the affection he showed my little sister. I liked Manny's patience, intelligence, and unrelenting determination. It was like I had gained a cousin and an uncle.

Which is probably why Manny lost it when I decided it was time to put my skills to the test, and summon a demon.

"No," Manny said flatly. "Absolutely not."

I crossed my arms under my breasts and looked at him evenly. "What's the problem? It's not like I haven't killed them before."

"The danger is too great, Constance," he said. "Six weeks in demonology doesn't make you an expert in it. You don't know what you can let through. You could become possessed."

"We'll put it in a trap until it's time to kill it. I'm just going to ask it a couple questions," I insisted. "And I thought you said that Possessors can't be summoned because they choose their victims. I'm not going to let a demon run through the streets, if that's what you're really worried about."

His dark grey eyebrows knit together furiously. "I'm more worried about your heart being torn out of your chest."

I worried about that too, but I tried not to let it show. Manny's fear for my life was touching, and I was grateful to know he cared about me, but I had to do this. Books weren't getting us anywhere.

"Manny," I said, taking a step towards him, "I need to confirm that Dro is a Nephilim. If I get a Red, it might be enough to tell us if we're right. We can't keep guessing and hoping for the best, any more than we can stay here forever."

Hurt filled his eyes when I suggested that we were going to be leaving. The same hurt stung my own heart, but we couldn't stay. Not if we wanted to keep them alive.

"I can do this," I assured him, "but I need your help. Please."

By now, he knew me well enough to understand that 'please' wasn't a common word in my vocabulary. I used it around Dro when no one else was listening, but I had been raised hard. I didn't beg for anything, from anyone. Not unless I was truly, crushingly, desperate.

Manny exhaled. "You'd better tell your sister what you plan on doing, because I don't want to face her wrath."

Despite it all, I managed a weak laugh. Manny gave me a reassuring smile, then walked off to get the supplies for the summoning.

DRO WAS EVEN MORE upset than Manny when I told her what I was going to do a couple hours later.

"You're insane! You can't do that! You *won't* do that!"

"It isn't a matter or can't or won't, Dro," I said calmly. "It's something that has to be done. We have a pretty good idea of what you are now, but we need to figure out why the demons are chasing you. At least then we might have a chance at figuring out how to stop them."

"But you always thought that people who summon demons are idiots! You're contradicting yourself!"

"I know. But unlike them, I intend to be a lot more careful," I showed her the small bottle of holy water, my throwing knives, and my hatchet. The holy water was added on Manny's insistence, though I doubted I would use it. Blades were my specialty. The weapons weren't silvered yet, but they would still work on the demons. They were the best things I could use since I didn't trust my faith.

None of it made Dro any happier. "Constance, please don't do this. It's too dangerous."

I shifted across the mattress in the basement to be closer to her, putting my arm around her shoulders and giving her a reassuring shake. "It'll be okay, sis. The demon will be trapped, and Manny will be backing me up. I've killed these bastards before. At least this time I'll have a head start."

Dro put her head in her hands. "You're going to get hurt. I can't live with myself if something happens to you, Connie. I can't."

"All that's going to happen is me summoning a demon, questioning it, then killing it. Nothing else, Dro. I promise."

"You can't promise me anything. You don't know what will happen. This is a bad idea."

I paused. "You're right. But I'm not going to let anything hurt me, or you. Just trust me, all right?"

Dro bit her lip and looked away from me. She hunched herself over her knees and made a hurt noise. I almost gave in right then, but if we didn't know the complete truth, we would linger here. The longer we stayed, the greater the risk that demons would track us, and Manny and Max would be caught in the crossfire.

I squeezed Dro's shoulders. "I won't hold it long, Dro. But you should stay inside. I don't want it to see you."

She shook her head. "I want to be out there with you. If something happens."

"Manny will look out for me. Stay with Max, okay?"

Dro sighed again, and I was grateful to have mentioned her

not-quite-boyfriend's name. He was the only other person I mostly trusted around her, and the only one who could keep her distracted while I was gone.

"I'll be back in a little while. I promise," I said, leaning to kiss the top of her snow-white head.

Dro nodded, knowing there was nothing she could do to stop me. I thought about ditching the idea, but then I remembered how scared she was when a demon appeared and tried to kill us. I wanted her to be free from that fear.

So I pushed off the mattress and started walking to the stairs, hoping that I hadn't just told a huge lie to my little sister.

CHAPTER TWELVE

Summoning the demon wasn't hard. Keeping it contained was the challenge.

As the town exorcist and expert demonologist, Manny Garcia knew what it took to summon a demon. I hoped it would be enough, but his expertise was expelling demons instead of calling them.

I looked at the chalk pentagram drawn on the driveway of an abandoned warehouse he knew of. Thankfully it was midnight on a Wednesday and no one was nearby to see us.

The circle was made of thick salt lines that had been sprinkled with holy water and peppered with sage. When the demon was summoned, it would be trapped, and really, *really* pissed. I had one hand on my hip, the other on the hilt of my hatchet.

"Are you sure this will be enough?" I asked.

Manny laughed sarcastically. "Don't tell me you're backing out now," he teased.

"Let me rephrase. Have you done this before?"

Manny flipped through his Bible, glancing up from the silver, half moon reading glasses he'd placed on his nose. "Of course not. I'm an exorcist. I don't summon demons. No sane person summons a demon."

I sighed, running my hand over my face. "That's reassuring."

"The theory for this idea—which I remind you, was yours—is simple," Manny continued. "I can contain the demon until you're ready to destroy it, but I don't think you'll be looking forward to that."

"Guess it will depend which of us is quicker."

Manny looked at me, his dark eyes serious. "You can still change your mind, Constance. No one will think any less of you. We understand why you're doing this."

That should have made me feel better, right along with the comforting look in Manny's eyes. But it was too late. I had been running blind for far too long.

"Thanks. But let's just get this over with."

Manny nodded solemnly, disappointed that I hadn't backed out. He stepped behind me and began the summoning. My Latin sucked, so Manny did the chanting. About midway through, I reached for one of my knives. Throwing knives had been a skill I'd learned during in my time with the Blood Thorns. I had excellent hand-eye coordination, and I'd only gotten better as I practiced. But that wasn't why I was taking the knife out now.

I drew the blade across my palm and dripped my blood into the center of the trap. I stepped back, carefully keeping away from the chalk and the salt-sage lines, then picked out a match from the pocket and scraped it along the side of its box. The match flared to life, and I tossed it into the middle of the circle on the drops of my blood.

My blood caught fire and the air rippled. A tear broken through the world, revealing a gaping wound of fire. My breathing hitched. It had been months since I'd seen this wound, and I'd forgotten how fearsome and unnatural it was. The scent of sulfur and smoke hit me like a slap, and I forced myself not to gag. This close, I could feel the heat from Hell making me sweat, beads of it trickling down my face.

Dro, Dro, this is for her, for answers, we need this—

A shape moved through the tear. Familiar, and unwelcome. A scrawny Red demon tumbled out of the portal, landing right in the trap as the wound in the world closer over behind it. Manny immediately switched to English and read from the Bible, his voice shaking but his words unfaltering. The demon got to its feet, glanced at its trap, then snarled and paced back and forth.

Yup. I had officially pissed off a demon.

"Do you understand me?" I asked. Demons knew all sorts of languages, so it wouldn't hurt to ask in the ones I knew.

It hissed and choked something at me. I couldn't tell if it was attempting to speak, or deliberately making animal noises. I asked again in Spanish, and got the same ugly response.

"I take that as a no." I huffed out a breath. Time to try another tactic. "If you understand me, nod your head."

The demon snarled harshly. I frowned. So far this interrogation was not going as planned. Not that I'd focused on the details of said plan. I waited a second longer, then moved onto my next question.

"Do you know my sister?"

The demon's lips contorted. I wasn't sure what it was doing, until I realized the corners of its mouth were twitched up. It started snapping, chittering and jumping up and down. It definitely knew about my sister.

"Is she a cambion?"

It snorted and snarled harshly. *Okay then.*

"Is she a Nephilim?"

The demon got excited and paced even quicker, chattering something I couldn't have kept up with even if I spoke demon-tongue.

"Are you trying to kill her?" I asked the demon.

It started convulsing. My free hand dropped to my hip,

finding the hilt of my hatchet. My other hand gripped my knife tightly as the demon started to make a sharp, hacking sound, like it was trying to choke down broken glass.

Then I realized it was laughing at me.

No. It didn't want to kill her. It wants her for something worse.

Knowing I wouldn't get any more information from it unless I got a crash course in demon-tongue, I decided the conversation was over. I turned my head slightly so I could keep my eyes on the demon while talking to Manny.

"Get ready," I told him.

Manny stopped the prayer. I walked towards the edges of the salt circle. The demon slowed its chuckling and watched me intently.

I hesitated for a moment longer. Usually when I got this close to demons, things turned chaotic. I had no time to process what happened outside of my reactions. It couldn't reach me. I should have felt calmer. But I couldn't hold back the fear that made my heart rattle in my chest. I couldn't keep myself from thinking that when I let the demon out of the circle, it was going to be faster than me. I had plenty of scars to prove just how quick and savage demons could be.

But my fear didn't matter. Dro did. Manny and Max did. If I let that fear overcome me, the demon would go after them. That was something I could not– *would not*– let happen.

I gripped my weapons tighter, then broke the circle with my boot.

My first mistake was assuming I knew what the demon would do. I thought it would jump at me the first chance it got.

Instead, it ran in the opposite direction. Down the street.

"Shit," I hissed, taking off after it.

Manny called after me, but I kept running. I had loosed the demon from the trap. I was the one who had to kill it before it slaughtered some blissfully ignorant Texan in the middle of the night.

The Red demon was fast, weaving its lean body around cars and through down the empty street, toward the center of the town. It had a head start on me, but I had spent a good portion of my life running from cops, feds, thugs, and monsters. The only difference was that I was the one doing the chasing this time.

When we hit downtown Amarillo, the Red made a sharp turn into an alley that almost tripped me up. I caught my footing and swerved around the alley after it.

That was when the Red jumped me. It rammed into me with the force of a linebacker, knocking me hard onto my back. My head smacked the pavement, dazing me for a second. That one second was all the opening the Red needed.

Its claws slashed across my chest, right under my throat. I gasped from the pain, and again when its claws sliced along my stomach, not deep enough to eviscerate me but deep enough to hurt. I wondered why the demon hadn't taken the chance to kill me yet. Then I saw the gleam in its black eyes and the twisted smile on its face.

It was playing with me, the same way a cat plays with a mouse in its paws.

While the demon slowly cut me to ribbons, I pried my hands free from under the Red's weight. My knife was in my hands, but I couldn't find an angle to attack with. It leaned forward and raked its claws across the side of my face, just barely missing my eye. I winced, but didn't scream. In my experience, the more you screamed, the more your attacker wanted to hurt you.

I shoved against the Red's leg, pushing the throwing knife into its smooth skin. It howled, but didn't loosen its grip. I got my arm under it and forced it up, relieving some pressure on my chest. It leaned forward and slashed at my throat with its claws. I bit back the scream this time because I thought it had killed me. All it took was an ounce or two of pressure to make someone bleed out from a neck wound. But the Red had shifted just enough for me to buck my hips and throw it off before my throat was ripped out. All I got were paper cuts.

We turned and twisted on the hard concrete. The Red didn't want to let me go, but I came up slashing with the knife, just as the demon lashed out with its claws. They tore through my jacket and shredded the flesh beneath.

Pain was everywhere, but I didn't stop moving. I grabbed my hatchet with my free hand, swinging and catching the Red in the arm with it. I'd been going to its neck, but I took what I got.

We were on our feet when the Red started slashing at me again. Now I had *really* made it angry. I stayed away from its claws, but was completely aware that I was being backed toward the wall. I kicked out, catching the Red in the shin. I roared in fury and swung at my head. I ducked low and shoved out with the knife. The demon batted the blade away, making it clatter on the ground.

The Red grabbed my arm and squeezed, its claws puncturing my bicep. I dodged its other strike and kicked its knee. The demon tried to pull me down with it, but I reached for another blade. My fingers closed around holy water instead. *That'll have to do.* I popped open the plastic cap and threw it on the Red.

It let me go and screamed as the blessed water boiled on its face. I winced at the awful, screeching sound, then darted forward and used my hatchet to cut open the Red's throat. Hot, black demon blood splashed onto my shirt, like bubbling oil from a skillet. I hammered my hatchet into the Red's chest. It scratched wildly at my shoulders. I ripped out the hatchet and pounded it into the demon's face. Then again. And again.

It finally stopped moving, disintegrating to a pile of ash at my feet. I scattered the ash with my boot. I'd never seen a demon reform from ash, but who knew what supernatural monsters were capable of. I stepped away, and then the swell of pain hit me.

My chest and stomach ached, my throat and face stung

fiercely, my arm burned angrily, and my head pounded. Adrenaline sent tremors through my hand and rattled my heart. I picked up the fallen knife and sheathed, then put the hatchet back on my hip. I closed my eyes, inhaling the cool night air. Trying to come down from the fear and power.

Dro would kill me for coming back like this, but it hadn't been for nothing. Dro was almost certainly a Nephilim, and the demons wanted her alive. This would be the first and last time I summoned a demon. I couldn't say I enjoyed the experience.

I tilted my head back, wincing as I stretched out my neck. I opened my eyes and caught sight of something on the roof of the building in front of me.

Two human shapes stood vigilantly next to one another, their attention on me. I couldn't really see their faces, but one of them had light hair, the other dark. Both of them wore long white coats, which made no sense in the hot Texas night.

They stared, not moving. I thought about something to do, whether to run or fight or shot. Before I could do anything, they turned and vanished into the night, blinking out of existence, like they had never been there at all. Maybe I had imagined them after all. I'd taken some good hits to the head. Even if they were real, I was in no shape to scale a building and confront them. One ass-kicking per night was good enough for me.

Still, imagined or not, I would be on the lookout for them. Just because they looked humanoid and hadn't attacked me, didn't mean they would be my friends.

CHAPTER THIRTEEN

Manny's eyes nearly bulged from his head when I returned, but I promised Dro would set me to rights when we got back. Sure enough, he drove us back and while Dro had been waiting, it was Max's reaction that surprised me the most.

"Seriously, did you want to be Terminator as a kid or something?" he scolded from the porch as I gingerly peeled off my lucky jacket.

"Never saw it," I muttered, checking the wounds on my body.

"You should. You would notice a lot of similarities."

I nearly rolled my eyes at him, but Dro stopped me.

"Get your butt in the house so I can heal you, Constance," She ordered, pointing at the door angrily.

I raised my eyebrows, then gave her a small smile. "Bossy, bossy," I teased.

She wasn't in the mood. "I wouldn't have to be if you had been careful."

"I don't always hunt demons on week nights," I pointed out, walking into the living room.

"And you had better not do so again," Manny said. He quickly found a large blanket and draped it over the couch so I wouldn't stain the cushions. "We never should have gone there."

"Relax," I sighed, dropping onto the couch. My muscles ached, even as I tried to get comfortable. "It's off my bucket list now."

He narrowed his eyes. "That doesn't fill me with encouragement."

Dro's fingers pressed to my damaged flesh. The hot and cold pins-and-needles feeling zipped over my skin, lighting up my nerves. I couldn't keep from wincing. Dro pressed her lips together and tried to hide the pain in her eyes. But it wasn't her fault. It was mine, and I'd tell her that when we had our talk later.

"Sorry about the blanket," I murmured to Manny.

He watched with a small smile, waving a hand impassively. "It's just fabric. I never cared much for the blanket anyway."

As Dro healed me, Max came out of the kitchen with a cloth and a bowl of water. He sat beside Dro and began mopping up my blood. I raised an eyebrow at him as he wiped my skin clean.

"What's with the pampering?" I asked. "I'm not your type," I said, tilting my head toward Dro.

Max snorted. "Definitely not. I like sane women."

I glared at Max, but he was getting used to my attitude and angry stares. He just shrugged it off and moved for the wound on my neck.

"But I figure I can do this, so the girl who actually *is* my type won't have to..."

He fell silent. Alarmingly silent. I turned my head to see what his problem was. Then I realized he had pushed my hair up from my neck, and seen my tattoo.

Max looked horrified, edging away from me slowly. "Are you... Are you really?" His voice was barely above a whisper.

"Is she really a what?" Manny asked suspiciously.

I brushed my hair with my hand, hiding the tattoo behind my ear. Dro gave me a worried look.

"One of the *Espanis de Sangre*," Max breathed. "A Blood Thorn."

The room fell into a deadly silence, everyone suddenly nervous about what I would do. Didn't matter that I wouldn't hurt Max or Manny any sooner than I would Dro. Once someone hears about the Blood Thorns, they tend to get anxious.

I couldn't blame them. The *Espanis de Sangre* were about as ruthless a drug cartel could get. They controlled the drug and trafficking trade just beyond the Texan border, terrorizing people living in Ciudad Juárez. They had a highly trained security team with more guns than the cops, more money than the Mexican president, and a reputation for killing their enemies gruesomely. They were heartless, soulless butchers with no tolerance for disrespect or disloyalty.

And I had been one of them.

Dro spoke in a careful whisper. "She isn't one of them anymore. We never had a choice."

"What the hell did you do for them?" Max asked.

"And why didn't you tell us?" Manny demanded right after.

I said nothing, suddenly finding my hands more interesting. I'd done terrible things for the Blood Thorns to keep us breathing. Things that still haunted me. I'd never be able to get rid of the memories, but ignoring them helped. Sometimes.

"She isn't going to hurt either of you," Dro insisted. "Constance did what she had to do to keep us safe. She always has."

"Which was what?" Manny asked with a hint of bitterness.

"Hurt other people," I answered grimly, setting the silence again. "Killed them if I had to."

"Connie," my sister pleaded.

"It's too late, Dro," I sighed. "They were going to find out sooner or later. They should know."

I looked at the Garcias, knowing that as soon as they heard my story, they were going to throw us out of their house and call the Marshals, or the police, or both. But they had been kind to us, the first people to genuinely care for us since our parents. They deserved the truth.

"I started off as a falcon when I was fourteen," I said. "I got information, brought it back. On one run, I was almost killed. I wanted to move up after that, become stronger. So I had them make me an enforcer. I became the person who went after the people who paid late, or didn't pay at all. And I usually beat them within an inch of their lives."

Max winced, but Manny's face was unreadable. Pressure crushed through my chest. I suddenly felt too heavy.

"You never would have taken us in if you knew who I used to work for," I admitted.

"But you wouldn't have told us at all if Max hadn't found your tattoo," Manny stated.

"No. I wouldn't have."

"We were running from the demons," Dro tried to reason. "We thought we could lose ourselves in Mexico, but the Blood Thorns found us and Con..." She looked at me with a strange mix of pride and anxiety. "Con fought them off. She made a deal with them." She glanced at Manny and Max desperately. "It isn't her fault. Please, please don't call the police on her."

Max might be weak for the despair in Dro's voice, but Manny remained stony.

"How did you convince them?" Max asked.

I sighed, running a hand through my hair. "Dad was a falcon for them before we came here. He had enough of a reputation for me to be considered. I told them I would repay his debt, and then some. Which is what I did, and in half the time they thought I could."

"Why did you leave them?" he asked. "I heard that no one leaves the Blood Thorns. At least, not alive."

"They betrayed us. They were going to give Dro to a witch who would have done something horrible to her. We had no other option but escape."

Manny stared at me for a long time, and I stared back. It pained me to hold his stare. I barely deserved to be in his home, let alone meeting his gaze.

After a very, very, long time, Manny asked me another question.

"Do you regret the things you did?"

I flashed back to my past in Ciudad Juárez. Riding in the back of a dumpy truck with my scared little sister. Making the deal with Emilio. Getting the tattoo, a black thorn that looked like it was weaving in and out of my bleeding skin, when I passed initiation. The late night runs in dark alleys. Nearly being raped and beaten to death. Advancing up the ranks. Standing by while people were tortured and slaughtered in front of me. Pretending not to care. Kicking down doors. Making people scream. Using my fists to give a message. Cutting off fingers. Sliding my blade across a man's throat. Being stronger than everyone else in the room.

Feeling hollower with every breath I took.

"Every day," I muttered. "Every day, I wish I could wipe the slate clean. But I can't."

"Because you don't think you can be redeemed, or because you don't want to be?"

"Both."

Dro took my hand and gave it a hard squeeze. I couldn't look at her. Of all the things I didn't deserve, her love was the strongest.

"God forgives anyone who asks for it," Manny said quietly, "especially when someone means it with all of their soul. He forgave me."

I raised an eyebrow. Max looked away, clasping his elbows and looking uncomfortable.

Manny took one of the chairs from the desk and sat down on it across from us. "I don't suppose you ever wondered why I became an exorcist?"

If I were perfectly honest, it had never crossed my mind at all. I knew better than most that some things in the past should stay there. He hadn't pushed me, so I hadn't pushed him. But all ghosts rose from the grave with a little time.

Manny reached under the collar of his shirt, and pulled out a gold wedding band on a simple chain.

"My wife, Marianna, became possessed when she was pregnant with Max. I was young back then. I didn't know about demons. I didn't understand the damage they could do. Marianna would have violent fits, breaking everything she could get her hands on, lashing out at me, hurting herself, trying to pry Max out of her stomach with her bare hands..."

I heard Dro's steady intake of breath. My heart ached for Manny. Max was eighteen, and all this time Manny had been living with the pain of losing his wife, and probably almost losing his son, too. I remembered the deaths of my parents, and kept quiet.

"No one could understand what was wrong, and eventually I ran out of options. I called an exorcist. He told me that my wife had a demon inside her, and that it wanted to kill my wife and possess my son. He asked my permission to remove the demon, and I consented." Manny looked at the ring around his neck. "Fate was erratic that day, because the same day the exorcism happened, was the same day Max was born."

The grief in his eyes was unbelievable. It seemed stretch from his eyes to the very center of his soul, tearing through his heart on the way down. I don't think I had ever seen such a broken-hearted man before.

"The doctor saved Max, and baptized him almost immediately. The demon couldn't get to him. But Marianna was bleeding too heavily. The demon tried to break out of her, and it couldn't escape her body. It became too much, and Marianna died."

I couldn't begin to express how sorry I felt for him. I looked over at Max. He had curled his arms around his knees like a lost kid. He looked guilty, like he thought his mother's death was his fault. He relaxed a little when Dro reached out with her other hand to take his. I saw him squeeze it tightly, like he could draw strength from her. I hoped he would feel her kindness. It wouldn't heal the wound, but she would take away as much pain as she could.

Her ice blue eyes and my dark brown ones fixed on Manny again.

"I learned about true evil that night. I could barely rejoice about the birth of my son because a demon had tortured my wife to death."

His face was hard and solemn, but his eyes were still filled with a sorrow I couldn't even begin to comprehend.

"That night I cursed God. He took the woman I loved from me, made me fear for my son, showed me true monsters. But the exorcist said that it wasn't the will of God or failure that killed Marianna. It was demons. Creatures who continued to take any helpless soul they wanted. If I wanted to channel my rage, it ought to be directed at them. So I followed exorcists, watched houses where victims of possession lived. Then I broke into those houses, and tried to beat out the demon trapped inside the human."

I tried to imagine Manny as a younger, brokenhearted man, ruthlessly beating on a possessed victim to relieve the pain in his heart. The picture I had didn't match that of the man in front of me, but I could also tell that Manny wasn't lying.

"One of the people I attacked turned out to be a woman who looked like my Marianna. And then I thought about what I was destroying. How I couldn't help her, and that Marianna would be ashamed that I was focusing on my anger, and not our son."

Manny slipped his wedding ring back under his shirt. "After that, I repented and asked God for forgiveness. It was granted when I remembered He provided me with a strong, kind, healthy son." He looked at Max, undying love crystal clear in his eyes. "He gave me a purpose, a way to help others when their need was dire."

Manny looked at me, his gaze wise and haunted. "I don't blame you for any wrongs you've done to protect your sister. But I will not continue to help either of you if you revert to whatever old habits you might have taken from the Blood Thorns. I do not want them in my house where my son can be harmed. I have been lenient because I understand how hard life has made you. But knowing this does change things. I can't pretend otherwise. And if you bring immediate danger to my son from your old employers, I will alert the authorities." His gaze turned sad. "Believe me, I would rather face demons than the Blood Thorns."

"I understand," I told him softly. And I did. God, he had every right to call the cops on me right here and now. I wouldn't even stop him if he did.

Instead, he still agreed to help us. There were no words to express my gratitude.

He got up from his chair and stood in front of me, putting his hand on my shoulder. The sadness hadn't left his aged eyes yet, but his smile had returned.

"God will forgive anyone, Constance. But first you have to forgive yourself."

I didn't know what Manny expected from me. To have a breakdown? To throw myself into his arms and accept God into my life? To begin forgiving myself for everything I'd done?

Better to say nothing. Better to let him believe maybe I could forgive myself for the choice I'd made and what I'd done. Even though in reality, I never would.

I kept my dark eyes locked on his, wondering what I should

say. I felt awful about what happened to his wife and how his life was nearly destroyed, but I also loosely admitted to not only being a murderer for one of the most dangerous criminal organizations on the planet. I had to know what Manny was going to do.

"Are," I started, unable to find my voice at first. "Are you certain you want to keep us here? Knowing what you know?"

"Logic tells me I should. Even justice does. Except that I know if I send you away without giving you a chance," he shook his head. "It wouldn't give you the chance at redemption you want. And I know you want that."

I could have lied. I lie to people all the time. It's almost as natural as breathing. But Manny was one of the best people I had ever met. He deserved better than that.

"I won't let any harm come to you or Max," I promised. "I can't say the same for everyone hunting us if they find us, but if I hear they're nearby, we'll be gone. I'll turn them away from you. There will be nothing that connects you to us. I'll make sure of it."

The old man's eyes darkened, sensing my meaning, weariness creeping in again. Still, he smiled, though weakly.

"Thank you for your honesty, Constance. I believe we can make a righteous woman out of you yet."

A laugh huffed out of me. "That would be a miracle."

He nodded, his smile strengthening. "We'll let you get some rest," he said. "Come on, Max."

The kid's mood hadn't improved. He stood up, and Dro stood with him. She wrapped her arms around his neck and held him tight. Max buried his face in her neck and shoulder. No amount of hugging could make Max feel better about the mother he had never known, but at least he could go to sleep knowing that Dro cared.

After agiving him a quick kiss on the cheek, she stepped back and sat next to me. Max's eyes lingered on my sister for a minute before he walked over to his father. Manny slung his arm over his son's shoulder and led him out of the living room to give us some privacy. When they were gone, Dro looked at me sadly.

"How much longer do you think we have here, Constance?"

I reclined back against the couch. "You really want the answer to that?"

She sighed and watched the empty doorframe. "No, not really."

Of course she didn't. I saw the way she looked at Max. Dro wanted to stay with him. We both knew that if we left, she might never find someone who would look at her the way Max always did. After a long silence, she turned her head to look at me.

"Did you find anything out on your little lunacy escapade?"

"Not as much as I hoped. Demons hate Nephilim, and that's likely what you are."

She frowned. "I don't know how I feel now that it isn't a mystery. But I still think you shouldn't have gone out there and talked to that demon for me."

"Trial and error, Dro. I'm fine."

"But it wasn't your responsibility. You're human. I'm not. I should have been the one to talk to it. They're after me."

"Which is exactly why I didn't let you. The demon knew about you, little sister. If it had seen you..." I shook my head, all sorts of horrible scenarios running through my mind. "It would have gone very, very badly."

She stifled a laugh. "You're saying the way you did it went well?"

"I'm saying I took a risk for you, and that I'll do it again if I have to. You have enough on your plate with the powers and the nightmares. If I don't help you every way I can, then I'm not being a good sister."

Dro flinched, suddenly regretting having said anything. "I'm sorry," she said. "I just... I..."

"I know."

My dark gold hand circled her pale shoulder and gave it a gentle squeeze. "Let's get some sleep, Dro. We'll be safe for tonight."

She nodded and stood up, starting to walk back to the basement. I stayed on the couch, remembering another time where being a good sister meant more than caring about consequences...

DAD WAS STUNNED *when I walked back in the house without so much as a mark. Dro was still crying, unable to sob out the truth to him. I thought that was a good thing. Dad loved us, but he wouldn't believe even me if I told him Dro healed me with a single touch.*

I felt fine, better than fine, but Mom told Dad to take me to the hospital to make sure I didn't have a concussion.

Mom met us there, still wearing her restaurant uniform. She raced over and hugged me as tight as a mother could.

"Mom," I wheezed, "Mom, I can't breathe."

She pulled back but kept her arms on my shoulders, looking at my head. "Your father said you were bleeding."

"It wasn't as bad as it looked. It just hurt a lot."

"Which doesn't make sense," Dad said from behind me. "I saw the cut. Your head was cracked wide open. When you came in, there wasn't even a scratch."

I glanced at Dro, who was holding Dad's hand and looking at the floor.

"Maybe it was just bleeding too much for you to see the wound," Mom offered.

Dad shook his head. "I've seen injuries like that at work, Carmen. It takes weeks to heal, not minutes."

Mom looked at me again. I didn't let my face betray

anything. Mom was trying to reason it out with Dad while we waited for the doctor. Dro looked at me like she wanted to tell them the truth– that she healed me with magic.

I carefully shook my head at her. This wasn't the time or place to explain anything to Mom and Dad.

We waited five hours before the doctor could see us. Mom held Dad's hand, talking quietly in Spanish. Dro fell asleep on my shoulder within the first hour. My little sister could sleep through a hurricane. She twitched a bit, but slept peacefully otherwise. I nudged her when the doctor came in. She raised her head wearily, yawning and rubbing her eyes.

"How was your nap, sleepyhead?" I asked with a smile.

Dro pouted at me as we hopped off the chairs with Mom and Dad. "Fine," she said.

Her tone of voice didn't make me believe her, but I didn't think anything of it.

The doctor ordered tests and scans for my head after asking me endless questions. He didn't have any answers for why I had healed so quickly given the circumstances. I still said nothing and Dro didn't make eye contact with anyone. She held Mom's hand and stayed close to her leg.

After another hour of waiting, the doctor came back with a puzzled expression and some black and white prints of my skull.

"Well Mr. and Mrs. Ramirez, I'm not sure I can explain it. Constance seems to have escaped a concussion, and there don't seem to be any fractures. She's a very strong girl."

Dad put his hand on my shoulder. "You can just say that our little trouble maker is a bonehead, doctor."

I frowned and shoved his hand off of me. He chuckled and Mom smiled. Dro stared at the floor.

"That's one way to put it," the doctor laughed. He looked at me. "But to be on the safe side, take it easy at school tomorrow, Constance. You look fine, but we shouldn't take any chances."

I nodded at him. There was no point in making a promise I likely wasn't going to keep.

Dro stayed quiet, even after we left the hospital. She hadn't said a word, even to me. Mom and Dad knew something was wrong, and we were going to be in for it when we got home. They led us to the living room and sat us on the couch. Dad was beside me while Mom sat on the far side next to Dro, putting her arms around her adopted girl.

"Bella, you heard the doctor. Constance is okay. What's wrong?" Dro tried to fold herself together, but Mom just pulled her closer. "Miles won't come back and hurt either of you. Daddy and I will make sure of that."

Dad was tough, but I got the feeling that if Mom ever saw Miles again, she would make him more afraid of her than Dad ever could.

Dro looked over at me, and I read her mind. She took a deep breath. "It isn't Miles."

"Dro–" I tried.

"It was me."

Mom and Dad were silent. "What do you mean, sweetheart?" Dad asked after a long time. "What was you?"

Before I could stop her, lie to our parents for her, Dro confessed. "I fixed Connie."

Dad and Mom exchanged confused looks. "What are you talking about, bella*?" Mom asked.*

"Connie was hurt, so I touched her and made the hurt go away. Like magic."

"Andromeda, you heard what the doctor said," Dad told her patiently. "Your sister–"

Dro reached for one of the magazines on the coffee table and put some papers between her fingers. She pulled them along the tender skin, giving herself a massive paper cut.

Mom gasped and grabbed her hand. "Andromeda! What did you..."

She fell quiet when Dro put her fingers on the bleeding skin, her fingers starting to glow. Mom and Dad watched with amazement as Dro's wound knit closed. They were frozen, staring at their adopted daughter with shock, and horror. Dro's eyes lifted to meet mine sadly.

"I'm sorry, Connie," said Dro. "They had to know."

I couldn't even speak. I was the big sister. I was supposed to take all the responsibility and make the hard choices.

Sometimes I forgot that a sister's love was supposed to go both ways.

Dro took a deep breath and looked at our parents. "Mommy, Daddy, there's something I should tell you..."

MY FINGERS PLAYED along the hilt of the hatchet at my hip as I thought about the night Dro told our parents about her powers. How she told them for the sake of us all. They still loved her, but after that they looked at her with caution. And a little fear.

I hadn't been afraid of Dro in years, but now that I knew what she was, I couldn't stop that creeping feeling in my stomach again. The one that told me the worst of our problems were only beginning.

CHAPTER FOURTEEN

D ro slept fitfully that night, making it hard for me to sleep. If she was going to get dragged into a nightmare, then I had to react as fast as possible to keep her from burning the house down. I didn't get anymore sleep than she did, so when she woke up and decided to make breakfast the next morning, I agreed to help her.

"Maybe you should just sit back and watch," she suggested as we walked out of the basement into the kitchen.

"What? I can kind of cook."

"Burning macaroni and cheese isn't cooking."

"It's not my fault that I get the faulty boxes and shitty stoves."

Dro laughed and started looking for cooking pans. She'd always known her way around a kitchen and loved to cook. She used to do it all the time with Mom. An old sadness tugged at my heart as I remembered eating cookie dough and getting into flour throwing fights.

I made a cup of coffee and glanced at my sister. Despite being happily focused on her task, I could see how tired Dro was. Her hair had been loosely braided down her back, exposing the dark circles under her eyes. Max came in the kitchen about half an hour later with a heavy textbook under his arm. He yawned as he sat down at the island across from me. "Something smells insanely awesome," he said.

He didn't look like he had slept very well, either. Probably staying up late working on his essay or math test or whatever, if the textbook were a sign. But when he looked at Dro, he immediately brightened.

"Chocolate and blueberry pancakes," she announced. "Would you like some?"

He grinned. "You had me at chocolate."

She smiled at him, a flush coming into her cheeks before she went back to cooking. I played with the cup of coffee in my hands, spinning it on the counter. "Shouldn't you be studying?" I teased.

Max shrugged. "Yeah, but it's boring."

"Shouldn't you be at least trying to focus on it?"

He looked at me innocently. "Are you trying to get rid of me, Constance? I was hoping you'd be thrilled by my charming presence."

I stifled a laugh and took a sip of coffee. Dro walked over to us with some plates and a huge stack of chocolate blueberry pancakes. I stared at them like they were sent from the gods, but felt a pinch in my chest. The last time Dro cooked something like this had been when we worked for the Blood Thorns. She'd been one of the kitchen helpers, and no harm was allowed to come to her. It had been a small comfort to me, because I had never fully trusted a single member of the *Espanis de Sangre*.

"Actually, I skipped studying because I might have found something out last night," he said as Dro sat down close to him.

Max became distracted by Dro's closeness, so I cleared my throat.

He looked over at me. "What did you say?"

I rolled my eyes. "What did you find out?"

"Oh, right. Well, I guess you could say I had a vision. Sometimes my dreams hint at things to come."

"So you dream the future?"

He pouted. "It sounds so much less dramatic when you say it like that."

I shrugged, slapping some pancakes onto a plate and starting to devour them like there was no tomorrow. They were light and fluffy, the blueberries warm and the chocolate melting in my mouth. I might not eat like this again for a long, long time, so I enjoyed every bit of them. Max took a bite of the pancakes, and from the look on his face, I guessed he was having a minor orgasm. Given how amazing Dro's cooking was, I couldn't blame him, but I my impatience was getting to me again.

"Come on, Max, don't keep us waiting."

Max glanced at me, slowing his chewing. "I think we should step back from looking for demons and trying to look for angels."

My fork stopped halfway to my mouth. "Say again?"

He held out his hands, "In my dream, there were these two guys in long white trench coats. I could almost feel how powerful they were in the dream. They were trying to talk to me."

"Talk to you?" I repeated, thinking back to the men who watched me from the roof. "About what?"

"Not about what." He looked at my sister, who'd been nibbling at her food. "About who."

I played his words over in my head. We had spent so much time running from demons that angels had never really crossed our line of thought.

"How do you know they were angels?" I asked.

Max shrugged as if he knew I wouldn't believe the truth. "They told me they were. They said they'd be meeting us soon."

"No offence, Max, but it sounds like you just had a weird dream."

"Is it really that hard to believe? Your sister is half-angel."

I tried not to think about the implications of that. Angels were the original badasses, and I wasn't sure their intentions would be any nobler than the demons. I picked at the pancakes, forcing myself to eat.

"I wish I could believe it was just a dream, that it doesn't matter. But when I woke up, I got this feeling deep in my gut. I just... I *knew*."

The extent of Max's talents as a psychic still eluded me, but I trusted him enough to know he wouldn't lie about anything concerning my sister.

"What did they say about me?" Dro asked quietly.

Max turned to her, concerned. "That you were chosen for something important. Something that will change the world."

His words sunk in, and I tried to lighten the mood by saying, "Good of the angels to be so specific."

My attempt utterly failed. Max stared at his food with troubled eyes. Dro hugged her arms around herself. I played with the pancakes on my plate, hoping I would find the will to keep eating, but I just couldn't get the motivation.

I set my fork onto my plate and rubbed my forehead. "Did they say what they wanted? Anything about Dro being Nephilim or what it means?"

"No," Max answered. "All they said was that Dro had to be protected above all costs."

"Did they seem hostile at all?"

"Not exactly. I mean, they didn't threaten to rain down holy vengeance on me or anything, but I got the feeling that if I messed with them, it would be a huge mistake."

That's comforting. "I got that feeling too," I murmured.

"What do you mean?" Dro asked.

I told them about the two people in white coats that I had seen on the rooftop when I'd finished killing the demon. I wondered how long they'd been watching over us, feeling uncomfortable and a little bit angry. If they were supposed to protect Dro, what the hell had they been doing while we'd been running and fighting for our lives? I didn't mind that they were more concerned about her safety than mine, but shouldn't they have at least done something when she'd been having those terrible nightmares? When she'd been burning?

"Great," Max said. "So we've got demons who want to kill you and angel stalkers who like invading people's heads." He smiled lopsidedly. "Never let it be said that you ladies don't keep interesting company."

I looked at my little sister. She stared into space, toying with her braid over her shoulder.

"You okay, Dro?" I asked.

She nodded, but I didn't believe her for a second.

"I just wish I could be normal," she said sadly, releasing her hair.

Max reached over and took one of her pale hands in his, gently squeezing it so she knew he was there. Physical contact was important to Dro. She always felt like an outcast, that she was a freak and people wouldn't want to touch her so softly. She slowly leaned her cheek onto Max's shoulder while he rested his head on top of hers. For him to be so selfless and tender with my sister when she needed it made my admiration and respect for him grow tenfold.

She deserved every moment of this.

The door behind me opened and I whirled, my hand slapping to the hatchet on my hip on reflex. Manny walked in, looking well rested for once.

He glanced at the pancakes on the table. "I'm glad you left enough for me," he said with a grin.

His cheer faded when he realized none of us were smiling back. "Is everything all right?" he asked.

Max kept himself wrapped around Dro, so I filled him in on the angel theory. Manny sat down at the far end of the island closest to me and listened intently. When I finished the spiel, Manny looked grim.

"It's fair to believe that where there are demons there are also angels, but I've never heard of them coming to earth like this. Let alone entering someone's dream."

"So we're screwed," I established. "That's basically what you're telling us."

"Not at all, Constance. I'm saying there is something else going on behind the scenes. Something we don't understand, and it's clearly dangerous. We all need to tread carefully from here on out."

"And do what? We know what Dro is, but what's the endgame? Why do they all want her so badly? It can't simply be because of what she is. The angels never cared enough to stop any demons from chasing us."

"Your guess is as good as mine, Constance. As I said, it's all the more reason for us to be wary. There is just as much lore on angels as there is on demons, so later today we can–"

Something pounded on the front door. I tensed, my hand going down to my side again.

Max looked at his father. "Were you expecting anyone, Dad?"

"No," Manny replied. "There aren't any appointments for today. It could be a walk-in."

Or it could be something else, I thought.

The pounding started up again. Whoever was out there seemed to be impatient. Manny slipped off the stool and headed for the door.

"Go into the basement," he said. "I'll see who it is."

"Dad," Max said hesitantly.

"It's okay, Max. Stay by the basement door. Keep the girls out of sight."

Max frowned, but got off the barstool and hurried with us into the hallway to the basement under the stairs. We opened the door, slipped down the stairs and closed the door as Manny opened the front entrance.

We didn't completely hide like Manny had asked. I crouched next to the basement door with Max, keeping my hand low on my hip. Dro stood a couple steps beneath me, watching with big, scared eyes. I couldn't hear exactly what was being said, but the new man sounded rough. Probably big, given the depth of his voice. Max stared at the door his father had walked through with a pinched expression.

"Something's wrong," he muttered. His voice sounded tense, like he was in deep concentration. He must have been trying to see into the future. I pressed myself to the door and eased it open enough to see who Manny was talking to.

The guy looked like a shaved bear. At least six foot three, a solid two hundred fifty pounds of muscle. He wore a long black duster that had seen better days, black camouflage pants, and a dark shirt. His head was buzzed, dark stubble forming on the top of it and around his chin. From where I hid, his eyes looked black.

This man was bad news. A criminal, maybe even a murderer. He stood in the hallway near the front table, picking things up then putting them back down, just for something to do. I'd been around a lot of men like this. They thought that when they entered a room, they owned everyone inside it.

The problem is sometimes they're right.

"I already told you," Manny insisted. "I don't know who those young women are. I don't know where you're getting your information from–"

"Oh, I got sources you wouldn't believe, old man," the guy said in his deep, Texas drawl. "I know those sneaky little bitches are here. Just like I know you got a kid somewhere here. Do yourself a favor and tell me where they are, and he won't get hurt."

Manny clenched his fists. "If you try to threaten my son–"

"I don't make threats, geezer. I make promises. Now tell me what the fuck I want to know."

The man was getting restless. He wouldn't hesitate to hurt Manny to get what he wanted. The son of a bitch would probably enjoy it.

But I wasn't going to let that happen.

CHAPTER FIFTEEN

The man started to walk forward, shouldering past Manny to get a better look around the house. While Manny's voice started getting more aggressive, I leaned back down and looked at Max and Dro. They were so tense I thought they might snap.

"It's one guy, but we have to stay out of sight," I whispered, looking at my sister. "He knows our faces, and he knows about you, Max."

"I'm not leaving my dad," he said firmly.

"Neither am I. But we have to be smart about this. Find a way to take him by surprise."

Max clenched his jaw, but nodded sternly. I looked back through the crack in the door and saw the man now had his back to me. Manny's eyes shifted in my direction. He betrayed nothing as the big man pressed on, steadily moving to the front door and holding it open.

"Stay behind me," I warned the others.

I took out my hatchet. I eased the door open quietly, and snuck toward the man's back. He made no motion that he sensed me coming.

"This is the last time I'm going to tell you," Manny said tightly by the door. "I don't know who they are and if I had seen them, I would have called the police."

The man lolled his head. "Well, this is gonna be the last time I tell you to quit with the fucking lies."

His hand went into his coat and he brought out a huge Magnum revolver and he pointed it directly at Manny's chest.

I froze. I figured the man would have a gun, but seeing it pointed at someone I cared about startled me. But old habits and instincts wove into my muscles. When the gun didn't go off, I sprung.

I was five foot eight and significantly smaller than this asshole, so I grabbed the back collar of his jacket, jerking his head down and placed the blade of my hatchet under his Adam's apple.

"Make a move and you die," I hissed.

The man chuckled. "They said you were a lively one. Full of surprises."

"Drop the gun," I said.

"No."

"Do it or I'll kill you."

"Not before I shoot the old timer. Sure you wanna risk it, *chica?*"

I didn't. My mind raced between killing him outright or wounding him and getting answers.

I could almost see the man smiling. "Too long. I'm a busy guy."

The man raised the gun half an inch before I could stop him, and squeezed the trigger.

The gunshot echoed through the house like thunder. I watched in horror as Manny stumbled and collapsed onto the rug by the door. Dro screamed behind me, but her cry wasn't half as loud as Max's when he saw his father fall.

"Dad!"

I snapped out of my trance a second too late. The big man slammed his elbow into my face so hard I almost blacked out. I pitched backward and he whirled on me, swinging out with his fist. I ducked the blow and slashed with my hatchet, but he stepped away before I could cut him.

He was quicker than he should have been for a man his size. Definitely an experienced fighter. His punches were heavy and meant for instant knockouts. I leaned back from a hit that would have caught me in the cheek, kicking at his ribs. He let me kick him, then held my foot to his side and yanked me close.

I had to hop on one foot so I wouldn't drop, swinging the hatchet again. He caught my wrist, crushing the bones inside it. He slammed his forehead into my face once, then again, making me see stars. He dropped my foot and punched me in the kidney. I gasped in pain, but backed away before he could hit me again. I reached inside my jacket for another knife, only to have him kick me in the stomach. I doubled over from the powerful hit that sent me into the living room, my back slamming against the hardwood floor.

He stalked inside when I heard an outraged scream. I turned my head, seeing Max throw himself at the big man. My heart stalled with panic. Max wasn't trained enough. He didn't have a lot of muscle on him. He would have been better off punching a brick wall. At least a brick wall didn't hit back.

The man batted Max's arms away, then grabbed a fistful of his shirt and slammed his fist into Max's face with terrifying speed. I put my hatchet and knife back into their sheaths, pushed myself up, and raced for the desk. I reached under it and grabbed Manny's shotgun. When I turned again, Max was motionless on the floor, and the man was out of sight.

Shit!

Dro screamed and I forced myself to move, gripping the shotgun tightly. I raced for the hallway, skidding to a stop when the man entered the living room again. With my sister.

The big man had his fist twisted in Dro's braid, holding her in front of him and pressing the barrel of his gun to her chin. My sister's hands were bloody. She'd been trying to save Manny when the man had grabbed her. He looked positively thrilled.

"Now, now, *chica*, don't do anything stupid. Your sister has a pretty face, and I don't think you want to see it blasted onto the other side of the wall."

Son of a bitch. Son of a fucking *bitch.*

Anger like nothing I'd felt in a long time burned in my heart. My lips peeled back in a snarl. I imagine I looked like a wild woman, my face bruised and bloody, my hair a tangled storm that matched the fury in my eyes.

But I couldn't do anything without him hurting Dro. And the asshole knew it, because he fucking *smiled* at me. The nasty smile of a man who dared me to try something. A man looking for a reason to hurt my sister and make me suffer.

He proved it when he teased the gun barrel along Dro's jaw. She winced, as if the barrel of the gun was still hot, but didn't whimper. She wouldn't be able to reach the knives that I insisted she keep in her boots without getting the man's attention, and her powers didn't work on command. We were trapped.

"Besides," the man purred, leaning in close to Dro. He sniffed her hair and made her cringe. "As pretty as she is, she's not the one I'm here for." His pitch black eyes turned to mine. "So drop the fucking gun, or she loses her face."

I had no choice. Not with Dro as a human shield, Max unconscious, and Manny dying. My breath caught in my throat. *Oh God, Manny...*

I slowly lowered the shotgun, keeping my eyes on him as I placed it on the floor.

"Good," he said. "My boss tells me you carry an arsenal with you, so lay it all out next to the gun. And I mean all of it. If I find out you're packing some hidden knife or some shit like that," he twisted the gun barrel under Dro's chin, "She's gonna pay the price."

"Fine," I said, resigned, "but if it's me you want, then let the rest of them go."

The man frowned. Then he spun the revolver in his hand and hit Dro across the cheek with it. She yelped in pain as a nasty wound opened along her face. I started to run forward, but he spun the revolver again and pressed it into her stomach.

"Did you hear me say you could talk? Or did you hear me tell you to put all your fucking weapons on the floor?"

I clenched my fists, but did as he asked. Every second we stood here was another second off Manny's life. As I laid all my knives and my hatchet on the floor. I desperately tried to control my anger against the man buzzing in Dro's ear, I could see Max starting to wake up. He groaned in pain. I couldn't see Manny. Something in my chest twist painfully.

Now that I had given up all my weapons, I slowly rose back to my full height. The man whistled.

"She learns quickly," he said. "Now, Snow White here is gonna cuff your hands behind your back. Snow, if you try anything stupid, remember your boyfriend is still alive, and my gun is still full of bullets."

Dro swallowed nervously, taking the handcuffs when the man put them in her hand. She stepped away from him, watching him point the gun at Max. My sister walked toward me, her head hung low. I turned my back to her so she could place the handcuffs on my wrists.

"Tighter," ordered the man. "Tight enough that it hurts. There's a good girl."

I made no expression once the cuffs bit into my skin, facing the man as he walked closer to us. He grabbed Dro's arm and jerked her close.

"Well, now that all the excitement's over, I can introduce myself." He grinned. "Name's Drake Talbot. Ever heard of me?"

Had I heard of Drake Talbot, the famous bounty hunter employed by mobs and gangs to pick up the traitors and strays? The man who had dragged a runaway drug dealer back to his employers by the back of his car? The man who tortured an informant's fourteen year old daughter before his eyes to get information before stabbing them both to death? The man who brought back the tongues of snitches, leaving them to choke to death on their own blood?

I nodded slowly.

"Good," approved Drake. "So this is the plan. We're gonna turn and walk out of here. You, me, and this pretty piece of leverage here," he gave Dro a rough shake. "We'll all be nice and close, since you're not going to do anything stupid, are you Constance?"

I shook my head. Fury and panic sent shivers through me.

"Smart choice. Now start walking."

I avoided looking at Max as I walked past him through the doorway, hoping to draw attention away from him. But I did glance at Manny's body, saw blood soaking his shirt and pooling around his back. He was too pale, his eyes were closed, and he didn't seem to be breathing. My heart crushed in on itself. *I did this. This is because of me.*

Dro whimpered behind me. Drake brushed against me and kicked open the screen door. He took another step, then stopped.

"Oh, damn it, I almost forgot."

Drake pulled out his gun and shot Max.

Drake's bulk blocked my sight, so I couldn't see exactly where he'd been hit, but Dro's scream was enough to let me know it was somewhere awful.

"Max!"

Drake pistol whipped Dro again, silencing her. "Relax, bitch," he said, dragging her toward me. "He's got some time to bleed out with his daddy. Pretty generous, you ask me."

I gritted my teeth so hard I thought I would destroy my

molars, but I did nothing. I had just cost two innocent people–two *friends*– their lives. I couldn't fight, or Dro would die too. My heart wrenched with hatred and grief.

"Okay, ladies, lets go. Mateo isn't my most patient client."

Fear turned the blood in my veins to ice. Drake saw it and smiled. He was working for Mateo Rocha. The son of my former employer, the current leader of the Blood Thorns.

The man who wanted to kill me.

CHAPTER SIXTEEN

Driving in a truck with Drake was worse than I imagined it would be. We were crammed in the cab, Dro seated between Drake and myself so I couldn't stop anything he wanted to do to her. The entire uncomfortable drive to El Paso consisted of few bathroom breaks, no food, Drake casually stroking my sister's hair and thigh, and me thinking about I could kill him from where I was sitting with my hands cuffed behind me.

My heart ached as my brain replayed Manny and Max's shooting. I didn't even know for sure if they'd died or were dying. Manny had been shot in the chest, and Max had been bleeding out from somewhere vital. I'd seen enough gunshot wounds in my life to know bleeding out from one was agonizing, and if you didn't get help in time, you died.

I turned my head to look at Dro. Her head was down, most of her braid gone, but the falling strands of white hair weren't doing much to hide the tears streaking her face. Dro kept her crying silent and controlled so Drake wouldn't notice, but the pain on her face was heart breaking.

It was my fault. I should have known that sooner or later Mateo and the Blood Thorns would catch up to me to get their revenge. It was just like them to send a sadistic fuck like Drake Talbot after me. But it hadn't stopped me from getting close to Manny and Max. It hadn't stopped me from caring about my new strange, little family.

We arrived at the Mexican border later that night. The road led to a tollbooth next to the wall. Two tall towers with pacing sharpshooters stood on either side of the booth while an expansive metal fence stretched out for miles beyond them. Fear spiked me as I stared past the windshield into the darkness. Mateo was just miles away now. Waiting patiently, probably thinking of ways to hurt me. I'd seen him deliver punishments personally, everything from breaking bones with a hammer to pouring burning oil on someone's face. Since Drake had taken Dro too, there were endless ways for Mateo to break me. The bastard wouldn't even have to touch me to make me scream for mercy.

Drake pulled the truck to a stop outside the gates and looked at the border guards, grinning at them.

"Evening officers," he drawled, showing some kind of badge.

The guard frowned and shone a flashlight into the cab, gaping a little when he saw our bruised and bloody faces. He whirled the flashlight at Drake.

"What the hell is this?" he asked.

"Bounty collection," Drake answered happily. "Cartel enforcer and her sister. They're nastier than they look, trust me."

The guard hesitated, looking between us and Drake. "I think you should get out of the truck, sir."

Drake's smile dropped. "What the fuck for?"

"We received a report that two battered women would be trying to leave the country in the company of a bounty hunter." The guard's voice turned cold and angry. "Who I assume is you."

Dro and I looked at each other, thinking the same thing. Only two people knew about Drake capturing us, which meant either Max or Manny were still alive. Or had been, recently.

Drake tightened his hand on the wheel. "What's your point?"

"They belong in the custody of the United States Marshals in conjunction with the DEA." The guard's hand went to his hip, resting right above his gun. "Are you going to be a problem, sir?"

I looked around. In the booth past the guard talking to Drake, another man was speaking on a phone. Maybe to the snipers in the towers. He glanced at a piece of paper in his hand, his eyes flicking from it to me. Damn Wanted list.

"They're my pickup," Drake continued to argue. "I'm not turning them over to the Marshals."

"You'll get a reward for–"

"Their shit reward isn't half of what I'd get if I took them across the border. Now raise the gate and let me through."

"That isn't going to happen. Now, I advise you to get out of the car–"

It happened so fast. Dro sucking in a deep breath, the subtle reek of sulfur, the air ripping open and breathing fire. A demon pouncing on the border guard. He screamed as the demon tore into him. I thought I heard gunshots, but if they weren't silver or filled with rock salt and sage, they weren't going to do enough.

The window beside me punched open, glass and a powerful fist scraping past my jaw. A Red demon wrenched open the door of the truck. I twisted and kicked it in the face with all my strength, cursing my handcuffed hands.

The demon growled and grabbed my legs, yanking me out of the cab. It tossed me onto the pavement and reached into the cab again. Another man screamed and gunshots cracked. The border guards fought for their lives, but it wouldn't be enough.

I pushed myself up and saw the Red pulling Dro out of the truck. I ran for her, driving my foot into the demon's ribs and forced it to focus on me.

"Get the handcuff keys!" I screamed.

The demon howled and lunged at me. I swept its legs out from under it and kicked its head, dancing away when it tried to snatch my ankle. It twisted into a crouch, looking like a big red spider. It scrambled toward me, and I jumped aside right before it pounced.

The Red slammed into the truck with a loud crunch and punched for my head. The blow glanced off the side of my face and I quickly backed around the side of the truck. Dro had made it to the other side of the cab and snatched the keys from Drake as he shot at another Red demon.

Drake felt her movement and snarled, right before the Red sank its claws into him. Drake roared and grappled with the creature.

My own Red demon chased me as I raced around the truck, hoping to lure it to Drake. It clambered into the truck bed and leaped. This time I didn't get far enough back.

The demon knocked me onto the ground, my arms howling in protest from the awkward position. I tried to buck the demon off, but my hips couldn't move its weight quickly enough. Its hands circled my throat and squeezed. Claws pricked my skin and its rough palms crushed my windpipe.

Suddenly, it whipped its head to the side, right as Dro stabbed her pocketknife into one of its black eyes. Its shriek of pain deafened me.

My sister stayed out of range of the Red's arms and stabbed the demon in the face again, and again, until the ash of its corpse rained dust over me. I coughed and winced, but rolled onto my side so Dro could unlock my handcuffs.

As soon as I was free, I got to my feet. Dro handed me the knife without question and stood at my side.

Carnage overtook the station. Demons poured out of the tear in the world one at a time, scrabbling through the door, heads whipping left and right and leaping at the first Hunan they saw. There were at least six of them now.

I hoped one of the guards managed to call for backup, because this was too much for us.

As I glanced around, I noticed Drake was gone. Dead or alive, I didn't know or care. He was one less thing to worry about now. Especially since another pair of Red demons had noticed us.

They shrieked and charged us at the same time. Dro reached in her boot and took out the other foldout knife she had stored in it. She was ready to fight with me.

I lashed out at the demons, kicking at the one on the left and punching at the one on the right. Dro came up from behind me and took the Red on the left. My sore arms protested at the way I was swinging them, but I pushed through the pain to keep fighting.

I swiped down, missing the Red's chest, but stabbing its leg. The Red howled and grabbed a fistful of my hair, jerking my head up. I yanked the knife free and stabbed it into the Red's stomach, then its chest, and then under its chin. The Red exploded into black ash.

My sister held her own against the other Red, keeping out of range. It toyed with her, like it didn't want to kill her.

I ran for my sister when something plowed into me and sent me to the ground. I looked up in fury, and found myself staring at a humanoid demon shrouded in black smoke. Its eyes were glassy, silver orbs. Its arms were too thin, its fingers too long. Tiny, sharp teeth filled its mouth when it smiled. My heart stopped. I knew that smile. This was the demon that had escaped Manny's exorcism. It was back, just like it promised.

"Those idiots always do things the hard way," the Possessor hissed in English.

It was the first time I had heard a demon speak a language I understood. It leaned in closer, cold smoke curling around my face. It reeked of wood smoke and rotten eggs.

"There are more entertaining, and effective methods."

The demon began to dissolve and move closer to my face. I thrashed and roared, but it kept me pinned. I couldn't even scream when it slipped into my mouth and nose.

It tasted like fire, burning my throat and sliding deeper into my body. I felt it reach my heart, twirling around it and holding on tightly. The smoky demon slithered through my veins, taking control of my nerves, wrapping around my spine, and soaked into my brain.

I felt something drape over me like a wet blanket, smothering the very fabric of my soul. A sudden lance of pain cut into my spirit, dismantling the person I used to be, and making me something else.

CHAPTER SEVENTEEN

I smiled with my new lips and stood on my new feet, loving how I felt. I would enjoy this one. I let the burning pain force the body's former owner down, locking her up tightly. I liked this body. It was tough and quick. My new senses took in everything around me. The darkness, the screams, the smell of blood.

The halfbreed.

I turned and fix my vessel's eyes on her. Somewhere deep in this new body of mine, the owner cried out. I pushed her down again. She would stay there until she broke. Until I had what I wanted, and the rewards that would come from it.

The halfbreed spun and kiced the red oni in the head, knocking it off balance so she can drive a knife into its throat. The oni turned to ash and dissolved. She turned to face me, and gasped sharply.

"Your eyes," she breathed. "Connie..."

I made the lips grin. "Not here, sweetheart. She's a little tied up at the moment."

Anger filled her bright blue eyes. So strong I could feel it pulsing through the air. Good.

"Let her go," the halfbreed demanded.

I kept the smile going as I walked toward to her. "She taught you well."

My captive screamed inside me, but I pushed her back. I was more than strong enough to control her.

"This is what's going to happen," I explained. "You're going to give yourself up and come with me. Or I'm going to rip this body to pieces. It won't hurt me, but when I let her go, it'll be a really painful death for her."

Fear flickered through the halfbreed's eyes. She knew I wasn't messing around. I licked my vessel's lips, loving the salty taste. We'd been told their bond was strong, almost more powerful than any magic we can use on them. But their fear for each other's safety was just as strong, and it was a delicious tease. I wondered if my Lord would forgive me if I took a quick bite. We needed the halfbreed alive, but not necessarily unharmed.

Defiance crept back into the girl, which surprised me. I felt a surge of the halfbreed's power, enough to halt me. I almost forgot what she was, who she'd been made from. She was destined to open the Gate for us, to be the key to our true freedom. Only her father matched her in power. She might have given him a run for his money, if she didn't have the prowess of a mouse with a panic disorder.

But mouse or no, there was no question that her blood would work.

"I said, let her go," the halfbreed grit out again.

I narrowed my stolen eyes. "So you're going to do things the hard way, huh? You're going to let your sister suffer? After everything she gave up for you? After you ruined her life? That's not a very nice thing to do."

I gripped my vessel's knife and draw it across her arm, cutting from elbow to wrist. I didn't feel any pain, but my captive's nerves twitched.

"No, don't!" the halfbreed screamed. The smell of her fear excited me.

"Do you know how scared she is of you? How she's always thinking you're going to lose control and burn her alive? Do you know how sick she is of having to watch out for you because you're not strong enough? Because you're just a weak little girl?"

Tears streamed down the halfbreed's face. Inside me, I felt another push against the trap I made. I had to give a little credit to the human who's body I possessed; she had persistence.

I sliced open the other arm. Blood snaked down the vessel's fingers onto the pavement. If it weren't for the surges of power that kept ebbing off her and us needing her to open the Gates, I would consider this halfbreed to be a waste of time. No creature with this much power should be such a sniveling weakling.

"Please," she begged. *Begged.* Her, of all people. "Please, stop."

Still, I loved it when they begged. "Are you going to come quietly? No muss, no fuss? Or am I gonna have to start chopping off feisty little Connie's fingers?"

The halfbreed made a pitiful choking sound instead of answering. I should cut off the sister's fingers anyway. I'm felt a little hungry, and human fingers were a great snack.

But I had to move quickly. The brainless oni who came through the portal with me were busy gorging themselves on human meat now that the gunfire stopped. They wouldn't remember what we came here for. I wanted to join the feast, but we had a schedule to keep, and the Boss wasn't very patient. Or lenient. Or understanding. Or merciful.

The portal closed after the six of them came through, so the witch needed to make another one to summon us back to Hell, unless Weepy Miss Halfbreed could do it herself. Not that I expected her to–

"Dro?" someone called. "Constance?"

I growled and whirl around to see a black SUV pulled up across from us, two humans making their way over. One of them was a kid who rang a bell in the memory I now controlled. He looked just as scared as the halfbreed. Sweat plastered his face and a bandage had been wrapped around his shoulder. I could smell his blood and pain twisted his face. Wish I'd been there for that party.

The second man didn't trigger any memories. Tall and strong, he'd dressed for battle. Dark blue jeans, a rugged leather jacket, a dark green shirt, and a Kevlar vest across his broad chest. Handsome, but in a rugged way. Strong boned and perfectly angled, his oak-colored hair cut nicely near his head. A dark scar rested under his left eye. His eyes were the best part of the package. A green so bright they practically glowed.

It's guys like this that made me understand why demons like coupling with humans every few centuries.

He held a sawed-off shotgun with confidence and experience. I didn't sense any fear off him, which was strange. The kid stared at the halfbreed, then looked at me and the blood on my vessel's arms.

"Max!" cried the girl, "Max, Con's possessed! You have to–"

I lunged and tackled the halfbreed. I searched my captive's memories and know the boy was a minor psychic and his father was an exorcist. I couldn't have him expel me. Not now, not when I had the little bitch. Not when we were so damn close.

She writhed underneath me until I grabbed her wrists. The halfbreed refused to damage the body I'm in. All she saw was her black-eyed sister. That's sweet, in a pitiful way. Even now, when I wouldn't hesitate to cause the halfbreed as much physical damage as possible without getting in trouble, she won't stop me.

Finally, it got easy–

Hands wrapped around my stolen body and hauled me off. I kicked and screamed in frustration, snapping my head back and connecting with whoever held me. I wrenched free and whipped around, coming face to face with Green Eyes. I hadn't busted his nose like I hoped, but he still didn't look scared. He even pointed the shotgun at me. Another idiot I had to deal with. The shotgun blast wouldn't kill me, just destroy the vessel and inconvenience me.

Though I did smell something strange, something coming from the gun...

"Get out of her, demon."

Now it clicked. The smell. *Sage.* He was one of *them*. I might have a problem.

"You slayers are so demanding," I taunted. "You didn't even say please."

His eyes were ice cold. "Don't make me repeat myself."

Jeez. Some people couldn't take a joke.

I turned my back on him to saw the crying halfbreed being held by the boy. I snarled and dashed for them, completely ignoring the pump of the shotgun and the shout behind me. I picked up the boy and tossed him away easily. I wrapped my hand around the halfbreed's throat, squeezing tightly because I'm done playing around. She clutched my wrist, trying to pry my fingers off, but still too scared to hurt me. Deep down in the trap, the vessel's scream became louder and more tortured. Excellent.

"Connie," she rasped, bright eyes desperate. "I know you're in there, big sister. Fight back."

I leaned in close, letting her see the blackness of my eyes. That I had taken control. "Shut the fuck up," I growled. "You're coming home."

"Stop!" shouted Green Eyes. "This is your last warning, demon!"

Like I cared. I had what I need. He could shoot my stolen body if it got him off.

Then I felt it. The shiver in the air. The heat and otherworldly presence. I spun in its direction. Goddamn it.

They shimmered into existence, and as usual, they looked fucking perfect. Dressed in the same white leather trench coats they always wore with the buttons closed up to the collar, white pants and white leather boots. Other than that, they looked nothing alike. The one on the right was taller with white blond hair and silver-grey eyes. The one on the left had wavy, shoulder-length auburn hair and bright blue eyes. Both of them looked so serious that a fool would think they had constipation.

But only a fool made jokes in the faces of angels.

"Release the Nephilim, Ohzlan," said Auburn.

I hated it when angels knew my true name.

"Fly away home, little birdies," I said. I never said I wasn't a fool. "We've got something special for this little halfbreed," I added giving her a shake. Auburn flinched when I shake the girl.

"She is a vessel for the Heavenly Host," said Bleach, taking a step forward, "and you will not harm her."

"You angels are so up tight. If you didn't want someone messing around with your toys, you shouldn't have left them out in the first place. Especially when they're so rare."

I shook the halfbreed again, and the woman in my trap fought some more, pressing against my cold barriers. I'd finally gotten sick of that, so I tightened the walls around her, getting satisfaction when I felt the bitter rush of her pain.

"This is not a negotiation, hellspawn," spat Bleach, who still moved for me. "You will leave the vessel you have stolen, and unhand the Nephilim."

I grinned. "You keep using that word, Blondie. But I don't think it means what you think it means."

My other arm was suddenly grabbed and twisted behind me, cold metal cuffs latching onto my wrist. Silver burns through the vessel's skin and into me. I spun around in anger, meeting a pair of brilliant green eyes.

"You cheating son of a bitch," I hissed, letting him see the demon through a stolen human's eyes.

He didn't flinch or back away. Damn demon slayers.

I had to let go of the halfbreed since I needed both hands to kill the slayer. I swung a fist at his face. He stood too close, so the blow caught him in the jaw and knocked him back—

Heavenfire ripped through the body, burning right through the skin until I felt it. It might not expel me, but it hurt so bad I barely took pleasure in knowing it hurt my captive as well. I whirled to see which of the two birdies took the cheap shot, only to see Blondie's fist connecting with my vessel's face. The son of a bitch must have put some angelic power into the hit, because two seconds later, I was out.

CHAPTER EIGHTEEN

I still had control of the vessel when I woke up, but those damn angels ensured I couldn't do anything else. They bound me to a chair with blessed silver cuffs, which seared the skin of my vessel and made me very uncomfortable. I looked around and see they also placed me in a salt-sage circle so I couldn't escape.

I glanced up at my captors. The two angels stood in front of me, looking stylish and grim. The boy stood next to them, sounding exhausted and distraught as he talked to Green Eyes. No sign of the halfbreed, but she wouldn't be far.

It looked like we'd taken residence in a cheap motel room with stained and cracked yellow walls. The angels probably cloaked the room so my screaming wouldn't be heard. Angels weren't past torture.

"Leave the vessel, Ohzlan," ordered Auburn.

"Fuck you," I spat. "I like it in here. This bitch can take a lot of hurt." I glanced around the room again when I didn't sense the halfbreed appearing at the sound of her sister's voice. "Where's the halfbreed? I didn't think she'd want to miss out on her sister getting punched up by angels."

At this, the kid and Green Eyes looked over. They glanced at the angels uncertainly, but the birdies didn't even blink.

"What do you want with the Nephilim?" asked Bleach.

I almost laughed. Like I'd tell him that. "You know my name, but I don't know yours. You're not archangels, that much is certain. Seraphs maybe?"

"What do you want with the Nephilim?" Auburn parroted.

"Bring her out here and I'll tell you."

"Do not attempt to fool us, hellspawn," Bleach said sharply, taking a step forward.

"I already have," I grinned maliciously.

Bleach puncheed me in the head, snapping it to the side. I wouldn't feel any pain the way the vessel would, so I just sat back and enjoyed the taste of human blood in my mouth.

"Whoa, hey, you said you weren't going to hurt her!" the kid shouted.

"We must find out what the plan is." Bleach drew his fist back again.

Green Eyes stepped forward and grabbed Bleach's arm. "That's enough. She's possessed, so exorcise her."

"You do not understand the implications of that request, slayer," Bleach said, clearly not liking that he had to explain himself to a lesser being. "Attacking a Nephilim is a direct threat to Heaven. The demons are planning something, and we must uncover what it is, no matter what the cost."

He tried to pull away from Green Eyes, but the human didn't let go. "I won't stand here and condone her torture."

I chuckled. "Look at you boys, fighting over me. You're making me blush."

Bleach held out his other hand and blasted me full in the chest with heavenfire. It blazed deep through the vessel into me. I screamed long and loud. The other humans in the motel might not be able to hear me, but the halfbreed would. Probably crying buckets wherever she hid. If it weren't for the damn trap and the damn angels, I would've called more demons. But that would make things easy.

"Perhaps there is another way," said Auburn. "It is possible the vessel Constance Ramirez will remember her possession. As such, she might be able to tell us what Ohzlan knows."

Oh shit.

I pulled on the cuffs. I was in trouble now.

"It is worth a try," Auburn continued. "She is important to the Nephilim."

Bleach finally jerked away from Green Eyes. "Very well. You may try. But if it does not work, we shall continue with my method."

Auburn inclineed his head in agreement, then looked at the kid and the slayer. "Are you schooled in exorcism?"

The kid nodded. "My... my dad used to do them."

The green-eyed slayer nodded as well, but said nothing.

The angel walked toward me, pulling back the cuffs of his sleeves. "Perform the exorcism. The vessel will scream, but you must not stop, no matter what. Ohzlan is a powerful Possessor, and has likely placed a trap on your friend. Removing it will be difficult."

The kid looked nervous. "Is it going to hurt Constance?"

"Yes," he replied heavily. "But we shall heal her. She will live. I swear on the sword of Michael, archangel and commander of the Heavenly Host."

Wow. A tall order for this pretty Seraph to fill. The Oath of Michael was not something angels used unless they meant business. Auburn looked at me, his blue eyes glowing electrically as he focuses his power.

"Begin," he instructed.

The kid took a breath and began chanting. I winced as the words of God burned me, blessing the vessel and trying to pull me out. I hooked onto the woman in the trap and held on tight. I always wanted to make an angel break the Oath of Michael, and this whole operation had turned into a disaster. If making the angels kill the halfbreed's sister was the only compensation I could get, then I'd damn sure take it.

Auburn's hands glowed with gold light, his heavenly power clashing with my hell power. I gritted my teeth and dug into the mortal soul again. I ripped and tore and damage as much as I could. The angel reached out, his hands glowing a bright gold, and touched my forehead.

I scream as white-hot fire poured into the vessel, slowly severing me from the human. He worked delicately, snipping away the threads of possession I had so carefully made to tie me to Constance Ramirez. It's like stitches were being cut away from a deep gash, stinging and burning every nerve. I gripped her soul and hold on mercilessly, letting her feel an excruciating pain she'd never felt before. One that would leave scars on her soul.

Whether it took minutes or hours, I can't tell, but the angel severed my connection to Constance. He left her in agony, but intact. I felt my true self pulled up and out of the vessel, my demonic scream tearing through the throat that had once belonged to me. Oxygen and vile angelic presence swirlled around me...

Then a crushing wave of pain hit me, and I screamed until I passed out.

CHAPTER NINETEEN

I don't know how long it was before I woke again. When I
did, I felt like I'd been set on fire, thrown down a cliff, then
crushed for good measure. I was lying on a comfortable bed, but
even that hurt. Didn't matter what I did– breathing, blinking,
existing– the pain refused to leave. I could tell it wasn't a
physical pain, though. It was a pain deep in my soul, as if
someone had sliced me open, stuffed something acidic inside me,
sewn me up, then torn me open again to take it out. I vowed
never to let myself get possessed again. I wouldn't survive it.

I wasn't alone. Someone lay in the bed beside me, and while
moving my neck felt like I was tearing apart the bruised tendons
in it, I turned my head to see who it was.

Dro looked wretched. Her eyes were completely red from
tears, her face paler than usual, her hair tangled and knotted. She
lay next to me under the blankets, snuggled close like she used to
do as a kid when she was scared. She felt me moving and looked
up. Her eyes widened before she threw her arms around me.

The hug felt like she'd slapped all my internal bruises at
once, but I held her tightly. We both needed it.

"It's okay, Dro, I told her. "I'm okay. It's gone." I prayed she couldn't hear the tremble in my voice. I must not have done a good job, because Dro let out a shaking breath and hugged me tighter.

"You are awake," a new voice said.

I slowly looked up and saw the angel with auburn hair, the one who did the exorcism with Max, staring at Dro and me. Recent memories started coming back. Their plan was to make me remember what happened under my possession, and they'd done too good of a job. I remembered everything I did, everything I said, and everything I felt. It came in quick flashes, but it was there. I wished it weren't.

"I trust that you are well," he said.

I recalled the sensation of my body burning from the inside out, the smoky darkness that drowned my soul before capturing and torturing it. I finally understood why people screamed so much during exorcisms.

"That's not exactly the word I would use," I muttered.

"We completely destroyed the demon when he exited your body. He shall not return."

I guess he said it to comfort me, but it didn't take away the horrible memories of being locked in my own body, trapped under a net that seemed to have been made of razors. I could still feel them slicing deep whenever I tried to escape the possession, the pain so horrific it would have cut me to the bone if it had been physical.

"Thanks," I mumbled, even though I didn't look in his eyes.

The angel didn't seem bothered by my reaction. He didn't have any expression at all. He looked at Dro, who still clung to me. "She has not left your side since the end of the exorcism. She healed your injuries and refused to eat or sleep."

I stroked Dro's hair. "I know. She's stubborn like that."

Dro sat up. "You were out for two days. We thought you'd gone into a coma."

Images of Max, a pissy blond angel, and a green- eyed

demon slayer flashed through my mind. "Where's everyone else? Is Max okay?"

She nodded. "He's all right. I healed him."

I was grateful, but there was one more person I needed to know about. I swallowed. "Manny?"

Tears filled in Dro's eyes. She shook her head. Heartache pierced me, yet another injury added to my soul. I quickly replaced it with anger, hoping Drake had died horribly, and very, very, slowly at the hands of a demon or six.

The door to the motel room opened and the rest of the group entered– Max, the white blond angel, and the green-eyed demon slayer. They all seemed surprised to see me awake, but only Max was happy about it. He smiled and raced across the room to sit on the other side of the bed.

"About time. How was your stay in La- La-Land?"

I gave him a sarcastic smile. "Not as comfortable as it sounds."

He flinched a little, but clasped my hand. "I'm glad you're okay, Constance." He read my eyes, then grinned. "Screw it, I'm freaking *relieved*."

He threw his arms around me and hugged me.

I grimaced at the next round of pain, then patted him on the back. It felt… nice.

Max pulled away and shifted on the bed so he could put his arm around Dro's shoulders. Sorrow was still raw on her face, and he looked like he needed someone to hang onto as well.

I looked at the other three men in the room. The two angels were expressionless, but the slayer didn't look happy. That was a shame because if he would have relaxed, I would have appreciated his eyes even more. They were amazing, the color of leaves under the sun.

"Do the three strangers have names?" I asked, keeping my eyes on all of them.

"Yeah," Max pointed to the auburn-haired angel. "That's

Sephiel," he pointed to the white blond angel, "Rorikel," his finger moved to the slayer, "and that's John Warrick. I called him then used a little precognition to see where you were. He's the emergency demon slayer my dad knew."

Pain filled Max's voice. He didn't look at me, and I wasn't eager to meet his eyes either. It was still hard for me to accept that Manny was gone. I composed myself as the three of them stared at me. I focused on the slayer, Warrick.

"So you guys do exist after all," I said wryly. "I wasn't sure. Manny made you seem like myths. How much do you know?"

He didn't even blink. "Max told me all of it."

"We are Seraphim," said Rorikel. "We have been instructed by Heaven to take up our vessels on earth and watch over the Nephilim you call Dro."

"Why?" I asked.

"We are her protectors."

"So that's why you were following us."

Sephiel's face still looked blank, but Rorikel frowned. He probably didn't think I'd seen them on the rooftops after I'd summoned the Red. There wasn't a lot of trust going around right now, so at least we were on the same page.

"But what are you supposed to protect her from? I don't know if you noticed, but you weren't exactly helpful the last few years when demons were fucking up our lives."

A muscle in Rorikel's wide jaw twitched. "We have guarded her more than you realize, human. We have defended you from horrors you cannot begin to comprehend."

"I was just possessed by a fucking demon," I said bitterly. "I can comprehend quite a bit. What do you really want with her?"

"To protect her," Sephiel's tone wasn't robotic like Rorikel's. He seemed sincere, like Manny had been. Maybe another woman would have taken a chance and trusted him outright. But I wasn't ready to do that. Not yet. Not when I knew nothing about this person or his intentions.

"Why? What's so special about Nephilim?"

"They–"

"Sephiel," Rorikel interrupted. "This is neither the time nor the place."

"Yes it is," I countered. "Tell us."

Rorikel gave me a steely look. "You have obtained knowledge from the Possessor demon known as Ohzlan. Reveal what you have discovered."

"Why should I, when you aren't going to tell me what I want to know?"

He narrowed his creepy, pale eyes. I started to wonder what mental powers Seraphim had. Having my brain fried by an angel after it had just been controlled by a demon was something that would absolutely kill me.

"We cannot tell you, but we must tell the Nephilim," said Sephiel. "And it is apparent to me that you will not leave her side, as she will not leave yours." He looked at Max. "Nor shall you, it seems," he looked at Warrick, "and John Warrick is a demon slayer. He must have knowledge of angels."

I glanced at Warrick. He looked impassive. I turned away from his intense green eyes when Rorikel began to argue with Sephiel.

"They are mortals, Sephiel. Their involvement in the matters of Heaven is expressly forbidden."

"You heard Ohzlan. There is something we do not know, and perhaps their experience with demons shall provide us with the information we truly need." Sephiel's blue eyes became serious. "We do not have time to argue politics and semantics." He looked at me. "Tell us what you remember, Constance, and we shall tell you what you wish to know."

He gave me that sincere look of his, and I wanted to trust him. I could use the power of Heaven on my side. Trust didn't come easy for me, but what other options was I supposed to have?

I pressed my lips together. I didn't want to think about being a prisoner in my own body again. I didn't want to think about the crushing, severing pain that tore into me when Ohzlan refused to give me up. But mostly I didn't want to remember the horrible things he made me say to Dro. The look on her face as he lied to her, when she didn't realize I was trapped inside myself, screaming none of it wasn't true. I took a deep breath, and tried not to shake.

"The demons want to open the Gates of Hell and escape to earth." I looked at Dro. "Using her blood."

Dro gaped. Max pulled her close, wrapping both arms around her as if that was all he needed to do to keep her safe. It was heartbreakingly sweet, and I wish it had been enough. I looked at the angels, who were still unreadable.

"Who's bringing them over to do that?" Warrick asked. "There aren't many cults capable of summoning that many demons at one time."

"They were summoned by some kind of witch. I didn't get a name." I paused, then went on. "I don't think Ohzlan knew how it worked. He was on a need-to-know basis."

Sephiel frowned. "That is worrisome."

Rorikel nodded. "Very troublesome."

A headache formed behind my eyes. I hoped not all angels were like this. I looked at Dro, who hadn't moved from Max's arms.

"There's something else." Everyone looked at me, but I focused on Dro. "I don't... I don't think that Dro is Nephilim."

I hated the heavy silence that followed.

"What do you mean?" Max asked. "We checked, and her powers are weird but it's the only thing that makes sense–"

"Ohzlan said we weren't using the phrase 'Nephilim' properly. He never strictly said what she was, but he knew she wasn't a Nephilim." I looked at my sister. "You might be something else."

She looked like she might be sick, turning and burying herself in Max's shoulder.

"I'm sorry, little sister," I said, meaning it with every bit of my heart.

"Demons are false more often than not," Rorikel said sourly. "The Nephilim called Dro is simply that, a Nephilim. Born of angel and human and destined for glorious purpose."

"Which is what?" I asked.

Sephiel faced me. "The Nephilim are the vessels for the archangels. Angels cannot take corporeal forms on earth. We must gain permission to enter a human's body to use our powers. Many times we appear in dreams and ask the vessel's concession. Sometimes a human may realize what we are and reject us. When an archangel asks a Nephilim, however, it is much more difficult for them to decline."

The pieces started to fit together slowly. "So, an archangel wants to use Dro's body?"

He nodded. "Through her, the spirit of the archangel will flow and give tremendous power to combat Hell's forces."

"It is as great an honor as a half human could receive," Rorikel added.

"What would happen if I said no?" Dro asked quietly.

Rorikel looked at her and frowned, his pale eyes hard. "It is not wise. The archangels do not take kindly to insult."

"Is that a threat?" I challenged.

"Not at all," he replied. "Merely a statement." He looked at Dro again. "I highly suggest you surrender yourself to your archangel when the time comes. They are resilient beings."

I was about to speak, but Dro had seen my eyes and cut me off. "How would I even know when they would want me? Assuming I'll do what they ask."

"Anyone with angel blood in their veins has a connection to Heaven, to other angels and Nephilim through a telepathic link," Sephiel said.

"You guys can read each others minds and communicate mentally?" Max asked.

Sephiel nodded once. "It is how the archangels will coordinate their attacks against the demons should the need ever arise. They will create a plan to strike the demons from earth."

"What about us humans? Would we be caught in the crossfire?" Warrick said.

Rorikel glanced at him. "The archangels would be saving your world. Collateral damage is irrelevant."

Warrick looked like he wanted to hit Rorikel. As much as I wanted to see a demon slayer throw down with an angel, we had bigger problems. I looked at Sephiel. At least I could actually get answers from him.

"Ohzlan felt that Dro was powerful," I informed. "More powerful than anything he'd ever encountered."

Sephiel's eyes were heavy, as if he knew exactly what I meant. "We will protect you," he said, looking at Dro. "Keeping the children of angels safe is a sacred duty."

"We were chosen to protect the Nephilim called Dro," Rorikel added. "She shall not come to harm."

I relaxed, but didn't let them see it. Their claims to protect Dro sounded nice enough, but angel or not, I didn't trust either of them. They already wanted to use her as a conduit for an archangel. It wasn't a stretch to think they would be after more than that.

"How do we stop the demons?" Dro asked.

That immediately got my attention. It wasn't our responsibility to take out the demons. The best thing we could do was run from them all— the angels, demons, Drake, Warrick. Things were simpler when it was just Dro and I. But things had changed. I could see the firm determination in Dro's eyes. If we didn't try to stop the demons from opening the Gates of Hell, she would never forgive me. Maybe she thought that if we stopped their plans, they would finally leave us alone. I couldn't really argue with that. I gave her a small nod.

"We must uncover the identity of this witch and subdue them. A mortal with the power to summon such powerful demons is distressingly vexing."

I looked at Warrick. "Know any demon slayers willing to help us out?"

His eyes were guarded. "Not really. We're not an army."

I glared. "Are you gonna ask or not?"

Warrick kept his eyes on me for another long minute. I should have felt guilty for snapping at him. He helped save me, but I was tired, in pain, stressed out, and didn't like being under that laser green stare.

Well, I like it a little. His eyes are pretty.

I ignored that stupid voice and looked away before he could read my eyes. Warrick took his cell phone out of his jean pocket and walked out of the hotel room to make whatever calls he had to make. I didn't trust him not to turn me in to the Marshals for that hefty bounty, but he was Max's emergency contact. Even though it went against my rules, I trusted Max.

"I want to help," Max said. "There has to be something I can do."

For my father, went unsaid. The grief was still too raw for us. I wanted to tell him no, that it was too dangerous and he didn't know nearly enough to survive in combat, especially against a demon, but Max wouldn't give a damn about what I thought. He would fight demons to honor his father, and defend my sister as much as he could.

"You are gifted with psychic abilities," said Sephiel, reminding me the angels had been watching with silence and interest. Well, maybe only Sephiel found it interesting. Rorikel was a blank slate. "Those gifts could be very useful."

Max relaxed. "I'll do whatever I can. Just let me stay."

His last words were so quiet and tender I knew I couldn't

refuse them. My sister reached over and touched Max's hands, smiling at him.

He grinned back at her, yet again looking at Dro like she held the light of the stars. A bomb could have gone off two doors down and Max wouldn't have noticed.

Sephiel smiled, looking strangely sad as he shook his head. He said exactly what I was thinking.

"Humans are strange creatures indeed."

CHAPTER TWENTY

After the dramatic reveals, arguments, and compromises, we all needed space. Warrick was still trying to get in contact other demon slayers. Rorikel went on a perimeter check of the Odessa motel we were currently occupying. Sephiel had used some kind of teleportation magic to take Max back to his house so they could bury Manny's body. I wanted to go with them, but I was only just getting my strength back. Dro was torn for not going with Max, but she refused to leave me alone.

So we sat in the motel room, eating the leftover burgers and fries that had been ordered a couple hours earlier. Angels didn't need to eat, and Max and Warrick hadn't been very hungry, so I ate all the fries they left behind. I was a skinny girl, but being possessed by a demon, exorcised, and sleeping for two days famished me. I wasn't about to let the food go to waste.

Dro had been quiet for most of the night, nibbling on her food instead of scarfing it down like me. She needed to talk, but didn't want to. Not a good sign, and there could only be a couple things she wanted to talk about in this mood.

"You might as well tell me what's on your mind before the

Testosterone Team comes back," I tried, munching on another French fry.

She didn't answer me right away, which was fine. I could be patient for Dro.

"How much of it was true?" she asked quietly.

"How much of what?"

Dro gave me a regretful look. "How much do I scare you?"

Damn it. Of all the things I wanted to avoid talking about with her, that was at the top of the list. Since my memories were given back to me during the exorcism, I was all too aware of what Ohzlan said to Dro using my voice. He wanted to hurt us both. And he had.

"Dro, listen to me. That was Ohzlan talking. Not me. I would never say or think those things of you."

"You didn't answer my question." She looked crestfallen. "I terrify you."

"No you don't," I said, wishing it didn't sound like a lie.

Dro dropped her head into her hands and clutched her snow-white hair as it spilled over her shoulders. "I knew it. I always knew I dragged you down. You're scared of what I might do."

"That isn't true," I told her, shifting on the bed to get closer to her. "Dro, the demon said those things."

Dro's head snapped up. "Why are you lying to me?"

I froze. She looked spiritless, tears building in her eyes. Dro was starting to run down like a machine that lost its batteries. I could have lied, told her what she wanted to hear. But good sisters don't lie to each other. I didn't have a lot of virtues to be proud of, but being a good sister was one of them.

"It was the demon," I repeated cautiously. "He went into the worst parts of my head and twisting my thoughts." I held my breath, ready to jump into the deep end. "I am afraid, Dro. I wish I wasn't, but I just don't understand all this. I understand you, but not your powers. Every time you lose control, I worry that it will be for the last time. It's torture to watch you have those nightmares and see you burn, knowing there isn't anything I can do."

I touched her shoulder. "I'm tired of running, but I don't blame you for anything. You haven't ruined my life. I wouldn't change anything, Dro. I would do it all again if I had to."

She exhaled heavily. "He was right, though. You'd be safer away from this. Away from me."

I almost took my hand back. "Are you trying to get me to leave?" I asked, saying the words I never thought I would say, hoping I was jumping to conclusions.

One look in her eyes told me I wasn't.

"Things are only going to get more dangerous, Constance," she said. "You're going to get hurt again. I can't change what I am, or know where my life will go. But you have a chance. You can escape and find a normal life. You can take Max with you. I would understand."

I lifted my hand from her shoulder. "No."

"Constance–"

"No fucking way. I haven't left your side in sixteen years. I'm not going to start now."

"The demons will be out for blood, and–"

"You think I care about that? Or about being scared? Ohzlan might have fucked around in my head and bent my thoughts to get to you, but leaving you has never once crossed my mind. Never. Didn't matter after Mom and Dad died, didn't matter when we joined the Blood Thorns, didn't matter all the times the demons almost killed me, doesn't matter now. I am not leaving you, Dro."

Instead of taking comfort in my words, Dro burst into tears. She shook her head. "I can't keep doing it, Connie. I can't keep living with your blood on my hands."

I put my arm around her shoulder. "Just like I can't live

without making sure you're safe. So we're kind of at an awkward impasse, aren't we?"

Dro choked on her laugh and threw her arms around my neck, hugging me tightly and sobbing onto my shoulder. I let her. The poor girl had so much weight on her soul, so much pain I couldn't understand or take away, no matter how badly I wanted to. She was allowed to fall apart sometimes, because she was strong enough to put herself back together again.

"I'm your sister," I told her. "Your pain is my pain. There's nothing you can do to make me leave, Dro. You're stuck with me."

"You promise?" she sobbed.

I stroked her hair. "I promise."

Dro started to calm down. I wouldn't ask if she believed me or not. I just had to trust her.

As we pulled away from each other, the door opened.

Max walked in, his red from crying. Sephiel walked behind him with an equally sad expression. Max's eyes shifted to Dro, the slump in his shoulders starting to lessen. He managed a weak smile when she looked at him. His dark eyes turned to me.

"I brought you these back," he said, holding out his hands.

I could have cried at the welcome sight of my weapons. My heart ached at the sight of my father's hatchet.

"I noticed them on the floor, after..." His voice trailed off. Tears built in his eyes again.

"Thank you," I said quietly. "You didn't need to do that."

He nodded, still avoiding my eyes. After a long time, he sniffed and raised his head. "I was also talking to Sephiel, and I know how we can keep demons from possessing us."

"How?"

He grinned, some of the familiar sparkle coming back into his eyes. "We've got to get tattoos."

THREE HOURS LATER, I was getting inked again. This time the tattoo was on my chest, just over my heart. I didn't have to worry about exposing half of my breast to a psychic, a demon slayer, and two angels, because they didn't seem to care. The needle stabbed and buzzed into my skin, and I set my jaw so I wouldn't show how much it hurt.

Max had drawn out the anti-possession sigil and shown it to the tattoo artist after we made sure he wasn't going to call in my arrest. I didn't think I needed to worry. Twenty- five thousand dollars was a lot of money to keep quiet.

The tattoo being drawn on me was a line with two loops on the left above a horizontal cross. The line extended right and shaped into an 'X' and a 'V' near its end. Max said it was the sigil of Michael, meant to protect us from evil. Only Max, Warrick, and I were getting the tattoo. Angels couldn't be possessed in their current vessels, and neither could Dro as a hypothetical Nephilim. Warrick seemed impressed with Max's knowledge. He hadn't known there was a way to avoid possession until Max explained it. Max had been on Cloud Nine ever since.

The bulky artist finished my tattoo and set down the ink gun.

"Keep it covered and watch for signs of infection," he mumbled.

I nodded and got out of the chair. I walked over to the mirror and took a look at my latest ink. Dro slid up behind me to get a peek, tilting her head to see the black lines on my slightly inflamed skin.

"It's not a bad design," she said.

"Yeah, well I didn't get it to look pretty," I grumbled, lifting my shirt back onto its place and taping a cloth bandage over it to protect the raw mark.

Dro looked over my shoulder. "Whoa, speaking of pretty..."

I turned, wondering what Max was doing that she found so

damn lovely. Except she was looking at Warrick, who had just sat down in the tattoo artist's chair, taken off his leather jacket, and lifted off his shirt.

I admit it– I stared. He was well muscled everywhere, like a mixed martial arts fighter. His arms were big and looked strong, his stomach toned and washboard flat. My eyes drifted all the way across his body, taking in the V-shape of his hipbones as well as the thin white scars that could only have come from demon claws.

My trance was broken when Dro nudged my ribs. She waggled her eyebrows at me and grinned.

"Rawr," she teased, making a claw with her hands.

I stifled a laugh and put my hand on the top of her head, turning it away from me. I made sure not to stare at Warrick again as his chest was tattooed. No man should be that hypnotic.

Lucky for me, Rorkiel was making a scene.

"Hey buddy, we don't take crazies in here," said one of the skinnier artists. "Keep a lid on it."

"All of them shall be damned," he proclaimed. "There are no saints here, only sinners."

I walked away from Dro to Rorikel, who stood in the skinny artist's face. Sephiel stood next to him, but said nothing. He seemed more interested in the way tattoo guns were working than keeping his friend from freaking out all the people in the parlor.

"What the hell do you care, Blondie?" one of the customers said. "Why don't you just keep your thoughts to your own damn self?"

Rorikel glared daggers. "You have failed as mortal souls, condemning and corrupting yourselves to pettiness and sin. You all disgust me."

I finally made it over and grabbed Rorikel's arm, dragging him away from the artist and the customer.

After three long steps, he wrenched free from me. "What are you doing?" he demanded.

"I should be asking you that question." I kept my tone low. "Look, I'm guessing you don't usually visit your human forms, but you can't start talking shit about people. Especially not in a place like this."

"You believe that I fear them? They are merely damned humans. Nothing more."

"They have free will. Let them make their own choices."

He scoffed. "You would side with them, wouldn't you? You, one with so many stains on her soul? Do you tell yourself it was for a noble cause? That you had no other choice? Do you think it will make a difference come Judgment Day?"

I am not in the mood for this. "Get the fuck out, Rori," I said coldly. "Go stand outside and be a good little watchdog."

He clenched his fists. "Do not presume to direct me, human. I am an angel of Heaven, tasked with protecting the vessel of an archangel. That protection does not extend to you."

"Ask me if I give a shit. Get out."

His eyes suddenly glowed, and I could see the heavenly power bubbling under his control. I tensed, feeling phantom fire tearing through my skin and scorching my soul. I never wanted to feel it again.

"Do not command me," he warned.

The thought of being burned by heavenly fire again sent a terrified chill down my spine, but I forced myself to look tough.

"Rori, you're on my last nerve. Stop being dramatic and do your fucking job."

I thought he would hit me. He looked ready to, and he was right– I wasn't the one who needed to be kept safe. Only Dro had to be. Then Sephiel walked up to Rorikel and touched his shoulder.

"Constance has a point. We need to guard the entrance. This

place could be a lure for Possessors. I will stay here and watch over the Nephilim, Rorikel."

The bitchy white-blond angel glared at his friend, but stormed out of the tattoo parlor.

"What the hell is his problem?" I asked when he was gone.

"Rorikel has never been known for his admiration of the human race. Nor is he famed for his patience."

"So he has a permanent stick up his ass," I muttered.

To my surprise, Sephiel smiled a little. "That is a sufficient definition, yes."

"Why do you like him then?"

"I do not understand what you mean."

"Why choose him as your partner?"

Sephiel frowned. "You are under the assumption I had a choice in the matter. Rorikel and I were assigned one another by Michael himself. His orders are not ones you defy."

"So if you defy your orders, what, you get fired?"

"I believe humans call it 'vaporization.'"

I blinked. "Oh. Wow. That's harsh."

"Heaven can be a stern place at times, but there is order there. Structure. A sense of stability you do not find in Hell, or earth for that matter." A fondness twinkled in his bright blue eyes, which shifted over my shoulder to where Dro stood. "But that lack of stability has led me to respect the human race. Despite their flaws, they can be decent and kind. Unique creatures, in their own strange ways."

I looked over with him and spotted Dro, who sat in a chair next to Max. This must have been his first tattoo because he eyed the needle nervously as it hovered above his skin. But Dro's presence relaxed him. They talked and flirted without restraint. She held Max's hand, gently touched his non-tattooed shoulder. I wondered if he felt all the happiness and softness she had for him with his power. I hoped he did. The kid deserved it.

I turned to talk to Sephiel again, but he was gone. I hadn't even heard him move, but he wasn't in the parlor anymore.

"Making new friends, or new enemies?" a voice rumbled from behind me.

I turned to Warrick. He'd put his shirt and jacket back on. Underneath it I could just make out the edges of the bandage on his chest. I pushed away the weird, slight disappointment I felt now that he wasn't shirtless, and found myself focusing on an even more dangerous feature. His bright green eyes.

They reminded me of the times I had walked in the forest, seeing crisp green leaves and feeling relaxed as warm summer air filled my lungs. I'd stared at the world around me, allowing myself to be lost in time and forgetting everything around me. Kind of like now.

What the hell are you doing, Constance? You don't know anything about this guy. Sometimes mistrust is a good thing.

"Bit of both," I said. I crossed my arms, nodding to his chest. "First time getting inked?"

He looked at me curiously. "Are you guessing or assuming?"

I shrugged. My patience had been thin with him earlier, and even though I didn't trust him, it wasn't fair for me to keep the bitchy attitude up. At least until I figured out if he was going to turn me into the Marshals or not.

Warrick turned up his right wrist, showing me a small tattoo of a name with two hummingbirds on either side of it. The name read 'Emma'.

"Second," he said.

I wondered who Emma was. Probably a girlfriend, or a woman he loved and couldn't let go. Warrick must've been the sentimental type.

This was the first time I had been more or less alone with the demon slayer. It was as good a time as any to get answers and tips from him. It would keep me from getting distracted by those spellbinding eyes that seemed to warm the very center of my being.

But first, I had to know why he was sticking around.

"So, why are you here?" I asked.

Warrick looked at me curiously. "What do you mean?"

"Why are you here getting inked with us? There are probably demons out there for you to kill, and you haven't taken off to chase them."

He held my eyes for a moment, then dropped them to my boots. "I knew Max's dad. Met with him a couple times when I needed information. He was a good man, and when Max told me what happened... I had to help."

The memory came back, the one of Drake standing in front of me, lifting the gun and pulling the trigger on Manny. The way he had instantly crumpled, not even able to scream. The amount of blood that had pooled underneath him staining the carpet and the hardwood underneath...

All because Drake had been looking for me.

"Max told me about your sister," Warrick added quietly. "I know what she can do."

I tensed, looking as dangerous as I could. But Warrick didn't seem to be intimidated. He raised one of his hands, as if he could stop me with that simple gesture.

"Don't worry, I'm not going to hurt her." He looked over my shoulder at Dro. "She seems like a sweet girl, and you all really care about her. I only kill demons, and your sister is anything but."

I wasn't too sure about that, but I wasn't going to voice my doubts to anyone. Especially not to a demon slayer.

"How long have you been slaying?" I asked, leaning against the wall.

"About five years." He chuckled mirthlessly. "At this point, I'm a veteran."

"What's your secret?" I asked curiously.

Warrick smiled at me. It was a nice smile, if a little sad. "Lots of belief, and lots of bullets."

I stifled a laugh. "Didn't peg you for the church-type."

"I'm more agnostic, really," he clarified. "But I believe there's something out there stronger and wiser than us. At least I hope so. People can be pretty crazy sometimes."

"No lie there. Is that why you became a slayer? Do you believe in destiny and all that noble stuff?"

His green eyes turned haunted, and I stopped pushing him. I recognized a look of pain when I saw one.

Warrick took a seat near the wall. He started rubbing the 'Emma' tattoo with his thumb.

"My sister was a medium," he said, eyes on the ink. "She could see the dead. Around Halloween she would tell me that she could see more than just spirits. She saw creatures, things that couldn't exist. It turned out she was seeing demons." He was quiet for a long time. "I did it for her. To keep her safe. I wanted to protect her from them."

Part of me wanted to ask more. The other part of me knew better. Prying into Warrick's past wasn't going to win me any points with him.

After a moment, I asked, "What did your parents think?"

"Nothing, because they didn't know. I was the only one Emma ever told. She knew I would believe her when no one else would." His eyes lifted to mine. "Kind of like you and Dro, I'm guessing."

I was quiet for a long time. Mom and Dad had known Dro was special from the moment they saw her. It hadn't just been the way she looked. There was something different about her, something you knew when you saw her. Only we never knew how much, or what it would cost us in the end.

But we had loved her anyway. That was what family did. They loved each other, no matter how different and strange some of that family was.

"Is that why you got her name tattooed on you?"

Warrick's eyes clouded, my first warning that I was starting to walk on shaky ground.

"No," he replied. "I got it as a tribute."

Oh. "I'm sorry," I said honestly.

I didn't need to know the details. Whatever had happened to Warrick's sister was obviously painful for him. I was a sister myself, and I couldn't imagine the idea of losing Dro.

Then his eyes filled with anger, and he whispered, "Not as sorry as Drake Talbot is going to be."

I blinked, shock stealing the words from my mouth. He knew Drake? How? What did he do to Warrick's sister to make him so furious?

I thought about the way Drake had been touching and threatening Dro in front of me, and then decided I didn't want to know the details to that story either.

Warrick's phone rang from the pocket of his dark jeans. He stood up, checking the caller ID on the screen. He gave me an apologetic look, then brushed past me and walked outside the tattoo parlor to take the call. I watched him from beyond the glass, wondering if another slayer had finally gotten back to him.

Trusting Warrick was a bad idea, but for some reason I wanted to. He was fearless and confident at the border when I was possessed. He was willing to put his life on the line to help us stop the demons, and he hadn't accused Dro of being some monster when he learned what she was. The man had even let himself get tattooed so he would be better at his job.

But he was a mystery, and mysterious men had betrayed me in the past.

I turned away from the door and looked at Dro, who was sitting next to her almost-boyfriend. I walked across the parlor to them. Like Warrick, Max had removed his shirt for the tattooing. Unlike Warrick, Max wasn't rippling with the muscle of a boxer. He was a little on the scrawny side, but I wasn't the one chasing after him. Dro, however, had a faint blush in her cheeks.

My eyes shifted over Max's chest to the spot where he had been shot. There wasn't a raw, gaping wound since someone healed him, but there was a small circular scar near his shoulder. Dro must have healed him, just not fast enough to take away the scar. My heart ached then twisted in anger for Drake. Warrick might want a piece of him, but if I found Drake first, I was going to kill him. And I would smile when I did it.

"How do you like getting tattooed?" I asked, pushing away the dark thoughts.

Max couldn't lift his shoulder, so he grimaced and shrugged his eyebrows. "It's like a day at the spa, right? A day at the spa with a million needles all the time."

I stifled a laugh. "It's not that bad, wuss."

"Says the badass who's done this before."

My laugh was more genuine this time. I was glad to have met Max. He was the only honest person I knew who wasn't my sister. I could never thank him enough for taking us in and showing Dro a kindness I never thought she would see. But at the same time, I regretted it. I'd brought pain and suffering to his door, been the reason he was shot, and the reason his father was dead. He should have hated me. I would have, if I were him.

"You know it wasn't your fault, right?" Max said.

I glanced up at him. For a moment I'd forgotten that he could sense things about people around him if he concentrated enough. He reached out and gently touched my hand. I wanted to pull away, not wanting him to see all the terrible things swirling around inside my heart. But he refused to let go.

"I'm not mad at you," he assured me, his eyes showing no hint of pain, "and I definitely don't blame you for what happened." Max's eyes went dark. "It was *his* fault."

He wasn't wrong, but he wasn't right, either. Drake had been after me. Might still be after me if he'd somehow survived the demons at the border. I had to live with that for the rest of my life, no matter how short it was going to be.

"Don't think like that." Max squeezed my hand. "You did everything you could. I'm grateful, and Dad would have been proud."

It wasn't Max's intention to hurt me, but his words knifed into my heart. Manny had been patient and understanding when I'd pushed him away. He hadn't blamed or scolded me for the things I had done, thinking that I could still save myself.

Max looked ready to say something else, but I put my hand on his shoulder to silence him.

"Noted," I said quietly. I yanked my hand back. "Now stay out of my head."

Max must have seen that I wasn't joking around, because his expression wasn't as playful anymore. Dro sighed and shook her head at me.

The tattoo artist finished up on Max's ink and let him out of the chair. Dro would speed up his healing, just as she would for Warrick and me. The last thing we needed was to fight demons with an infected anti- possession tattoo.

I heard the door open behind me and turned quickly, my hand resting at my hip where I could reach my hatchet. The people in the tattoo parlor couldn't see it underneath my lucky jacket and were probably wondered what the hell I was doing, but I didn't care. If a demon stormed through the doors, I would be ready.

But the only person who walked through the door was Warrick. He slid his phone back into his pocket and walked through the parlor to us.

"That was my contact with the Marshals," he said. "No one's seen Drake or anyone matching his description. He might have crossed the border."

Warrick wasn't pleased with that. I wasn't pleased with him knowing the Marshals.

"You do a lot of work with the law?"

"Of course. It's not like slaying pays my rent."

I turned to Max, who was standing next to Dro beside the chair. I gripped Max's elbow and dragged him over to me.

"It would have been nice to know your emergency demon slayer does work for the U.S. Marshals," I said in a quiet, dangerous voice.

Max frowned, pulling free from my grip. "If I'd have known, you'd have known."

There goes all the trust I could have given Warrick. Taking up one bounty would be one thing, but if he collected them for a living, there was no way he didn't know about me. No way he wouldn't want that twenty-five grand. My body tensed. If he were on the phone with the Marshals, he might have told them I was with him, and that he would bring me in. I kept my eyes from Warrick, already planning on how to cut him loose.

"That's not a bad thing though, right?" Dro said, knowing the problems Warrick might bring but focusing on distracting him. "Maybe Drake will give up on the bounty now that he knows demons are involved."

Warrick gave her a cold look, but the hatred wasn't directed at her. "You don't know Drake Talbot. Once he sets a goal or takes a job, he sees it through to the bloody end."

Dro looked at me, as if I knew something she didn't. I shrugged. Her guess about Warrick and Drake's history was as good as mine.

Warrick didn't elaborate, stalking off to the wall to be alone while Max finished getting patched up. When we started leaving the tattoo parlor, I tried to ignore the whispers of the tattoo artists and customers at my back. I couldn't quite hear what they were saying, couldn't tell if they were going to call in the bounty on me now that my face had been seen. Going back to threaten them wouldn't help my case. I was just going to have to keep my guard up and watch the shadows.

Sephiel and Rorikel weren't in sight when we got outside. I

wasn't about to start shouting for them, but I didn't like that they were gone.

"Where the hell did they go?" I asked, scanning the dark streets.

As I said it, the world seemed to shiver. Sephiel and Rorikel suddenly appeared out of thin air, literally in the blink of an eye. I frowned, really not liking how they could do that. Angels showing up randomly didn't sit well with me.

"We must go to Athens," Rorikel stated, as if materializing out of nothingness was normal and humans should expect it all the time.

"Athens?" I said with heavy sarcasm. "You mean we get a trip to Greece out of this mess?"

He glared. "No. Athens, Texas."

I sighed, and solemnly vowed never to try and humor Rorikel again. His brain probably couldn't comprehend jokes of any kind.

"What's in Athens?" Warrick asked.

"We have sensed a powerful magic presence there," Sephiel answered. "Dark magic. It seems prudent to investigate the possibility that the witch is summoning demons there, and perhaps uncover clues to stopping the Opening ritual."

"I can feel it too," Dro whispered. I looked at her, and she at me. "It's faint, but I can feel the darkness coming from there. Almost like it's in my blood."

Dro sounded calm, though she was the opposite. I wasn't about to question her judgment, though I did see the nervous look Rorikel and Sephiel gave each other.

"What?" I asked.

Rorikel looked away. Sephiel turned to face us. "To feel black magic in her blood like that... It is, unusual for a Nephilim to do."

"But they can do it, right?" Dro asked. "I'm not the only one?"

He looked at her sadly. "If there is another Nephilim with that skill, they are not known to us."

Of course not, I thought grimly. *That would mean Dro is actually a Nephilim. And she isn't.*

"We'll worry about what that means later," I said, hoping it wasn't anything serious. And knowing I was probably wrong.

CHAPTER TWENTY-ONE

Since only Rorikel and Sephiel could teleport, we were forced to drive. Sephiel produced a car from somewhere (since Rorikel was probably too virtuous to steal) and we decided to stop at a motel in Abilene for rest.

The angels checked us into an almost decent motel that took cash for joint rooms. Rorikel, Max, and Warrick took one while me, Dro, and Sephiel took the other. The angels took some time to set up invisible walls– wards, apparently– and spells that would avert human attention and soundproof the rooms. There was no telling who might be possessed since the incident at the border. We hadn't really listened to the news in the last few days, but I hardly imagined all of those demons had been killed yet, even if the portal was closed. I just hoped no one else had been killed. Well, except for Drake. I hoped the demons had torn him to shreds.

Despite the joint rooms, there wasn't much privacy. The guys wanted the room doors open in case they needed to come in and rescue us from a demonic attack, as if we were helpless damsels. I swear they forgot I was carrying a jacket full of throwing knives and a well used hatchet.

We didn't have much to do, so we spread ourselves around our room. I sat on the edge of the bed. Warrick leaned against the dresser with his hands at his sides. Sephiel and Rorikel stood like white statues on either side of the front door. Max decided to sit at the blocky table in the corner with Dro and use his cell phone to find clues about the town of Athens. He stopped when he came across information regarding a place called Fuller Park. The Park was famous for its haunted gravesite, and the satanic rituals that often went on there.

"They have a tunnel system shaped like a pentagram," he added.

"Seriously?" I said.

"Yup. There are five stone markers for each of the entrances."

"Is it occupied?"

"Not for a long time. Only paranormal hunters and Satanists venture out that way, but these days they seem to be staying away from it. Like even they can tell it's a messed up place." He held my eyes. "They say it's cursed."

"Probably because it is," muttered Warrick. "Slayers get called out to this part of Texas all the time to deal with possessions."

"How many of you are there?" I asked, suddenly wanting to know how much backup we might have if things went straight to... Well, if they went straight to Hell.

He hesitated. "Most of us like to stay under the radar, but we make sure to keep up on one another's movements. Passing warnings, updates, that kind of thing." He took a deep breath. "Right now, there are six living slayers. Including me."

"Only six?" I said, shocked. "In all of the States?"

"In all of North America."

I dropped my head into my hands and let out an angry sigh.

"It's not a career people get into, Constance. If you're not born into it, you find a damn good reason to join. Then you pray you're good enough to stay alive."

I lifted my head when he said that. From the hurt expression on his face, I realized I had hit a sore spot.

"Sorry," I said, meaning it. "So we can't expect any more slayers." I looked at Rorikel. "What about other angels?"

Rorikel snorted like I'd just asked a stupid question. "Angels avoid the affairs of demons at all costs," he proclaimed in a 'no-duh' tone of voice. Which I hated.

"To have the power they have, the witch must be willing to give themselves to possession, regardless of the consequences to their body, mind and soul," said Sephiel, quickly diffusing the hostility between Rorikel and me. "We may encounter resistance from possessed individuals."

Unwanted memories pressed into my mind. The excruciating pain, being trapped in my own body with no way to escape. I wrapped my arms around my middle. My brain couldn't comprehend a single reason why anyone would think demonic possession was something worth doing.

"However, if they have astrally projected, we must heed even more caution." Rorikel added.

His arms were crossed over his chest, and he looked every inch the tough, no B.S. bodyguard he was supposed to be.

I blinked at him, then looked at Sephiel, Warrick and Max. "Say again."

Rorikel scoffed at me. I expected nothing less.

"It's an out of body experience," Max clarified. "Basically you share your spirit with something of your choice. You have to be careful and totally prepared when you do it, otherwise you can get possessed by something you don't intend to."

"Like me?"

"In a way," Sephiel confirmed, "but your soul remained inside your body, so Ohzlan's abilities were limited by it. When a person's spirit opens completely to a demon, they are far more formidable. That is why most dark magic practitioners often use blood to entice the demon they are calling. The more blood that is used, the more powerful the spell, and therefore the possession."

I thought back to the night at Owl Creek six years ago. "Is that how you create portals? Blood magic?"

Sephiel nodded. "Only a human sharing a demon's soul can open a portal. The potency and length of time the portal can remain open depends on the strength of the demon. Possessors can only have a portal open for a minute or two, but a Higher demon could leave a portal open for hours."

I cringed internally. It had definitely been a Higher demon that night at the camp. "How often do people get possessed by Higher demons?"

"Rarely," said Rorikel. "They are far too difficult to control. They often ask permission of their vessel before entering it. That semblance of trust makes the human easier to manipulate."

"So, just to be clear," Max said, "you have to bleed yourself or someone else to the point of death, make your spirit an open door, then say yes when the big bad demon comes asking for a body-buddy."

"That is the idea, essentially," Sephiel said grimly.

Max sighed. "It's a nightmare. But real life." he muttered.

"What would happen if someone said yes to the archangels?"

We all turned our heads to look at Dro. She saw my expression and backtracked almost immediately. "I'm not saying yes, but I want to know what would happen if I did."

"The archangel chosen for you would need to be summoned in a ritual," said Rorikel, all too happy to answer. "Your soul would be taken out and replaced with the spirit of the archangel to fulfill its purpose."

Dro winced, and Sephiel stepped in.

"It is… uncomfortable… for humans. But there is not as much pain as you think."

"What happens to my soul? Would I get it back?"

He hesitated for a fraction of a second, just enough for me to see. "After the demons have been defeated, your soul would be transported to Heaven, where it would belong with honor."

"But her body would die," I said, getting his attention. "Her soul wouldn't be in her human body ever again."

Sephiel tried to answer, but Rorikel chose to get into the conversation instead.

"You do not know what a privilege it is to be the vessel of an archangel," he defended fiercely. "If she is as powerful as Ohzlan claimed, she might have been chosen by one of the most powerful archangels. Perhaps Raphael or Gabriel, or even Michael himself. With their combined strength, the demon hordes would cower in fear, and victory would be assured."

"What if it wasn't?" I argued.

He looked like he wanted to hit me. Again. "You dare question the fortitude of the Heavenly Host?"

"I question that everything that's supposed to go according to plan, yeah. What if she is hurt, or injured?"

"If the vessel is destroyed, the archangel could vacate and choose another Nephilim to inhabit to complete his mission. Time would tell when such an act would occur, as Andromeda is currently the only Nephilim we know of, but there are almost no demons that can stop an archangel. They are much too powerful."

I was ready to fight him some more, but Dro asked another question.

"What would happen if the demons caught me?"

Sephiel looked at her with deadly seriousness. "That will not happen, Andromeda."

"But Constance is right," she countered. "Plans can be screwed up. If Max knew something would go wrong, he would have said something by now," she said, looking at her friend.

Max nodded a little stiffly. "I'm still only getting flashes. Nothing really concrete. I don't know what's going to happen."

Dro looked at the angels again. "I can't sense anything but the power coming from that place in Athens. It's spreading like a virus. I want to know," she said, sounding braver than she looked. "I need to know."

Sephiel read her eyes carefully. I wondered why he took such an interest with my sister. He looked at Dro with fondness, like she were the most precious thing in the world. I didn't mind it, but I didn't understand it.

"The demon's ritual requires blood," Sephiel explained. "A copious amount of it. As the bleeding begins, a Higher demon must be summoned to complete the final piece of the spell and open the Gates."

"What's the final piece?" Dro asked when he didn't keep going.

His bright blue eyes met her own, and he looked oddly uncomfortable.

"Hell contains the dead souls of sinners, and sin began with Eve when Lucifer tempted her with the apple in the Garden of Eden. Eve was created from Adam's rib as per God's design to open the gates of human life, so must another rib be given to open the Gates of Hell."

Dro paled slightly, and I felt a surge of disgust and anger build up.

"That's pretty Old Testament," Max said uncomfortably.

Sephiel looked at him. "We have been alive for millennia. The Old Testament is familiar to us. It is how things used to be, and all the most dynamic summonings and spells are used with the similar mindset."

"Taking out an innocent person's rib is a touch on the dramatic side," Warrick griped, "even for the Old Testament."

"It kept the human populace obedient," Rorikel replied sharply. "These new generations of humans are even more disgraceful than the last. They blatantly sin, and find no shame in it."

"Not everyone can be a perfect little angel," I threw at him.

He glared daggers at me. "Certainly not you."

"Don't pretend you know anything about my big sister," Dro snapped.

I could only imagine the things going through her head, all the memories of the horrific things I had done, but she was still ready to drop all her problems to defend my honor, just as I would have done for her. "You have no idea what we've been through."

Rorikel stared at her. "God allows you free will," he said, toning back his anger only because she was important to his mission, "but humans abuse it for their own selfishness. All of you are more likely to choose sin than not." He looked at me. "And most of you have."

"Then why bother protecting us all?" Warrick disputed, to my surprise. "If you find us so repulsive, what the hell are you doing here?"

"I am here to protect the Nephilim until her archangel comes for her. Nothing more. Heaven does not accept sinners, and I see none of you attempting to repent."

"You're probably not going to either," I seethed. "I did what I had to do to keep Dro alive. If you think I'm going to regret killing murderers, rapists, and monsters, you clearly haven't faced off with any of them. You're just an angelic asshole who's never tried to save someone's life and never given them the chance to change their mistakes."

Rorikel straightened his back, and I was suddenly very aware of how tall he was. A warrior with thousands of years of experience on me, he had powers I couldn't imagine.

"Oh, but I have," he said, ice in his tone, "and I have discovered that humans do not change. They will never place their beliefs above their own personal goals. There is no justification for murder, which is why you will never see Paradise, Constance Ramirez."

He turned and stormed out of the motel room, slamming the door so hard it rattled in the frame. I shouldn't have cared, but Rorikel's words bothered me. I'd always known I would never go to Heaven, but I wished there had been some kind of hope for me. That maybe I could be forgiven just enough to go to the same afterlife as my sister. The idea of spending such a short human lifetime with Dro only to lose her when I died didn't sit well with me. I knew that was how life went, but as a kid I thought we would stay with each other forever. I held onto that hope as we got older. It had motivated me, reminded me I wasn't going to lose her.

Now I wasn't so sure.

"What the hell crawled up his ass, laid eggs and died?" Max grumbled, reaching under the table to take Dro's hand.

Sephiel sighed. "Rorikel is what you might call a close-minded individual. He does not like change, and does not appreciate those who scorn or dishonor the goodness of God."

Yup. That sounds like Rorikel. "What about you? Do you think all us sinners should burn in Hell and have demons stab us in the ass with pitchforks all the time?"

Sephiel forced a smile. "I think humans have stumbled, and not all of them have regretted the mistakes they have made. Not all of them deserve to be saved. But perhaps that is what makes them so different from us. They have the chance to learn from their misfortunes and mishaps. Angels do not. We must always be the image of grace and strength. We cannot fail."

Sephiel's bright blue eyes had gone dark with almost human emotions. I thought I spotted guilt, sorrow, and a bit of anger.

"I take it not many angels feel the way you do," guessed Warrick.

"Very few," he replied. "Certainly none of the archangels."

Sephiel looked at Dro. "Your mother and I were one of the few who respect humans."

"You know my birth mother?" Dro asked, perking up in her chair as her face brightened with curiosity and surprise.

Sephiel nodded. "Her name was Everiel."

Dro quickly picked up on the 'was,' but couldn't hold back her interest. "What was she like?"

"Gentle and strong, kind and just. Never afraid to speak her mind and stand up for others." Deep sorrow creased his eyes. "She looked like you. She was beautiful."

"What happened to her?" Dro asked quietly.

Sephiel looked away. "She died."

The angel's silence made it very clear that he wasn't going into any more details. Knowing more about Dro's angel mother seemed important, but I didn't want to piss off the only angel who seemed to like us.

"What about my father?" Dro asked. "Did you know him? Is he still alive?"

Sephiel's eyes flicked up, and I didn't miss the quick spark of rage in them.

"I do not know the answer to either of those questions."

Liar. He knew Dro's father, and he hated him.

Before I could press the issue any further, Sephiel turned for the door. "I must seek out Rorikel and bring him back. I do not wish for him to remain angry with any of you."

Sephiel closed his eyes and winked out, leaving an empty space where he'd once stood. I was getting really sick of that. I looked at Dro, who was still holding Max's hand and looking troubled.

"You okay, Dro?" I asked her.

She looked at me nervously. "I thought angels would be easier to deal with than demons."

"You're assuming this was supposed to be easy to begin

with," I said, leaning back and rubbing my eyes with the heel of my palm.

"Do you think we can trust either of them?" Warrick asked.

He was still near the dresser, now with his arms folded over his chest, and his green eyes piercing into my dark brown ones.

"Sephiel, maybe," I said. "The only thing we can trust Rorikel not to do is hurt Dro. He doesn't give a fuck about the rest of us." I turned my eyes from him to Max. "Sense anything we should be looking out for?"

Max hesitated, then closed his eyes and focused. He breathed out and I could see his eyes moving behind his eyelids as he stretched his ability. After a minute or two, he opened his eyes and looked at us.

"Not really," he said. "Just a lot of red. Can't even tell if it's fire or blood or both."

"Terrific," I muttered.

Max frowned sharply. "It's not easy trying to look into the future and knowing you might hate what you see. You can cut me some slack, Constance."

He was right. He'd been doing everything he could, giving us all the knowledge he could and supporting my little sister at every turn. He didn't deserve to be an outlet for my frustration.

"Yeah," I said. "I guess I can. Sorry."

The words were hard for me to say. I'd had a lot of time to feel the sting of regret. But Max had done more for me than I could thank him for. I owed him. Hopefully, one day, I could find a way to repay him with something worthwhile.

CHAPTER TWENTY-TWO

We decided to get as much sleep as possible before leaving for Athens. The angels patrolled the motel, since Rorikel still didn't want to be near a naughty little sinner like me.

I tried to sleep, holding my hatchet close to my chest and running my thumb up its neck. The last thing my father ever gave me. A gift I never wanted. He'd known I would fight to keep my mother and sister safe, but he'd intended to get the hatchet back. He didn't know he would be among the first to die that night.

Despite the terrible memories it carried, I felt stronger when I held it. The blade was chipped and the leather wrapping on the handle had been cracking lately. The weapon truly reminded me of... me.

Dro tossed and turned on the bed across from me.

"You can't sleep either?" I asked.

Dro rolled onto her side and looked at me. Her long white hair spilled over her shoulder and glowed in the dark motel room.

"What gave it away?" she said wryly.

I shrugged, grinning a little. "Big sister intuition."

"Uh huh." Dro didn't quite manage a smile.

"What's on your mind?"

She sighed, twirling the ends of her hair around her finger. "Everything," she confessed. "What Rorikel said about the archangels and sinners, the rituals, Sephiel talking about my mother. It's a lot to process."

"You're right. It is."

Dro started twirling her hair around her finger slowly. "I wish she were still alive," she said softly. "Then I could talk to her about what I am. She could help me understand it all."

"Sephiel seemed really care about her. He'll help us."

"But you don't trust him."

"Just because I don't trust him doesn't mean he won't help you. You're the one this is all about."

Dro dropped her hair. "Only because I'm a vessel. I wouldn't matter to anyone if I was just a normal human."

I frowned. "You would matter to me."

"That isn't what I mean, Con. I know you love me, and no matter what I'll still love you, too. But think about all the problems that have been caused because of what I am. If it weren't for me, Mom and Dad would still be alive."

A chill crept into my heart. "Don't say that, Dro. What happened to Mom and Dad wasn't your fault."

My sister's icy blue eyes looked heavy. "You know that it was."

"No. It was the demons. Not you. You–"

"The only reason the demons were there was because of me. If I hadn't been, we'd all still be a family."

"What about Max?" I asked, grasping at straws. "You never would have met him if it hadn't been for everything that happened."

Dro shifted, resting her head on the pillow and wrapping her arms around her middle. "No. But Manny might still be alive."

This wasn't going to work. Even if I told her that Manny's death was on my conscience, I couldn't deny that Dro's family history had brought some horrible circumstances on us. I would never convince her all the darkness and pain we carried wasn't her fault. I would never put that guilt on her. She did it to herself.

"That's why I asked Rorikel about what would happen if I said yes," Dro said.

I looked at her again. "You're thinking about giving in?"

"If it means stopping the demons, what choice do I have?"

"We stop the demons by figuring out what the witch is doing, then throw a wrench in it. We don't do something that will get you possessed and killed by an angel."

"Con, we have no clue who the witch is. Who knows what will be waiting for us in Athens. Saying yes might be the only thing that keeps us alive. At least if the archangel takes me, we'll have a chance to stop them."

I pushed myself up into a sitting position. "No. I am not going to let you do that."

She sat up to meet my eyes. "It isn't your choice, Constance. It's mine. You have to consider the possibility that we won't be able to handle whatever we face there."

"I'm not going to let an angel take you over and kill you just so it can have your body."

I turned my eyes away from her, remembering the horrible, violating pain of my own possession. How completely I had been dominated, stripped of my safety, and trapped as the demon said and did things I couldn't stop.

"You don't know what it's like, Dro," I whispered shakily. "You don't know..."

I couldn't go on. Even now, I could taste Ohzlan's thick, smoky body winding down my throat, burning me as he crawled toward my heart. I could feel the sudden, hard shove as he pushed me aside and stood on top of me. The sharp slices of the net as it was thrown over me, how savagely it cut whenever I moved, begging and screaming for him to leave my sister alone, the tear of his claws in my soul as the angels tried to rip him out–

I jumped when Dro touched my hand. I looked at it, beginning to calm down as she gave it a gentle squeeze. I took a deep breath and looked in her pale blue eyes. Seeing all her kindness, pride, and love was all that kept me from having a panic attack. The pressure and pain in my heart started to fade, and suddenly I was me again.

"I didn't say I was going to do it," she assured me. "But if it comes down to your life or mine, I won't hesitate. You can't keep me safe all the time, Con. You're human. I'm not. I can handle things you can't."

I narrowed my eyes. "I don't give a shit about pain."

"But I do." Dro shook her head. "I'm tired of this, Connie. I'm tired of being hunted and being the reason everything gets messed up. If something ever happened to you..." Dro looked away, blinking rapidly and tightening her grip on my hand. "I wouldn't be able to live with myself. I'd rather die."

"Don't say that. Don't ever say that. None of this is your fault, Dro. It's the demons fault. Even the angels are to blame. But not you. I won't let you slip. I promise. We'll find a way to stop them. You can start fresh. We'll get through this, little sister."

Dro looked at me, desperate and afraid to hope. "You make it sound so easy."

"It won't be. But we can't give up. That's never been us."

A half smile came over her face. Better than nothing. "No, I guess not."

I wished there was more for me to tell her, a way to make her believe that both of us would make it through alive. But I couldn't lie to her, and it would be safe to assume that I might die. I'd refuse to let my sister die, but as she had pointed out, I was human. It was so easy for me to be killed.

"Get some sleep, Dro. Think about everything else in the morning."

She nodded, finally releasing my hand and starting to tuck herself back into the bed. She glanced up at me. "You need to sleep too, Constance. You look more tired than usual."

I stifled a laugh. "Thanks, sis. Nice to hear that kind of thing."

She shrugged. For a second, she looked like a sixteen year old girl again, and not a young woman growing up far too fast in a dangerous life. Dro dropped her head onto her pillow, closed her eyes, and fell asleep.

I watched for signs of a nightmare, but nothing happened. I lay on my back and looked at the ceiling. I closed my eyes, but didn't feel tired. I was thinking too much about Dro's willingness to sacrifice herself so the demons could be stopped. It was just like her to give herself up like that for the greater good, but I wouldn't let it happen. I had fought my possession, and nearly died because of it. Dro wouldn't fight, too convinced she might deserve the pain, and die because of it. I couldn't survive if something happened to her.

She was my rock, my purpose and foundation. Without her, I was lost. An earth without a moon. Deep down, I was broken. Something inside me had snapped years ago, and only Dro held me together. She'd been with me so long I couldn't even remember a day without her. She was the last bit of normality in my life. The last familiar thing. When something threatened her, I was the first one at her defence...

***

"I DON'T THINK I'm doing this right, little sister," I said, trying to weave the plastic flowers into Dro's braid. "They keep falling out."

She sat patiently on the porch with her back to me, dainty pale hands clasped in her lap on her flower printed dress. Dro would be ten years old in a couple weeks, and she was taking advantage of her birthday month by making me braid flowers into her hair.

"You'll get it," Dro promised with a smile.

My sister had every confidence in me, even though I had no clue what I was doing. She was in a good mood today. The last few years had been difficult, every day a challenge for our family to cope with Dro's strange gifts. Mom and Dad hadn't believed her until she proved them by mentioning things no one could know. We never said anything or looked for help, because we were afraid she would be taken away. Mom and Dad still treated her like a princess, but they were careful around her. I had steadily gotten used to the things Dro could do. They were a part of who she was and couldn't be changed. Dro always felt like she was a freak, so I treated her like she were a normal girl.

I just wish I knew how to braid her hair.

"It's not hard," she said, as if reading my thoughts.

My fingers hesitated in her hair. I was still learning the extent of her weird abilities. I had thought mind reading wasn't one of them, but I was never sure of anything when it came to Dro's gifts.

"Maybe not for you," I grumbled. "I've got butterfingers."

Dro giggled. I smiled softly.

"What a beautiful little girl," someone said.

I'd been so absorbed in trying to get the freaking braid right that I hadn't noticed her walk up. I lifted my head, forgetting the braid and moving to stand in front of my sister.

It was the woman from across the street. Isabel.

Up close, she was even more beautiful. Long black hair lay perfectly straight on either side of her face. She was slim but curvy, and she showed off her body by wearing a black blazer that revealed the top part of her breasts, tight black leggings, and black boots that went to her knees. Her lips were the color of blood, her eyes ringed by black eyeliner.

There was something wrong with her eyes. I'd seen that look from bad guys in movies and the bullies on the streets. I didn't know what it meant, but I didn't like it.

I didn't like her.

"Do you want something?" I asked, trying to force her attention onto me.

Isabel's eyes slid up to mine. A chill went down my back, anxiety coiling around my spine like a snake ready to squeeze the life out of its prey. I balled my fists. Getting ready to hit something made me feel stronger. Even if I wasn't.

Isabel smiled. "I noticed your sister out here and had to see what all the fuss was about." Her eyes went back to my sister. "I've heard so much about you, little Andromeda."

I tensed, the phantom snake twisting tighter inside me. Only our parents called Dro by her full name. Isabel shouldn't have known it.

Isabel went back to ignoring me, bending at the waist and putting her hands on her knees so she could look into Dro's eyes. That creepy smile hadn't left her face.

"You truly are extraordinary, aren't you Andromeda?" she crooned. "So beautiful, so special. But you know how special you are, don't you?"

I tried to move in front of Dro again, but I couldn't. Something locked me in place. I pushed against it, but it felt like an invisible force had clamped onto me and rooted me to the ground.

"Do you ever wonder about your parents, little Andromeda? Do you wonder who they really are?"

Dro shook her head. "I have a Mommy and Daddy and sister who love me."

"But they aren't your blood." She leaned in closer to Dro.

"What if I could take you to your father? Would you like that, little Andromeda?"

My heart pounded so loud I could hear it in my ears. I tried to move again, but that weird invisible force wouldn't let me.

Dro shook her head again. "No," she said. "I like it here. I love my family."

Isabel actually looked surprised, like she thought Dro would throw away everything she knew to meet her birth father, the man who'd abandoned her to die in the woods.

Nice try, lady.

"What's going on?" Dad's voice sounded.

We looked over. Mom and Dad stood next to each other, covered in dirt from working in the backyard. They glanced from us to Isabel. The creepy, gorgeous woman straightened up slowly, as if she wanted to use her body as a weapon. Which she probably could.

Suddenly I could move again. I scurried in front of Dro to block her from Isabel's view. Not that Isabel was looking at us anymore.

"Your daughter is wonderful, isn't she, Luis?"

Dad stiffened at the sound of his name. Mom left his side and stood beside us, wrapping her arm around my shoulder and reaching back to hold Dro's hand.

"Is there something you want, Isabel?" she asked.

The woman smiled at my mother, but there was nothing friendly about the twist in her lips.

"I just want to make sure that she's being taken care of." Her dark eyes found Dro's again. "She is such a unique girl, after all."

Dad found himself and took slow steps toward her. "My wife asked you a question. Tell her the truth."

Isabel gave him a bored look. "Calm yourself, Luis. I'm not here to step on toes."

"You work for the government, don't you?" Mom asked, her

arm tightening around me. We hadn't legally adopted Dro. Isabel could file a report and have them take Dro away from us.

"Why are you jumping to conclusions, Carmen?" She looked between Mom and Dad. "Can it be you really don't know what you have? That you don't know her power?"

Dad stood inches away from her. He looked angry, but he only looked this way if he were scared for us.

"We've done nothing to you. Leave my family alone. Stay away from my children. Both of them."

Isabel faced him, calm and composed. "My, my, you're quite defensive over what doesn't belong to you, aren't you, Luis?"

My dad had never hit a woman in his whole life. He never would. But in that second, I was almost certain he was going to punch Isabel's head off.

"Leave," my dad growled.

Isabel backed off instead of continuing to push my father. Maybe she had some survival instinct after all.

"If you insist," she said with that dark smile of hers. Her eyes moved to Mom, Dro, and me. "Take good care of her." Isabel looked at Dro. The flash of evil burned in her eyes. "Goodbye, little Andromeda."

Isabel turned and walked across the street to her house. Dad walked up to stand beside us on the porch, keeping his eyes on Isabel's back. Once she was in her house, he sat down next to Dro and put his arm around her shoulder, rubbing her arm.

"You okay, sweetheart?"

Dro bit her lip, but nodded. "She was thinking really weird things."

"Like what, bella?" Mom asked, kneeling down beside her.

Dro hesitated again. Even five years after telling Mom and Dad the truth, she was still nervous about confessing that she had any abilities at all. Dro took a deep breath.

"She kept thinking that she had finally found me, and that

her master would be happy." She looked away. "She thought I was a monster."

Dad let out a long string of curses in Spanish. I'd learned a few of them, and raised my eyebrows. Mom brushed strands of white hair behind Dro's ear.

"She's wrong, bella. She couldn't be more wrong. You're not a monster. You're an angel."

Mom kissed Dro's pale head. My sister relaxed. Mom looked at the half braid at the back of Dro's head, toying with the hair there.

"Did Constance try to braid your hair?" she asked.

Dad glanced at it, tilting his head. "Is it supposed to look like that?"

I pouted and crossed my arms. Dro giggled. Mom turned her so she could fix the braid I'd made a disaster of. My parents comforted Dro and made her feel normal. I wanted to join them, but I didn't. Instead, I watched the house across the street. Isabel stared at us through the windows. She looked at Dro the same way that hungry lion looked at a zebra.

That snake around my spine just wouldn't let go. Isabel wouldn't listen to Dad's warning. It might not be tomorrow or the day after, but she would torment Dro again. I thought about how I hadn't been able to move or react. Maybe Isabel had magic, just like Dro

For the first time in years, I wondered about who my sister's real father was, and if there was nothing I could do to keep my little sister safe...

CHAPTER TWENTY-THREE

The memory of Isabel had hit me like cold water, and I knew I wouldn't sleep again. I silently pushed myself off the bed and hooked my hatchet onto my belt. I threw on my lucky jacket and opened the door, gently shutting it behind me so Dro wouldn't wake up.

I tilted my head back and let the cool night air brush over my face. Standing out here on the second story of a cheap motel seemed like the only place where I didn't have to worry about my sister, the people trying to kill me, demons, and all my other problems. Until I heard someone else having problems of their own.

"What do you mean you can't find his body?"

I looked to my left and saw Warrick standing outside the door of his motel room, his back to me and his cell phone pressed to his ear. Tension radiated off him in waves.

"I get that, but there has to be some trace of him. No way he could have bled out that much and then just vanished. If he'd been eaten there would have been leftover bones or something," Warrick said as he shifted from side to side, gripping the railing. "No, this isn't about Emma. I need backup. Can you get here or not?" He paused. "I have my sources, and I trust them. I need your help."

Warrick fell silent as the other person spoke for a long time. "No, I haven't forgotten, but I..."

The voice on the other end turned sharp. Warrick hung his head in defeat.

"Yes. Yes, I understand... No. I'll do it myself."

Warrick hung up and shoved the phone back into his pocket. He ran his hands over his face, then finally noticed me.

He looked just as tired as Dro did, if not more. There were dark circles under his eyes that I hadn't noticed before, making his irises seem even greener. "How much did you hear?"

I shrugged and crossed my arms. "Enough. What was that about?"

"Slayer stuff. Nothing I can explain to you."

I gave him a hard look. "You're making this whole trust thing very difficult."

"Rich, coming from you."

I deserved that, but refused to admit it.

Wait, why am I thinking that? I don't know this guy. He'll turn me in as soon as he's held up his end of whatever deal he made with Max.

"Fine. You can do your whole 'no one understands me' thing on your own." I turned to leave.

"Wait," he said.

I should have kept walking, but the slight pleading in his voice had me stopping and turning. He had pushed away from the railing, but was still gripping it like he needed support. He hesitated, then let out the breath he'd been holding.

"I'm sorry," he said.

That caused my eyebrows to ride up my forehead a little bit. I waited for him to go on.

"I'm just stressed right now. The slayers are moving down to Texas, but they've been looking for the demons that escaped the border. They won't come to help us. We're on our own." He met my eyes. "I really did try, Constance."

He sounded so sincere I almost believed him. But I hadn't heard the other end of the conversation. For all I knew, he could have been telling them Dro was connected to demons. He said he wouldn't hurt her, that he was here to help Max, but I hadn't been here for the whole conversation. He could have told them too much. He could have said something to make them suspect she was something demonic instead of being a Nephilim. He could have easily betrayed us all.

But the pain in his eyes seemed too real.

"I appreciate that," I told him. "And I'm sorry for being bitchy. When I don't get enough sleep, claws come out."

He grinned. "I'm amazed you put them away at all."

I laughed. "Never away. Just a little duller at times."

His gaze softened. He was too damn handsome when he smiled. I should have kept it that way, calm and easy, but I remembered his conversation all too clearly. "So Drake might still be alive."

Warrick's hand tightened on the railing. "Yeah. He might have been wounded by the demons, but his body is missing." Green eyes blazed. "There was enough blood to suggest he's dead, but I know him. He's a fucking cockroach."

I should have dropped it then, but I couldn't avoid asking any longer. "What's your deal with him?"

Warrick looked at his feet. "I've chased him for years. We've had it out a couple times. He put me in the hospital more than once. Gave me this," Warrick pointed to the dark brown scar under his left eye.

"But what started it all?" I said, taking a careful step closer. "Why do you hate him so much?"

"Because he's a vile, sick, twisted son of a bitch who has no problem raping, torturing, and killing. Who doesn't hate those sort of people?"

"I can tell it's more than that," I pressed, taking another step. "You mentioned Emma. Your sister. Whatever problem you have with him is personal."

Warrick didn't look at me.

"Listen, Warrick, I'm a sister too. I know what it's like to see your family hurt and scared. I can understand whatever pain you were going through."

This time he did look at me, his forest green eyes filled with so much fury I was actually nervous, even though his anger wasn't directed at me.

"No you can't," he told me in an icy voice. "Because Dro is still alive."

That stopped me from saying anything else. He was right. That was something I couldn't imagine. I stood there in silence as Warrick leaned back against the railing and ran the pad of his thumb along the name tattooed on his wrist. It seemed like forever before he spoke again.

"I was helping the Marshals out," he said quietly. "There were some drug traffickers running around west Texas causing problems and I heard rumors of a Possessor involved with them. I was part of the team that went in for the arrest. I exorcised the Possessor, but the man he'd been using died. I didn't know he'd been a man Drake Talbot was trying to collect a bounty for."

Warrick pressed harder on the tattoo. "He was pissed. Really pissed. I found out later that I'd cost him about half a million dollars, but back then I didn't know who he was. He tracked me down and made it his mission to ruin my life. It wasn't long before he found out I had an older sister."

"Jesus," I said under my breath.

"Drake took her when she was leaving my house one night. He called me the next day and said I had three days to come up with double the money I'd cost him or he would kill her. I did everything I could. I emptied my savings, sold my house and my car, got money from my parents, even the Marshals I worked with gave me some money. In three days, I had enough. Drake called back and told me where the drop was going to be. I went there and left the money like he told me to. I waited, but Drake never showed. He called again and said I would find my sister at the house I just sold. So I went back."

Warrick let go of his wrist and gripped the railing. He looked so furious that I thought he might actually bend the metal.

"Emma was there, lying on the front porch of my old house. Her clothes were gone. It took me a full minute to recognize her past all the bruises. She'd been dead for days."

My stomach twisted. I'd known Drake was an animal, but to do that to an innocent person out of pure spite... I couldn't imagine the pain.

"Drake ghosted after that," he continued. "He'd taken the money and vanished, probably laughing the whole fucking time. After that, I swore I would hunt him down. I would make him suffer for torturing and murdering my sister. I followed every lead I got, I had some close calls, but the bastard always seemed to be one step ahead."

"Then you heard he was after us," I caught on.

Warrick nodded. "Max told me on the way to find you. I was hoping to catch him at the border, but he was gone by the time we got there. I've been chasing him for almost three years, and I'm not any closer to catching him."

I'd never heard someone's voice so full of pain before. The first thing that crossed my mind was comforting him. A touch on his shoulder, my hand on his, holding him and letting him know someone cared. Drake had made Warrick suffer in the worst possible way I could think of. My possession probably didn't feel half as bad as the heartache Warrick felt right now.

I took another step toward him. "He'll turn up again," I said. "The Blood Thorns hired him to get me, and I know they're offering him a fortune for it. If Drake's as money-crazed as you say he is, he won't stop until he has me."

Warrick turned his head to meet my eyes. The pain was still there, but there was also gratitude, respect, and utter relief. He didn't seem like he the kind of guy who was open with other people, let alone a wanted criminal he just met, but talking to me appeared to relax him.

"You're not offering yourself as bait, I take it," he said with a dry smile.

I smirked. "Not a chance. I have a reputation to keep."

He grinned, but it didn't hold for very long. I felt sorry for him. I hated seeing him this way. I'd been terrible to him. I might not trust him, but it wasn't fair for me to treat him this way when he'd helped us.

"I'll help you catch him if I can, Warrick," I said suddenly. Memories flashed again. "I want him to suffer for what he did to Manny and Max."

Warrick's playfulness left him, his green eyes shockingly cold. "Just don't get in my way when it comes down to him and me."

The amount of anger in his voice kept me from arguing. I wanted to kill Drake, to make him bleed the way Manny and Max had bled, but there was no wavering in Warrick's face. Warrick, who deserved vengeance for his sister more than I did for my sake.

In the end, it didn't really matter who pulled the trigger. Just as long as Drake Talbot died.

"Deal," I agreed. Then I touched his hand. "And I'm sorry about what happened to your sister. I really am."

He nodded sorrowfully, turning his hand so it clasped mine. "Thanks."

I became aware of how close we'd gotten to each other. He stood only a few inches away from me, and when the wind picked up, I could catch the smell of his musky pine cologne. His hands were callused from years of fighting, but his touch was warm and gentle. He had the exact build and confident aura that I looked for in a man.

It had been years since I'd been with someone. Dro had started something with Max, and I was glad for it, but seeing them together reminded me how lonely I could get. My last relationship had ended with betrayal and rage on both sides, and I hadn't been able to trust another man since. But something about Warrick made me want to try.

He took another step closer, still holding my hand. Our chests almost touched, and I stayed completely still.

"You're a better woman than I thought, Constance."

I laughed. "I'm really not. But I'm glad you think so."

Warrick chuckled, eyes sparkling under the dim lights of the motel. I forgot all my problems and my paranoia. Right then, it was just Warrick and me. I must have looked like an idiot, staring into his eyes and letting them speed my heartbeat. A warm, fluttery feeling filled my stomach, and all I wanted to do was kiss him.

It *had* to be physical attraction. I wondered what he'd do if I did kiss him. I wondered if he would try and kiss me.

Warrick opened his mouth, like he was about to say something I was aching to hear. He suddenly backed away, looking serious. I wondered why, and then I smelled it. A rotten, smoky scent. A smell I would know anywhere.

Sulfur.

CHAPTER TWENTY-FOUR

We jumped apart and I yanked the hatchet from my belt. Warrick took a handgun from inside his jacket.

"Can't see 'em, but they've gotta be close." His eyes darted across the motel parking lot. "Go inside, Constance."

I gave him an impatient look. "You need to get Dro out of there. They're here for her. I can handle myself and will follow behind you."

Warrick turned to argue when thunder cracked the air. I whirled and stared across the landing, watching the flaming red portal open to a wall of flames.

I whipped my head to look at Warrick. "Go! Get Dro! I'll be fine!"

He hesitated for one more second, but turned and ran for the room my sister slept in. I trusted Warrick to guard her. The gun would do more damage, and with any luck, Sephiel and Rorikel would come back and help me.

Not that luck and I were fast friends.

I had to focus on keeping the demon away from my sister. I just needed seconds. I was fast, and I could—

Lurching through the portal came the biggest demon I had

ever seen. It stood two feet taller than me and was compacted with muscle. Pale, bumps and white scars riddled its flesh. Oil black hair hung in strings down to its shoulders. It had a blocky face and milky white eyes. Jagged teeth were slick behind its snarling lips and huge bony claws protruded from the end of its fingers.

Okay, let's call this one a Shredder, I thought.

I was starting to regret sending Warrick away. I didn't have many weapons on me. I had my hatchet and a silver knife in each of my boots, and that was it.

Not that I had much time to complain when it roared and charged me.

I threw myself against the door, feeling air rush past as the Shredder barrelled past me. It skidded to a stop and whipped its elbow around. I ducked and stepped back from its rapid slashes and swipes. The motel's narrow landing made it hard to move, and harder to hide.

Any time now, angels. Some guardians they were turning out to be.

The Shredder kicked out and I jumped back, the tip of its clawed foot scratching down my shin. Pain screamed down my and I stumbled into the wall. One cut and I'd almost lost a limb. The Shredded punched its claws at my head. I ducked, the claws slamming through the door over me. Splinters of wood spilled into my hair and down my neck. But I had my shot. I swiped the hatchet along the Shredder's exposed stomach, the blade peeling through thick hide.

The Shredder growled, more a sound of anger than pain. It reach for me with its free hand. I flattened myself to the door, but the claws still ripped through my jacket along my stomach. They scraped through the fabric and skimmed the surface of my skin. Another inch, and my guts would have been tumbling out onto the floor.

Heart pounding, I slashed at the demon, but it caught my

wrist. Pain ruptured in my hand and I grabbed the hatchet with my free hand, then slammed the blade into the demon's face.

Black blood gushed out of the wound just under its eye. The Shredder roared and let me go. My hand swelled and throbbed with pain, likely half broken now, but I didn't stop. I jumped and slammed the hatchet into the Shredder's face over and over, keeping one eye on its claws. If I blinded it, I could run—

It thrust upward with its claws and I twisted my head. Rough bone scraped along my face, wrenching my hair. The demon kicked me in the chest and sent me flying through the door. I slammed hard against the far wall and collapsed onto my face. Sharp pain filled my torso, each breath coming ragged. I coughed and forced myself to breathe. The floor vibrated as the demon stomped over to me, its bulk barely squeezing through the door frame. It jabbed its claws down toward my face. I rolled away as fast and as far as I could, the bony claws digging through the door and tangling on my hair. I grimaced at the pain shooting through my scalp, then jumped. Four bone-claws plunged into the door half an inch from my ear. That hair-pulling saved my life.

The demon scraped its claws toward either side of my head, trying to pierce my temples. I pushed between its legs and tearing out hair by the roots but escaping. I twisted into a crouch at the Shredder's back, and watched its heel clobber into my head.

My sight blurred and I hit something hard. I couldn't see. Pain bloomed black stars into my vision, and then clawed hands wrapped around my throat. I dangled, smelling sulfur, blood, and greasy body odor. I wanted to puke, but I couldn't even breathe.

I hacked weakly at the demon's arm with my hatchet while reaching for the knife in my boot. The demon slammed its head into mine, white hot pain exploding in my head. My fingers fumbled the knife. Had to fight, had to keep going. I drunkenly raised the knife and threw it at the demon. The monster was close enough that I couldn't miss. The blade sank into its shoulder. It howled and dropped me onto the floor. I rubbed my throat, fighting for air, and watched its shadow loom. I wouldn't be fast enough this time–

A blast of gold light struck the Shredder in the back, knocking it off balance. Sephiel and Rorikel stood in the doorway, gold heavenfire gleaming in their hands. Their faces were hard, their bodies were ready for a fight.

I crab-walked backward then pushed to my feet, gasping for air. The sudden motion almost made me pass out again, but I bent my knees and let my vision refocus. My left eye was swelling closed, cutting off more of my sight. My head throbbed and my body burned with pain, but I could still stand. Which meant I could fight.

"About fucking time!" I shouted.

The angels ignored me. Typical. "Obtain the Nephilim," Rorikel ordered. "We shall dispatch the demon."

For once, I didn't argue with him. I didn't know where Dro, Warrick, or Max were. Something was wrong. I took the knife out of my other boot and turned for the adjoining room. My head swirled for a moment until I blinked to clear the haze from it. Running on adrenaline and anger, I kicked the door open.

The room stank of sulfur and demon blood. A Red demon was crumpling into a heap of ash on the floor, probably killed by Warrick. But the demon had never been the problem.

Drake Talbot was.

Manny's killer fought Warrick with more power and strength than I remembered.

I should have known it was going to be a losing fight. Warrick wasn't a lightweight, but Drake had at least thirty pounds on him. He also looked well rested and didn't seem to have any injuries. Warrick was covered in so much blood I couldn't tell what was from the dead demon or from him.

Max lay slumped on the floor near the bathroom door. I

couldn't tell if he was breathing. Dro bled from a long scratch along the side of her face and a wounded shoulder, another pile of demon ash next to her, fighting to get up.

I hobbled into the room, my eyes turning to the fistfight. Warrick punched at Drake, but the bounty hunter grabbed his fist and jabbed Warrick in the face and kidneys. He took a step back and kept Warrick's arm outstretched, then jerked him forward and clotheslined him. Warrick landed hard on the coffee table, his pain- filled shout mixing with sound of breaking wood. He rolled on the splinters of the table, but couldn't get to his feet before Drake started kicking him in the ribs.

"Can't let anything go, can you, Johnny boy?" Drake sneered.

"Neither can I," I said.

Drake looked up at the exact moment I hurled my knife at him.

He turned at the last second, so my knife landed in his shoulder instead of his chest like I'd hoped. That was okay. I had a perfectly good hatchet that was dying to be used some more.

Drake yanked the blade out with an angry grunt, grimacing at the blood on my blade before throwing it onto the floor. He stomped toward me, and soon it was my hatchet versus his newly drawn Bowie knife. It didn't take him long to slash at my neck with the blade, but I kept my distance.

He tried to stab me in the chest, but I twisted and kicked the inside of his knee. I slashed back with my hatchet, the blade still slicing across his face and nose. I turned on my heel and drove my foot into his head. He staggered, and I grinned.

Damn, that felt good.

Drake jumped back before I could kick him again. His face was a bloody mask of hate and rage, but also a maniacal glee. It was disgusting. Only freaks and sadists enjoy bleeding and pain.

"Don't be shy, bitch," he taunted. "You're a good little fight."

"Fuck you," I growled. "This ends now, Drake. Warrick won't let you live, and I'm not going anywhere with you."

Drake laughed. "You're not very smart are you, sweetheart? I might love giving Warrick the runaround, but what makes you think I'm back for you?"

Harsh realization hit me. I whirled, and saw that I'd been fucking set up.

There was a reason that Dro hadn't been running over to help me. Two Red demons had slipped through the broken bathroom window and were dragging her toward it. One of them had placed its clawed hand over her mouth so she couldn't scream. If I'd known, I would have said 'fuck Drake' and gone to save my sister.

But I'd been tricked, and now they had her.

Dro thrashed and tried to fight back, but couldn't break free from the demons gripping her arms and hair. Panic filled her bright blue eyes. The air behind the demons tore open, revealing a black space instead of red. Not Hell, but somewhere else. Somewhere worse?

"Seph! Rori!" I screamed. The angels would drop everything to help Dro. Not that I intended to wait for them.

I rushed toward the demons, only to be jerked back by a strong hand on snared my shoulder. I screamed with fury as I was spun, just in time to see Drake's knife plunge into my belly.

Pain exploded through my torso. Drake smiled and twisted the blade. A horrible, piercing agony filled me, unlike anything I'd ever felt before. It swept through me like fire, blistering and relentless.

I choked on my scream as he shoved me off the knife. I landed hard on my back, fresh pain wrenching through me again. Blood spilled out of my stomach, hot and sticky. So much, how could there be so much? My entire body burned. I couldn't move. I'd seen enough of these wounds to know that once you twisted the knife, there was no fixing it. You just bled out and died.

Everything blurred. Distantly, I heard Dro screaming. I tilted my head, trying to find her. She stood on the edge of the tub, fighting the demons hauling her away. Tears streaked her cheeks, her face twisted with rage. Heat swelled out from the bathroom, a sign she would burst into flames. One of the Reds stopped her by punching her in the back of the head. She slumped forward, unconscious.

I couldn't move, couldn't scream my sister's name or cry out for help. I couldn't do a single fucking thing when the demons hauled her away into the black portal behind them.

Tears slid down my cheeks. Agony pulsed rapidly, in tune with my strained breaths. Blood still pumped from the wound, too deep to be closed.

Drake's heavy knee thunked beside my head. His eyes raked over my body, and then his hands followed. Bastard. Fucking *bastard.*

"You know," he purred with a smile as his fingers brushed under my breasts. "I wish Warrick were awake to see this. I did to you what I did to his sister. Stabbed her so she couldn't move, then took my time." His black eyes met mine. "It's better when they're in pain. They fight you less."

"I'm going to fucking kill you," I rasped.

Draked chuckled, then straddled me and sat on my chest. Scorching pain shot through my stomach, crushed by his weight and torn muscle body. He closed a thick hand around my, choking off my scream. He squeezed and pressed harder, leaning over my face so I could smell the stale mugginess of his breath. My head spun. I couldn't even think past the pain.

"Shh, don't make promises you can't keep." He considered me. "Kind of a pity, though. I'd like to spend more time with you. The stronger ones are so much more fun to break."

A sharp, jabbing bite of pain rent through my side. Drake

turned my head, forcing me to watch as he slowly slid the knife into my side, just under my ribcage. I twitched and gasped, too weak to fight, my throat crushed in his hand. The hilt of the blade sank deep. Close enough to cut a lung.

My torso felt doused in lava. I could only lie there, smelling blood, feeling knives, and staring at Drake as he smiled.

"But your sister will do just fine. I'll take good care of her." He grinned coldly. "I wonder what she'll think when I fuck her with your blood on me."

Drake dragged the knife out of me slowly, making sure I felt the entire length of the blade. His pin was too strong, his body too heavy. I couldn't move, not even when he gave the knife a few vicious tugs. Drake let go of my throat, and I tasted blood.

He stood up, and fresh waves of pain lanced through me. "Sorry, sweetheart. Duty calls."

Then he was gone. I didn't even see him leave. My entire body blazed with agony. Blood warmed the floor around me while my body shivered. I was so cold, and each twitch wrenched my nerves. The edges of my vision were getting fuzzy. I couldn't move. I thought someone called my name, but I didn't know who they were.

I had failed. I'd been stupid. I hadn't stayed with Dro, and now she was in the very clutches of the people I swore to keep her away from. There was nothing I could do to save her.

I'm sorry, Dro. I'm so sorry.

It was my last thought before the world went black.

CHAPTER TWENTY-FIVE

The pain hadn't lessened, it only changed. I couldn't focus on thoughts, only sensations. My side and stomach tingled with an icy burn, and my head pounded. Thankfully the mattress was soft. There were people on it. One of them felt like warm sunlight, and the other smelled like pine. I groaned and rolled toward the one who smelled like pine. A warm, callused hand placed itself on my cheek and stroked my skin.

"It's okay, Constance," a deep, comforting voice rumbled. "Sephiel's almost finished. You're going to be all right."

I nestled closer to him, glad the pain had begun to lessen. But something felt wrong. Like something important was missing.

No, not something. Someone.

I pushed myself up and opened my eyes. Dizziness hit and I swayed. Someone put their arms around me, holding me to their chest. "Take it slow," Warrick murmured.

But I couldn't. I had to move.

After the dizzy spell ended, I pushed myself away from Warrick and looked around. I was in the motel room, Warrick on one side of me, Sephiel on the other, his hands covered in blood.

My blood. He'd healed injuries I had gotten from the Shredder and Drake.

Drake.

His name was poison on my soul. I could still feel his hand on my neck, his weight on my stomach. That fucking grin of his.

Max was sitting across from me at the table by the window, his head in his hands. He probably felt as wretched as I did. Next to him, Rorikel leaned against a wall with his arms folded over his chest, a stormy look on his face. He clearly wasn't happy. Not that I cared about his happiness. I had to find Dro.

"How long was I out?" I asked, trying to get off the bed.

Warrick's hand slid up to my shoulder and held me in place. "You shouldn't move. Sephiel might have healed you, but your body need real rest."

I turned on him sharply. "I'll rest when my sister is back here or I'm dead. How much time did we lose?"

"About six hours," Sephiel answered grimly.

"What the hell?!" I shouted. "What happened? Why did it take you so long to get in here?!"

"Traps had been left for us that hindered quick travel. Once we arrived and saw the Severance demon, we believed it to be the true adversary. We did not expect such a prolonged distraction–"

"There are *two* of you!" I screamed. "You should have stopped Drake then dealt with the Shredder after!"

"Do not blame us for your lack of preparation," Rorikel retorted icily. "That man was human, yet two of you could not defeat him."

"Don't you dare blame me for Drake, Rorikel."

He didn't hear the warning in my voice. "You let yourself become distracted and grievously injured. Be grateful that Sephiel saw fit to heal you, though I cannot comprehend his reasoning."

I tried to get up from the bed, but Warrick held me down.

"Get your hand off me, Warrick," I growled.

"Constance, please, we haven't been sitting on our asses doing nothing. We're trying to find her. Max is reaching out with all his telepathy and the angels have been splitting their time ushering off witnesses and cops while trying to use a mental link to find her."

"Then why isn't it working?" I demanded, hardly stopping to think or care about the mess that must have been left behind after the fight. "It's been six hours!"

"Max cannot appear to focus his powers directly," said Rorikel with disdain. "His emotions are obscuring his concentration."

Max lifted his head and slammed his fist on the table. "Fuck you, bird brain! I'm trying! Give me a fucking break so I can find my friend, okay?!"

No one said anything to that. I didn't know Max was capable of such fury, but he cared deeply for Dro. I knew he would do everything he could to find her.

Rorikel on the other hand...

"What about you?" I asked, not wanting to turn my anger on Sephiel. He'd just saved my life. "What the hell's stopping you from tracking her down?"

"There appears to be a spell blocking our mental link with the Nephilim. Unless she opens her power and lets us in, we will not be able to locate her. She has not been formally trained in her powers." His pale eyes narrowed on me. "It seems someone has been shielding her from her full potential."

"Are you putting that on me too? What the fuck is your problem?!"

"Constance, you need to calm down," Warrick said.

I finally jerked free from his hand. "Don't tell me to calm down! She's *gone*!"

Warrick got up and gently took my elbow. I tried to shake him off, but he tightened his grip and refused to let go.

"Come on," he said, "let's give them some space to concentrate. You aren't going to help anyone by shouting."

No, but I could damn well try. I shoved Warrick's hand away and stood up, storming out of the room. The air was icy and dry, like the life had been stolen from it. I gripped the cold railing outside the motel door and tried to breathe as the closed the door behind me.

I couldn't get Dro's face out of my mind. How scared and desperate she had been to warn me of the trap. How horrified she had looked when I was stabbed.

I gasped and choked out sobs that wracked my already strained body. I placed my hand over my mouth to get myself under control, but it didn't work. My heart ached with every breath, like someone had wrapped it in barbed wire.

She was gone. My little sister was in the hands of the worst monsters I could imagine. It was my fault.

A careful hand placed itself on my shoulder and started drawing me back. Warrick. Part of me tried to fight him, not wanting to be seen weak like this, but the other part was too damaged. The pain was too intense for me to fight. It clouded my vision and stripped away every ounce of strength I thought I had.

Somewhere along the way, I was turned around and pressed against Warrick's chest. I tried to push away, but he wrapped his arms around my back and held me close.

That was when I let it all go. All the tenacity from years of fighting, struggling, bleeding, and promising I would never let anyone hurt my sister, disappeared in an instant.

Keep her safe. That was the only thing I had to do right. And I'd failed.

Violent sobs choked out of my throat. My face burned with tears. My screams were muffled against Warrick's chest. I don't know how he was able to hold the emotional storm I had become, but he did. He said nothing as my tears soaked into his shirt. Warrick rested his head on top of mine. Comforting me, and almost tricked me into thinking everything would be okay.

But my safety and comfort didn't matter. I had to pull it together, or I would never be able to save Dro. I jerked my head back and shoved Warrick away. This time he let me go. I wiped at my eyes, purposefully avoiding his face. I couldn't handle whatever I might do if I looked in his eyes.

"You didn't have to do that," I mumbled.

"Yes I did," he whispered. "I've been there, Constance. You can't be indestructible all the time."

I thought about everything that had happened. Battling for my life and my sister's life long before we knew what hunted us. Learning Dro's secrets and how much harder it would be to protect her. Losing a man who mentored me, and getting untrustworthy, supernatural allies. Not understanding how to deal with a man who wanted to keep me away one minute then hold me the next. Failing my sister and almost dying because of it. Enduring a grief that was strong enough to break me in half.

I pushed it all down, hid it away, and drew on all my anger. My rage was stronger than any pain. If anything could hold me together long enough to rescue Dro, that would be it.

When I looked at Warrick again. "Watch me."

I walked past him and opened the motel door. The angels looked up when I came back in. Something awful must have been on my face because even Rorikel kept his mouth shut. *Thank God for small favors.*

I moved past them and sat at the table across from Max. The poor kid looked exhausted and distraught with worry. I reached over to clutch his hand. Max squeezed back, and I hoped he knew better than to read my emotions right now. He needed peace more than I did.

"Did you find anything?" I asked.

"No. All I'm seeing is Athens. I can't really tell what's happening."

"Take your time. Tell me what you see."

Max blew out a breath and closed his eyes. "I can see the town. No one's on the streets. There's rooms filled with demons. There's a lot of blood, and I hear someone screaming." Max winced, hurt clear in his gentle, dark eyes."It might be Dro."

We were both silent when he said that. I leashed my emotions so I wouldn't start screaming and tearing down the wallpaper.

"Then there's this guy," Max continued once he was mostly composed. "He's surrounded by shadow. I can't make out his face, but he's powerful, and definitely not human. He may be more powerful than Dro." He opened his eyes, looking defeated. "It ends after that. I don't see anything else."

I kept my hand in his. Max looked at me for guidance, to stay strong while we searched for Dro. He hadn't seen the way I'd fallen apart on the balcony with Warrick. He needed me to be the strongest version of myself. And the strongest version of me worked to get things done.

"Must have something to do with those underground tunnels in Athens," I gave him a weak smile. "Thanks, Max. That's good enough for now. Let's go."

"We do not know for certain when his next vision will occur," said Rorikel. "His powers are sporadic at best."

I glared. "This isn't Max's fault."

Rorikel frowned. "He is human. His mind and emotional state are not trustworthy at this time."

"Dude, I'm right here," Max said.

Rorikel ignored him. "For all we know, the things he has seen have happened already."

"Doesn't matter," I argued, my temper rising to a boil. "Dro's missing. We have to get her back. If Athens is the source of all this power you guys are feeling and that's where Max's vision is leading him, then she must be there."

"Perhaps it is a ruse to bring you into a trap." He gave me a dark look. "It would not be the first one you fell into."

I stared at him for a long time. Then I let go of Max's hand and stood up and walked across the room. There was a lamp on the dresser, which I took and threw it at Rorikel's head.

One more broken piece of furniture wouldn't matter at this point. If the angels had averted all other eyes from us, then I could break anything I wanted.

The lamp shattered against the wall, and a few shards of it scratched along Rorikel's face. He swiped at his cheek, shocked when his fingers came away bloody. Fury burned in his eyes.

"You dare–"

"*Shut up*," I snapped. "I am not in the mood to be picked apart by you. My sister is missing, and we can all share the blame for being tricked. So if you don't have anything useful to contribute in the next five seconds, you can get the fuck out of my way. I'm going to Athens. And you are not strong enough to stop me."

The angry angel drew himself up to his full height and took a step toward me. Someone moved up to my side. Warrick. I don't know what the hell he planned to do against an angelic warrior-asshole like Rorikel, but it was nice to have some support.

Then Rorikel stopped abruptly, as if something else had caught his attention. Behind him, Sephiel had the same kind of startled look. Max gasped sharply. I whirled around and saw him clutching his head.

"Max? What's wrong?"

"Another vision," he said in a breath. "Damn it, ow–"

"Andromeda has opened her connection to us," Sephiel said.

Just as I turned to him, Sephiel rushed over and slapped his hand against my forehead. I had one second to breathe before I was taken–

–to the room where she was being held. Her feet and ankles were chained to the floor, warded with powerful spells to ensure

she couldn't escape. The skin around the shackles was raw and bloody. She was scared and in pain, her head throbbing from the pounding it had taken in the fight and her capture. She pushed again, trying to get the message out so they could find her.

"Come on, someone please," she whispered.

The door opened. Dro pushed herself back. A tall, lean woman entered the room with two burly men behind her. One of them was Drake. Dro felt bile rise in her stomach when Drake sneered at her, pure liquid hate for what he'd done to Constance burning in her heart. But then she saw the woman. The bile was replaced with anger, and fear.

Six years had aged her, but she still carried herself regally. Her body was covered in an elegant black cloak that bared her shoulders, her feet cased in heavy leather boots. Her arms were concealed in long silky gloves, her night black hair pulled up in a tight bun at the top of her head. Her dark eyes were surrounded with eye shadow and mascara, but Dro could see the bruised circles of exhaustion under them. Staring at her face was like looking into an endless, black abyss.

"Isabel," Dro breathed. Memories rushed through her, glimpses of a time she'd wanted to forget. Pieces that had never fit before, or become shadows in her mind, reformed into the truth. "This was all you."

The witch smiled. "Of course it was. The demons couldn't break through by themselves, after all. Not even the most powerful ones had access to this plane. I offered my services to them, and was rewarded with enough power to bring them over. To find you."

Dro grinned wickedly, defiance coming through. "But you failed. I didn't go with the demons that night. My sister got me free."

Isabel's smile faltered, anger flashing through her dark eyes. "An unforeseen circumstance that will not happen twice. Your sister is dead. Drake saw to that himself."

Drake smiled.

Dro looked between them, hoping to find their lie.

But they just kept smiling. Dro started shaking her head. "No," she whispered, barely a breath. "No."

Isabel smiled almost sympathetically, and took another step into the dark room. "Don't cry, Andromeda. Rejoice. The time is almost upon us. You shall set them free. All the souls condemned to Hell. You will be a savior for the lost."

"No. I'm not doing anything for you." Dro's voice trembled with sorrow and anger. Her power surged under her skin. "Because of you, all those people at Owl Creek are dead." The air became heated and heavy. "Because of you, my parents are dead. Constance is..." She couldn't say it. She didn't want to say it. Doing so would make it true.

Isabel's eyes turned completely black. She held out her hand to Dro and concentrated. A thousand invisible knives stabbed into Dro's nerves. She screamed as pain consumed her, numbing out her building powers. Dro dropped onto her side and cried out again as Isabel twisted her hand, like she was twisting all the knives at once.

She lowered her hand and the torture stopped. Dro's body convulsed in agony. Tears seeped past her eyelids.

"Know this, halfbreed. Just because your father desires you, does not mean you can't be harmed."

Dro twisted her head to look up at Isabel. "How can you know my father? He was human."

Isabel smiled. "Was he?"

She held out her hand and shot the painful spell at Dro. She screamed as the invisible knives ripped in her body again. The pain was so intense she began to black out–

–I stepped back from Sephiel, wondering why the room was shaking. Then I realized that it wasn't the room. It was me.

CHAPTER TWENTY-SIX

I replayed the whole scene. Isabel was alive. On the side of the demons. Torturing Dro. Feeling her pain was enough to threaten tears again, but I held them back and looked for the rage. It was easier to find, and didn't hurt half as much.

I looked over and saw that Rorikel had taken his hand away from Warrick's head. The demon slayer looked at me with horror, then with pity. I turned away from him. I didn't need pity. I needed to save Dro, and kill Isabel.

"The pull was definitely from Athens," Max whispered from behind me. He sounded so broken-hearted that I couldn't look at him. "She's there. I'm positive."

"Do you know that woman, Constance?" Sephiel asked. "Isabel?"

Just hearing her name almost sent me over the edge. I put my hand on the hilt of my hatchet and gripped it tightly.

"Yeah, I know her," I said. "She's the one who caused the Owl Creek Slaughter."

The angels may not have been familiar with the slaughter, but Warrick and Max were. They knew the background, what the media had released. But they didn't know the details as intimately as I did. They didn't have nightmares of blood and screams. They didn't wake up with fear at the first smell of smoke.

I moved over to the bed and sat down, taking the hatchet from my hip and turning it in my hands. I sighed, and told them what really happened at Owl Creek...

Dro was turning ten years old. Her birthday was on a weekend, but both Mom and Dad were able to get time off to spend it with us. I was fourteen, so while Dro was inside the camper baking and cooking with Mom, I was helping Dad chop the firewood. He was busy carving Dro's gift from a leftover piece of wood.

I looked up and glanced around the camp, not really looking for anything or anyone.

Until I saw her. Isabel.

I'd never seen her here before. That was my first clue that something was wrong. The second was that she wasn't dressed for camping. No fleece jacket, hiking boots, or jeans. Instead she wore a strapless black cloak, long black gloves, and black boots. I gripped the hatchet tightly.

"Dad," I said. "Isabel's here."

My father was confused until he followed my line of sight. Isabel's eyes found him. She smiled.

Dad turned to me and gripped my shoulders. "Go inside with your Mom and your sister."

I didn't like the way his voice sounded. "But–"

"Just do it, Constance."

Dad was more than capable of protecting himself, but the feeling in my gut, the one that told me something awful was about to happen, just wouldn't leave. But I listened to him and hurried into the camper, the door slamming shut behind me. Mom and Dro looked up from the kitchenette, confusion and worry on their faces. Dro knew immediately that something was happening. She could read me better than anyone.

"Constance?" Mom said. "What's going on? Where's your father?"

Just as I was about to speak, I heard raised voices from outside the camper.

"Stay back, Dro," I ordered as Mom and I rushed toward the window.

We huddled together and looked outside into the darkness, where my father was facing off with Isabel. He was taller and stronger than she was, but I didn't think she would stand up against him if she couldn't fight for herself.

"I don't give a damn," my father shouted angrily. "You aren't taking her."

Isabel scowled. "You don't understand the implications of refusing like this."

"I don't care. I warned you. She isn't going anywhere with you."

Isabel's eyes changed, turning pitch black. I felt a chill go through my bones. Dad took a step back.

"What the—"

"Return the child to me, mortal," commanded Isabel. In two voices.

One was hers, but another one layered over it. A deep, imposing voice. The voice a monster might have. "Or you and yours shall suffer greatly."

I wondered what was on Dad's face. If he was as scared as I was. Other people were coming out of their trailers, curious to see what was going on.

"What are you?" I barely heard my father say.

"Something you cannot comprehend," Isabel said in her dual voice. "Give her to me."

Dad took another step back and gripped his carving knife tightly. "No."

Fury was on Isabel's face, but I couldn't tell if it was her own rage, or the rage of the thing controlling her. "Then this shall be on your head."

Isabel turned and held out her hands to the air. The world split open like a raw, bloody wound, and creatures poured out. Dozens of them, some of them were red and humanoid, others grey and sickly. There were black wisps of smoke, huge dogs, bulky brutes, and things that moved too fast for me to see. As soon as their feet touched the grass, they scattered and began killing everyone they could.

I saw the red monsters tear out people's innards with their claws. The grey ones ripped apart whoever they could and stuffed chunks of torn skin into their hungry maws. Smoke-monsters forced themselves down human throats and made them attack their loved ones. Dogs leaped and tore limbs clean off. The brutes grabbed anyone in range and used their massive fists to turn people into pulps of red flesh. Some of the campers were dragged toward the hole in the world, gripping at tufts of grass as desperately as they could. Flames curled around RV's and tents, turning the night black and red with smoke and fire.

It was literally Hell on earth.

Isabel threw back her head and laughed. The sound that came from her sounded raw, guttural, and inhuman. My father rushed her and stabbed her in the back with his carving knife. The sound she made was definitely from her, a short bark of pain. Isabel whirled before Dad could pull the knife out. The thing inside her was furious, but it made Isabel smile.

"You are brave, mortal," she remarked with her two voices. "But foolish. You can kill this body, but you cannot kill me."

Isabel tore the knife from her back, and sliced it across my father's throat.

I couldn't understand it. One moment my father was standing there facing off with Isabel, then there was a spray of red liquid across her face, and then Dad was lying on the ground.

Mom screamed like someone was tearing her heart out. Dro started to cry. I ran for the door, just as monsters kicked it in. The monster was human- shaped and had dark red skin, and blood in its disgustingly wide smile.

The monster shrieked and launched itself at me at the same time I swung the hatchet that I still held. Its claws grazed my shoulder and chest, just as the hatchet connected with its upper arm. The monster was surprised that I attacked it, though not half as surprised when my mom charged it with a furious roar, a butcher knife in her hand. She and the monster tumbled out of the RV. She stabbed wildly at it, lost in a grief-stricken rage.

But it wasn't enough.

Another red monster appeared behind her and tore her off the one she was trying to kill, throwing her onto the ground. The monster she attacked sprang up like its wounds were nothing more than papercuts. One of them trapped her arms over her head while the second straddled her body. The one near her head sank its teeth into her throat while the one pinning her slashed its claws wildly across her chest, cutting her to ribbons. Mom screamed again, but it was a scream of pain as the monsters ripped her apart.

Shock and fear froze me until I heard Dro sob. I whirled to face my little sister. Tears streamed her pale face. She looked terrified. So was I, but I couldn't let it show right now. I had to get her out of here, or the monsters would kill her too.

I grabbed her shoulders and shook her once so she would look at me. "Back window, run!"

Dro jumped, but ran for the back of the camper. I was right behind her when another monster crashed through the broken door. I shoved Dro toward the window, hoping she would focus on escaping. I had to buy her time. The red monster slammed into me and knocked me onto my back. Its chin was smeared with my mother's blood.

I bit back a scream and tried to push it off, but it was

stronger than me. I kicked and thrashed, hacking at it with the hatchet. Out of the corner of my eye, I could see Dro half out of the back window, hesitating.

"Go!" I screamed, slicing the hatchet into the monster's face.

I didn't know if she listened to me or if she made it, because the monster threw me out of the RV's door. I hit the ground hard, rolling on the grass and getting fresh bruises. The hatchet nicked me a couple times, small, stinging bites.

The monster jumped on me and yanked my arm. I screamed in pain as it pulled harder and harder, muscles and tendons stretching to the point of snapping. My finger clenched around the hatchet. I slammed it up into the monster's chest, then into its face. It finally recoiled and let me go. I couldn't tell if I'd killed it or not. I clutched my arm and winced, rolling to see the camp.

Blood was everywhere. Fires and bodies lay scattered across the clearing. Heavy smoke rolled into the sky. Adrenaline and fear were the only things that kept me moving. I got to my feet and started looking for my little sister, running through the slaughter. Looking anywhere but at the people I used to know, even when they reached out and begged for help.

I screamed when someone grabbed my ankles and pulled me down. I twisted, kicking and screaming at my attacker. But it wasn't a monster. It was one of the campers. Blood painted his chin and was splattered on his cheeks. Both of his legs were ragged stumps of shredded flesh, missing at the knee. He was way too pale.

"Please," he gurgled through bloody lips. "Please kill me."

I couldn't move. I was too scared. One of the big dogs suddenly appeared at his side, huge teeth chomping down into his stumped legs and dragging him away. I don't know if it was him who screamed, or if it was me.

I heard a familiar scream through all the chaos and twisted on the grass. I saw Dro by the tree line in the grip of a red monster. I got up and ran as fast as I could. She cried and struggled, and I ran faster.

Dro's icy blue eyes were wide and terrified. "Connie!" she screamed.

The monster hit her across the face, sending her sprawling onto the grass. I slammed into it, sending us both onto the ground. I tried to hit it with the hatchet, but it was so much stronger than me. It punched me in the stomach and knocked me onto my back. I rolled on the ground to avoid its claws. It snapped its sharp teeth and hissed at me. Somehow I found my footing and swung the hatchet again. This time I hit the monster in the arm with the weapon, black blood gushing out of its wound. The back of the monster's hand cracked against my face, sending me crashing onto the charred ground. I panicked, my breathing ragged. I'd lost the hatchet and was looking for something, anything, to fight back with–

The monster screamed.

I twisted on the ground, and saw that it was on fire. Not a normal, red and orange fire, but a fierce, white-hot flame blazing hotter than any bonfire I'd ever been close to. The heat was sweltering, a thick, humid air that coated my throat and made it hard to breathe. The white fire destroyed the demon, turning into black ash.

The white fire came from my sister's hand. My sister… who was on fire.

It wrapped around her like a shroud, illuminating her, yet she made no sound of pain. Not even her clothes were singed. Tears streaked her face. She looked at me, crying and consumed by flames.

"Help me, Constance."

I was confused, scared, and hurt, but her words still cut me to the core. Finally the blaze vanished and she collapsed onto the ground. The grass ignited around her.

I surged forward, carefully dodging the line of white fire.

Flames reached for my ankles, but I was quick. I hauled her up, the heat from the ground making it hard to breathe. She was barely conscious. The fire didn't seem to have harmed her physically, but now wasn't the time to wonder why.

I draped Dro's arm over my shoulder, found the hatchet and picked it up. I navigated us behind the burning grass, and carried her to a car parked well away from the camp site. I knew that car. The driver always forgot to lock the doors. I put Dro in the front seat and got into the driver's side. Dad showed me how to drive a couple times, getting me ready for my license. I wasn't an expert, but my feet could reach the pedals. I fumbled around for the keys, finding them in the compartment by the coffee holders. I started the car and looked up, and saw Isabel.

She stared at me, blocked from us by a wall of white flame. She couldn't get through now, and she was furious. Her eyes promised vengeance. The fire had spread too far, engulfing the edge of the trees and she was trapped behind it, along with the monsters. None of them could walk around that fire.

I glared at her with just as much hatred. If I saw her again, I would make her pay.

I started the car, shifted, and drove into the forest, turning my back on the massacre...

CHAPTER TWENTY-SEVEN

W hen I looked up, the men were staring at me. Max looked horrified, the angels were unreadable, and Warrick was looking at me sadly again.

I straightened my back and ignored it all. I hadn't thought about Owl Creek in years, and couldn't linger on it now. I had to focus on getting Dro back.

"After that we ran," I said. "We tried to find out what Dro was, why she could do the things she could, but we never stopped running." A thought occurred to me. "That's probably how she kept track of us, and found us here."

"What do you mean?" Warrick asked.

"Isabel had been following us back then, keeping an eye on Dro. She must have found another demon to work with. Maybe she made a spell to have the demons sense Dro, then set them on us whenever she felt we were close."

"You think she can do that?"

I glanced at Max, quickly considering his question. "Yeah. I don't know what she's fully capable of, but I know she's a dangerous bitch." I looked away from him, thoughts still churning through my mind. "She's being all buddy-buddy with the demons of her own free will. And that it's been making her powerful. Really powerful. The demon she's serving is giving her more strength than she needs."

"Do you know which demon it is?" Sephiel asked Max.

The kid shook his head. "Whenever I look, all I get is a vision of the shadow-guy. But I don't think he's anyone I want to shake hands with."

Sephiel said nothing more, going back to his own thoughts.

"We need to get more weapons," I said. "Can you guys get us some?"

Sephiel nodded at me. "We shall return shortly." He glanced at Rorikel, who frowned, but blinked out of existence with him.

"What about Drake?" Max asked.

The name burned in me again. "She probably hired him after he escaped the border. Probably offered him more money for Dro than the Blood Thorns did for me."

"Drake is mine," Warrick said, making me turn my head to where he was sitting next to me on the mattress. There was no humor on his face.

I narrowed my eyes. "How about we call it first come, first serve?" I was half serious.

He didn't even blink. "No."

I frowned. I was going to make sure I got some literal kicks in Drake before Warrick killed him, but getting revenge wasn't my real concern at the moment. Saving my sister's life was.

The air shivered and the angels returned with an arsenal. They had silver knives, holy water, salt, sage, silver bullets, handguns, a sawed-off shotgun, rock-salt shells, full body weapon rigs and clip-on flashlights.

"Holy shit," said Max. "Did you guys raid the angel armory or something?"

"More or less," smirked Sephiel, placing the weapons on the bed next to me.

I stood up and went for one of the rigs, sliding it over my

shoulders and clicking together the buckles around my hips and thighs. I adjusted the shoulders straps so they were tight, then grabbed all the knives I could and slipped them into the rig. There were two sheaths at my ribs, two on my hips, and even a sheath for my hatchet. A girl could never have too many blades when she prepared to hunt demons, but I decided to slip a bottle of holy water onto my belt. You never knew when it could come in handy.

While I put on my lucky jacket, Warrick was going for the sawed-off shotgun and filling it with shells. He took a handgun and loaded it while I glanced at Max. His eyes were closed again, so I assumed that he was pushing his ability to find out more about the shadow-guy. Or more likely, trying to see what was happening to Dro.

Sephiel suddenly asked, "Why do you use a hatchet?"

I looked at the auburn-haired angel, who'd been staring at me. "It was my father's," I said. That was all I was going to say.

Sephiel glanced at the hatchet again, then met my eyes. "Would you like me to bless it?"

I stared at him for a second. It made sense that an angel could bless whatever he wanted, but I hadn't exactly been expecting to hear it. "What difference would that make?"

He grinned a little. "The blessing of an angel would be more powerful than the blessing of a mortal priest. It would cause demons infinitely more pain."

He sold me there. I turned the hatchet in my hand and held it out to Sephiel, handle first. He took it from me and examined the weapon from top to bottom. Once he was done assessing it, he closed his eyes and began blessing.

"*Sancte Michael Archangele, defende nos in proelio, contra nequitiam et insidias diaboli esto praesidium. Imperat illi Deus, supplices deprecamur: tuque, Princeps militiae coelestis, Satanam aliosque spiritus malignos, qui ad perditionem animarum pervagantur in mundo, divina virtute in infernum detrude. Amen."*

After finishing the prayer, Sephiel looked in my eyes. *"Anima potentis, cor sororis."*

I took my hatchet back from Sephiel when he handed it back and looked at it. The weapon didn't look any different. Same ratty wooden handle, same chipped and scratched blade. But it felt strange, and I swore I could feel a slight tremor in it. I lifted my eyes to look at Sephiel.

"What did that last bit mean?" I asked.

"It means 'soul of a warrior, heart of a sister'," he answered.

It was no secret I would do anything for Dro, that I had fought and killed for her and would do so again. But Sephiel looked at me with that soft, grateful look again. He cared about Dro, not because she was Nephilim, but because she was, well, Dro.

"Thank you," was all I could think to say to Sephiel. I looked at the rest of the group. "Can you get in touch with Dro? Tell her we're on our way?"

His bright blue eyes were sad. "The connection has been closed. Whether or not due to a spell or unconsciousness, I cannot tell."

My heart ached. "Can you do that blinking thing? Teleport us to Athens? We can't waste anymore time."

Sephiel hesitated. "It is possible, but it will be extremely uncomfortable for your human bodies."

"I don't care," I said, stepping forward. "Do it."

The blue-eyed angel nodded. "As you wish."

He reached out and took my hand. The effect was almost immediate. I felt as though I was being sucked through a vacuum hose. My entire body seemed to snap and compress, and I sucked in a breath to keep from crying out in pain. I snapped my eyes shut, the world rioting around me.

Then my feet hit solid ground, and I was rolling away from

Sephiel. As fast as it happened, it was over. I almost thought I had imagined it. I staggered to my feet and breathed in deep, feeling my body tremble and twitch away the uncomfortable sensation of teleporting. I slowly lifted my head and inhaled, then looked at the ghost town.

I'd never been to Athens before, but I had heard some old stories about the supernatural here. Ghost hunts, grave robberies, animal mutilations, black magic cults, satanic rituals, and of course, the underground tunnel system shaped like a pentagram.

These days it was known for its paranormal society, being a little more secretive about its history when it came to the supernatural. I hadn't expected many people out this late at night, but I also hadn't expected the town to be so empty. No lights were on in the shops and restaurants, no one walked the streets, no dogs barked, no cars drove by. Nothing but empty buildings and flickering street lamps.

It felt wrong.

I looked over my shoulder to see Warrick and Max handling Rorikel and Sephiel's teleportation about as well as I had. Warrick was on his feet, but looking incredibly uncomfortable. Max looked like he was going to throw up.

"You guys okay?" I asked.

Warrick's face was tight, but he nodded. Max blew out some air, lifting his head and looking a little more grounded.

"Angel Airlines is not gonna be my first choice for travel, that's for sure." He looked at Sephiel. "No offence, Seph."

Sephiel waved it off. "None is taken, Max."

Warrick walked from Rorikel to me, looking at the surroundings. "Where is everyone?"

I glanced forward again. "Good question. Not sure I wanna know the answer. Max, how far is it to the tunnels?"

He walked up to my side, closing his eyes and focusing. A couple seconds later, he opened his eyes and pointed to our left. "That way. Half an hour's walk and we're there."

"What about Dro? Can you sense what's happening to her?"

He looked nervous and shook his head. "I tried, but I can't see anything."

His sounded guilty, but I didn't blame him. Despite all he'd gone through, he still did everything he could to help us.

"Okay. Then let's go."

I didn't wait for them to follow me. If I didn't start moving, I was going to lose my mind. Dro had been gone for way too long. I focused on ways to ruin Isabel and Drake's day. It was easier than thinking about all the shame weighing on me.

CHAPTER TWENTY-EIGHT

I made it to the edge of Fuller's Park in less than half an hour because I ran. The guys only caught up with me because I slowed down when I saw the grave plot surrounded by brick pillars linked by heavy chains and metal bars to obviously encourage people away from this place.

Just in case the two heavyset men standing in front of it didn't work.

I stayed off the trail and crouched low in the bushes, watching them carefully. They wore red plaid shirts, dirty jeans, trucker hats. They might have been men from the town, but there was something wrong with them. They didn't seem to be moving, or even blinking.

Warrick appear at my side. In the distance, I could make out the shapes of Max and the angels. I raised a hand to my lips, ushering them to be quiet.

"They're probably from the town," Warrick whispered. He frowned at them. "They might be possessed."

"Then they don't deserve to die." I looked at Warrick. "Take my hand."

He blinked at me, green eyes flashing. "Why?"

"We'll pretend we're on a date and got lost. When we're up close, we'll be able to know for sure."

Warrick read my eyes, then quickly nodded and took my hand. We stood up and started walking toward the men. He put his other arm over my shoulder as we moved out onto the main path.

I was abruptly aware of how well built and warm Warrick was. I could smell his earthy, musky scent, and it was easy for me to tilt my head to the side and rest it against his shoulder. It wasn't long before the men noticed us.

"Maybe they'll know," I said, trying to sound like a ditz. "Excuse me, my boyfriend and I are looking for the grave site that's supposed to be here. Is this the right one?"

The two men stared at us blankly. I would have been unnerved if I didn't have to get past them. I edged closer.

"It's supposed to be, like, haunted or something, and we thought it would be cool to check it out."

Their eyes fixed on me and flashed black, the Possessors revealing themselves.

"Well, look who showed up," the one on the left said. "We were wondering if you would make it."

I pulled away from Warrick just as the possessed men attacked us. He took the one on the right while I took the one on the left. He charged me, getting ready for a tackle. He was a big guy, and if I let him get his arms around me, I was screwed.

Shock rippled up my leg when my foot connected with his face. He stumbled and roared in fury. I reached for holy water to try and expel the demon, but the possessed man swung his huge fist at my head. I ducked low, feeling air sweep over my hair. I leaned back when he tried to knee me in the face, but wasn't able to avoid his meaty hand slapping onto my skull and twisting my hair.

Pain shot through my scalp, but the short distance gave me the chance to drive my elbow into his face. His head rocked back and he lost his grip. I kicked him once in the ribs and then spun in a roundhouse kick. My heel connected with his cheek and dropped him. I reached for the holy water and poured it on the man. The demon inside him screamed as the blessed water burned it. He started thrashing wildly as I dropped to my knees next to him, gripping his chin to pry his mouth open and pour the holy water down his throat.

Black smoke exploded out of the possessed man's mouth, the demon unable to stand it. I stepped back as the Possessor darted for me. It stopped abruptly, hissed, then spiraled over my head and into the darkness. I pressed a hand to the sigil inked over my heart. I couldn't be possessed again. *Thank God.*

I turned my head sharply to see Warrick still fighting the other possessed man. Warrick matched him evenly, blocking every punch and never letting up his attacks, but never seeming to get his own.

Then the possessed man drew a hunting knife.

I don't even remember moving. One second I was watching Warrick fight, the next I grabbed the knife and punched the possessed man in the face. He growled and lashed out at me, but I drove a sidekick into his stomach. Warrick finished him off with two more jabs to the face and a splash of holy water. The Possessor ripped out of the man's body, coiled up toward the sky, and disappeared into the night.

Warrick and I were breathing heavily as we looked at the two men on the ground, and then at each other. Respect and gratefulness filled his eyes, but there was also a trace of impatience.

"I had him," he said.

I rolled my eyes. "You could just say thank you."

"Thank you," he muttered quietly.

I smirked. "See? That wasn't so hard."

He grinned and I quickly turned my head away so he wouldn't see the sudden blush I got in my cheeks.

"Can you check on the others? They should have made it here by now."

While Warrick walked off the path to find Max and the angels, I knelt down by the man we had both fought. He was dazed and in pain, since Warrick had broken his nose.

"Hey," I said, getting his attention by nudging him with my boot.

He blinked up at me, looking around with confusion. "Where am I? What the hell happened?"

"You're from Athens?" I asked, ignoring his questions.

"Yeah, I... Oh, God, what happened to the town?"

That should have been my question. "Tell me what you remember."

He pushed himself up and collected his thoughts. "They came out of nowhere. There was this lady, she did something that made this door out of thin air, and these black mists came out of it. They started taking over people. Some of them ran, but most couldn't get far." He cringed. "I tried to get away, but that smoky mist thing took me over." He started to choke. "It was horrible. The things it made me do..."

"I know," I said. "It happened to me once."

He turned his head to look at me, eyes wide. "You believe me?"

I nodded. "Tell me why you were you waiting for me."

The man nodded. "We got told someone might come looking for the pale girl."

My heart started beating faster. "Do you know where she is?"

"In the tunnels, last I heard."

"Is she alive?"

I relaxed heavily when the man nodded. I couldn't allow myself to think that Dro was all right, but I'd needed to know that she was alive. *Hang on, little sister.*

The man flinched when he saw the rest of my group come out of the bushes. I looked over my shoulder.

"What took you guys so long?" I asked the angels. "We were confronted by a small horde of possessed," said Rorikel blandly. "Complications ensued, and were dealt with."

Max looked uncomfortable. I had the feeling that 'dealt with' meant 'killed.'

I turned back to the man. "Do you know how to get in the tunnels?"

He looked at me with horror. "Are you crazy?! You can't go in there! They'll kill you!"

I stared at him with so much intensity he backed down. "The pale girl is my sister. I'm going in there whether you help me or not. Considering we got rid of your demon without killing you, I'd say you owe us."

The man became flustered and started stammering. I just waited. "There's a pentagram marking in the brick back there. You put some blood on it and say this phrase, ah, *spes relinquite omnes, o vos intrantes,* and it'll open."

"Good. Can you get your friend out of here?"

He looked at the unconscious man. "Yeah, I think so."

"Then do that. Call the cops if you want, but then get the hell out of the state."

I started to stand up and he followed me quickly. "You know what this is? Tell me."

"Trust me, buddy. You're better off not knowing."

I turned my back on him and walked for the brick pillars. I could hear Warrick giving him some advice. As the resident demon slayer, he was probably giving him information he needed to cope with what had happened. The poor man was in for some hard times.

I crouched down and looked at the pillar, trying to find where the pentagram was. I plucked the flashlight from my belt and switched it on. The dull light illuminated the brick, and the pentagram etched into it. The symbol was covered in dirt and faded from time, so I brushed away some of the dirt so the symbol would be clearer. I stood up, took a throwing knife out of my jacket and sliced open my hand. I didn't doubt that I would bleed more before I found my sister, so what was one more cut? I smeared my blood on the pentagram, then said the phrase.

"Spes relinquite omnes, o vos intrantes."

Behind me, Rorikel stifled a laugh and muttered something I didn't catch. Inside the plot where the graves were, the ground shifted and the tombstone in the center began to tremble. It slowly sank into the earth, grinding against something stony on its way down. A couple seconds later, it stopped, and the forest was silent again.

I stepped into the plot and peered down into the secret entrance. All I could see was blackness surrounded by dirt and cold stone. Even when I shone my flashlight into the open door, I could barely make out the ground. I took out one of the silver knives and dropped it through the door. It clattered on the stone floor after a couple seconds, but nothing shot out of the darkness to see what the noise had been.

Still, the trap door screamed, *'danger danger don't go in don't go in.'*

"Here," Warrick said.

I looked over, seeing that he'd come over to my side and taken a bandage out of his leather jacket. He nodded at my wounded hand. I tried to take it from him, but instead he took my hand and wrapped the cut himself. His hands were warm and gentle, and I wished I wasn't so worried about my sister so I could thank him. But if I showed any softness now, I might fall apart again. That couldn't happen, so I focused on the trap door and the blackness beyond it.

"What did the phrase mean?" I asked no one in particular as Warrick bound my hand.

"Oh you'll love it," Max grumped from the other side of me. "I remember if from high school. It's classic Dante." His big brown eyes found mine. "Abandon all hope, ye who enter here.' "

I sighed. "Lovely."

"You must enter the door now," Sephiel said urgently.

I looked over my shoulder. Both he and Rorikel were facing the trees, their backs tense and their hands gripping silver broadswords I swore hadn't been with them when we left the motel. Damn angels and their randomly appearing weapons. I looked past them, but couldn't see anything.

"What's wrong?"

"The Possessors that escaped have called for reinforcements," Rorikel said. "The remainder of the town, most likely."

"Shit," I breathed.

"You're not going to kill them, are you?" Warrick asked. "They're still people. The demons are just controlling them."

An ear-piercing shriek echoed from the woods. Rorikel took a step forward. Sephiel turned and ushered us towards the trap door. He grabbed Max's arms and lowered him down before he could protest. Then he moved onto the annoyed demon slayer. Sephiel stopped in front of me and looked at me with his bright blue eyes.

"Save her, Constance," he whispered, sounding desperate.

Then he lifted me down into the trap door, closed it over our heads, and locked us in shadow.

CHAPTER TWENTY-NINE

Warrick, Max and I stared at the closed off ceiling. Our angel guardians were about to fight an entire town of possessed humans. I couldn't stand the thought of how much blood would be shed up there, or if either angel would survive. Hopefully they would keep it to a minimum. Those people hadn't done anything but be in the wrong place in the wrong time.

Max said what we were all thinking. "Well, this is just fucking great."

"There's nothing we can do now," I said. "Come on."

I pointed the flashlight around the tunnel. It was larger than I expected, with cracks in the old stone, and smelling of dust. The only direction was straight ahead, so I clipped the flashlight to my belt and started walking.

"Did you know these tunnels were used to help liberate the slaves during the Civil War?" Max said. "Then from the 1920's to 1930's, they were used to transport moonshine."

"That's fascinating, Max," I snarked. "Did you also know that sound echoes down tunnels?"

"Sorry," he whispered. "I'm nervous."

I turned my head to give him a semi-understanding look, but his eyes were on the floor. His eyebrows were pulled together, worry clear in his eyes. He looked heartsick, and I knew he was thinking about my sister. I reached out to pat his shoulder, bhe ache in my chest kept me from saying anymore.

We walked in silence for another five minutes before I pulled back to talk to Max again. "How much of these tunnels have you seen?"

"Flashes," he answered. "But I have a general idea where to go."

We stopped at a fork in the tunnels, and I looked at him. "Time to prove it."

Max hesitated only for a second, then took a step forward and began to concentrate. Warrick walked up beside me, getting way too close once again.

"Getting out of here isn't going to be easy," he muttered.

"Are you saying that because the only entrance we know of has been closed off, or because when we get Dro back we're going to be chased by a bunch of pissed off demons?"

"Both," he admitted. "We have to be careful, Constance. Without Sephiel and Rorikel here, there won't be anyone to heal us if we get hurt."

I held Warrick's piercing green gaze with my own dark brown one. "I know." I glanced at Max, who was still concentrating. "Look, I know I've been a bitch to you more often and not, but I really am grateful that you're here helping us. And for... the thing on the balcony."

I mumbled it as much as I could so he wouldn't think I was being mushy. The truth of the matter was that we were probably going to die down here, and I didn't want him to think I wasn't thankful for everything he'd done. Warrick smiled a little, making my heart sigh.

"You don't need to thank me. I would be acting the same as you if it was Emma who'd been taken."

There was a flash of sadness in his eyes. Once again, I wished we were in a different place. That I had the heart to comfort him. That my sister was safe, and not in danger of dying.

I fumbled for something to say, but Warrick's anguish was gone when he looked at Max. I followed his gaze. The psychic walked over to us.

"Well, some concentration and one killer headache later, I get how all this works."

Headache? "Are you all right?"

"Oh yeah," he said. "Just happens when I push myself too hard too often." He grinned. "I'm always happy to see that soft side of you, Constance."

I rolled my eyes, and Max explained.

"First, we go left. Then we'll come to a door. There was a lot of commotion, so there must will be some kind of trial behind it, and before you ask, no, I don't know what that's going to be. That part was fuzzy. If we survive that, we go left again and face another door and another trial. I got a blackout for that too, but after that we hang a third left and go through the last trial. If we live through all of those, we make a final left, and that should lead us to the center of the tunnels. That's where Dro should be."

My heart began hammering. She was so close.

"Are you sure? If Isabel is as strong as Constance says, what is to stop her from putting those images in your head?" Warrick asked.

Max and I both winced. "I don't know what you want me to say," he told Warrick. "I've stretched my abilities as far as they can go. There isn't anything else I can do, and we can't go back."

I pointed my flashlight into the shadows past Max. Both men made valid points, but we couldn't go back. And there were only three turns and three doors between me and my sister.

I turned left.

It took all of my willpower not to run. If I had three trials ahead of me, fine. It was the price I had to pay for failing to protect Dro when she needed me most.

THE FIRST DOOR was a huge slab made from the same rough stone as the tunnel with demonic symbols etched across it. I couldn't read them, but I did see the same pentagram that had been carved into the pillar by the grave plot. I assumed the idea was the same, so I shifted the bandage Warrick placed on my hand, squeezing the wound until fresh blood flowed. I smeared my blood onto the pentagram.

There was a heavy *thunk* that made me step back. The door made a crunching, grinding noise as it lazily dragged itself open. I fixed the bandage and took the hatchet from my hip.

We stepped inside, a huge, empty chamber opening up to us, at least three time as large as the tunnel.

A weird crunching and squishing sound came from the corner. I turned, and saw twelve demons ravenously eating a corpse. Their heads snapped up and they shrieked when our flashlights hit them. I'd seen them at Owl Creek, but had no clue what they were. They were scrawny and humanoid in shape with oversized heads and gigantic eyes the color of spoiled milk. Their skin was covered in rough, patchy scales, their claws and teeth yellowed and short, but still sharp enough to tear flesh from bone.

"What the fuck are these?" I asked, pulling out my hatchet.

"Corpse eating demons," Max said nervously from behind me.

"Ghouls," Warrick rumbled, taking a calm step forward.

It was the first time I'd really seen Warrick in action against demons, and I was momentarily stunned. He held out the sawed-off and fired a blast of rock salt at the ghouls. The crack of gunfire echoed through the cavern. The blast hit two of them and sent them sprawling across the room. They moved fast, but Warrick fired another shot that sent a ghoul flying away from him, then turned and flipped the shotgun, using the butt of it to hit the face of a ghoul that had been coming up on his side.

He was good. *Very* good. But he didn't see the one making its way behind him.

I slammed my hatchet into the demon's head and saved Warrick's life.

Sharp fangs grated along the back of my arm. It wrenched me back and forth, and pulled me off my feet. I dropped onto my back, hearing a metallic click behind me, and pushed free from the ghoul. I twisted and backed up, just in time to see silver spikes shoot out of the floor and impale the ghoul through its skull, throat, and heart. It twitched on the spikes, then began to dissolve as the trap snapped back into the floor.

I turned to warn Max and Warrick, but was punched in the head by another ghoul instead. I was having a really rough start.

The demon jumped onto me and let out a terrible hiss, opening its jaws to bite my face off. I caught it by the throat to hold it back and swung my hatchet into the side of the ghoul's head.

Sephiel had been right about my hatchet. It felt *much* more powerful now. The blade drove deeper, and delivered a stronger blow while feeling light as a feather.

Black ghoul blood oozing down the side of its face as its body began to disintegrate. I rolled to my feet and looked at the ground. They were well hidden all over the floor, but I saw the series of holes running horizontally through the room. I stood up and ran for Warrick and Max.

Warrick held his own against two ghouls, now using a silver knife and some fast martial arts moves, but Max was in trouble. One ghoul corroded near his feet, and he struggled against another one. He used techniques and skills I taught him, but claw marks ran dow his face and his shirt had been shredded. Even worse, the ghoul pushed him back towards the line of spikes.

"Max, don't move!" I screamed, hefting my hatchet.

He froze, but covered his face as the ghoul raised its claws. I threw my hatchet at the ghoul, hitting it in the skull. It crumpled into a heap of ash. I grabbed Max by the shirt and swung him around, watching my footing for any signs of the pressurized spikes. I let go of him when I knew he was in a safe spot, then took my hatchet back from the ashy remnants of the ghoul. I took out a silver knife and pressed the flat of it onto his chest.

"Watch where you step," I ordered.

I turned away from Max and ran to help Warrick. There were three ghouls left standing, and all of them were focused on the slayer. He did his best to keep from being surrounded, but they were moving fast. I gripped my hatchet and took out another silver knife, spinning it into a reverse grip.

One of the ghouls slashed at Warrick's face, claws scratching thin lines along his forehead. Warrick spun and kicked back to get the demon away, only to have another one jump on top of him and drive him onto the ground. The other two ghouls hovered, ready to leap on him and rip him to pieces.

I slammed my hatchet into the back of one of the ghouls, then lashed out with my knife and cut the other ghoul across the chest. The hits didn't kill them, so they both faced me and charged at the same time. I backed up, ducking and turning away from their swipes. Once or twice I felt claws skim across my jacket or my stomach, but I kept them at bay.

One of the ghouls crouched low and lunged for my gut. I buckled forward and kneed it in the chin, looking up to see the second ghoul aiming a slash at my face. I leaned my head back and kicked the ghoul around my waist away. I hurled my silver knife into the chest of another ghoul, turning my attention to the last one. I took control of the fight, forcing the demon back towards the line of spikes. Its claws caught me in the shoulder, but I followed the turn and kicked it in the head. The ghoul was knocked onto the line of spikes. I heard the click, and watched the spikes jut through its chest, killing it instantly.

When I turned again, the last ghoul wrapped its hands around my throat. It squeezed tight, crushing my neck. I swung my hatchet at its head. It throttled me furiously, snapping my head back and forth. We toppled onto the ground and I lost my grip on my hatchet. My vision started to blur. I drove my knee into its stomach and pushed the demon over my head, sending it flying back, its claws making shallow scratches along my neck.

I coughed air back into my lungs, rolled, and grabbed my hatchet. I looked up as the ghoul lunged for me again, and swung my hatchet. The metal cracked against its face, driving it back. I lashed out with my foot, catching it in the chest. It stumbled back, stopping when it heard the metal clicking noise.

Heavy metal spikes jolted up from the floor and skewered the ghoul. I shuddered as the spike protruded through its legs to the top of its head. Another, quieter click, and the metal spikes snapped back down into the floor, the demon's remains bursting into an ashy cloud.

Someone touched my arm. I jumped, but it was only Warrick. "Are you all right?" he asked, helping me to my feet.

I looked at the injuries he'd taken. Shallow claw marks on his chest and arms, as well as the bloody gash on his forehead.

"Fine," I said. "You look worse than I do."

He grinned a little. "Don't be so sure."

Good point. "Max, you okay?"

He was scratched, holding a silver knife dripping black blood, and looking rattled, but he was breathing. That was all that mattered.

"I really hate ghouls," he pouted. "And floors that shoot spikes."

"You're not the only one," I stated.

I looked at the floor again, then took out a knife resting

sheathed at my ribs. I tossed it over the spikes, hoping there was a space we could walk onto.

The knife clattered on the stone floor, but I didn't hear a click. Tentatively, I stepped over the line. When I wasn't spitted like a pig, I relaxed and beckoned the guys.

"Come on, it's safe."

Max gaped at me. "You're joking."

I picked up my knife, spinning it between my fingers. "Just watch where you walk and you'll be fine. Don't be a wuss."

I turned and looked at the floor, taking small steps until I saw the next line of holes. I continued my testing method of tossing a knife over the line of holes and stepping over carefully if I didn't hear a click. I glanced back, ensuring Warrick and Max followed behind me. After crossing another four steps, we made it to the other side of the room. I turned and looked at the guys.

"Everyone all right?"

"We're not full of holes, if that's what you mean," Max muttered.

Accepting his yes, I turned forward. The exit door was made of rotting wood and didn't have any markings on it, so I didn't have to cut my hand open again. I was about to push forward when Warrick stood across from me, holding out his hand and pressing his ear against the door. He must not have heard anything, because he backed up and pulled it open. We turned left and walked in silence until we reached the next door.

CHAPTER THIRTY

I t took us about twenty minutes of power-walking—which hurt, thanks to our wounds—to reach the next door. It looked identical to the one leading through the spiked chamber, so finding the pentagram wasn't hard. I peeled back the bandage on my hand, ready to tear my wound open again. Warrick placed his hand on my uninjured shoulder, getting my attention.

"What?" I asked.

He let go of me and took out one of his own knives, cutting open his palm before I could say anything. "It doesn't always have to be you," he said.

Warrick turned and smeared his blood on the pentagram.

The door unlocked with a series of heavy *thunks*, then a steadily grated open. Max moved closer and our collective flashlights illuminated the room before us.

"Fuck," I breathed.

White, silky strands of cobwebs and spider silk curved along the corners of the a cavern, some of it looking shiny and fresh while other parts looked dusted and old. Strands hung in between the floor and the ceiling like stringy stalactites and stalagmites.

Even worse were the large, oval shaped cocoons randomly spread around the room. All of them were around four to six feet tall, sticking to the walls, the floor, the corners, and the roof. I got a little nauseated when I thought about what might be in those cocoons.

"No chance we can skip this room?" I asked, unease rising within me.

Max looked at me. "Uh, no? Why, are you afraid of spiders?"

"I have a strong dislike for them."

Max raised his eyebrows. "Holy shit, are you seriously afraid of spiders? *You*, the big badass who kills demons and argue with angels and scares people off with a look."

I glared at him, hating that he'd found me out. Spiders had too many eyes, too many legs, and could crawl on you when you weren't looking. I hated that. My glare no longer worked on Max, though I was glad. It was the first time in hours that he'd sounded like himself.

"I get the feeling that after this, you'll be thinking differently," I grumbled before I walked into the room. The only way to fight fear was to face it.

The cobwebs clung to our feet and sank a little with every step we took. We stumbled often, and had to grab each other to stay upright.

We were about a quarter of the way through the room when I heard the first skittering noise behind me. I whirled in the direction of the sound, but saw nothing. Max and Warrick turned with me, the beams of the flashlights on our belts whipping every time we turned. We could barely see through this room, the shadows thick and encompassing. All we could hear were those damned, skittering noises.

Then Warrick shouted in alarm. I whirled and saw a spider the size of a pitbull latched to his back.

He used knife to stab the spider in the face. It screeched

once, then dropped off his back into a black, ashy heap. Warrick glared at the spider's remains, small punctures in his jacket and superficial scratches on his skin.

Warrick handed Max a handgun. "Keep them off us!" he shouted.

More skittering and chittering echoed in the cavern, and at least eight spiders poured into view, peeking through cobwebs and dropping from the ceiling. Their bodies were black, lithe, and covered in coarse hair and white cobwebs, the feelers on the back of their eight legs hooked and sharp. They had four antlike pincers, and six blood red eyes on the top of their head. They came on so fast, way faster than I expected. They must have been starved to jump on us so quickly.

Goddamn *demon* spiders.

I twisted and slashed at the spider I saw coming out of the corner of my eye. It squealed when my blessed blade slammed its head, black blood squirting onto the underside of my arm. It smelled ferociously sour. I wrenched the hatchet out as the spider dissolved.

Gunfire cracked through the room as Warrick shot any spider he could see. One creature jumped for his flank, and I kicked it away. The move saved him, but caused me to stumble forward and hold my arms out for balance. Right into a pair of pincers.

I cried out as the pincers sank deep into my left arm above the elbow. I hacked at the spider's face until it let go, only to launch itself at me again. My feet were trapped in the cobwebs, but I turned my upper body so the spider didn't slam into me. Its clawed legs still brushed along my stomach and there was enough weight behind the graze to throw me off balance. I slammed my hatchet into the spider's back, tumbling right onto the spider and the cobwebs.

The smells of sulfur and sourness had been dull before, but now they reeked in front of me, almost making me gag as the spider wriggled to escape. I raised my hatchet and slammed it down again and again until the spider collapsed in on itself. I was covered in black, demon-spider blood, my left arm was throbbing with pain, and I couldn't unstick myself from the webbed floor. My flashlight swung wildly from my hip as I tried to move, and spotted something in the shadows.

Peeling out from the dark came the mother spider. Nearly nine feet tall and just as wide as her offspring, she had a dozen glowing red eyes and ten legs instead of eight. Her pincers snapped and she let out a shriek of rage that pierced my ears.

When she charged me, I flipped my back so I was underneath the mother spider. I hacked at her legs with my hatchet, but after two strikes, she had moved again. She raised her thorax and I saw the sharp spinnerets under her belly. She slammed the spinnerets at my legs. I yanked my feet back, feeling tremors in the cobwebs at the force of her weight. She jabbed the spinnerets at me again, getting closer, her body skimming my boot. God, this had been a bad idea.

Sharp gunshots popped through the room. The mother spider screeched, a bloom of dark blood punching out of her head. She stumbled away from me, and I twisted. Max stood a few feet away, his eyes and jaw wide, his hands gripping the gun. Arms suddenly hooked under mine and hauled me to my feet. Warrick stood behind me, black blood and cobwebs singing to his face and hair, angry red scratches across his upper chest.

I pulled out of his arms and watched the mother spider approach Max. The other smaller spiders seemed to be dead or hiding, but the mother spider was tougher. Max stepped back and fired another shot at her as she crawled up the wall to get height on him. His shot missed as she crouched, ready to strike. I reached for a silver knife on my hip. Max took a step back and stumbled, horrified at her size and speed, landing on his ass on the webbed floor. The mother spider hissed and bunched her legs when I threw my silver blade. The knife hit punched into one of her crimson eyes, bursting it. The spider screamed and staggered in pain, swinging her face toward us. Her pincers clacked furiously.

"Good job pissing it off," Warrick hissed sharply.

"Not the time," I shot back.

The mother spider stomped angrily in our direction, the webbed floor trembling with every step she made. Warrick and I split off from each other, and she went for me. I ducked and dodged to avoid her, but there was nowhere to hide.

The mother spider swiped at me with one of her legs, tearing through the back of my jacket. Warrick lunged and stabbed the mother spider in her thorax. She shrieked as he twisted the blade before one of her legs lashed out and kicked him hard in the chest. Warrick flew across the room, and I lost sight of him in the darkness.

I jumped up and wrenched my silver knife out of the mother spider's eye, her horrifying arachnid face snapping back to mine. I slashed my hatchet across her face, the blade cutting into two more eyes. The mother spider screamed and slammed her head into my chest before I could back up. I landed on the floor, and she drove her huge head into my chest again with the force of a truck. I gasped, pain blooming in my torso. God, she might have cracked something.

As she came down again, I pushed up with my silver knife, driving it straight into her head. The mother spider whipped her head back and forth, yanking my grip on the knife. Then she scooped me up in her pincers and started pulling me towards her mouth.

The adrenaline pounding through my heart started to crack and give way to fear. I pushed out with my arms and legs to keep her from completely crushing me, forcing the strength of my whole body against her mandibles. She was just so fucking *strong*. Sharp, snakelike fangs and a tiny black tongue flickering inside her mouth. She squeezed and my limbs buckled inward, body condensed again.

I shifted my hatchet into my other hand and slammed it into the mother spider's top pincer, hacking it wildly until it was half dangling from her face. She howled and dropped me. I landed on my back, my body aching even though it was freed. The mother spider took another step toward me, black blood leaking from her face, too fast for me to stop.

A shotgun boomed on my left, the blast hitting the spider in the side of the face. She screeched and turned to the person who had shot her.

Warrick.

His face was hard with determination. He never blinked when he fired a second blast into the demon's face. She recoiled and started backing away. He swiftly reloaded the shotgun and kept shooting her in the head. Something moved out of the corner of my eye, making me jump. But it was just Max trying to help me up. He was covered in cobwebs, black blood, and scratches. He had gotten it easy.

"I take it back," he said. "Spiders are fucking scary."

There was another high-pitched screech, the blast of a shotgun, and then silence. We turned to see Warrick walking over to us with the shotgun at his side, calm and confident as ever. He was covered in demon blood and bruises. Behind him, the mother spider was buckling and crumbling into chunky pieces of ash.

I'd never wanted to kiss a man so much in my whole life.

I halted all the fantasies building in my mind when he stopped in front of me. His eyes traced my injuries, focusing on my left arm.

"How bad is that?" he asked.

I shrugged, acting like my arm wasn't burning. "It hurts, but I can still move it."

"I'll take a look. Max, can you look for the exit?" He

hesitated. "You killed all the spiders, right?" "If we didn't, call for help."

Max frowned. "Not encouraging, dude."

Warrick handed over his shotgun. "Feel better now?"

"No."

But Max started walking deeper into the room anyways. Warrick turned to me and waited. He wasn't going to let me go anywhere until he was done playing doctor, so I peeled off my jacket and looked at my arm.

It looked like someone had placed a mini bear-trap near my elbow, leaving a nasty, bite-like bruise. Blood seeped out of some of the tenderized flesh. My forearm was slicked with demon-spider saliva. I handled the grotesque very well, but the sight of my ravaged arm made my head spin. Or maybe that was the exhaustion.

Warrick frowned and started reaching for the med- kit in his jacket, taking out some more gauze.

"Lucky for you, their venom isn't poisonous," he said, beginning to wrap my arm gently.

"You know this from experience?"

"Research, actually. Only the mother spiders have venom, and only in their smaller fangs. The little ones don't have any."

"I wouldn't have called those little."

He smiled at me, sending another warm ripple through my heart. When he finished with the gauze he took a step back so I could put my jacket back on.

"You're still going to wear that thing?" Warrick said.

"Yup. It's my lucky jacket."

"It's ripped shreds, covered in blood and dirt and God knows what else. It's literally holding together by a thread."

"The key word is lucky. I got this jacket when I was last employed."

There was bitterness in my voice and hesitance in his eyes, but Warrick didn't look entirely stunned. He knew who I'd run with, maybe even the things I'd done. If Max hadn't told him, he would have figured it out himself.

"Doesn't seem like it would be a happy reminder."

"It isn't. That's why I kept it."

Warrick raised an eyebrow, waiting for me to continue. I shouldn't have said anything, but it was too late to go back now.

"I was on a run that went bad," I explained. "My target caught me spying on him. We got into a fight. I took the jacket from him when it was over and used it to cover my wounds until I got back to the house." I paused to remember. "He was the first man I killed."

Warrick was quiet for a moment. "And you wanted a reminder of what you did," he stated quietly.

I nodded. "After that, I knew what I would become. What I *had* to become to keep Dro safe. As soon as I accepted it, the jacket started bringing me luck."

"Pretty strange luck," he said, half amused, half serious.

I shrugged. "You make your own, right?"

I flexed my arm back and forth, trying not to wince. It was sore and I'd need to watch it, but it was useable. I could feel Warrick staring at me again with that gentle, understanding look. I really wished he would stop doing that. It made me want to be closer to him.

"I found the door," Max called. "Can we get the hell out of here now?"

I walked away before Warrick could say anything else. He gave me a fair amount of distance before he stared following me. I decided that was a good thing. The only people I wanted to be close to right now were Isabel and Drake, so I could shove a knife into their hearts.

Max pulled open the door and walked through it into the tunnel. I took a deep breath and felt the pain from my latest fight. My body was sore from being crushed, I had new bruises, and my arm throbbed. Never mind the latest mental damage I'd gotten.

I had to push it all down. If I thought about it, the fear might cause me to falter, and I would get the three of us killed. I couldn't allow that. Not when Warrick and Max were already risking so much by coming on this brutal adventure with me.

I walked ahead of them.

CHAPTER THIRTY-ONE

Nearly thirty minutes later, we made the next left and came to a stop at the door. Max walked up to it and quickly found the pentagram. He sighed and held out his hand, looking at me.

"My turn," he said.

I gave him a respectful nod, then took out a silver knife and drew a shallow cut along his palm.

"Ow," he complained.

I rolled my eyes. "It's a scratch."

He made a sour face at me, reaching forward to touch the wall. "You are not the person who should be telling me the difference between a scratch and a serious injury."

Warrick chuckled behind me.

The lock on the door clicked and the door ground open. The light from our dull, and shockingly durable, flashlights showed nothing. No ghouls, no spiders, no traps. Just blackness.

It made me more nervous than anything I'd seen in the other rooms.

This door moved with excruciating slowness. I felt like I could run back through all the other rooms and endure all their trials again before it widened any further. Just when I thought we would be trapped in the hallway for ages, the door shuddered to a halt. We waited, but it didn't open any further. There was no way we could get through all at once.

"Perfect," I growled. "Just fucking perfect."

"I'll say," echoed Max. He paused, then added, "Makes you think something bad is behind that door."

I scoffed. "Ha, ha." I started to walk for the crevice. It wasn't even wide enough for me to walk straight through. I would have to press my back to the wall and slide in. "Maybe something s blocking it."

The moment I put my spine to the wall, Warrick grabbed my wrist. "You sure you want to go first?" He looked worried.

"Yeah," I lied. "It'll be a tight squeeze, so let me go through first. If the door starts acting up, I don't want one of you to be crushed."

The worry lines around Warrick's eyes deepened, but let go of me. Before I lost my resolve, I shuffled along the rough wall and into the room. Aside from my dim, flashlight beam, the room was black as pitch. I kept stalking forward, narrowing my eyes to see better, and then I heard it. A distant, angry growl. The door began to close behind me.

I whirled around. Warrick and Max shouted at me to come back, and they couldn't push it open. I wasn't fast enough. The door crunched shut, and I was in complete darkness.

Max and Warrick's yells were muffled from beyond the stone, telling me to hold on. It wasn't the most comforting thought, since I was alone in blackness with something that sounded very, very angry. My heart pounded violently in my chest. I couldn't wait. Maybe if I opened the exit door across the room, the entrance one would unlock and let the guys in. I had to do something. I couldn't just stand here. The flashlight on my belt was as effective to my surroundings as a penlight, but I could use it. I took careful steps and looked for any wires or mismatched steps that would spring a trap. There didn't seem to be any. I focused on going straight ahead, but it wasn't long before the shadows were playing tricks on me. I would imagine something streaking past my vision, but when I looked for it, I just saw black.

Then I heard it again, that low growling noise. I froze in place, listening carefully. I thought I was starting to hear things, until whatever it was growled again. I gripped my hatchet tightly.

A huge mass slammed into my back and knocked me onto the cold stone floor, yanking a scream from me. It was big, strong, and ripping through my oversized jacket, hunting for flesh. It shook me back and forth like a chew toy. Something like heavy paws were pressed onto my lower back as the creature continued to whip my torso back and forth. My muscles screamed at the thrashing, the monster trying to snap me in half. The flashlight was tossed from my belt, clattering away. I swung back with the hatchet, catching the monster in the leg. It roared angrily and let me go. I twisted onto my back to see what it was.

The beast stood as tall as an Irish wolfhound. It had no hair, but oily black skin and vicious looking claws on its feet. Its eyes were solid black except for a few red veins, and its serrated teeth poked over its snarling lips. Two small, curved horns were behind its sharp ears. Its body was lean and well muscled. It smelled like wet fur, blood, and sulfur.

My heart froze in chest. I had seen these things at Owl Creek. They'd been the creatures I'd feared the most. Even before Manny's demonology lessons, I had known what they were.

Hellhound.

The beast tensed and snarled. I got ready for it to jump on me again, but it didn't. Instead, it let out a vicious roar, and then disappeared back into the shadows of the room. I scrambled for the flashlight, hooking it onto my belt as best as I could with fumbling fingers. I grabbed a knife to calm myself. It didn't work. I could hear the hellhound growling in the shadows, but every time I thought I knew where it was, the sound would come from somewhere new.

I was toying with me.

A heavy swipe crashed into my right side and whipped me around, tearing apart more of my ragged jacket. Wincing, I fought to keep my balance and the monster leaped onto my chest, knocking me onto the ground and sinking its fangs into my shoulder.

I screamed as it ripped into my flesh, shaking its head from side to side, fighting to rip my arm off at the shoulder. I slammed my hatchet into the side of its head and stabbed the knife into its stomach. The hellhound's skin was tough and leathery, but I broke through and damaged it enough to let me go. Blood coated my chest, mine and the hellhounds and I barely had a second to breathe before the hellhound latched its teeth into my lower leg and threw me across the room.

I screamed at the pain in my bitten calf and wrenched hip, rolling violently across the hard, dark floor. I felt around my leg. Still there, thank god.

The hellhound smashed its head into my ribs, pummelling then, and turned me onto my side, jaws open and ready to clamp down for the kill.

I stabbed the hellhound in the eye. It howled and backed away into the shadows. I needed to do something, *fast*. It would rip me apart before I stabbed it. I went for the holy water on my hip, unscrewing the cap. The hellhound was suddenly behind me, its teeth sinking into my undamaged shoulder.

More pain tore through my upper body, blood soaking my clothes. Gritting my teeth, I threw the holy water over my shoulder into the hellhound's face. It roared and released me again. I could smell burning demon flesh, and now I could also see smoke. I got to my feet, fiery pain shooting down my injured leg and raging through my shoulders. I narrowed my eyes on the trail of smoke catching in my flashlight beam, followed its acrid scent. I lunged forward and hammered my hatchet down onto the back of the hellhound's neck. It barked angrily as it crumpled, but I kept driving the hatchet down as fast as my injured shoulders would allow. Every strike cut deeper. I poured holy water on the hellhound to keep it in too much pain to escape.

I reached the bone in the hellhound's neck, and kept hacking away.

I don't know how long it took until I had all but severed the hellhound's head from its body. By the time it dissolved into ash, my arms felt like lines of fire. There wasn't an inch of me that didn't hurt. Adrenaline and fear made my whole body tremble. I screamed it all away.

I stood there and let some of the pain fade until I was sure I wasn't going to collapse, then breathed again. I took the flashlight off my belt and shone it around the room, finding the door I'd entered. I tested my weight on my injured shin. It was stiff, but I forced myself to get used to it.

Warrick and Max were still shouting, trying to find a way in. I limped to the door and found another pentagram symbol. Rather than cut open my hand again, I smeared some of the fresh blood from one of my shoulders onto my fingers and painted it over the symbol. The door clicked and rumbled open. I planted my feet, fighting to stay upright.

Max and Warrick rushed into the chamber, their eyes wide with horror as they looked at me.

"Jesus," Max breathed, "did you get into a fight with a fucking dog or something?"

"Actually, yes," I mumbled.

Warrick moved up to my side and looked at my latest injuries, frowning intensely.

"It looks worse than it is," I said, carefully taking off my jacket and trying not to wince very much.

He narrowed his eyes. "I doubt that."

"I'll be fine," I told him stubbornly.

I glanced down at the bites on my shoulders. They burned fiercely, but weren't as deep as I thought. The jacket's leather protected me, once again. The hellhound really had just wanted to toy with me. I shrugged them, wincing as tense pain flared in them. I gritted my teeth and forced myself to adapt to the pain. The hurt was just something I would have to deal with.

I started walking back into the room. Warrick stepped in front of me. "You should stay here," he said. "Max and I will bring Andromeda back."

My eyes narrowed. "I'm not going to sit here and hope for the best. I'm going to save my sister."

I tried to get past him, but Warrick didn't move. "You've been through enough, Constance. You look like you can barely stand. No one would think less of you if you stopped and let us do this."

I clenched my fists. "No." Dro was so close– *so close*. I couldn't give up now. I wouldn't.

"Warrick," said Max, "she's gonna come no matter what you tell her. Might as well stop trying."

He glanced between us and read my eyes for a long, grim time. Then he looked at my shoulders and leg. "Will you at least let me stop your bleeding?"

I sighed. "Fine. But hurry up."

Warrick frowned, then knelt down and started wrapping my leg. To distract myself from the pain and his too soft touch, I looked at Max.

"That door was probably meant to stay locked until the hellhound was killed," I said.

Max blinked. "Wait, you fought and killed a *hellhound?!*"

"Yeah."

"What did it look like?"

I described it to him as best as I could. He blinked again, a boyish grin starting to play on his face. "Holy shit, you fought and killed a hellhound! That's gonna piss off the bad guys for sure."

"Great. More demons hating me. Just what I need."

"Hey, at least you're giving them a hard time." He grinned. "It's your favourite thing!"

Rolling my eyes, I watched Warrick stand and gently touch my elbows, nudging them upright. I winced at the pull in my arms, but raised them as much as I could. He leaned close, wrapping me in a light embrace, and tenderly coiled the gauze under my arms and around my shoulders. He radiated so much heat, and I could smell the blood and sweat from the earlier fights, but also that musky pine scent of his.

"Thanks," I murmured.

"Try not to run off alone again." He sighed, and I felt the breath tease my hair. "It's a miracle you're still standing. Lucky jacket indeed."

I swallowed the lump in my throat and looked at Max seriously while Warrick finished turning me into a mummy. "Can you see what's going on with Dro?"

The grin left his face. "They're doing that ritual, trying to open the Hell Gate. She's trapped with them. I..." He held his breath. "It doesn't look good, Constance."

I didn't ask him what he meant. I'd find out soon enough.

Warrick finally backed away from me, reaching into the small med pouch strapped to his waist—I'd forgotten about those—and took out a bottle of painkillers. He skimmed the label, opened, the top, and gave me the prescribed amount. I took the little pills and dry swallowed them. My shin and shoulders still throbbed and burned, but the painkillers would do wonders soon. I tried to smile at the demon slayer, but there was no humor in his stern eyes.

I walked past him and Max, moving as quickly as I could to the other end of the room. I had no idea how I was going to rescue my sister given the state I was in. From what Max had said, Dro was probably going to have to be carried out.

Doesn't matter. She needs you.

I walked faster.

I reached the far wall and pulled the door open, slipping out into the tunnels. A faint red glow flickered on the left, so I turned in its direction. We turned off our flashlights and Warrick moved up to my side. As we got closer to the light, we heard faint chanting. It didn't sound Latin, or any human language for that matter. It was all growls and snarls.

We saw an archway ahead leading to a stone staircase and wide, shadow-draped outcroppings. We got on our stomachs and tucked into the outcroppings, staring down into a wide cavern about a hundred feet across in both directions, torches spotted into the wall to add more ominous light. The floor was about forty feet below us, keeping us hidden for a now, though we'd be seen before long.

I skimmed over the cavern, passing the details until I found my sister. And when I did, I saw her covered in blood.

CHAPTER THIRTY-TWO

I t took every ounce of sense and willpower not to run for her, screaming like a Valkyrie for revenge. If we were going to save Dro, we had to be smart.

But there was so much blood...

Dro lay on a grey stone altar, her wrists and ankles shackled with iron cuffs, leaving her spread eagled and completely vulnerable. Her snow-white hair spilled around her head and down the sides of the stone. She wore what might have been a simple white gown once, but now it was drenched in red. Her hands and feet were soaked in it, faint streaks were in her hair, and more on her face. I couldn't tell if it was her blood or someone else's, but it didn't matter. Dro wasn't moving. She might be unconscious, but she had to be alive. Isabel needed her for the summoning, and the ritual didn't seem to be over yet. But it was completely possible that she was being bled to death.

On either side of me, the guys were as speechless. Warrick was still, but Max trembled. Or maybe that was me. Focus, I needed to focus, or I would never save my sister or keep my friends alive.

I looked around at the rest of the cavern. The tunnel walls

had been smoothed out and curved in the center. The altar itself was on a small stage washed with even more blood, a thirty foot pentagram circling the stone and ignited by fire. The flames were close to Dro, but not hurting her. I had to squint my eyes to see her blood steadily dripping into the fire.

At the head of stone altar, dressed in a black robe and chanting in demon tongue, was Isabel. She was completely focused on what she was doing, clearly excited about it.

I turned my head back to the center of the cavern, seeing a bulky frame against the wall. *Drake.*

Warrick noticed him too, tensing beside me. I put my hand on his arm to keep him from moving. We needed a plan, and like me, he knew it. But also like me, he wasn't happy about it.

"Oh my God," Max breathed next to me.

We looked over and followed the direction of his finger as he pointed to the far right corner of the room. I squinted, not sure what I was looking at. It just looked like a huge pile of...

Bodies.

Dozens of them, heaped like trash. I understood where all the blood had come from. Sephiel had said that opening the Gates of Hell would require a lot of blood, but seeing it was worse than I imagined. Innocent people had been slaughtered for no fucking reason. Anger and disgust built in me, and I struggled to keep myself under control. I turned my head back in Isabel's direction as she performed the ritual.

"What do we do?" Warrick whispered in my ear.

I looked into the cavern as Isabel chanted. The area was too open. Drake was on guard, his head turned in the direction of the ritual. There were no other demons I could see, but it hardly mattered when Isabel could call them with a snap of her fingers.

"I don't suppose anyone is carrying a sniper rifle?" Max muttered.

"Yeah, in my pocket full of dreams," I replied. I frowned. "We can't get past without Drake seeing."

Warrick carefully cracked open his shotgun and loaded it quickly. He clicked it shut, then handed it to me.

"We need a diversion. I'll get Drake's attention, and give you and Max the chance to get Andromeda out of here."

I raised my eyebrows at him, remembering how badly he'd been hurt the last time he fought Drake. "Then take your gun so he doesn't shoot you."

Warrick's eyes were lasers. "He won't shoot me. He'll go for the up close and personal kill."

He didn't need to explain anymore. Bad blood ran deep for some people. Drake and Warrick had enough to fill an ocean.

"John," I said, hoping he would listen if I used his first name. "It's not a good idea. It's too dangerous." Somehow, in the past few days, I'd gotten used to him being around. Of his big heart, kindness, and patience.

He smirked. "I seem to remember saying similar things to you." The smile left his face as quickly as it came. "This is the best way, and you know it. Dro is only going to suffer more if we keep waiting. Let me do what I can for you, then get her out of here."

"John–"

He put his hand on my face, stilling my words. Its warmth pulsed into me, and my heart strained.

"I couldn't protect my sister, Constance. Let me help you protect yours."

Warrick suddenly pushed forward and kissed me. I could have pushed him away, but… I didn't want to. How long had it been since I kissed someone? Since I let myself dream of doing so? His lips were soft, his kiss passionate. His scent filled every breath, long dark eyelashes brushing against my cheek. Desire rushed through me, and I pushed myself closer to him. I was lost, and craving more. I had become attached to him, and now I didn't want him to leave. If he did, I might never see him again. I gave in, gave him something to come back to.

Kissing him hard, sweeping my tongue long his, nipping his lower lip.

He pulled back, green eyes sparkling like emeralds under the sun. They were filled with longing, satisfaction, and hunger for more.

He broke my heart even more when he smiled sadly and said, "Be safe, Constance."

Warrick pushed himself off the ground and walked down the staircase before I could beg him to stay. Max and I pressed low to the ground, trying to stay small, hoping Warrick wasn't about to get himself killed.

"Well, well, well," Drake jeered as he walked toward Warrick. His husky drawl echoed off the cavern walls. "What are you doing here all alone, Johnny-boy? Did you ditch that dead bitch's crew? Or did you just miss me?"

"I'm not here because of her," Warrick growled. "I'm here because I'm going to kill you."

Drake laughed. "I've always liked your ambition, Johnny-boy. It's nice to have a dream."

I looked at Max. "Get ready to move," I whispered, clutching the shotgun. "Don't go near Isabel. Work on getting Dro free."

"How? Did you bring massive bolt cutters, or are those in your pocket full of dreams, too?" I shot him a look. "Sorry. I'm stressed out."

I patted his hand. "Isabel probably has the keys. I'll get them from her. Just be ready."

"But you're right," I heard the bounty hunter say, his grating voice carrying across the cavern. "It's been years since we started this. Tonight seems like a good night to finish it."

Drake's words sent a chill down my spine. He wasn't going to let Warrick get away this time, and I couldn't get involved. I continued to watch them as I moved down the steps. Warrick raised his fists, holding himself in a boxing stance. He circled around so Drake's back was to us.

Max and I raced down the stairs as Warrick and Drake launched themselves at each other. Warrick barely missed a hit that would have knocked his lights out. He drove his fist into Drake's stomach, then punched him in the jaw, and kicked Drake in the ribs. He tried again, but the bounty hunter lunged forward and punched him in the chest. Warrick stumbled back, stepping aside when Drake's fist flew past him again. They were too close, and Drake's elbow slammed into the side of Warrick's head. The demon slayer stumbled, and was kicked to the ground.

I *hated* seeing Warrick getting hurt to buy us time, but I couldn't be in two places at once. I had to hold onto the belief that the demon slayer would turn the fight around, and that Drake would be the one lying broken at the end.

I sprinted for the stage, where Isabel's chanting grew intense and loud. If she noticed a deadly fistfight in the cavern, she didn't seem to care. Which meant the spell was drawing to a close.

Isabel shouted the last words of her spell, throwing her hands out on either side of her body. Dro suddenly woke up. Her body snapped back and forth. She screamed at the same time the portal opened.

It was the biggest huge, at least triple my size. Hellish flames twisted out of it, the heat so intense that I started to sweat. Dro thrashed and screamed on the altar. Isabel laughed manically behind her, but we were almost there.

Then a demon stepped through the portal.

It had the shape of a devastatingly beautiful man. Seven feet tall, his skin marble white and flawless, his muscles clear and defined. All he wore was a black loincloth lined with gold. Long, white hair hung straight down to the base of his spine, not a lock of it out of place. Growing out of his back were four horned, bat-like wings, the larger ones on his shoulder blades while the smaller ones exited from his lower ribs. His eyes were black from lid to lid. A cold, devastating, merciless black.

For a moment I was frozen with fear and wonder. I'd never seen a creature so mesmerizing, so extraordinary. I didn't know whether to run away screaming in terror, or to drop to the ground and kiss his feet. Power pulsed off him like a heartbeat, washing over my body and nearly crippling me. He could do anything to me, and I wouldn't care. Whatever this demon was, he was stronger than anything I had ever known was able to exist. More than the angels. More than Dro.

Isabel smiled. "Lord Lucifer," she breathed. "You have come."

CHAPTER THIRTY-THREE

My heart skipped a beat.

Lucifer. Satan. The Antichrist. She had summoned *the fucking Devil.*

I might not know everything about angels and demons, but I knew Lucifer was the biggest and nastiest of them. He would crush me between his fingers before I could get within ten feet of stopping him.

So I didn't try to stop him. I went for Isabel.

Everyone was so shocked that *the Devil himself* had been successfully called up, that I was able to raise the shotgun and aim it at Isabel.

She stared at Lucifer with wide, gleaming eyes, tears of joy shining down her grinning cheeks. She was so wrapped in bliss that I thought she wouldn't see me preparing to blast a hole through her.

Then she raised her hands and threw a spell at me.

I didn't even have the chance to scream when an invisible hand gripped my heart, twisting and wrenching it brutally, trying to pull it from its valves. The shotgun clattered from my hands as I dropped and gasped in air, but I couldn't breathe. It was excruciating, feeling the organ being jerked back and forth inside my chest. Isabel gave my heart another sharp squeeze and I thought for sure she had crushed it. Pain exploded inside me, a horrible, tearing feeling.

A blaze of light from the altar in front of me, and Isabel let out a sharp yelp. The grip on my heart was suddenly gone, expanding quickly and painfully. I forced myself to breathe, fighting the nausea and coppery taste of blood in my mouth, and looked up from the floor.

Isabel placed a hand over her face, stumbling around as if she'd been blinded. I looked to my right, and saw my little sister through the flames, one hand shaking, but outstretched. She used her power to save my life. Her icy blue eyes were filled with emotions that moved too fast for me to read. Relief. Fear. Desperation. Regret.

But she knew I was here, and that I would save her. I shot to my feet, my previous injuries numbed thanks to the painkillers. Adrenaline coursed through my veins to fuel me. I jumped up onto the stage, blood soaking the bottom of my boots. I looked at the flaming, bloody pentagram, trying to see how I could get past it.

I turned my head, and then I was staring into the eyes of Lucifer.

Fear and desire made me ache for him, and I couldn't move. I wanted to run from him. I wanted to run to him. He read my eyes, and a sharp sensation filled my head, like clawed fingers probing me. But not controlling. I had to move. I wasn't letting him near Dro.

I heard a furious war cry behind me. I turned just as Isabel arched her arm, dagger raised high. I pulled my hatchet out and hooked her on the blade. I caught a small glimpse of silver on her belt. *Keys.* I punched her in the face, then yanked the keys from her belt.

Lucifer was too powerful for me to do anything against, but Isabel was someone I could fight.

I kicked Isabel in the stomach to get distance between us then looked over my shoulder, finding Max. He stared at Lucifer with a mix of shock, awe, and horror.

"Max!" I screamed, throwing the keys toward him. "Get Dro!"

I turned to Isabel, and we stared to dance. She proved to be more competent than I expected. She ducked and weaved from a lot of my strikes, lashing out with some nasty moves of her own. Like me, she fought dirty. Like me, she was determined to win.

I swiped my hatchet at her head, but she ducked, staying low and trying to stab me in the ribs. I kicked her hand away, but the move exposed the other side of my body. She punched me in the kidneys, sharp pain filling my already damaged side. I hooked Isabel's dagger with my hatchet again when she tried to cut my throat, pulling it away from me. I kicked the inside of her leg then pushed forward, driving my knee into her ribs a couple times. Isabel tried to stab me in the neck again, but I grabbed her wrist and held it down. Then I slammed my forehead into her nose, feeling it crunch under my skull.

Then Isabel cheated and used another spell.

I gasped and felt my body tighten as pain consumed me. It felt like a million flaming needles were prodding me over and over again. My nerves seared and my insides contracted sharply. Even if I wanted to scream, I don't think I could have found the air to do so, given how brutally my lungs were burning. The pain was so intense that I couldn't fight back.

As suddenly as it happened, it ended. Isabel let me go and I dropped heavily onto the bloody floor. I heard Dro scream Max's name and looked up. Max lay crumpled on the stage, his back to me, unmoving. I tried to crawl to Max, but saw a shadow shift from the corner of my eye.

Lucifer stepped through the fires into the pentagram, and stood by Dro's side.

I shot to my feet, swaying in pain, and lifted my hatchet, arching my arm to throw it at the fallen angel, but someone seized my arm and stopped me. I whirled my head felt Isabel's fist slam into my face. Through the haze of pain, I watched her recover her dagger and arch her arm to stab me with it.

Desperation and rage fuelled me. I swatted her arm away and slashed up with my hatchet. The blade sliced along her chest, through her throat, and out of her chin. Her eyes went wide. I swiped with my hatchet again, the blade slicing across her neck and spraying more blood onto me. Isabel collapsed onto the ground, blood squirting out of her severed throat. After a couple seconds, her raspy breathing stopped and she stared up at the ceiling with unseeing eyes.

I didn't give her body a second look. I turned and hurled my hatchet at Lucifer.

He caught the fucking weapon in his hand, not even needing to see it. Lucifer examined the hatchet, then dropped it. He looked at me, then clawed his way into my head. He searched through my brain and saw everything that made me who I was. He knew all my secrets, all my passions and fears. He clawed up memories and emotions, creating a maelstrom inside me. There wasn't a fucking thing I could do to stop him, and part of me didn't want to. I was human, and he was the most incredible, most terrifying being I had ever encountered. I loved that I wanted to hate him. I hated that I wanted to love him.

I sucked in a heavy breath when he finished reading me, tasting the smoke, dust, and blood in the air. Fear crept back into my heart like it had when I was fourteen years old, desperately taking my sister away from the slaughter at Owl Creek.

Lucifer's black eyes never left mine, never blinked once. I clenched my fists, but I couldn't stop shaking.

"Don't fucking touch her," I warned him, voice trembling.

Nothing passed over Lucifer's face. No anger, no disdain, no amusement. If I hadn't seen him grab my hatchet out of the air, I would have thought he was just a statue. A mesmerizing, fearsome statue.

"Why do you love her?" Lucifer finally asked me.

The perfection and power in his voice almost had my knees buckling. A flawless, rolling baritone that could belong to a commander as easily as a passionate lover. It was as beautiful as the rest of him.

There's no way I can fight him.

But I wouldn't leave Dro to him. I wouldn't run. "She's my sister," I said. Simple, and the truth. Lucifer would know if I lied.

"She has brought you nothing but sorrow and pain. She is the reason your family is dead. The reason you became a killer. The reason you live in constant fear. The reason you are damned. Why do you love her?"

Dro had said similar things to me not long ago. She thought my life would have been different if I had never found her. That I would have been safe and normal. But I wasn't a person who spent much time imaging the 'what-ifs' and 'maybes.' There was no changing my actions. There was only dealing with the consequences. I was facing off with Lucifer, and there was going to be a consequence for it. Just as there would be if I did what Dro had suggested, and run.

Living with the Devil as an enemy was easier than living without Dro. I couldn't stop my fear, but I wouldn't survive without her. She was the only person who kept me whole and sane. She was the only person who made me feel human.

"Because she's my sister," I repeated.

Lucifer stared at me for a long time. I desperately wanted to look away, though I never wanted to turn my eyes. I wanted to get Dro free, to do *anything*. But I couldn't. I was in way over my head and a thousand miles from shore.

"Do you think I love her any less?" Lucifer said. He slowly turned his head to Dro. "She is my child."

I didn't take the time to comprehend what he said, because he reached out to touch Dro's hair.

"I said don't fucking—"

Lucifer lifted his hand. A huge force of energy slammed into my chest and hurled me across the stage into the wall. I crashed into it brutally and felt my ribs finally crack. Pain exploded everywhere when I landed on the ground. Then he lifted me up and threw me into the wall again. Something else cracked. Then he threw me one more time just because he could.

"Stop!" Dro screamed.

Lucifer dropped me. Now that the painkillers were wearing off, I felt like I'd been run over by a train. I was completely covered in blood from rolling on the stage floor, tasted it in my mouth and felt it soaking my hair, had broken bones everywhere, and was all but immobilized by pain.

Lucifer hadn't moved from where he stood. He looked at Dro like she held the key to all his dreams.

"Please," I heard Dro whisper shakily. "Please, let her go. Let them all go. I'll stay. Just don't hurt them."

My heart crumbled. *Don't do it, little sister. Don't give up. Please don't give up.*

Lucifer didn't seem to have heard her desperate request. The demon continued to stroke her hair and face without emotion.

"I have waited so long for you, my child," he crooned. "You are exactly as I created you to be. So beautiful, so powerful. You are the key to saving those of your blood."

His hand slid down her throat, between her breasts, and stopped at her ribs.

"Now it is time for you to bring them salvation."

Lucifer's hand plunged into Dro's side like a knife, disappearing up to his wrist. Blood pooled around his hand. Her back arched and she strained against the cuffs holding her down, screaming from a pain so agonizing I couldn't even begin to imagine it.

I crawled across the bloody floor as fast as I could. I pushed myself up and collapsed. I lifted my head again when Dro stopped screaming.

Lucifer's hand had left her body. He held one of her blood-soaked ribs in his fist.

Sephiel's words about the spell to open the Gates of Hell shot through my brain.

Lucifer had chosen my sister to be the key to Hell on earth.

I forced myself to my feet. My vision was swimming, but I had to do something. I couldn't lie down on the floor and pray for it to be over quickly. I had to act, even if I had no fucking clue what to do. Even when I knew Lucifer would kill me with a flick of his wrist.

He held my sister's rib high in the air, then raked his fingernails along his chest. Black demon blood welled from the four scratches, but his face was empty. He smeared his blood on his clean hand, then ran it along the length of Dro's rib.

A blast of red fire consumed it, followed by a small explosion of white light. Dro's rib shattered into a million tiny shards that dissolved into ash. A sudden wind picked up from Lucifer, flattening me onto the ground. I winced and rolled again, picking myself up. I was almost at the altar–

Dro's body arched again, a steady white glow coming from her chest. Lucifer was watching intently. White flame suddenly burst from Dro's skin. She was living a nightmare.

But she isn't screaming.

Panic filled my chest and I tried to run without passing out. I wasn't moving nearly fast enough.

The white-hot fire consuming my sister began to glow brighter. So bright I had to stop and cover my eyes so I wouldn't be blinded. A high-pitched buzz followed. I dropped to my knees, squeezing my eyes shut and holding my ears.

There was a crack in the air. Heat swelled in the room. It became so hot I could feel blisters forming on my skin. A blast of that light and heat rippled through the air, just over my head as I ducked down. I felt it slam into the stone walls around me, rising into the ceiling. I had never witnessed so much power come from Dro before.

Suddenly it was over. The world went dark and the temperature dropped so rapidly I got goose bumps. My ears were ringing and I had to blink to adjust my eyesight, but I spotted the altar.

The flames on the pentagram were out. Lucifer was gone. Dro was motionless on the stone.

I got to my feet and shambled toward her, hearing a sharp crack. I turned my head and saw the wall across from me had a huge crease in it that was growing wider. I looked up. The roof had the same splintering lines running along it.

I finally made it to the altar and looked at Dro. The chains had been melted off her wrists and ankles. Her eyes were closed and her skin deathly pale. Blood and sweat soaked her hair. Gore spread across the gown, tightening it to Dro's body. The fist-sized hole in her side oozed, turning the side of her dress almost black with blood. Gasping in shaking breaths, I pulled off my jacket and cinched it tightly around her torso. Not a flinch from Dro. Tears blurred my eyes. I pressed my hands against the wound. Rubble started dropping from the roof above me, slowly at first, then faster and faster.

We weren't getting out of this. I could barely stand. I couldn't carry my sister so far with so many injuries. But I could stay with her.

I lifted Dro off the altar and slid onto the ground with her, my back pressed against the stone slab. I around her, my chin resting on her head and my arms wrapped around her back and her shins. Her blood warmed my stomach.

The pieces of the roof fell harder and in larger chunks,

booming in the cavern. I thought I heard my name screamed once or twice, but the sound was lost in the collapsing chamber. I closed my eyes and hugged my sister tightly, pressing one of my hands to the back of her head.

"I tried," I whispered. "I swear I tried."

I always knew it would end this way. That I would die with my sister in darkness and pain, covered in blood. I'd done my best. My only regret was that it hadn't been enough.

The roof collapsed, and everything went black.

CHAPTER THIRTY-FOUR

Awareness came slowly to my broken body. First the terrible, thumping pain of broken and bruised bones, then the pounding in my head, and tightly pinched limbs.

I held something. Dro. She felt warm. If she was still warm, then she had to be alive.

My fingers protested as I moved them. They were covered in blood and dust, but they found their way to Dro's neck. There was a flicker of a pulse. We were both still alive. I could get her out of here.

Holding my sister close to my chest, I felt around me. Rock pressed surrounded us. They must have fallen and bounced around the altar, creating a strange bubble of stone. No light shone through the rubble covering us. We didn't have a lot of air. Much as I enjoyed not being crushed, I didn't want to suffocate. Dro was breathing slowly, but this air wouldn't keep her alive. I didn't know if Warrick, Max, or the angels had survived. I wasn't going to be counting on them, either.

I carefully shifted Dro so she was resting against the altar, tightening my jacket around her body to slow the blood flow from her ribs. The ribs that remained. I cringed at the thought, but kept working. My body felt rubbery and agonized as I struggled to move. I bit down on my lip to stop a scream, then lifted a hand to work at the rubble. None of my fingers were broken, but every twitch sent waves of pain down my arm. I had to be very careful and watch what I was doing. One wrong shift and I might move a supporting rock. After that, the rubble would drop onto my head and kill me.

I worked and worked, shifting smaller, cracked rocks, finding more air, staying calm and breathing in as few breaths as possible. I checked on Dro, found her breathing, and dug some more. Eventually, I made a space wide enough for my head. Then for my arm. I pulled my trembling legs underneath me, lifted my sore shoulder, and carefully slid my arm through the hole, gingerly feeling around above me. Pain shot down the limb. God, I hope it didn't get trapped in the stone. I could only work by feel. I couldn't see, the flashlight broken when Lucifer turned me into a rag doll. His image ripped through my mind, standing tall and confident, holding my sister's bloody rib in his hand while she screamed and burned...

Tears streamed down my eyes, but I pushed away the tumult in my chest and felt around. The tips of my fingers brushed something flaky and dry. *Dirt.* My heart leaped. Maybe just our section of the roof crumbled and filled the chamber? I hoped so. If the whole thing collapsed, we might been in a tomb. I wiggled my fingers a little more, turning my head so the dust wouldn't go into my mouth or eyes. I kept moving my fingers, dirt tumbling down my shirt and dusting my aching shoulder. After a minute, more dirt than I expected crumbled down. I quickly yanked my hand back and landed on my ass. Pain sparked through my legs and up my battered back. God. Had I ever been this hurt?

I scooted back next to Dro as dirt spilled through the hole I had made. I covered my hand with my mouth to control my breathing and keep from inhaling dirt. I shielded Dro and hoped I hadn't caused a cave-in.

After a few seconds, the flow stopped, forming a small pile at the tip of my boots. . I smoothed out the pile, spreading it flat on the floor. Once it was gone, I moved back to the hole and looked through. I carefully slid my arm back in the crevice and pushed up as high as I could, straining my shoulder. My fingernails caught dirt and pulled it away from the surface. More soil started crumbling down, and I moved back to Dro again.

I did this two times before I felt fresh air above me. I blinked in confusion. I couldn't have gotten that far. I stopped moving my hand, hearing dirt being scraped above me.

As if people were trying to dig us out.

I pulled my hand back and sat down, crab-walking back to Dro. I checked her pulse. It had gotten weaker. Then I heard something, like distant shouting. I twisted around the altar and listened to the voices above me.

Voices that sounded like they belonged to Max and Warrick.

I crawled to the hole and looked up. I could see a thread of light. Dirt was being forced away from the hole. The far end of the hole I had made became wider as rubble was yanked away from the path I'd made. A couple minutes later, light blinded me. I winced and blocked it with my hand. I blinked to adjust my eyes, then lowered my hand as rock was shifted above me.

Sephiel and Rorikel moved dirt and rock faster at supernatural speeds, but Max and Warrick tried to keep pace with them. They were all covered in dirt and blood, though Max and Warrick looked far worse than the angels. Warrick dropped into the gap, green eyes shining with relief and concern. He held out his hand to me.

I reached up and clasped it to let him know I was okay. It was solid, warm, and alive. He squeezed my hand tightly, a weak smile spreading across his face. Relief swarmed my raw heart, so strong I could have cried.

"You're alive," I rasped.

He grinned. "Drake's not as strong as he thinks he is."

I laughed weakly, then pulled back, getting a confused look from him. "Dro's down here." Tears filled my throat, and I almost couldn't say, "She's hurt."

Warrick nodded, understanding. Behind him, Max and Sephiel dug faster. I crawled back to my sister and scooped her up as best as I could. My lucky jacket had soaked up almost all of her blood. She felt too light, too limp.

"It's okay, Dro," I whispered in her ear. "You're almost out of here. Max is waiting for you."

Dro made no movement and no sound. My heart twisted and sobs choked me as I brought her into the light. Warrick and Rorikel were digging more rock away. Sephiel dropped into the newly created space, only a couple feet away from me. His auburn hair was disheveled and blood caked the side of his face, but his blue eyes were alive and burning.

I lifted Dro up and looked Sephiel in the eyes. "She's lost blood," I managed to say. "He tore out her rib."

For a second, he froze with more terror than I thought an angel possible. But the second ended, and he lowered himself down, placed Dro over his shoulder and lifted her out of the tunnel. I watched my little sister disappear with Sephiel, Max and Rorikel right on his heels.

They would be able to save her. They had to. She was breathing. She had a pulse. They just had to heal her. I closed my eyes and swayed.

"Constance!"

I blinked and looked up just as Warrick reached down and grabbed my hand. My shoulders were still roaring in pain, but Warrick gripped my hands and lifted me out of the tunnel. I whimpered, but didn't fight him.

Fresh morning air was a welcome chill in my lungs. I drank in as much of it as I could, so much that I choked on it. Dizziness hit in a wave. I swayed again, but strong arms caught me and held me up. I closed my eyes and pressed against a warm body.

Fingers moved through my hair. I breathed in the smell of dirt, blood, and musky pine. I held him tighter.

"I got you," Warrick murmured. "You're safe."

I blinked slowly, unable to think of anything to say to Warrick. I couldn't begin to tell him how grateful I was that he'd saved us, or how happy I was that he was alive. I pulled back to look at him.

A bruise was forming on his jaw and around one of his eyes. Dust coated his oaky hair, scratches and blood covering his face and chest. He must have been in pain, but he didn't seem to care about it. Instead, Warrick focused on me, gently brushing my hair behind my ear. Concern and relief sparkled in his eyes. I was so glad to see him I almost couldn't breathe.

Breathing. "Dro."

Warrick nodded, and helped me limp past the churned earth to the rest of the group.

Sephiel, Rorikel, and Max were kneeling on the ground beside Dro. Both angels had their hands over Dro's torn skin, glowing light coming from their hands and fierce determination in their eyes. Max clasped one of Dro's hands in both of his, muttering a prayer. Tears lined his cheeks.

Warrick helped lower me down to Dro's side next to Max. Pain shrieked trough me, but I touched my sister's arm and stared at her face. Warrick place his jacket over my shoulders and sat next to me, keeping me close. I leaned against him, feeling his heart pounding in his chest. I felt so glad for it, because I was falling apart, and I needed someone to hold me together. I didn't know if Dro would survive. Tears wouldn't stop leaking from my eyes. My little sister had suffered more than any other sixteen year old girl ought to. I needed to see her survive this. It would be too much, otherwise. Too unfair.

The healing glow from the angels stopped. Sephiel put his hand on Dro's forehead.

"She will live," he said. "But for now she must rest. Her

body has to restore itself. We have accommodated for the missing rib as much as possible. But it will never grow back."

Max made a low groan next to me. Warrick squeezed my hand.

"What happened?" I asked with a scratchy voice.

"Drake hit me pretty hard when the roof started falling. When I got up, he was gone." Warrick looked down, his face tight and grim. "After that pulse came from Dro and the roof began caving in, Sephiel and Rorikel appeared and got us out. They were going to come back for you, but..."

"We could not sense the Nephilim," Rorikel answered flatly. "We were not aware if she was alive or dead. We needed to retrieve those we knew had survived."

I focused on Dro. If I looked at Rorikel, I might try to use the rest of my strength to stand up and punch him.

"Constance," Warrick said, "that... That thing Isabel summoned. What was it?"

I shivered, remembering his exquisite beauty. His glorious wings and power. The way I'd nearly drowned in despair and desire for him. His stony face and consuming black eyes.

The way he called Dro his 'child', and then ripped out her rib.

I shivered again and Warrick gently rubbed my arm to calm me down, mindful of its damage. I steeled myself and took a deep breath.

"Lucifer. Isabel summoned Lucifer."

The air became so silent you could have heard a pin drop ten feet away. I could feel everyone staring at me, but I never shifted my eyes from Dro. I knew she needed sleep and the angels had healed her, but I wished she would open her eyes. I needed to see for myself that she was okay.

"That is not possible," Rorikel breathed. For once, he sounded like he actually could emote something other than anger and disdain for myself and the human race. But Rorikel sounding afraid wasn't helping the situation.

"It was him," I said. "I know it." I held my breath. "He called her his child."

The angels went still again. After another long time, Rorikel spoke again.

"It is not possible," he repeated. "She is Nephilim. Lucifer is a fallen angel, King of Hell and demons. She cannot be of his blood, unless..."

He trailed off and it was like someone had switched on a light in his head. He reached over and touched some of Dro's blood. He lifted it to his nose and smelled it. He pulled back and got to his feet. He looked repulsed.

"I thought she smelled like demon blood because she had it spilled upon her. But her blood *is* demon."

Sephiel got to his feet. "She is Nephilim, Rorikel. You know–"

"She is *both*."

Shock and fear began to settle in Rorikel's grey eyes. "She is the blood of both an angel and a demon. Everiel lived long enough to birth the ultimate abomination."

"Don't call her that," I growled.

Rorikel turned on me. "You do not understand. That force she released has now opened not only the Gates of Hell, but the Gates of Heaven. If Lucifer has been freed, there is nothing stopping him from entering the Heaven Gate and destroying Paradise."

I knew that was bad. *Apocalyptically* bad. The weight of what he'd said should have sunk into me more, the way it had for Warrick and Max. The demon slayer and the gifted boy were looking at Rorikel like the fire was already falling from the sky. I probably would have looked the same, but I couldn't focus on anything but Dro.

Until Rorikel pulled out his sword.

Max shot to his feet. "What the fuck are you doing?" he demanded.

"There is only one way to prevent further destruction," the angel said. "The abomination must die."

He raised his sword and plunged it down. I wrenched away from Warrick, but I wasn't going to be fast enough to stop Rorikel.

A blast of gold light hit the white-blond angel in the chest, knocking him back and away from Dro. Sephiel stepped in front of us, his sword in one hand and heavenfire in the other. Rorikel looked stunned, but his expression quickly became infuriated.

"Traitor," Rorikel hissed.

"We were tasked with protecting this child," Sephiel said. "She must not come to harm."

"Our orders were given before we knew what she was," he barked. "The abomination shall be the doom of Heaven, Sephiel. You know this. She cannot live."

Rorikel took a step forward, but Sephiel blasted him again, pushing his partner back. Or ex-partner, from the look of hatred that crossed the other angel's face.

"I will not let you harm her, Rorikel. Not you, or any other angel. We failed to protect her from Lucifer once. We must not do so again." Sephiel took a careful step forward. "There is still a chance, brother. We can stop Lucifer. She has the power to open the Gates, but he will also have given her the power to close them. Killing her will accomplish nothing. She does not deserve to die."

Sephiel sounded as reasonable as he always did. He made excellent points. He spoke the truth. Rorikel just refused to listen.

He shook his head, looking almost sad for a moment. "You choose them, the humans, over your own kind. You always have. But that isn't why you want to keep that creature alive, Sephiel.

You're holding onto a memory, and your clemency shall be your downfall."

Rorikel threw a blast of heavenfire at Sephiel so fast I was sure it was going to hit him. Rorikel never did anything half way. He meant to kill his partner.

But Sephiel was faster. He moved like lightning, snapping out his hand and using some sort of invisible force to push the light away. Rorikel let out a furious shout and charged, his sword raised high. Sephiel blocked his strike, and all the ones that followed it. The angels moved with such speed and grace it was like watching a deadly ballet.

Their white coats arched and spun as they slashed and parried one another. I'd never seen two fighters more evenly matched. I was rooting for Sephiel, but Rorikel was angry enough to be a serious threat.

Rorikel spun and drew his sword up, the tip of the blade slicing diagonally across Sephiel's chest. The blue- eyed angel stumbled back, a thin line of blood visible on the front. Rorikel pressed on the attacks, hacking at Sephiel with a two handed grip on his sword. I tried to push myself up, but Max put his hand on my shoulder.

"Wait," he whispered. "Sephiel knows what he's doing." He looked at the fight again. "Watch."

Sephiel was still on the defense, Rorikel getting closer and closer to him. Because Sephiel was letting it happen.

Their swords crossed and Sephiel made his move. He shone heavenly light in Rorikel's eyes with a free hand, temporarily blinding the white-blond angel and making him cry out angrily. Sephiel wrenched Rorikel's sword away and caught him around the waist, flipping him over his shoulder. He spun on his heel and pressed the tip of his sword to Rorikel's chest. The beaten angel made no move to stop him. Sephiel looked like a stone-cold killer, emotion drained off his face.

"You are still my brother, Rorikel," he said. "As your brother,

I am asking you to help us. We can stop Lucifer. But we cannot do it alone. Please, help us."

Once again, Sephiel was sincere and honest enough to be completely convincing. His 'please' hadn't been forced or half-hearted. He actually had hope that Rorikel would listen to him.

But once again, Rorikel didn't care.

"Kill me if you wish, but Heaven shall hear of this, Sephiel. They shall all know of your falseness. That you chose the humans and Lucifer's abomination over your own kind. You shall not know safety. The Heavenly Host shall pursue you just as readily as the fiends of Hell will. All you shall do is prolong the suffering of those you have chosen to protect."

His words were so cold and heartless I was almost certain that Sephiel was going to kill him for them. If I'd had any strength, I would have done it myself. But instead, Sephiel lifted his sword from Rorikel's chest and placed its tip on the dirt.

"So be it," he said.

Rorikel scowled and quickly got to his feet. He hadn't put any fear in Sephiel like he hoped. He looked at us, grey eyes scanning our dirty human faces. His eyes lingered on Dro for a long time, even when I hunched over her and protected him from his bitter gaze. Then he blinked out of sight, and was gone.

I remained tense, my eyes scanning the forest around me, ready to throw myself on Dro if Rorikel came back.

"He has gone," Sephiel said, slowly making his way back towards us. "If he is to return, I shall feel it and forewarn you all."

"You should have killed him," I said. "He's just going to try and do the same to us. Sooner rather than later, judging by how pissed off you made him."

Sephiel stared at the ground, looking tired and sad. "It would not have given us time. The Heavenly Host knows both of the Gates are opened. We all felt the power Andromeda unleashed when Lucifer used her. Killing Rorikel would have achieved nothing." His voice was filled with guilt. "And he is still my brother."

I made myself understand. I was a sister who would never hurt her younger sibling.

But you did. You couldn't protect her, and she nearly died.

I slumped against Warrick's shoulder. He hadn't let me go since he pulled me from the collapsed tunnel.

"Sephiel, she needs to be healed," Warrick urged, keeping me circled in his arms. "She's lost a lot of blood and her injuries–"

"You are right, John Warrick. We shall leave this place. But I fear we cannot go anywhere safe."

"Why not?" Max asked.

Sephiel looked at him seriously. "Because there are no safe places anymore."

CHAPTER THIRTY-FIVE

Somewhere between Sephiel's ominous reply to Max and our preparation for teleporting, I passed out. When I woke up again, I felt no pain, except a pressing need to pee.

I took a deep breath and opened my eyes, looking at my surroundings. I was in a large bedroom with white walls, lying on a mattress with plain white sheets and a warm comforter. I pushed myself up, suddenly aware that I was in dark blue scrubs instead of my blood- covered clothes and jacket. I stretched my muscles then threw off the comforter and got to my feet, glancing over my shoulder at the sky beyond the window.

The clouds were heavy and dark. A big storm was coming. I frowned, wondering if it was a natural storm, or if Lucifer's emergence into the world had something to do with it.

There would be consequences for what I had done, what I failed to stop. More choices I couldn't be forgiven for. Would I ever do something truly, genuinely *good*?

I stretched my limbs, padded out of the bedroom, used the bathroom, and looked around the hallway. There was nothing distinguishable about this home, no decor or adornments or anything to suggest it was actually lived in. Everything seemed too empty. I made my way down the stairs, not even seeing any furniture. We must have been taken to a show home, or a house under renovation. I turned a corner and found Warrick and Sephiel in the living room.

Warrick sat on the floor with a variety of take-out food and pizza boxes around him, thumbing through his phone with a frown. He looked decidedly rumpled, with dark jeans and a white T-shirt stretched over his hard muscles. Something about the dark socks he wore made him look so... normal. His dark brown hair looked soft and clean, and a days worth of stubble darkened his jaw. I remembered the feel of it against my lips when he kissed me.

My stomach chose to rumble then. Warrick looked up, green eyes bright and shining with amusement. He chuckled at the noise my stomach made, and I felt my heart skip a beat. He was unfairly attractive when he smiled.

"Please tell me there's leftovers," I said.

Warrick grinned and motioned to the boxes. "Take your pick. After the last two days, we thought a buffet was a good idea."

I raised my eyebrows as I sat cross-legged on the floor next to Warrick. "I was out for two days?"

His smile faltered and he nodded. "You really damaged yourself, Constance. Sephiel healed you, gave you new clothes, then put a sleeping spell on you so you could get undisturbed rest. You needed it."

"You changed my clothes while I was sleeping?"

"I did." Sephiel's voice startled me. He stood by the window with his hands clasped behind his back. He no longer wore his long, white coat, but donned simply grey trousers and a white shirt that spanned across impressive muscles. He was staring at the blackening clouds. From the reflection on the window, I could see his grave expression. "I assure you a great deal of modesty was afforded you. As for your leather jacket, the one Warrick claimed to be 'lucky,' I worked to remove the bloodstains and restore the tears as much as possible. No easy feat, but I needed to occupy my mind while you slept."

Shock went through me. I hadn't imagined he would do something like that for me. I glanced at Warrick. He lifted his hands and smiled. "I didn't want to be blamed if I shrank it, and my sewing skills aren't anything to write home about."

I looked at Sephiel. "Thanks, really." It felt weird to be so grateful for strangers. Usually, strangers wanted to kill me. "What about Dro? Is she awake? Is she okay?"

"She still rests," Sephiel said.

"I gotta go see her," I said, starting to stand up again.

Warrick quickly grabbed my hand. "She's all right, Constance. Max is with her. You need to eat something, and we have to talk."

"Warrick is right," Sephiel said. His eyes lowered. "There are pressing issues we must address. Once Andromeda wakes, we will leave this place."

I lowered myself back down, pulling my hand from Warrick's. I rummaged through the boxes, finding a slice of barbecued Heaven. I devoured the pizza in about four bites, then moved onto another piece. When I started on my third, I looked at Sephiel.

"Is it true?" I asked. "Is Dro Lucifer's daughter?"

The angel closed his eyes for a long time. "Yes."

My heart dropped to my stomach. I was still starving, but I had lost my will to eat. "Why would her mother do something like that? Be with Lucifer? Didn't she know what he was?"

"Of course she did," Sephiel said en edge entering his voice. "What happened to Everiel was of Lucifer's accord. Not her own."

Oh. *Oh.*

"He..." I didn't want to say or suggest it, but I needed to be sure. "He kidnapped her?"

Sephiel nodded. "Everiel was captured by a demon and

brought into Hell as a prize for Lucifer." His fists clenched tightly at his back. "For decades, she was his. He had been trying to birth a child of both angel and demon blood. He thought she would be another failure, but his plan finally worked. Everiel became pregnant with Andromeda while she was prisoner in Hell."

"Jesus Christ," Warrick said under his breath.

"Why did he let her go?" I asked carefully.

"He did not. Everiel escaped. She birthed Andromeda on Earth, but the process was too intense, even for an angel. She carried Lucifer's child. She was never meant to survive the birth." Sephiel lowered his head. "She died before I could heal her."

Grief deeper than anything I could imagine filled Sephiel's voice, mixed with enough guilt to fill an ocean. The angel slowly turned toward me, sorrow making him look a thousand years older.

"I cherished Everiel for centuries. Even now, my heart still yearns for her. That is why I shall not see harm come to Andromeda. She might be born of Lucifer, but she is of Everiel's blood as well. Everiel wanted me to protect her, and that is what I shall do."

I looked at him carefully, noted the deep pain in his eyes, the hard line of his jaw. Could I trust an angel in so much conflict? How much did he love Dro in comparison to Everiel? Would he use her as a way to hurt Lucifer. Nothing he'd done since I'd known him gave me that impression, but I knew all too well that kind faces could lie.

The problem was that I needed as many supernatural allies as I could get. Max's gifts were sporadic at the best of times and Dro's powers were virtually out of control. But I trusted Warrick, at least partially. I could do the same to Sephiel, couldn't I?

The angel probably read all my thoughts as if they were plastered on my face, but he didn't seem to be offended. After a long time, I spoke again. "What happens now that we know what Dro really is?"

Sephiel took a step towards us, sighing heavily. "It shall not be easy. There has never been a hybrid like Andromeda before. She is still growing into her powers. It will be easier for supernaturals to sense her now that Lucifer has fully awakened her abilities. I believe he shall hunt for her again, and use her to get into Heaven."

"Couldn't he just do that on his own?" Warrick questioned. "I thought you said the Gates were open."

"They are," Sephiel answered. "But the entrance to Heaven is guarded against demons, just as the entrance to Hell is guarded against angels. It will take an army to enter either."

"So he wants her on his side," I said, wishing my voice hadn't trembled.

"Yes. Aside from Michael, she is the most powerful being known to this world. Lucifer and Michael may be evenly matched, but with Andromeda on Lucifer's side, even the Heavenly Host could be powerless against her."

"What are they going to do in the mean time?" asked Warrick. "Why didn't Lucifer just take Dro when he had the chance?"

"Perhaps it was because Lucifer needed to return to Hell to unleash his forces. He is more patient than you can imagine. Lucifer has been waiting for thousands of years to begin his reign."

"How do you know that's what he wants?"

Sephiel's eyes darkened. "We have had traitors in the past who have since been cast out of Heaven. They told us after thorough interrogation."

From the grave look on Sephiel's face, I was guessing he might have been part of it once. I decided to switch the topic. "Are you going to be cast out?"

Sephiel thought for a moment. "Yes. But I would need to be

reclaimed, first. I have no intention of returning to Heaven soon."

I sighed. "So, what happens to Earth now?"

His lips formed a fine line. "Earth is now a stalking ground for all demon kind. I suspect we shall hear of their activities shortly. Lucifer thrives on chaos. He wishes to draw the archangels and the Heavenly Host out. If he kills them, there shall be no defense in Heaven. He shall command his forces to slaughter every human they can find, and increase the number of damned souls for his army."

"How do we stop him?" I asked.

"I do not know. Lucifer is more powerful and cunning than even I can comprehend."

"Is there any way we can plead our case to Michael? To the archangels?"

Sephiel shook his head. "They would kill Andromeda and me on the spot, and would bar you from Heaven. We are on our own."

I dropped my head into my hands. "Shit."

"I shall depart and gather information. When I return, we will leave this house. We are powerless against the forces of Heaven and Hell, and evasion is our best hope right now."

Sephiel started to walk out of the living room, then stopped beside me and reached inside his jacket. He held out a new, silver hatchet to me.

"I was not able to retrieve your father's hatchet," he said. "This was the best substitute I could create for you. The blade is solid silver that I have blessed and washed in salted holy water. It shall be a powerful weapon against demons."

I took the hatchet from Sephiel. The silver blade was wrapped in a black leather handle, the neck curved more to make it easier to throw. Despite it being made of solid metal, the hatchet was surprisingly light. Engraved into the hilt was the

Latin saying Sephiel had used the last time he blessed my weapon.

Anima potentis, cor sororis. Soul of a warrior, heart of a sister.

It was a beautiful gift and I was deeply honored. But I was sad to have lost the hatchet that originally belonged to my father. It was the last thing I'd had of my parents, something I could look at to remember when my life hadn't been so violent and dangerous. I would miss it, but... maybe I could use this new hatchet as a sign that I could heal, change. Become a better woman. The little things Sephiel and Warrick had done, like fixing my lucky jacket and giving me a new weapon, or promising to fight with me and tend my wounds, reminded me just how terrible I could be, and how I didn't want to be that way anymore.

I looked at the hatchet. "Thank you. Both of you."

I felt Sephiel watch me for a moment, and then the feeling was suddenly gone. I looked up to see he had vanished. I turned the hatchet around in my hands, quickly getting used to the weight and feel of it. Warrick watched me the whole time, a knowing smile on his lips.

Why did people have to stare at me until I said something? It was much easier when they just said it and got it over with.

I put the hatchet down. "So, you think the other demon slayers will throw a fit when they find out you were right?"

Warrick smirked a little. "Definitely."

"Do you need to warn them?"

"Most of them probably know."

"Hm." I reached for another piece of pizza, picking off the toppings and nibbling on them. "Well, be safe."

"What'd you say that for?"

"You have priorities as a demon slayer. You don't have any loyalty to us. The world needs heroes like you out there killing monsters."

I grinned at him, but he looked confused. "You think I'm going to leave?"

Now I was confused. "Yeah. Why wouldn't you?"

Warrick's eyes pierced me, and I looked away. I played with the hatchet, wishing I could think about something other than his eyes and the way he kissed me.

"You can't do this alone, Constance," he said. "Max isn't a fighter, Dro needs you to keep her safe, and Sephiel can only lift the weight so much. You need more help. I'm choosing to do this."

"Why?"

He was silent for a long time, and then he said, "Because Dro isn't safe. I loved my sister the way you love Dro, and my sister died. I don't know if I could live with myself, knowing Drake is still out there and looking for you both."

I can't really explain why I was disappointed. Warrick had told me the truth. Now that he knew Drake was on our tail, he was taking his chance for revenge. But a small, strange, girly part of me had hoped for something more intimate. That maybe he was staying because he cared about me.

I pushed the thought down quickly. Despite how much he'd proved himself, I couldn't trust Warrick in the end. If we survived the demons and the angels and things went back to normal-ish, he could still turn me in for the Marshal bounty. Or worse, let me read too much into his reaction around me.

"Thanks. I appreciate the honesty," I said. I pushed myself up from the floor. "I'm gonna go check on Dro." I started walking away.

"You still don't trust me, do you?" Warrick said, making me turn around. "You can, Constance. I won't be anything but honest with you."

I crossed my arms over my chest. "Really?"

He nodded once.

"Then tell me why you kissed me."

I never expected to see a demon slayer blush. He lowered his head, trying to hide it just the way I'd tried to hide all of mine from him. He composed himself and lifted his head.

"Because I thought Drake was going to kill me, and I wanted to go out with at least one good memory. Kissing a beautiful woman is always a good thing to remember."

Words escaped me. I clutched my arms tighter around my upper body, as if it would keep my heart from bouncing around my ribcage. No one but Dro had ever called me beautiful before. Warrick's eyes glittered, even in the shadows of the room. I hated and loved what he was doing to me. The way he was making my heart race, building up the desire to kiss him again. To see exactly how deep that desire ran. It had been a long time since I'd wanted anything for myself, but I wanted Warrick. A dangerous desire, and not one I could let distract me until Dro was safe, and never hunted again. Would Warrick even be around that long? Would he see a side of me that turned him away? Was it even worth the risk?

I left the room before I decided to be impulsive and stupid, feeling Warrick's eyes on my back until I was out of his sight. I should have said something, but what would I say? I made my way up the stairs and cleared my head from thoughts of Warrick.

CHAPTER THIRTY-SIX

I walked to the only room with a closed door and gently rapped on it. No one answered, so I turned the doorknob and gently pushed the door open.

The curtains were drawn, making the room just a little darker, but I could see Max lying on the sheets of a large mattress with his back to me, and another shape with him under the covers. I made my way over to the mattress and checked to see if either Dro or Max were awake.

My little sister slept heavily, her face ghost white, nearly as pale as the blue scrubs she wore. But she looked at peace. Max cuddled next to Dro, his own clothes appearing to be from the same wardrobe as Warrick, his forehead resting against hers. His hand cradled hers and tucked it under his chin. I smiled a little. Max was in love with Dro. He'd suffered so much– losing his father, being shot, struggling to manage his gifts, and nearly dying. Despite that, he still loved her. He had earned my approval.

He sighed and shifted on the bed, slowly blinking his eyes open. He jumped when he saw me.

"Holy shit, Constance, you scared the crap out of me!" he whispered harshly.

I chuckled. "Relax. I've only been here about a minute."

"That doesn't make it less creepy." Max propped himself up on his elbow, still holding Dro's hand.

"How is she?"

Max looked down at her. His thumb stroked the top of Dro's hand. "She hasn't woken up yet. Been sleeping like the dead. You were sleeping too, so I decided to stay with her in case she woke up." The fingers of his other hand combed through the top of her hair. "I didn't want her to be alone."

Yeah. He had definitely earned it.

"I never had a chance to thank you," I said. "For everything. Sticking with us, staying strong. Caring about Dro. I'll never be able to thank you enough."

He looked up and blinked at me. "Can you repeat that so I can put it in writing?"

I narrowed my eyes. "Nice try. One offer of gratitude is all you get."

He grinned. "I'll just have to log that in my brain somewhere."

I wished I could have smiled. Instead, I looked down at Dro. "Did you know what was going to happen to her?" I asked. "With Lucifer?"

Max shook his head. "No. All I saw was that shadow again. I didn't even know whose it was until Lucifer showed up. If I'd have known, I would've said something."

I believed him. It wasn't hard, considering how much guilt was in his voice. "Can you see what's going to happen to us?" I asked.

He had a hard time meeting my eyes. "No luck there either. I mean, I've tried, but every time I try to see what happens to you or to Dro, all I see is Lucifer's shadow." He swallowed nervously. "But the basic instincts are kicking in. It's gonna get worse, Constance. A lot worse. I don't know what will happen, but it won't be anything good."

I hadn't expected anything less, though it would have been nice to have the worst behind us for once. To think that maybe God was on our side, even if I didn't believe in Him. But God was on the side of the angels, and there was only one angel who didn't want to kill us.

"Do you want some time alone with her?" Max asked.

I nodded. Max tucked Dro's hand back under the covers, pulling them up to her shoulders. He quickly kissed her forehead, then slid off the mattress.

"It's polite to ask a girl permission before you lie in bed with her and kiss her in her sleep," I chided when Max was at the door.

He hesitated at the door, glancing at her. "I... I wanted comfort, too." Worried, he looked at me. "Would she have said no?"

I shook my head. Dro's heart was the biggest I'd met, and I'd seen the way she looked at Max. Shy, but interested. Wanting to explore, wanting to know what it would be like to have something as selfless and simple as teenage love.

"She would have said yes."

Max smiled with relief and left the room. I sat against the wall next to the bed with Dro for a long time, remembering how I had always been able to protect her when she was scared. I never let anyone hurt her. If they did, I hurt them worse. I had killed men and monsters for Dro.

But Lucifer wasn't just a monster. He was *the* monster. The King of Hell. The Devil. He probably couldn't even be killed. I would keep Dro as safe as I could and at any cost, but I had already failed her once. She'd been captured, tortured, and nearly died in a sacrifice. Those weren't failures that could be easily fixed or forgiven. They didn't deserve to be.

I let out a heavy sigh and pressed the back of my head

against the wall. It had been easier when we were ignorant, to just think Dro was gifted. I hadn't even minded so much when we thought demons were hunting her just because she was a Nephilim. At a base level, I could understand them at least. Monsters needed to be killed, and I was good at killing.

But protecting her from Lucifer and his demons, as well as the archangels and the Heavenly Host? I wasn't sure I could do that. Didn't mean I wouldn't try, but I wasn't nearly as confident as I had been a couple years ago. I was human. There was just so little I could do...

WHEN THE CAR ran out of gas, I didn't know where we were. I'd driven onto the main road until the car sputtered and died. We were alone on the road, the camp far behind us. My hands shook where I gripped the steering wheel. Grief was a lump in my throat. Tears I hadn't known I'd cried covered my cheeks.

Dad and Mom were dead.

Dro held back on crying for the drive, but as soon as the car stopped, she shivered and broke down. She'd never cried this hard before. I undid my seatbelt and reached over, putting my arms around her. I couldn't tell who was shaking more, her or me.

"What happened?" she sobbed out. "Why did I burn?"

"I don't know."

"What were those things? Why were they after us?" She cried harder. "Why did they kill Mommy and Daddy?"

Pain twisted in my stomach, like I had been punched in the gut. Tears blurred my eyes. "I don't know."

Dro trembled. "It's my fault. They were looking for me. They killed Mommy and Daddy because of me."

I pulled back to look at my sister. Half of me wanted to lie. To tell her that it wasn't anything to do with her and that it was a mistake. But that wouldn't bring Dro any more comfort than it would bring me. We were completely alone.

"It'll be okay, Dro. We'll be okay."

Fresh tears spilled down her cheeks. "No we won't. They're gonna look for us. I know it. They're gonna kill you, Connie. They're gonna kill us both."

I flashed back to the slaughter at the camp. So many bodies and creatures running across bloody-soaked earth. Dad having his throat cut by a madwoman. Mom being torn apart by monsters. Dro exploding into white fire.

The things looking for her were bigger than I was. They were stronger. All I had was my attitude and Dad's hatchet. That wouldn't be enough. Dro wasn't a fighter. She was too nice to everything and everyone. Someone had to be nasty and mean to beat the monsters, and that wasn't her.

It was me.

I took her hands and looked her in the eyes. "I won't let them get you, Andromeda. Not ever. I'll keep you safe. I promise."

Dro stopped crying for a second to read my eyes, so different from her own bright blue ones. They were filled with hope. She believed me. I even believed myself.

"But we have to run," I told her, "keep running and never ever look back."

She nodded. "Never look back..."

Dro breathed out a sleepy sigh and turned on the mattress, pulling me out of the memory. She blinked her eyes steadily, her eyes fixing on the ceiling. She frowned, her lips curving in confusion, and she glanced around the room until her gaze fell on me.

For a moment, Dro just stared, like she couldn't believe I was here. Dro didn't hesitate or seem to care about her injuries. I stood up from the floor to tell her to lie back down, but she pushed herself up to her knees and threw her arms around my neck, crushing me tight to her chest.

"I thought you were dead," she whispered, voice shaking.

I hugged her tighter, scared that I would lose her again if I let go. She always felt so small, but her body was warm, and alive, and she had that clean smell she always had. The ones that reminded me of a home I used to know.

"I could say the same thing about you," I replied. Guilt ached in my heart as I remembered how Isabel and Lucifer had tortured her. How I hadn't–

"Stop thinking about it, Connie," Dro breathed. "Stop it."

"Sorry," I said, remembering that she could sense my emotions. She knew me too well. "How are you feeling?"

Dro pushed back from me, looking down at her left side. A bandage was wrapped around the area where her rib had been torn out. There wasn't any blood on the cloth, but Sephiel and Rorikel hadn't been able to regrow her rib. It was probably going to cause her pain for the rest of her life.

"Sore, but okay. I can feel the piece of me that's missing," she said quietly. "It's… weird."

I almost broke down right then. I had to clench my fists and dig my nails into my palm and focus on the pain to stop.

"I'm so sorry, Dro," I said, too ashamed to look at her. "I should have stayed with you. This wouldn't have happened if I'd been in the room, but I…"

"Don't blame yourself for this. Please, big sister. You couldn't have known what would happen. None of us did. But I knew you would be looking for me. I knew you'd find me. That was what I kept telling myself when…"

Dro stopped and bit her lip. I noticed the tears in her eyes, just as I noticed how she was starting to shake. I scooted onto the bed and pulled her into my arms. She clutched my body and cried for a couple minutes. I joined her.

I didn't say anything to try and make her feel better. There was nothing I could say. I wasn't going to lie to my little sister and tell her everything was going to be okay.

Everything was *far* from okay.

Once we had calmed down, and I told her everything that happened while she'd been healing, Dro leaned back and looked at me. "He did it, didn't he?" she asked. "He opened both the Gates."

I wiped my eyes, looking at her seriously. "Yeah."

Dro slumped and shivered. "I felt it," she said, pulling her knees to her chest and wrapping her arms around them. "I was barely awake, but I still felt it. That power that rushed through me, the Gates opening," her eyes shone with fear. "Lucifer in my head, promising to find me again and take me home..."

I reached out and took one of her hands. "He's not taking you anywhere, Dro. We'll figure out how to stop him."

She lifted her head. "You don't get it. I know I'm his daughter. I can feel the connection in our blood. The angel in me might be able to hold him back for a bit, but he's too strong for me, Constance. If he wants to find me, he will."

I didn't try and tell her she was wrong. I squeezed her hand. "I won't let him take you, Dro. Never again. We've beaten the odds before. We can beat them this time."

But she was already shaking her head. "You don't understand how strong he is. He'll hurt you to get to me, and I'll give in to make him stop. We can't win against him, Connie–"

I took her other hand. "Andromeda," I said, holding my fear down as best as I could. "Please don't give up. I need you to stay strong, because if you can't be, then neither can I."

Deep down, I think Dro always knew how afraid I was of the things and the people hunting us. But I don't think she ever understood how intense that fear was for me. I would have to overcome it if we were going to fight back and live through this.

I wouldn't be able to do that if she gave up. Dro had always been my anchor. Without her, I drifted out to sea.

Dro started crying in earnest when she saw how scared I was, but that I still refused to give up. She couldn't stand to lose me anymore than I could lose her. I wan't the only one who needed an anchor.

I pulled Dro close again and held her as she continued to cry. She was the only one of her kind, but I let her know that she wasn't alone. That she would never be alone, even if neither of us knew what we were going to do next.

Only we had allies now. Friends, even. It was no longer just us. I once said I'd burn the world to a cinder to keep Dro safe. But for a moment, a single, quiet second, I let myself dream what it would be like to have something more. To have a future where we didn't just survived, but *lived*.

That was a dream worth holding onto.

Thank you so much for reading! Constance's story continues in DARK DIVINITY!

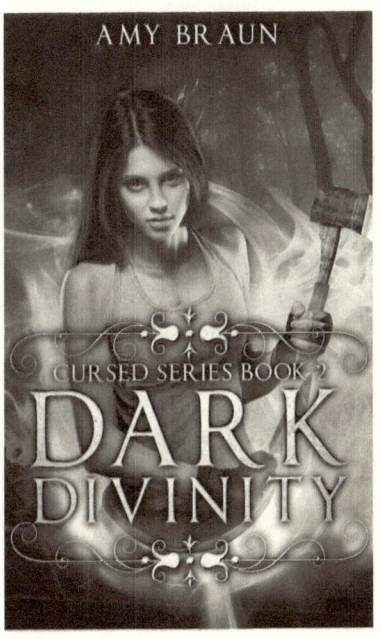

**Hell has risen. Heaven is descending.
Sacrifices are made...**

It's been two months since Constance Ramirez's adopted sister Andromeda was used as the Key to opening the Gates of Heaven and Hell. They escaped with their lives, but made countless enemies as a result.

Now that demons are beginning to weave into ordinary lives, their only hope is to find a way to close the Gates of Heaven and Hell before the angels and demons begin a war. Something that becomes only harder as one of Constance's deadliest enemies resurfaces.

But as they struggle to stay alive and find the Gates, they learn that a huge sacrifice will be required if they succeed, and this time, Constance isn't sure the cost will outweigh the reward...

ACKNOWLEDGMENTS

The *Cursed* story has been with me for years. At first it was just an idea that I thought would be fun. Then it became an obsession. I worked on it every second I had available to me, losing myself in mythology and research, developing characters that I think are memorable, and action scenes that had even me on the edge of my seat. Now that the first novel has finally reached completion, I feel like a mother watching her baby take its first steps. Nervous, but undeniably proud that it's come this far.

This accomplishment wouldn't have been possible without the love and encouragement I've gotten from my friends and family. There's nothing quite as wonderful as seeing the smiles on their faces when you tell them what you've achieved.

Huge thank you to Deranged Doctor Designs for the absolutely beautiful cover. You knocked it out of the park.

Big thanks to my editor Eden Royce for working with me and pointing out important details that were embarrassing to miss. Advice to new authors: *Always* hire an editor. You never know when you're going to accidently name a location after a salad dressing brand.

Tons of thanks to the lovely ladies of the Writing GIAM community, as well as the alpha and beta readers who helped me nitpick *Demon's Daughter*.

Last but not least, thank you reader for giving my story a chance. Considering this series is my figurative child, I can't tell you how much it means to know that someone, somewhere, picked it up and enjoyed it. Thank you for giving this story– and this indie author– a chance. I hope to be thanking you again soon.

ABOUT THE AUTHOR

 Amy is a Canadian urban fantasy and horror author. Her work revolves around monsters, magic, mythology, and mayhem. She started writing in her early teens, and never stopped. She loves building unique worlds filled with fun characters and intense action.

When she isn't writing, she's reading, watching movies, taking photos, gaming, struggling with chocoholism and ice cream addiction, and diving headfirst into danger in Dungeons & Dragons campaigns.

Never miss a new release, cover reveal, or giveaway! Sign up for Amy's newsletter today!

www.amybraunauthor.com

facebook.com/amybraunauthor

twitter.com/amybraunauthor

instagram.com/amybraunauthor